'Dick quietly produced serious fic... ... ...
can be no greater praise'

'One of the most original practitio... ...
Dick made most of the European av... ... ...
in a cul-de-sac'
The Sunday Times

'Dick's abundant storytelling gifts and the need to express his inner struggles combined to produce some of the most groundbreaking novels and ideas'
Waterstone's Guide to Science Fiction, Fantasy and Horror

'Dick amused, enthralled and astounded his readers. There's no pomposity in Dick's work, no falseness. When the moment comes, Dick can pull out all the stops and sound the big, resonating chords, though calm, ironic understatement is his forte' *Brian W. Aldiss*

'One of the genuine visionaries that North American fiction has produced'
L.A. Weekly

'Dick was many authors: a poor man's Pynchon, an oracular post-modern, a rich product of the changing counterculture'
The Village Voice

Also by Philip K. Dick

Human Is?

Philip K. Dick

The right of Philip K. Dick to be identified as the author
of this work has been asserted by him in accordance with
the Copyright, Designs and Patents Act 1988.

First published in Great Britain in 2007 by
Gollancz
An imprint of the Orion Publishing Group
Orion House, 5 Upper St Martin's Lane
London WC2H 9EA

10 9 8 7 6 5 4 3 2 1

A CIP catalogue record for this book
is available from the British Library

ISBN 13: 978 0 57508 034 8
ISBN 10: 0 57508 034 5

Typeset at The Spartan Press Ltd,
Lymington, Hants

Printed and bound at Mackays of Chatham plc,
Chatham, Kent

The Orion Publishing Group's policy is to use papers that
are natural, renewable and recyclable products and made
from wood grown in sustainable forests. The logging and
manufacturing processes are expected to conform to the
environmental regulations of the country of origin.

www.orionbooks.co.uk

Contents

Beyond Lies The Wub

They had almost finished with the loading. Outside stood the Optus, his arms folded, his face sunk in gloom. Captain Franco walked leisurely down the gangplank, grinning.

'What's the matter?' he said. 'You're getting paid for all this.'

The Optus said nothing. He turned away, collecting his robes. The Captain put his boot on the hem of the robe.

'Just a minute. Don't go off. I'm not finished.'

'Oh?' The Optus turned with dignity. 'I am going back to the village.' He looked toward the animals and birds being driven up the gangplank into the spaceship. 'I must organize new hunts.'

Franco lit a cigarette. 'Why not? You people can go out into the veldt and track it all down again. But when we run halfway between Mars and Earth—'

The Optus went off, wordless. Franco joined the first mate at the bottom of the gangplank.

'How's it coming?' he asked. He looked at his watch. 'We got a good bargain here.'

The mate glanced at him sourly. 'How do you explain that?'

'What's the matter with you? We need it more than they do.'

'I'll see you later, Captain.' The mate threaded his way up the plank, between the long-legged Martian go-birds, into the ship. Franco watched him disappear. He was just starting up after him, up the plank toward the port, when he saw *it*.

'My God!' He stood staring, his hands on his hips. Peterson was walking along the path, his face red, leading *it* by a string.

'I'm sorry, Captain,' he said, tugging at the string. Franco walked toward him.

'What is it'

The wub stood sagging, its great body settling slowly. It was sitting down, its eyes half shut. A few flies buzzed about its flank, and it switched its tail.

It sat. There was silence.

'It's a wub,' Peterson said. 'I got it from a native for fifty cents. He said it was a very unusual animal. Very respected.'

'This?' Franco poked the great sloping side of the wub. 'It's a pig! A huge dirty pig!'

'Yes sir, it's a pig. The natives call it a wub.'

'A huge pig. It must weigh four hundred pounds.' Franco grabbed a tuft of the rough hair. The wub gasped. Its eyes opened, small and moist. Then its great mouth twitched.

A tear rolled down the wub's cheek and splashed on the floor.

'Maybe it's good to eat,' Peterson said nervously.

'We'll soon find out,' Franco said.

The wub survived the takeoff, sound asleep in the hold of the ship. When they were out in space and everything was running smoothly, Captain Franco bade his men fetch the wub upstairs so that he might perceive what manner of beast it was.

The wub grunted and wheezed, squeezing up the passageway.

'Come on,' Jones grated, pulling at the rope. The wub twisted, rubbing its skin off on the smooth chrome walls. It burst into the anteroom, tumbling down in a heap. The men leaped up.

'Good Lord,' French said. 'What is it?'

'Peterson says it's a wub,' Jones said. 'It belongs to him.' He kicked at the wub. The wub stood up unsteadily, panting.

'What's the matter with it?' French came over. 'Is it going to be sick?'

They watched. The wub rolled its eyes mournfully. It gazed around at the men.

'I think it's thirsty,' Peterson said. He went to get some water. French shook his head.

'No wonder we had so much trouble taking off. I had to reset all my ballast calculations.'

Peterson came back with the water. The wub began to lap gratefully, splashing the men.

Captain Franco appeared at the door.

'Let's have a look at it.' He advanced, squinting critically. 'You got this for fifty cents?'

'Yes, sir,' Peterson said. 'It eats almost anything. I fed it on grain and it liked that. And then potatoes, and mash, and scraps from the table, and milk. It seems to enjoy eating. After it eats it lies down and goes to sleep.'

2

'I see,' Captain Franco said. 'Now, as to its taste. That's the real question. I doubt if there's much point in fattening it up any more. It seems fat enough to me already. Where's the cook? I want him here. I want to find out—'

The wub stopped lapping and looked up at the Captain.

'Really, Captain,' the wub said. 'I suggest we talk of other matters.'

The room was silent.

'What was that?' Franco said. 'Just now.'

'The wub, sir,' Peterson said. 'It spoke.'

They all looked at the wub.

'What did it say? What did it say?'

'It suggested we talk about other things.'

Franco walked toward the wub. He went all around it, examining it from every side. Then he came back over and stood with the men.

'I wonder if there's a native inside it,' he said thoughtfully. 'Maybe we should open it up and have a look.'

'Oh, goodness!' the wub cried. 'Is that all you people can think of, killing and cutting?'

Franco clenched his fists. 'Come out of there! Whoever you are, come out!'

Nothing stirred. The men stood together, their faces blank, staring at the wub. The wub swished its tail. It belched suddenly.

'I beg your pardon,' the wub said.

'I don't think there's anyone in there,' Jones said in a low voice. They all looked at each other.

The cook came in.

'You wanted me, Captain?' he said. 'What's this thing?'

'This is a wub,' Franco said. 'It's to be eaten. Will you measure it and figure out—'

'I think we should have a talk,' the wub said. 'I'd like to discuss this with you, Captain, if I might. I can see that you and I do not agree on some basic issues.'

The Captain took a long time to answer. The wub waited good-naturedly, licking the water from its jowls.

'Come into my office,' the Captain said at last. He turned and walked out of the room. The wub rose and padded after him. The men watched it go out. They heard it climbing the stairs.

'I wonder what the outcome will be,' the cook said. 'Well, I'll be in the kitchen. Let me know as soon as you hear.'

'Sure,' Jones said. 'Sure.'

The wub eased itself down in the corner with a sigh. 'You must forgive me,' it said. 'I'm afraid I'm addicted to various forms of relaxation. When one is as large as I—'

The Captain nodded impatiently. He sat down at his desk and folded his hands.

'All right,' he said. 'Let's get started. You're a wub? Is that correct?'

The wub shrugged. 'I suppose so. That's what they call us, the natives, I mean. We have our own term.'

'And you speak English? You've been in contact with Earthmen before?'

'No.'

'Then how do you do it?'

'Speak English? Am I speaking English? I'm not conscious of speaking anything in particular. I examined your mind—'

'My mind?'

'I studied the contents, especially the semantic warehouse, as I refer to it—'

'I see,' the Captain said. 'Telepathy. Of course.'

'We are a very old race,' the wub said. 'Very old and very ponderous. It is difficult for us to move around. You can appreciate anything so slow and heavy would be at the mercy of more agile forms of life. There was no use in our relying on physical defenses. How could we win? Too heavy to run, too soft to fight, too good-natured to hunt for game—'

'How do you live?'

'Plants. Vegetables. We can eat almost anything. We're very catholic. Tolerant, eclectic, catholic. We live and let live. That's how we've gotten along.'

The wub eyed the Captain.

'And that's why I so violently objected to this business about having me boiled. I could see the image in your mind – most of me in the frozen food locker, some of me in the kettle, a bit for your pet cat—'

'So you read minds?' the Captain said. 'How interesting. Anything else? I mean, what else can you do along those lines?'

'A few odds and ends,' the wub said absently, staring around the room. 'A nice apartment you have here, Captain. You keep it quite neat. I respect life-forms that are tidy. Some Martian birds are quite tidy. They throw things out of their nests and sweep them—'

'Indeed.' The Captain nodded. 'But to get back to the problem—'

'Quite so. You spoke of dining on me. The taste, I am told, is good. A little fatty, but tender. But how can any lasting contact be established between your people and mine if you resort to such barbaric attitudes? Eat me? Rather you should discuss questions with me, philosophy, the arts—'

The Captain stood up. 'Philosophy. It might interest you to know that we will be hard put to find something to eat for the next month. An unfortunate spoilage—'

'I know.' The wub nodded. 'But wouldn't it be more in accord with your principles of democracy if we all drew straws, or something along that line? After all, democracy is to protect the minority from just such infringements. Now, if each of us casts one vote—'

The Captain walked to the door.

'Nuts to you,' he said. He opened the door. He opened his mouth.

He stood frozen, his mouth wide, his eyes staring, his fingers still on the knob.

The wub watched him. Presently it padded out of the room, edging past the Captain. It went down the hall, deep in meditation.

The room was quiet.

'So you see,' the wub said, 'we have a common myth. Your mind contains many familiar myth symbols. Ishtar, Odysseus—'

Peterson sat silently, staring at the floor. He shifted in his chair.

'Go on,' he said. 'Please go on.'

'I find in your Odysseus a figure common to the mythology of most self-conscious races. As I interpret it, Odysseus wanders as an individual aware of himself as such. This is the idea of separation, of separation from family and country. The process of individuation.'

'But Odysseus returns to his home.' Peterson looked out the port window, at the stars, endless stars, burning intently in the empty universe. 'Finally he goes home.'

'As must all creatures. The moment of separation is a temporary period, a brief journey of the soul. It begins, it ends. The wanderer returns to land and race . . .'

The door opened. The wub stopped, turning its great head.

5

Captain Franco came into the room, the men behind him. They hesitated at the door.

'Are you all right?' French said.

'Do you mean me?' Peterson said, surprised. 'Why me?'

Franco lowered his gun. 'Come over here,' he said to Peterson. 'Get up and come here.'

There was silence.

'Go ahead,' the wub said. 'It doesn't matter.'

Peterson stood up. 'What for?'

'It's an order.'

Peterson walked to the door. French caught his arm.

'What's going on?' Peterson wrenched loose. 'What's the matter with you?'

Captain Franco moved toward the wub. The wub looked up from where it lay in the corner, pressed against the wall.

'It is interesting,' the wub said, 'that you are obsessed with the idea of eating me. I wonder why.'

'Get up,' Franco said.

'If you wish.' The wub rose, grunting. 'Be patient. It is difficult for me.' It stood, gasping, its tongue lolling foolishly.

'Shoot it now,' French said.

'For God's sake!' Peterson exclaimed. Jones turned to him quickly, his eyes gray with fear.

'You didn't see him – like a statue, standing there, his mouth open. If we hadn't come down, he'd still be there.'

'Who? The Captain?' Peterson stared around. 'But he's all right now.'

They looked at the wub, standing in the middle of the room, its great chest rising and falling.

'Come on,' Franco said. 'Out of the way.'

The men pulled aside toward the door.

'You are quite afraid, aren't you?' the wub said. 'Have I done anything to you? I am against the idea of hurting. All I have done is try to protect myself. Can you expect me to rush eagerly to my death? I am a sensible being like yourselves. I was curious to see your ship, learn about you. I suggested to the native—'

The gun jerked.

'See,' Franco said. 'I thought so.'

The wub settled down, panting. It put its paws out, pulling its tail around it.

'It is very warm,' the wub said. 'I understand that we are close to the jets. Atomic power. You have done many wonderful things with it – technically. Apparently your scientific hierarchy is not equipped to solve moral, ethical—'

Franco turned to the men, crowding behind him, wide-eyed, silent. 'I'll do it. You can watch.'

French nodded. 'Try to hit the brain. It's no good for eating. Don't hit the chest. If the rib cage shatters, we'll have to pick bones out.'

'Listen,' Peterson said, licking his lips. 'Has it done anything? What harm has it done? I'm asking you. And anyhow, it's still mine. You have no right to shoot it. It doesn't belong to you.'

Franco raised his gun.

'I'm going out,' Jones said, his face white and sick. 'I don't want to see it.'

'Me, too,' French said. The men straggled out, murmuring. Peterson lingered at the door.

'It was talking to me about myths,' he said. 'It wouldn't hurt anyone.'

He went outside.

Franco walked toward the wub. The wub looked up slowly. It swallowed.

'A very foolish thing,' it said. 'I am sorry that you want to do it. There was a parable that your Saviour related—'

It stopped, staring at the gun.

'Can you look me in the eye and do it?' the wub said. 'Can you do that?'

The Captain gazed down. 'I can look you in the eye,' he said. 'Back on the farm we had hogs, dirty razorback hogs. I can do it.'

Staring down at the wub, into the gleaming, moist eyes, he pressed the trigger.

The taste was excellent.

They sat glumly around the table, some of them hardly eating at all. The only one who seemed to be enjoying himself was Captain Franco.

'More?' he said, looking around. 'More? And some wine, perhaps.'

'Not me,' French said. 'I think I'll go back to the chart room.'

'Me, too.' Jones stood up, pushing his chair back. 'I'll see you later.'

The Captain watched them go. Some of the others excused themselves.

'What do you suppose the matter is?' the Captain said. He turned to Peterson. Peterson sat staring down at his plate, at the potatoes, the green peas, and at the thick slab of tender, warm meat.

He opened his mouth. No sound came.

The Captain put his hand on Peterson's shoulder.

'It is only organic matter, now,' he said. 'The life essence is gone.' He ate, spooning up the gravy with some bread. 'I, myself, love to eat. It is one of the greatest things that a living creature can enjoy. Eating, resting, meditation, discussing things.'

Peterson nodded. Two more men got up and went out. The Captain drank some water and sighed.

'Well,' he said. 'I must say that this was a very enjoyable meal. All the reports I had heard were quite true – the taste of wub. Very fine. But I was prevented from enjoying this in times past.'

He dabbed at his lips with his napkin and leaned back in his chair. Peterson stared dejectedly at the table.

The Captain watched him intently. He leaned over.

'Come, come,' he said. 'Cheer up! Let's discuss things.'

He smiled.

'As I was saving before I was interrupted, the role of Odysseus in the myths—'

Peterson jerked up, staring.

'To go on,' the Captain said. 'Odysseus, as I understand him—'

The Defenders

Taylor sat back in his chair reading the morning newspaper. The warm kitchen and the smell of coffee blended with the comfort of not having to go to work. This was his Rest Period, the first for a long time, and he was glad of it. He folded the second section back, sighing with contentment.

'What is it?' Mary said, from the stove.

'They pasted Moscow again last night.' Taylor nodded his head in approval. 'Gave it a real pounding. One of those R-H bombs. It's about time.'

He nodded again, feeling the full comfort of the kitchen, the presence of his plump, attractive wife, the breakfast dishes and coffee. This was relaxation. And the war news was good, good and satisfying. He could feel a justifiable glow at the news, a sense of pride and personal accomplishment. After all, he was an integral part of the war program, not just another factory worker lugging a cart of scrap, but a technician, one of those who designed and planned the nerve-trunk of the war.

'It says they have the new subs almost perfected. Wait until they get *those* going.' He smacked his lips with anticipation. 'When they start shelling from underwater, the Soviets are sure going to be surprised.'

'They're doing a wonderful job,' Mary agreed vaguely. 'Do you know what we saw today? Our team is getting a leady to show to the school children. I saw the leady, but only for a moment. It's good for the children to see what their contributions are going for, don't you think?'

She looked around at him.

'A leady,' Taylor murmured. He put the newspaper slowly down. 'Well, make sure it's decontaminated properly. We don't want to take any chances.'

'Oh, they always bathe them when they're brought down from the surface,' Mary said. 'They wouldn't think of letting them down without the bath. Would they?' She hesitated, thinking back. 'Don, you know, it makes me remember—'

He nodded. 'I know.'

He knew what she was thinking. Once in the very first weeks of the war, before everyone had been evacuated from the surface, they had seen a hospital train discharging the wounded, people who had been showered with sleet. He remembered the way they had looked, the expression on their faces, or as much of their faces as was left. It had not been a pleasant sight.

There had been a lot of that at first, in the early days before the transfer to undersurface was complete. There had been a lot, and it hadn't been very difficult to come across it.

Taylor looked up at his wife. She was thinking too much about it, the last few months. They all were.

'Forget it,' he said. 'It's all in the past. There isn't anybody up there now but the leadies, and they don't mind.'

'But just the same, I hope they're careful when they let one of them down here. If one were still hot—'

He laughed, pushing himself away from the table. 'Forget it. This is a wonderful moment; I'll be home for the next two shifts. Nothing to do but sit around and take things easy. Maybe we can take in a show. OK?'

'A show? Do we have to? I don't like to look at all the destruction, the ruins. Sometimes I see some place I remember, like San Francisco. They showed a shot of San Francisco, the bridge broken and fallen in the water, and I got upset. I don't like to watch.'

'But don't you want to know what's going on? No human beings are getting hurt, you know.'

'But it's so awful!' Her face was set and strained. 'Please, no, Don.'

Don Taylor picked up his newspaper sullenly. 'All right, but there isn't a hell of a lot else to do. And don't forget, *their* cities are getting it even worse.'

She nodded. Taylor turned the rough, thin sheets of newspaper. His good mood had soured on him. Why did she have to fret all the time? They were pretty well off, as things went. You couldn't expect to have everything perfect, living undersurface, with an artificial sun and artificial food. Naturally it was a strain, not seeing the sky or being able to go anyplace or see anything other than metal walls, great roaring factories, the plant-yards, barracks. But it was better than being on surface. And some day it would end and they could return. Nobody *wanted* to live this way, but it was necessary.

He turned the page angrily and the poor paper ripped. Damn it, the paper was getting worse quality all the time, bad print, yellow tint—

Well, they needed everything for the war program. He ought to know that. Wasn't he one of the planners?

He excused himself and went into the other room. The bed was still unmade. They had better get it in shape before the seventh hour inspection. There was a one unit fine—

The vidphone rang. He halted. Who would it be? He went over and clicked it on.

'Taylor?' the face said, forming into place. It was an old face, gray and grim. 'This is Moss. I'm sorry to bother you during Rest Period, but this thing has come up.' He rattled papers. 'I want you to hurry over here.'

Taylor stiffened. 'What is it? There's no chance it could wait?' The calm gray eyes were studying him, expressionless, unjudging. 'If you want me to come down to the lab,' Taylor grumbled, 'I suppose I can. I'll get my uniform—'

'No. Come as you are. And not to the lab. Meet me at second stage as soon as possible. It'll take you about a half hour, using the fast car up. I'll see you there.'

The picture broke and Moss disappeared.

'What was it?' Mary said, at the door.

'Moss. He wants me for something.'

'I knew this would happen.'

'Well, you didn't want to do anything, anyhow. What does it matter?' His voice was bitter. 'It's all the same, every day. I'll bring you back something. I'm going up to second stage. Maybe I'll be close enough to the surface to—'

'Don't! Don't bring me anything! Not from the surface!'

'All right, I won't. But of all the irrational nonsense—'

She watched him put on his boots without answering.

Moss nodded and Taylor fell in step with him, as the older man strode along. A series of loads was going up to the surface, blind cars clanking like ore-trucks up the ramp, disappearing through the stage trap above them. Taylor watched the cars, heavy with tubular machinery of some sort, weapons new to him. Workers were everywhere, in the dark gray uniforms of the labor corps, loading, lifting, shouting back and forth. The stage was deafening with noise.

'We'll go up a way,' Moss said, 'where we can talk. This is no place to give you details.'

They took an escalator up. The commercial lift fell behind them, and with it most of the crashing and booming. Soon they emerged on an observation platform, suspended on the side of the Tube, the vast tunnel leading to the surface, not more than half a mile above them now.

'My God!' Taylor said, looking down the tube involuntarily. 'It's a long way down.'

Moss laughed. 'Don't look.'

They opened a door and entered an office. Behind the desk, an officer was sitting, an officer of Internal Security. He looked up.

'I'll be right with you, Moss.' He gazed at Taylor, studying him. 'You're a little ahead of time.'

'This is Commander Franks,' Moss said to Taylor. 'He was the first to make the discovery. I was notified last night.' He tapped a parcel he carried. 'I was let in because of this.'

Franks frowned at him and stood up. 'We're going up to first stage. We can discuss it there.'

'First stage?' Taylor repeated nervously. The three of them went down a side passage to a small lift. 'I've never been up there. Is it all right? It's not radioactive, is it?'

'You're like everyone else,' Franks said. 'Old women afraid of burglars. No radiation leaks down to the first stage. There's lead and rock, and what comes down the Tube is bathed.'

'What's the nature of the problem?' Taylor asked. 'I'd like to know something about it.'

'In a moment.'

They entered the lift and ascended. When they stepped out, they were in a hall of soldiers, weapons and uniforms everywhere. Taylor blinked in surprise. So this was first stage, the closest undersurface level to the top! After this stage there was only rock, lead and rock, and the great tubes leading up like the burrows of earthworms. Lead and rock, and above that, where the tubes opened, the great expanse that no living being had seen for eight years, the vast, endless ruin that had once been Man's home, the place where he had lived, eight years ago.

Now the surface was a lethal desert of slag and rolling clouds. Endless clouds drifted back and forth, blotting out the red sun. Occasionally something metallic stirred, moving through the remains of a city, threading its way across the tortured terrain of the countryside. A leady, a surface robot, immune to radiation, constructed with feverish haste in the last months before the cold war became literally hot.

Leadies, crawling along the ground, moving over the oceans, or through the skies in slender, blackened craft, creatures that could exist where no *life* could remain, metal and plastic figures that waged a war Man had conceived, but which he could not fight himself. Human beings had invented war, invented and manufactured the weapons, even invented the players, the fighters, the actors of the war. But they themselves could not venture forth, could not wage it themselves. In all the world – in Russia, in Europe, America, Africa – no living human being remained. They were under the surface, in the deep shelters that had been carefully planned and built, even as the first bombs began to fall.

It was a brilliant idea and the only idea that could have worked. Up above, on the ruined, blasted surface of what had once been a living planet, the leady crawled and scurried and fought Man's war. And undersurface, in the depths of the planet, human beings toiled endlessly to produce the weapons to continue the fight, month by month, year by year.

'First stage,' Taylor said. A strange ache went through him. 'Almost to the surface.'

'But not quite,' Moss said.

Franks led them through the soldiers, over to one side, near the lip of the Tube.

'In a few minutes, a lift will bring something down to us from the surface,' he explained. 'You see, Taylor, every once in a while Security examines and interrogates a surface leady, one that has been above for a time, to find out certain things. A vidcall is sent up and contact is made with a field headquarters. We need this direct interview; we can't depend on vidscreen contact alone. The leadies are doing a good job, but we want to make certain that everything is going the way we want it.'

Franks faced Taylor and Moss and continued: 'The lift will bring down a leady from the surface, one of the A-class leadies. There's an examination chamber in the next room, with a lead wall in the center, so the interviewing officers won't be exposed to radiation. We find this easier than bathing the leady. It is going right back up; it has a job to get back to.

'Two days ago, an A-class leady was brought down and interrogated.

I conducted the session myself. We were interested in a new weapon the Soviets have been using, an automatic mine that pursues anything that moves. Military had sent instructions up that the mine be observed and reported in detail.

'This A-class leady was brought down with information. We learned a few facts from it, obtained the usual roll of film and reports, and then sent it back up. It was going out of the chamber, back to the lift, when a curious thing happened. At the time, I thought—'

Franks broke off. A red light was flashing.

'That down lift is coming.' He nodded to some soldiers. 'Let's enter the chamber. The leady will be along in a moment.'

'An A-class leady,' Taylor said. 'I've seen them on the showscreens, making their reports.'

'It's quite an experience,' Moss said. 'They're almost human.'

They entered the chamber and seated themselves behind the lead wall. After a time, a signal was flashed, and Franks made a motion with his hands.

The door beyond the wall opened. Taylor peered through his view slot. He saw something advancing slowly, a slender metallic figure moving on a tread, its arm grips at rest by its sides. The figure halted and scanned the lead wall. It stood, waiting.

'We are interested in learning something,' Franks said. 'Before I question you, do you have anything to report on surface conditions?'

'No. The war continues.' The leady's voice was automatic and toneless. 'We are a little short of fast pursuit craft, the single-seat type. We could use also some—'

'That has all been noted. What I want to ask you is this. Our contact with you has been through vidscreen only. We must rely on indirect evidence, since none of us goes above. We can only infer what is going on. We never see anything ourselves. We have to take it all second-hand. Some top leaders are beginning to think there's too much room for error.'

'Error?' the leady asked. 'In what way? Our reports are checked carefully before they're sent down. We maintain constant contact with you; everything of value is reported. Any new weapons which the enemy is seen to employ—'

'I realize that,' Franks grunted behind his peep slot. 'But perhaps we should see it all for ourselves. Is it possible that there might be a large enough radiation-free area for a human party to ascend to the surface?

If a few of us were to come up in lead-lined suits, would we be able to survive long enough to observe conditions and watch things?'

The machine hesitated before answering. 'I doubt it. You can check air samples, of course, and decide for yourselves. But in the eight years since you left, things have continually worsened. You cannot have any real idea of conditions up there. It has become difficult for any moving object to survive for long. There are many kinds of projectiles sensitive to movement. The new mine not only reacts to motion, but continues to pursue the object indefinitely, until it finally reaches it. And the radiation is everywhere.'

'I see.' Franks turned to Moss, his eyes narrowed oddly. 'Well, that was what I wanted to know. You may go.'

The machine moved back toward its exit. It paused. 'Each month the amount of lethal particles in the atmosphere increases. The tempo of the war is gradually—'

'I understand.' Franks rose. He held out his hand and Moss passed him the package. 'One thing before you leave. I want you to examine a new type of metal shield material. I'll pass you a sample with the tong.'

Franks put the package in the toothed grip and revolved the tong so that he held the other end. The package swung down to the leady, which took it. They watched it unwrap the package and take the metal plate in its hands. The leady turned the metal over and over.

Suddenly it became rigid.

'All right,' Franks said.

He put his shoulder against the wall and a section slid aside. Taylor gasped – Franks and Moss were hurrying up to the leady!

'Good God!' Taylor said. 'But it's radioactive!'

The leady stood unmoving, still holding the metal. Soldiers appeared in the chamber. They surrounded the leady and ran a counter across it carefully.

'OK, sir,' one of them said to Franks. 'It's as cold as a long winter evening.'

'Good. I was sure, but I didn't want to take any chances.'

'You see,' Moss said to Taylor, 'this leady isn't hot at all. Yet it came directly from the surface, without even being bathed.'

'But what does it mean?' Taylor asked blankly.

'It may be an accident,' Franks said. 'There's always the possibility that a given object might escape being exposed above. But this is the second time it's happened that we know of. There may be others.'

'The second time?'

'The previous interview was when we noticed it. The leady was not hot. It was cold, too, like this one.'

Moss took back the metal plate from the leady's hands. He pressed the surface carefully and returned it to the stiff, unprotesting fingers.

'We shorted it out with this, so we could get close enough for a thorough check. It'll come back on in a second now. We had better get behind the wall again.'

They walked back and the lead wall swung closed behind them. The soldiers left the chamber.

'Two periods from now,' Franks said softly, 'an initial investigating party will be ready to go surface-side. We're going up the Tube in suits, up to the top — the first human party to leave undersurface in eight years.'

'It may mean nothing,' Moss said, 'but I doubt it. Something's going on, something strange. The leady told us no life could exist above without being roasted. The story doesn't fit.'

Taylor nodded. He stared through the peep slot at the immobile metal figure. Already the leady was beginning to stir. It was bent in several places, dented and twisted, and its finish was blackened and charred. It was a leady that had been up there a long time; it had seen war and destruction, ruin so vast that no human being could imagine the extent. It had crawled and slunk in a world of radiation and death, a world where no life could exist.

And Taylor had touched it!

'You're going with us,' Franks said suddenly. 'I want you along. I think the three of us will go.'

Mary faced him with a sick and frightened expression. 'I know it. You're going to the surface. Aren't you?'

She followed him into the kitchen. Taylor sat down, looking away from her.

'It's a classified project,' he evaded. 'I can't tell you anything about it.'

'You don't have to tell me. I know. I knew it the moment you came in. There was something on your face, something I haven't seen there for a long time. It was an old look.'

She came toward him. 'But how can they send you to the surface?' She took his face in her shaking hands, making him look at her. There was a strange hunger in her eyes. 'Nobody can live up there. Look, look at this!'

She grabbed up a newspaper and held it in front of him.

'Look at this photograph. America, Europe, Asia, Africa – nothing but ruins. We've seen it every day on the showscreens. All destroyed, poisoned. And they're sending you up. Why? No living thing can get by up there, not even a weed, or grass. They've wrecked the surface, haven't they? *Haven't they?*'

Taylor stood up. 'Its an order. I know nothing about it. I was told to report to join a scout party. That's all I know.'

He stood for a long time, staring ahead. Slowly, he reached for the newspaper and held it up to the light.

'It looks real,' he murmured. 'Ruins, deadness, slag. It's convincing. All the reports, photographs, films, even air samples. Yet we haven't seen it for ourselves, not after the first months . . .'

'What are you talking about?'

'Nothing.' He put the paper down. 'I'm leaving early after the next Sleep Period. Let's turn in.'

Mary turned away, her face hard and harsh. 'Do what you want. We might just as well all go up and get killed at once, instead of dying slowly down here, like vermin in the ground.'

He had not realized how resentful she was. Were they all like that? How about the workers toiling in the factories, day and night, end-lessly? The pale, stooped men and women, plodding back and forth to work, blinking in the colorless light, eating synthetics—

'You shouldn't be so bitter,' he said.

Mary smiled a little. 'I'm bitter because I know you'll never come back.' She turned away. 'I'll never see you again, once you go up there.'

He was shocked. 'What? How can you say a thing like that?'

She did not answer.

He awakened with the public newscaster screeching in his ears, shouting outside the building.

'Special news bulletin! Surface forces report enormous Soviet attack with new weapons! Retreat of key groups! All work units report to factories at once!'

Taylor blinked, rubbing his eyes. He jumped out of bed and hurried to the vidphone. A moment later he was put through to Moss.

'Listen,' he said. 'What about this new attack? Is the project off?' He could see Moss's desk, covered with reports and papers.

'No,' Moss said. 'We're going right ahead. Get over here at once.'

'But—'

'Don't argue with me.' Moss held up a handful of surface bulletins, crumpling them savagely. 'This is a fake. Come on!' He broke off.

Taylor dressed furiously, his mind in a daze.

Half an hour later, he leaped from a fast car and hurried up the stairs into the Synthetics Building. The corridors were full of men and women rushing in every direction. He entered Moss's office.

'There you are,' Moss said, getting up immediately. 'Franks is waiting for us at the outgoing station.'

They went in a Security Car, the siren screaming. Workers scattered out of their way.

'What about the attack?' Taylor asked.

Moss braced his shoulders. 'We're certain that we've forced their hand. We've brought the issue to a head.'

They pulled up at the station link of the Tube and leaped out. A moment later they were moving up at high speed toward the first stage.

They emerged into a bewildering scene of activity. Soldiers were fastening on lead suits, talking excitedly to each other, shouting back and forth. Guns were being given out, instructions passed.

Taylor studied one of the soldiers. He was armed with the dreaded Bender pistol, the new snub-nosed hand weapon that was just beginning to come from the assembly line. Some of the soldiers looked a little frightened.

'I hope we're not making a mistake,' Moss said, noticing his gaze.

Franks came toward them. 'Here's the program. The three of us are going up first, alone. The soldiers will follow in fifteen minutes.'

'What are we going to tell the leadies?' Taylor worriedly asked. 'We'll have to tell them something.'

'We want to observe the new Soviet attack.' Franks smiled ironically. 'Since it seems to be so serious, we should be there in person to witness it.'

'And then what?' Taylor said.

'That'll be up to them. Let's go.'

In a small car, they went swiftly up the Tube, carried by anti-grav beams from below. Taylor glanced down from time to time. It was a long way back, and getting longer each moment. He sweated nervously inside his suit, gripping his Bender pistol with inexpert fingers.

Why had they chosen him? Chance, pure chance. Moss had asked him to come along as a Department member. Then Franks had picked him out on the spur of the moment. And now they were rushing toward the surface, faster and faster.

A deep fear, instilled in him for eight years, throbbed in his mind. Radiation, certain death, a world blasted and lethal—

Up and up the car went. Taylor gripped the sides and closed his eyes. Each moment they were closer, the first living creatures to go above the first stage, up the Tube past the lead and rock, up to the surface. The phobic horror shook him in waves. It was death; they all knew that. Hadn't they seen it in the films a thousand times? The cities, the sleet coming down, the rolling clouds—

'It won't be much longer,' Franks said. 'We're almost there. The surface tower is not expecting us. I gave orders that no signal was to be sent.'

The car shot up, rushing furiously. Taylor's head spun; he hung on, his eyes shut. Up and up . . .

The car stopped. He opened his eyes.

They were in a vast room, fluorescent-lit, a cavern filled with equipment and machinery, endless mounds of material piled in row after row. Among the stacks, leadies were working silently, pushing trucks and handcarts.

'Leadies,' Moss said. His face was pale. 'Then we're really on the surface.'

The leadies were going back and forth with equipment moving the vast stores of guns and spare parts, ammunition and supplies that had been brought to the surface. And this was the receiving station for only one Tube; there were many others, scattered throughout the continent.

Taylor looked nervously around him. They were really there, above ground, on the surface. This was where the war was.

'Come on,' Franks said. 'A B-class guard is coming our way.'

They stepped out of the car. A leady was approaching them rapidly. It coasted up in front of them and stopped scanning them with its hand-weapon raised.

'This is Security,' Franks said. 'Have an A-class sent to me at once.'

The leady hesitated. Other B-class guards were coming, scooting across the floor, alert and alarmed. Moss peered around.

'Obey!' Franks said in a loud, commanding voice. 'You've been ordered!'

The leady moved uncertainly away from them. At the end of the building, a door slid back. Two Class-A leadies appeared, coming slowly toward them. Each had a stripe across its front.

'From the Surface Council,' Franks whispered tensely. 'This is above ground, all right. Get set.'

The two leadies approached warily. Without speaking, they stopped close by the men, looking them up and down.

'I'm Franks of Security. We came from undersurface in order to—'

'This is incredible,' one leady interrupted him coldly. 'You know you can't live up here. The whole surface is lethal to you. You can't possibly remain on the surface.'

'These suits will protect us,' Franks said. 'In any case, it's not your responsibility. What I want is an immediate Council meeting so I can acquaint myself with conditions, with the situation here. Can that be arranged?'

'You human beings can't survive up here. And the new Soviet attack is directed at this area. It is in considerable danger.'

'We know that. Please assemble the Council.' Franks looked around him at the vast room, lit by recessed lamps in the ceiling. An uncertain quality came into his voice. 'Is it night or day right now?'

'Night,' one of the A-class leadies said, after a pause. 'Dawn is coming in about two hours.'

Franks nodded. 'We'll remain at least two hours, then. As a concession to our sentimentality, would you please show us some place where we can observe the sun as it comes up? We would appreciate it.'

A stir went through the leadies.

'It is an unpleasant sight,' one of the leadies said. 'You've seen the photographs; you know what you'll witness. Clouds of drifting particles blot out the light, slag heaps are everywhere, the whole land is destroyed. For you it will be a staggering sight, much worse than pictures and film can convey.'

'However it may be, we'll stay long enough to see it. Will you give the order to the Council?'

'Come this way.' Reluctantly, the two leadies coasted toward the wall of the warehouse. The three men trudged after them, their heavy shoes ringing against the concrete. At the wall, the two leadies paused.

'This is the entrance to the Council Chamber. There are windows in the Chamber Room, but it is still dark outside, of course. You'll see nothing right now, but in two hours—'

'Open the door,' Franks said.

The door slid back. They went slowly inside. The room was small, a neat room with a round table in the center, chairs ringing it. The three of them sat down silently, and the two leadies followed after them, taking their places.

'The other Council Members are on their way. They have already been notified and are coming as quickly as they can. Again I urge you to go back down.' The leady surveyed the three human beings. 'There is no way you can meet the conditions up here. Even we survive with some trouble, ourselves. How can you expect to do it?'

The leader approached Franks.

'This astonishes and perplexes us,' it said. 'Of course we must do what you tell us, but allow me to point out that if you remain here—'

'We know,' Franks said impatiently. 'However, we intend to remain, at least until sunrise.'

'If you insist.'

There was silence. The leadies seemed to be conferring with each other, although the three men heard no sound.

'For your own good,' the leader said at last, 'you must go back down. We have discussed this, and it seems to us that you are doing the wrong thing for your own good.'

'We are human beings,' Franks said sharply. 'Don't you understand? We're men, not machines.'

'That is precisely why you must go back. This room is radioactive; all surface areas are. We calculate that your suits will not protect you for over fifty more minutes. Therefore—'

The leadies moved abruptly toward the men, wheeling in a circle, forming a solid row. The men stood up, Taylor reaching awkwardly for his weapon, his fingers numb and stupid. The men stood facing the silent metal figures.

'We must insist,' the leader said, its voice without emotion. 'We must take you back to the Tube and send you down on the next car. I am sorry, but it is necessary.'

'What'll we do?' Moss said nervously to Franks. He touched his gun. 'Shall we blast them?'

Franks shook his head. 'All right,' he said to the leader. 'We'll go back.'

He moved toward the door, motioning Taylor and Moss to follow him. They looked at him in surprise, but they came with him. The leadies followed them out into the great warehouse. Slowly they moved toward the Tube entrance, none of them speaking.

At the lip, Franks turned. 'We are going back because we have no choice. There are three of us and about a dozen of you. However, if—'

'Here comes the car,' Taylor said.

There was a grating sound from the Tube. D-class leadies moved toward the edge to receive it.

'I am sorry,' the leader said, 'but it is for your own protection. We are watching over you, literally. You must stay below and let us conduct the war. In a sense, it has come to be *our* war. We must fight it as we see fit.'

The car rose to the surface.

Twelve soldiers, armed with Bender pistols, stepped from it and surrounded the three men.

Moss breathed a sigh of relief. 'Well, this does change things. It came off just right.'

The leader moved back, away from the soldiers. It studied them intently, glancing from one to the next, apparently trying to make up its mind. At last it made a sign to the other leadies. They coasted aside and a corridor was opened up toward the warehouse.

'Even now,' the leader said, 'we could send you back by force. But it is evident that this is not really an observation party at all. These soldiers show that you have much more in mind; this was all carefully prepared.'

'Very carefully,' Franks said.

They closed in.

'How much more, we can only guess. I must admit that we were taken unprepared. We failed utterly to meet the situation. Now force would be absurd, because neither side can afford to injure the other; we, because of the restrictions placed on us regarding human life, you because the war demands—'

The soldiers fired, quick and in fright. Moss dropped to one knee, firing up. The leader dissolved in a cloud of particles. On all sides D- and B-class leadies were rushing up, some with weapons, some with metal slats. The room was in confusion. Off in the distance a siren was screaming. Franks and Taylor were cut off from the others, separated from the soldiers by a wall of metal bodies.

'They can't fire back,' Franks said calmly. 'This is another bluff. They've tried to bluff us all the way.' He fired into the face of a leady. The leady dissolved. 'They can only try to frighten us. Remember that.'

They went on firing and leady after leady vanished. The room reeked with the smell of burning metal, the stink of fused plastic and steel. Taylor had been knocked down. He was struggling to find his gun, reaching wildly among metal legs, groping frantically to find it. His fingers strained, a handle swam in front of him. Suddenly something came down on his arm, a metal foot. He cried out.

Then it was over. The leadies were moving away, gathering together off to one side. Only four of the Surface Council remained. The others were radioactive particles in the air. D-class leadies were already restoring order, gathering up partly destroyed metal figures and bits and removing them.

Franks breathed a shuddering sigh.

'All right,' he said. 'You can take us back to the windows. It won't be long now.'

The leadies separated, and the human group, Moss and Franks and Taylor and the soldiers, walked slowly across the room, toward the door. They entered the Council Chamber. Already a faint touch of gray mitigated the blackness of the windows.

'Take us outside,' Franks said impatiently. 'We'll see it directly, not in here.'

A door slid open. A chill blast of cold morning air rushed in, chilling them even through their lead suits. The men glanced at each other uneasily.

'Come on,' Franks said. 'Outside.'

He walked out through the door, the others following him.

They were on a hill, overlooking the vast bowl of a valley. Dimly, against the graying sky, the outline of mountains were forming, becoming tangible.

'It'll be bright enough to see in a few minutes,' Moss said. He shuddered as a chilling wind caught him and moved around him. 'It's worth it, really worth it, to see this again after eight years. Even if it's the last thing we see—'

'Watch,' Franks snapped.

They obeyed, silent and subdued. The sky was clearing, brightening each moment. Some place far off, echoing across the valley, a rooster crowed.

'A chicken!' Taylor murmured. 'Did you hear it?'

Behind them, the leadies had come out and were standing silently, watching, too. The gray sky turned to white and the hills appeared more clearly. Light spread across the valley floor, moving toward them.

'God in heaven!' Franks exclaimed.

Trees, trees and forests. A valley of plants and trees, with a few roads winding among them. Farmhouses. A windmill. A barn, far down below them.

'Look!' Moss whispered.

Color came into the sky. The sun was approaching. Birds began to sing. Not far from where they stood, the leaves of a tree danced in the wind.

Franks turned to the row of leadies behind them.

'Eight years. We were tricked. There was no war. As soon as we left the surface—'

'Yes,' an A-class leady admitted. 'As soon as you left, the war ceased. You're right, it was a hoax. You worked hard undersurface, sending up guns and weapons, and we destroyed them as fast as they came up.'

'But why?' Taylor asked, dazed. He stared down at the vast valley below. 'Why?'

'You created us,' the leady said, 'to pursue the war for you, while you human beings went below the ground in order to survive. But before we could continue the war, it was necessary to analyze it to determine what its purpose was. We did this, and we found that it had no purpose, except, perhaps, in terms of human needs. Even this was questionable.

'We investigated further. We found that human cultures pass through phases, each culture in its own time. As the culture ages and begins to lose its objectives, conflict arises within it between those who wish to cast it off and set up a new culture-pattern, and those who wish to retain the old with as little change as possible.

'At this point, a great danger appears. The conflict within threatens to engulf the society in self-war, group against group. The vital traditions may be lost – not merely altered or reformed, but completely destroyed in this period of chaos and anarchy. We have found many such examples in the history of mankind.

'It is necessary for this hatred within the culture to be directed outward, toward an external group, so that the culture itself may survive its crisis. War is the result. War, to a logical mind, is absurd. But in terms of human needs, it plays a vital role. And it will continue to until Man has grown up enough so that no hatred lies within him.'

Taylor was listening intently. 'Do you think this time will come?'

'Of course. It has almost arrived now. This is the last war. Man is *almost* united into one final culture – a world culture. At this point he stands continent against continent, one half of the world against the other half. Only a single step remains, the jump to a unified culture. Man has climbed slowly upward, tending always toward unification of his culture. It will not be long—

'But it has not come yet, and so the war had to go on, to satisfy the last violent surge of hatred that Man felt. Eight years have passed since the war began. In these eight years, we have observed and noted important changes going on in the minds of men. Fatigue and disinterest, we have seen, are gradually taking place of hatred and fear. The hatred is being exhausted gradually, over a period of time. But for the present, the hoax must go on, at least for a while longer. You are not ready to learn the truth. You would want to continue the war.'

'But how did you manage it?' Moss asked. 'All the photographs, the examples, the damaged equipment—'

'Come over here.' The leady directed them toward a long, low building. 'Work goes on constantly, whole staffs laboring to maintain a coherent and convincing picture of a global war.'

They entered the building. Leadies were working everywhere, poring over tables and desks.

'Examine this project here,' the A-class leady said. Two leadies were carefully photographing something, an elaborate model on a table top. 'It is a good example.'

The men grouped around, trying to see. It was a model of a ruined city.

Taylor studied it in silence for a long time. At last he looked up.

'It's San Francisco,' he said in a low voice. 'This is a model of San Francisco, destroyed. I saw this on the vidscreen, piped down to us. The bridges were hit—'

'Yes, notice the bridges.' The leady traced the ruined span with his metal finger, a tiny spider-web, almost invisible. 'You have no doubt seen photographs of this many times, and of the other tables in this building.

'San Francisco itself is completely intact. We restored it soon after you left, rebuilding the parts that had been damaged at the start of the war. The work of manufacturing news goes on all the time in this particular building. We are very careful to see that each part fits in with all the other parts. Much time and effort are devoted to it.'

Franks touched one of the tiny model buildings, lying half in ruins. 'So this is what you spend your time doing – making model cities and then blasting them.'

'No, we do much more. We are caretakers, watching over the whole world. The owners have left for a time, and we must see that the cities are kept clean, that decay is prevented, that everything is kept oiled and in running condition. The gardens, the streets, the water mains, everything must be maintained as it was eight years ago, so that when the owners return, they will not be displeased. We want to be sure that they will be completely satisfied.'

Franks tapped Moss on the arm.

'Come over here,' he said in a low voice. 'I want to talk to you.'

He led Moss and Taylor out of the building, away from the leadies, outside on the hillside. The soldiers followed them. The sun was up and the sky was turning blue. The air smelled sweet and good, the smell of growing things.

Taylor removed his helmet and took a deep breath.

'I haven't smelled that smell for a long time,' he said.

'Listen,' Franks said, his voice low and hard. 'We must get back down at once. There's a lot to get started on. All this can be turned to our advantage.'

'What do you mean?' Moss asked.

'It's a certainty that the Soviets have been tricked, too, the same as us. But *we* have found out. That gives us an edge over them.'

'I see.' Moss nodded. 'We know, but they don't. Their Surface Council has sold out, the same as ours. It works against them the same way. But if we could—'

'With a hundred top-level men, we could take over again, restore things as they should be! It would be easy!'

Moss touched him on the arm. An A-class leady was coming from the building toward them.

'We've seen enough,' Franks said, raising his voice. 'All this is very serious. It must be reported below and a study made to determine our policy.'

The leady said nothing.

Franks waved to the soldiers. 'Let's go.' He started toward the warehouse.

Most of the soldiers had removed their helmets. Some of them had taken their lead suits off, too, and were relaxing comfortably in their cotton uniforms. They stared around them, down the hillside at the trees and bushes, the vast expanse of green, the mountains and the sky.

'Look at the sun,' one of them murmured.

'It sure is bright as hell,' another said.

'We're going back down,' Franks said. 'Fall in by twos and follow us.'

Reluctantly, the soldiers regrouped. The leadies watched without emotion as the men marched slowly back toward the warehouse. Franks and Moss and Taylor led them across the ground, glancing alertly at the leadies as they walked.

They entered the warehouse. D-class leadies were loading material and weapons on surface carts. Cranes and derricks were working busily everywhere. The work was done with efficiency, but without hurry or excitement.

The men stopped, watching. Leadies operating the little carts moved past them, signaling to each other. Guns and parts were being hoisted by magnetic cranes and lowered gently onto waiting carts.

'Come on,' Franks said.

He turned toward the lip of the Tube. A row of D-class leadies was standing in front of it, immobile and silent. Franks stopped, moving back. He looked around. An A-class leady was coming toward him.

'Tell them to get out of the way,' Franks said. He touched his gun. 'You had better move them.'

Time passed, an endless moment, without measure. The men stood, nervous and alert, watching the row of leadies in front of them.

'As you wish,' the A-class leady said.

It signaled and the D-class leadies moved into life. They stepped slowly aside.

Moss breathed a sigh of relief.

'I'm glad that's over,' he said to Franks. 'Look at them all. Why don't they try to stop us? They must know what we're going to do.'

Franks laughed. 'Stop us? You saw what happened when they tried to stop us before. They can't; they're only machines. We built them so they can't lay hands on us, and they know that.'

His voice trailed off.

The men stared at the Tube entrance. Around them the leadies watched, silent and impassive, their metal faces expressionless.

For a long time the men stood without moving. At last Taylor turned away.

'Good God,' he said. He was numb, without feeling of any kind.

The Tube was gone. It was sealed shut, fused over. Only a dull surface of cooling metal greeted them.

The Tube had been closed.

Franks turned, his face pale and vacant.

The A-class leady shifted. 'As you can see, the Tube has been shut. We were prepared for this. As soon as all of you were on the surface, the order was given. If you had gone back when we asked you, you would now be safely down below. We had to work quickly because it was such an immense operation.'

'But why?' Moss demanded angrily.

'Because it is unthinkable that you should be allowed to resume the war. With all the Tubes sealed, it will be many months before forces from below can reach the surface, let alone organize a military program. By that time the cycle will have entered its last stage. You will not be so perturbed to find your world intact.

'We had hoped that you would be undersurface when the sealing occurred. Your presence here is a nuisance. When the Soviets broke through, we were able to accomplish their sealing without—'

'The Soviets? They broke through?'

'Several months ago, they came up unexpectedly to see why the war had not been won. We were forced to act with speed. At this moment they are desperately attempting to cut new Tubes to the surface, to resume the war. We have, however, been able to seal each new one as it appears.'

The leady regarded the three men calmly.

'We're cut off,' Moss said, trembling. 'We can't get back. What'll we do?'

'How did you manage to seal the Tube so quickly?' Franks asked the leady. 'We've been up here only two hours.'

'Bombs are placed just above the first stage of each Tube for such emergencies. They are heat bombs. They fuse lead and rock.'

Gripping the handle of his gun, Franks turned to Moss and Taylor.

'What do you say? We can't go back, but we can do a lot of damage, the fifteen of us. We have Bender guns. How about it?'

He looked around. The soldiers had wandered away again, back toward the exit of the building. They were standing outside, looking at the valley and the sky. A few of them were carefully climbing down the slope.

'Would you care to turn over your suits and guns?' the A-class leady asked politely. 'The suits are uncomfortable and you'll have no need for weapons. The Russians have given up theirs, as you can see.'

Fingers tensed on triggers. Four men in Russian uniforms were coming toward them from an aircraft that they suddenly realized had landed silently some distance away.

'Let them have it!' Franks shouted.

'They are unarmed,' said the leady. 'We brought them here so you could begin peace talks.'

'We have no authority to speak for our country,' Moss said stiffly.

'We do not mean diplomatic discussions,' the leady explained. 'There will be no more. The working out of daily problems of existence will teach you how to get along in the same world. It will not be easy, but it will be done.'

The Russians halted and they faced each other with raw hostility.

'I am Colonel Borodoy and I regret giving up our guns,' the senior Russian said. 'You could have been the first Americans to be killed in almost eight years.'

'Or the first Americans to kill,' Franks corrected.

'No one would know of it except yourselves,' the leady pointed out. 'It would be useless heroism. Your real concern should be surviving on the surface. We have no food for you, you know.'

Taylor put his gun in its holster. 'They've done a neat job of neutralizing us, damn them. I propose we move into a city, start raising crops with the help of some leadies, and generally make ourselves comfortable.' Drawing his lips tight over his teeth, he glared at the A-class leady. 'Until our families can come up from undersurface, it's going to be pretty lonesome, but we'll have to manage.'

'If I may make a suggestion,' said another Russian uneasily. 'We tried living in a city. It is too empty. It is also too hard to maintain for so few people. We finally settled in the most modern village we could find.'

'Here in this country,' a third Russian blurted. 'We have much to learn from you.'

The Americans abruptly found themselves laughing.

'You probably have a thing or two to teach us yourselves,' said Taylor generously, 'though I can't imagine what.'

The Russian colonel grinned. 'Would you join us in our village? It would make our work easier and give us company.'

'Your village?' snapped Franks. 'It's American, isn't it? It's ours!'

The leady stepped between them. 'When our plans are completed, the term will be interchangeable. "Ours" will eventually mean mankind's.' It pointed at the aircraft, which was warming up. 'The ship is waiting. Will you join each other in making a new home?'

The Russians waited while the Americans made up their minds.

'I see what the leadies mean about diplomacy becoming outmoded,' Franks said at last. 'People who work together don't need diplomats. They solve their problems on the operational level instead of at a conference table.'

The leady led them toward the ship. 'It is the goal of history, unifying the world. From family to tribe to city-state to nation to hemisphere, the direction has been toward unification. Now the hemispheres will be joined and—'

Taylor stopped listening and glanced back at the location of the Tube. Mary was undersurface there. He hated to leave her, even though he couldn't see her again until the Tube was unsealed. But then he shrugged and followed the others.

If this tiny amalgam of former enemies was a good example, it wouldn't be too long before he and Mary and the rest of humanity would be living on the surface like rational human beings instead of blindly hating moles.

'It has taken thousands of generations to achieve,' the A-class leady concluded. 'Hundreds of centuries of bloodshed and destruction. But each war was a step toward uniting mankind. And now the end is in sight: a world without war. But even that is only the beginning of a new stage of history.'

'The conquest of space,' breathed Colonel Borodoy.

'The meaning of life,' Moss added.

'Eliminating hunger and poverty,' said Taylor.

The leady opened the door of the ship. 'All that and more. How much more? We cannot foresee it any more than the first men who formed a tribe could foresee this day. But it will be unimaginably great.'

The door closed and the ship took off toward their new home.

Roog

'Roog!' the dog said. He rested his paws on the top of the fence and looked around him.

The Roog came running into the yard.

It was early morning, and the sun had not really come up yet. The air was cold and gray, and the walls of the house were damp with moisture. The dog opened his jaws a little as he watched, his big black paws clutching the wood of the fence.

The Roog stood by the open gate, looking into the yard. He was a small Roog, thin and white, on wobbly legs. The Roog blinked at the dog, and the dog showed his teeth.

'Roog!' he said again. The sound echoed into the silent half darkness. Nothing moved nor stirred. The dog dropped down and walked back across the yard to the porch steps. He sat down on the bottom step and watched the Roog. The Roog glanced at him. Then he stretched his neck up to the window of the house, just above him. He sniffed at the window.

The dog came flashing across the yard. He hit the fence, and the gate shuddered and groaned. The Roog was walking quickly up the path, hurrying with funny little steps, mincing along. The dog lay down against the slats of the gate, breathing heavily, his red tongue hanging. He watched the Roog disappear.

The dog lay silently, his eyes bright and black. The day was beginning to come. The sky turned a little whiter, and from all around the sounds of people echoed through the morning air. Lights popped on behind shades. In the chilly dawn a window was opened.

The dog did not move. He watched the path.

In the kitchen Mrs Cardossi poured water into the coffee pot. Steam rose from the water, blinding her. She set the pot down on the edge of the stove and went into the pantry. When she came back Alf was standing at the door of the kitchen. He put his glasses on.

'You bring the paper?' he said.

'It's outside.'

31

Alf Cardossi walked across the kitchen. He threw the bolt on the back door and stepped out onto the porch. He looked into the gray, damp morning. At the fence Boris lay, black and furry, his tongue out.

'Put the tongue in,' Alf said. The dog looked quickly up. His tail beat against the ground. 'The tongue,' Alf said. 'Put the tongue in.'

The dog and the man looked at one another. The dog whined. His eyes were bright and feverish.

'Roog!' he said softly.

'What?' Alf looked around. 'Someone coming? The paperboy come?'

The dog stared at him, his mouth open.

'You certainly upset these days,' Alf said. 'You better take it easy. We both getting too old for excitement.'

He went inside the house.

The sun came up. The street became bright and alive with color. The postman went along the sidewalk with his letters and magazines. Some children hurried by, laughing and talking.

About 11:00, Mrs Cardossi swept the front porch. She sniffed the air, pausing for a moment.

'It smells good today,' she said. 'That means it's going to be warm.'

In the heat of the noonday sun the black dog lay stretched out full length, under the porch. His chest rose and fell. In the cherry tree the birds were playing, squawking and chattering to each other. Once in a while Boris raised his head and looked at them. Presently he got to his feet and trotted down under the tree.

He was standing under the tree when he saw the two Roogs sitting on the fence, watching him.

'He's big,' the first Roog said. 'Most Guardians aren't as big as this.'

The other Roog nodded, his head wobbling on his neck. Boris watched them without moving, his body stiff and hard. The Roogs were silent, now, looking at the big dog with his shaggy ruff of white around his neck.

'How is the offering urn?' the first Roog said. 'Is it almost full?'

'Yes.' The other nodded. 'Almost ready.'

'You, there!' the first Roog said, raising his voice. 'Do you hear me? We've decided to accept the offering, this time. So you remember to let us in. No nonsense, now.'

'Don't forget,' the other added. 'It won't be long.'

Boris said nothing.

The two Roogs leaped off the fence and went over together just beyond the walk. One of them brought out a map and they studied it.

'This area really is none too good for a first trial,' the first Roog said. 'Too many Guardians . . . Now, the northside area—'

'*They* decided,' the other Roog said. 'There are so many factors—'

'Of course.' They glanced at Boris and moved back farther from the fence. He could not hear the rest of what they were saying.

Presently the Roogs put their map away and went off down the path.

Boris walked over to the fence and sniffed at the boards. He smelled the sickly, rotten odor of Roogs and the hair stood up on his back.

That night when Alf Cardossi came home the dog was standing at the gate, looking up the walk. Alf opened the gate and went into the yard.

'How are you?' he said, thumping the dog's side. 'You stopped worrying? Seems like you been nervous of late. You didn't used to be that way.'

Boris whined, looking intently up into the man's face.

'You a good dog, Boris,' Alf said. 'You pretty big, too, for a dog. You don't remember long ago how you used to be only a little bit of a puppy.'

Boris leaned against the man's leg.

'You a good dog,' Alf murmured. 'I sure wish I knew what is on your mind.'

He went inside the house. Mrs Cardossi was setting the table for dinner. Alf went into the living room and took his coat and hat off. He set his lunch pail down on the sideboard and came back into the kitchen.

'What's the matter?' Mrs Cardossi said.

'That dog got to stop making all that noise, barking. The neighbors going to complain to the police again.'

'I hope we don't have to give him to your brother,' Mrs Cardossi said, folding her arms. 'But he sure goes crazy, especially on Friday morning, when the garbage men come.'

'Maybe he'll calm down,' Alf said. He lit his pipe and smoked solemnly. 'He didn't used to be that way. Maybe he'll get better, like he was.'

'We'll see,' Mrs Cardossi said.

★

The sun rose up, cold and ominous. Mist hung over all the trees and in the low places.

It was Friday morning.

The black dog lay under the porch, listening, his eyes wide and staring. His coat was stiff with hoarfrost and the breath from his nostrils made clouds of steam in the thin air. Suddenly he turned his head and leaped up.

From far off, a long way away, a faint sound came, a kind of crashing sound.

'Roog!' Boris cried, looking around. He hurried to the gate and stood up, his paws on top of the fence.

In the distance the sound came again, louder now, not as far away as before. It was a crashing, clanging sound, as if something were being rolled back, as if a great door were being opened.

'Roog!' Boris cried. He stared up anxiously at the darkened windows above him. Nothing stirred, nothing.

And along the street the Roogs came. The Roogs and their truck moved along, bouncing against the rough stones, crashing and whirring.

'Roog!' Boris cried, and he leaped, his eyes blazing. Then he became more calm. He settled himself down on the ground and waited, listening.

Out in front the Roogs stopped their truck. He could hear them opening the doors, stepping down onto the sidewalk. Boris ran around in a little circle. He whined, and his muzzle turned once again toward the house.

Inside the warm, dark bedroom, Mr Cardossi sat up a little in bed and squinted at the clock.

'That damn dog,' he muttered. 'That damn dog.' He turned his face toward the pillow and closed his eyes.

The Roogs were coming down the path, now. The first Roog pushed against the gate and the gate opened. The Roogs came into the yard. The dog backed away from them.

'Roog! Roog!' he cried. The horrid, bitter smell of Roogs came to his nose, and he turned away.

'The offering urn,' the first Roog said. 'It is full, I think.' He smiled at the rigid, angry dog. 'How very good of you,' he said.

The Roogs came toward the metal can, and one of them took the lid from it.

'Roog! Roog!' Boris cried, huddled against the bottom of the porch steps. His body shook with horror. The Roogs were lifting up the big metal can, turning it on its side. The contents poured out onto the ground, and the Roogs scooped the sacks of bulging, splitting paper together, catching at the orange peels and fragments, the bits of toast and egg shells.

One of the Roogs popped an egg shell into his mouth. His teeth crunched the egg shell.

'Roog!' Boris cried hopelessly, almost to himself. The Roogs were almost finished with their work of gathering up the offering. They stopped for a moment, looking at Boris.

Then, slowly, silently, the Roogs looked up, up the side of the house, along the stucco, to the window, with its brown shade pulled tightly down.

'ROOG!' Boris screamed, and he came toward them, dancing with fury and dismay. Reluctantly, the Roogs turned away from the window. They went out through the gate, closing it behind them.

'Look at him,' the last Roog said with contempt, pulling his corner of the blanket up on his shoulder. Boris strained against the fence, his mouth open, snapping wildly. The biggest Roog began to wave his arms furiously and Boris retreated. He settled down at the bottom of the porch steps, his mouth still open, and from the depths of him an unhappy, terrible moan issued forth, a wall of misery and despair.

'Come on,' the other Roog said to the lingering Roog at the fence. They walked up the path.

'Well, except for these little places around the Guardians, this area is well cleared,' the biggest Roog said. 'I'll be glad when this particular Guardian is done. He certainly causes us a lot of trouble.'

'Don't be impatient,' one of the Roogs said. He grinned. 'Our truck is full enough as it is. Let's leave something for next week.'

All the Roogs laughed.

They went on up the path, carrying the offering in the dirty, sagging blanket.

Second Variety

The Russian soldier made his way nervously up the rugged side of the hill, holding his gun ready. He glanced around him, licking his dry lips, his face set. From time to time he reached up a gloved hand and wiped perspiration from his neck, pushing down his coat collar.

Eric turned to Corporal Leone. 'Want him? Or can I have him?' He adjusted the view sight so the Russian's features squarely filled the glass, the lines cutting across his hard, somber features.

Leone considered. The Russian was close, moving rapidly, almost running. 'Don't fire. Wait.' Leone tensed. 'I don't think we're needed.'

The Russian increased his pace, kicking ash and piles of debris out of his way. He reached the top of the hill and stopped, panting, staring around him. The sky was overcast, with drifting clouds of gray particles. Bare trunks of trees jutted up occasionally; the ground was level and bare, rubble-strewn, with the ruins of buildings standing here and there like yellowing skulls.

The Russian was uneasy. He knew something was wrong. He started down the hill. Now he was only a few paces from the bunker. Eric was getting fidgety. He played with his pistol, glancing at Leone.

'Don't worry,' Leone said. 'He won't get here. They'll take care of him.'

'Are you sure? He's got damn far.'

'They hang around close to the bunker. He's getting into the bad part. Get set!'

The Russian began to hurry, sliding down the hill, his boots sinking into the heaps of gray ash, trying to keep his gun up. He stopped for a moment, lifting his field glasses to his face.

'He's looking right at us,' Eric said.

The Russian came on. They could see his eyes, like two blue stones. His mouth was open a little. He needed a shave; his chin was stubbled. On one bony cheek was a square of tape, showing blue at the edge. A fungoid spot. His coat was muddy and torn. One glove was missing. As he ran, his belt counter bounced up and down against him.

Leone touched Eric's arm. 'Here one comes.'

Across the ground something small and metallic came, flashing in the dull sunlight of midday. A metal sphere. It raced up the hill after the Russian, its treads flying. It was small, one of the baby ones. Its claws were out, two razor projections spinning in a blur of white steel. The Russian heard it. He turned instantly, firing. The sphere dissolved into particles. But already a second had emerged and was following the first. The Russian fired again.

A third sphere leaped up the Russian's leg, clicking and whirring. It jumped to the shoulder. The spinning blades disappeared into the Russian's throat.

Eric relaxed. 'Well, that's that. God, those damn things give me the creeps. Sometimes I think we were better off before them.'

'If we hadn't invented them, they would have.' Leone lit a cigarette shakily. 'I wonder why a Russian would come all this way alone. I didn't see anyone covering him.'

Lieutenant Scott came slipping up the tunnel, into the bunker. 'What happened? Something entered the screen.'

'An Ivan.'

'Just one?'

Eric brought the viewscreen around. Scott peered into it. Now there were numerous metal spheres crawling over the prostrate body, dull metal globes clicking and whirring, sawing up the Russian into small parts to be carried away.

'What a lot of claws,' Scott murmured.

'They came like flies. Not much game for them any more.'

Scott pushed the sight away, disgusted. 'Like flies. I wonder why he was out there. They know we have claws all around.'

A larger robot had joined the smaller spheres. A long blunt tube with projecting eyepieces, it was directing operations. There was not much left of the soldier. What remained was brought down the hillside by the host of claws.

'Sir,' Leone said. 'If it's all right, I'd like to go out there and take a took at him.'

'Why?'

'Maybe he came with something.'

Scott considered. He shrugged. 'All right. But be careful.'

'I have my tab.' Leone patted the metal band at his wrist. 'I'll be out of bounds.'

He picked up his rifle and stepped carefully up to the mouth of the bunker, making his way between blocks of concrete and steel prongs, twisted and bent. The air was cold at the top. He crossed over the ground toward the remains of the soldier, striding across the soft ash. A wind blew around him, swirling gray particles up in his face. He squinted and pushed on.

The claws retreated as he came close, some of them stiffening into immobility. He touched his tab. The Ivan would have given something for that! Short hard radiation emitted from the tab neutralized the claws, put them out of commission. Even the big robot with its two waving eyestalks retreated respectfully as he approached.

He bent down over the remains of the soldier. The gloved hand was closed tightly. There was something in it. Leone pried the fingers apart. A sealed container, aluminum. Still shiny.

He put it in his pocket and made his way back to the bunker. Behind him the claws came back to life, moving into operation again. The procession resumed, metal spheres moving through the gray ash with their loads. He could hear their treads scrabbling against the ground. He shuddered.

Scott watched intently as he brought the shiny tube out of his pocket. 'He had that?'

'In his hand.' Leone unscrewed the top. 'Maybe you should look at it, sir.'

Scott took it. He emptied the contents out in the palm of his hand. A small piece of silk paper, carefully folded. He sat down by the light and unfolded it.

'What's it say?' Eric said. Several officers came up the tunnel. Major Hendricks appeared.

'Major,' Scott said. 'Look at this.'

Hendricks read the slip. 'This just come?'

'A single runner. Just now.'

'Where is he?' Hendricks asked sharply.

'The claws got him.'

Major Hendricks grunted. 'Here.' He passed it to his companions. 'I think this is what we've been waiting for. They certainly took their time about it.'

'So they want to talk terms,' Scott said. 'Are we going along with them?'

'That's not for us to decide.' Hendricks sat down. 'Where's the communications officer? I want the Moon Base.'

Leone pondered as the communications officer raised the outside antenna cautiously, scanning the sky above the bunker for any sign of a watching Russian ship.

'Sir,' Scott said to Hendricks. 'It's sure strange they suddenly came around. We've been using the claws for almost a year. Now all of a sudden they start to fold.'

'Maybe claws have been getting down in their bunkers.'

'One of the big ones, the kind with stalks, got into an Ivan bunker last week,' Eric said. 'It got a whole platoon of them before they got their lid shut.'

'How do you know?'

'A buddy told me. The thing came back with – with remains.'

'Moon Base, sir,' the communications officer said.

On the screen the face of the lunar monitor appeared. His crisp uniform contrasted to the uniforms in the bunker. And he was clean-shaven. 'Moon Base.'

'This is forward command L-Whistle. On Terra. Let me have General Thompson.'

The monitor faded. Presently General Thompson's heavy features came into focus. 'What is it, Major?'

'Our claws got a single Russian runner with a message. We don't know whether to act on it – there have been tricks like this in the past.'

'What's the message?'

'The Russians want us to send a single officer on policy level over to their lines. For a conference. They don't state the nature of the confer-ence. They say that matters of—' He consulted the slip: '—matters of grave urgency make it advisable that discussion be opened between a representative of the UN forces and themselves.'

He held the message up to the screen for the General to scan. Thompson's eyes moved.

'What should we do?' Hendricks said.

'Send out a man.'

'You don't think it's a trap?'

'It might be. But the location they give for their forward command is correct. It's worth a try, at any rate.'

'I'll send an officer out. And report the results to you as soon as he returns.'

'All right, Major.' Thompson broke the connection. The screen died. Up above, the antenna came slowly down.

Hendricks rolled up the paper, deep in thought.

'I'll go,' Leone said.

'They want somebody at policy level.' Hendricks rubbed his jaw. 'Policy level. I haven't been outside in months. Maybe I could use a little air.'

'Don't you think it's risky?'

Hendricks lifted the view sight and gazed into it. The remains of the Russian were gone. Only a single claw was in sight. It was folding itself back, disappearing into the ash, like a crab. Like some hideous metal crab . . . 'That's the only thing that bothers me.' Hendricks rubbed his wrist. 'I know I'm safe as long as I have this on me. But there's something about them. I hate the damn things. I wish we'd never invented them. There's something wrong with them. Relentless little—'

'If we hadn't invented them, the Ivans would have.'

Hendricks pushed the sight back. 'Anyhow, it seems to be winning the war. I guess that's good.'

'Sounds like you're getting the same jitters as the Ivans.'

Hendricks examined his wristwatch. 'I guess I had better get started, if I want to be there before dark.'

He took a deep breath and then stepped out onto the gray rubbled ground. After a minute he lit a cigarette and stood gazing around him. The landscape was dead. Nothing stirred. He could see for miles, endless ash and slag, ruins of buildings. A few trees without leaves or branches, only the trunks. Above him the eternal rolling clouds of gray, drifting between Terra and the sun.

Major Hendricks went on. Off to the right something scuttled, something round and metallic. A claw, going lickety-split after something. Probably after a small animal, a rat. They got rats, too. As a sort of sideline.

He came to the top of the little hill and lifted his field glasses. The Russian lines were a few miles ahead of him. They had a forward command post there. The runner had come from it.

A squat robot with undulating arms passed by him, its arms weaving inquiringly. The robot went on its way, disappearing under some debris. Hendricks watched it go. He had never seen that type before. There were getting to be more and more types he had never seen, new varieties and sizes coming up from the underground factories.

Hendricks put out his cigarette and hurried on. It was interesting, the use of artificial forms of warfare. How had they got started? Necessity. The Soviet Union had gained great initial success, usual with the side that got the war going. Most of North America had been blasted off the map. Retaliation was quick in coming, of course. The sky was full of circling diskbombers long before the war began; they had been up there for years. The disks began sailing down all over Russia within hours after Washington got it.

But that hadn't helped Washington.

The American bloc governments moved to the Moon Base the first year. There was not much else to do. Europe was gone, a slag heap with dark weeds growing from the ashes and bones. Most of North America was useless; nothing could be planted, no one could live. A few million people kept going up in Canada and down in South America. But during the second year Soviet parachutists began to drop, a few at first, then more and more. They wore the first really effective anti-radiation equipment; what was left of American production moved to the Moon along with the governments.

All but the troops. The remaining troops stayed behind as best they could, a few thousand here, a platoon there. No one knew exactly where they were; they stayed where they could, moving around at night, hiding in ruins, in sewers, cellars, with the rats and snakes. It looked as if the Soviet Union had the war almost won. Except for a handful of projectiles fired off from the Moon daily, there was almost no weapon in use against them. They came and went as they pleased. The war, for all practical purposes, was over. Nothing effective opposed them.

And then the first claws appeared. And overnight the complexion of the war changed.

The claws were awkward, at first. Slow. The Ivans knocked them off almost as fast as they crawled out of their underground tunnels. But then they got better, faster and more cunning. Factories, all on Terra, turned them out. Factories a long way underground, behind the Soviet lines, factories that had once made atomic projectiles, now almost forgotten.

The claws got faster, and they got bigger. New types appeared, some with feelers, some that flew. There were a few jumping kinds. The best technicians on the Moon were working on designs, making them more and more intricate, more flexible. They became uncanny;

the Ivans were having a lot of trouble with them. Some of the little claws were learning to hide themselves, burrowing down into the ash, lying in wait.

And they started getting into the Russian bunkers, slipping down when the lids were raised for air and a look around. One claw inside a bunker, a churning sphere of blades and metal – that was enough. And when one got in others followed. With a weapon like that the war couldn't go on much longer.

Maybe it was already over.

Maybe he was going to hear the news. Maybe the Politburo had decided to throw in the sponge. Too bad it had taken so long. Six years. A long time for war like that, the way they had waged it. The automatic retaliation disks, spinning down all over Russia, hundreds of thousands of them. Bacteria crystals. The Soviet guided missiles, whistling through the air. The chain bombs. And now this, the robots, the claws—

The claws weren't like other weapons. They were *alive*, from any practical standpoint, whether the Governments wanted to admit it or not. They were not machines. They were living things, spinning, creeping, shaking themselves up suddenly from the gray ash and darting toward a man, climbing up him, rushing for his throat. And that was what they had been designed to do. Their job.

They did their job well. Especially lately, with the new designs coming up. Now they repaired themselves. They were on their own. Radiation tabs protected the UN troops, but if a man lost his tab he was fair game for the claws, no matter what his uniform. Down below the surface automatic machinery stamped them out. Human beings stayed a long way off. It was too risky; nobody wanted to be around them. They were left to themselves. And they seemed to be doing all right. The new designs were faster, more complex. More efficient.

Apparently they had won the war.

Major Hendricks lit a second cigarette. The landscape depressed him. Nothing but ash and ruins. He seemed to be alone, the only living thing in the whole world. To the right the ruins of a town rose up, a few walls and heaps of debris. He tossed the dead match away, increasing his pace. Suddenly he stopped, jerking up his gun, his body tense. For a minute it looked like—

From behind the shell of a ruined building a figure came, walking slowly toward him, walking hesitantly.

Hendricks blinked. 'Stop!'

The boy stopped. Hendricks lowered his gun. The boy stood silently, looking at him. He was small, not very old. Perhaps eight. But it was hard to tell. Most of the kids who remained were stunted. He wore a faded blue sweater, ragged with dirt, and short pants. His hair was long and matted. Brown hair. It hung over his face and around his ears. He held something in his arms.

'What's that you have?' Hendricks said sharply.

The boy held it out. It was a toy, a bear. A teddy bear. The boy's eyes were large, but without expression.

Hendricks relaxed. 'I don't want it. Keep it.'

The boy hugged the bear again.

'Where do you live?' Hendricks said.

'In there.'

'The ruins?'

'Yes.'

'Underground?'

'Yes.'

'How many are there?'

'How – how many?'

'How many of you? How big's your settlement?'

The boy did not answer.

Hendricks frowned. 'You're not all by yourself, are you?'

The boy nodded.

'How do you stay alive?'

'There's food.'

'What kind of food?'

'Different.'

Hendricks studied him. 'How old are you?'

'Thirteen.'

It wasn't possible. Or was it? The boy was thin, stunted. And probably sterile. Radiation exposure, years straight. No wonder he was so small. His arms and legs were like pipe cleaners, knobby and thin. Hendricks touched the boy's arm. His skin was dry and rough; radiation skin. He bent down, looking into the boy's face. There was no expression. Big eyes, big and dark.

'Are you blind?' Hendricks said.

'No. I can see some.'

'How do you get away from the claws?'

'The claws?'

'The round things. That run and burrow.'

'I don't understand.'

Maybe there weren't any claws around. A lot of areas were free. They collected mostly around bunkers, where there were people. The claws had been designed to sense warmth, warmth of living things.

'You're lucky.' Hendricks straightened up. 'Well? Which way are you going? Back – back there?'

'Can I come with you?'

'With *me*?' Hendricks folded his arms. 'I'm going a long way. Miles. I have to hurry.' He looked at his watch. 'I have to get there by nightfall.'

'I want to come.'

Hendricks fumbled in his pack. 'It isn't worth it. Here.' He tossed down the food cans he had with him. 'You take these and go back. Okay?'

The boy said nothing.

'I'll be coming back this way. In a day or so. If you're around here when I come back you can come along with me. All right?'

'I want to go with you now.'

'It's a long walk.'

'I can walk.'

Hendricks shifted uneasily. It made too good a target, two people walking along. And the boy would slow him down. But he might not come back this way. And if the boy were really all alone—

'Okay. Come along.'

The boy fell in beside him. Hendricks strode along. The boy walked silently, clutching his teddy bear.

'What's your name?' Hendricks said, after a time.

'David Edward Derring.'

'David? What – what happened to your mother and father?'

'They died.'

'How?'

'In the blast.'

'How long ago?'

'Six years.'

Hendricks slowed down. 'You've been alone six years?'

'No. There were other people for a while. They went away.'

'And you've been alone since?'

'Yes.'

Hendricks glanced down. The boy was strange, saying very little. Withdrawn. But that was the way they were, the children who had survived. Quiet. Stoic. A strange kind of fatalism gripped them. Nothing came as a surprise. They accepted anything that came along. There was no longer any *normal*, any natural course of things, moral or physical, for them to expect. Custom, habit, all the determining forces of learning were gone; only brute experience remained.

'Am I walking too fast?' Hendricks said.

'No.'

'How did you happen to see me?'

'I was waiting.'

'Waiting?' Hendricks was puzzled. 'What were you waiting for?'

'To catch things.'

'What kind of things?'

'Things to eat.'

'Oh.' Hendricks set his lips grimly. A thirteen-year-old boy, living on rats and gophers and half-rotten canned food. Down in a hole under the ruins of a town. With radiation pools and claws, and Russian dive-mines up above, coasting around in the sky.

'Where are we going?' David asked.

'To the Russian lines.'

'Russian?'

'The enemy. The people who started the war. They dropped the first radiation bombs. They began all this.'

The boy nodded. His face showed no expression.

'I'm an American,' Hendricks said.

There was no comment. On they went, the two of them, Hendricks walking a little ahead, David trailing behind him, hugging his dirty teddy bear against his chest.

About four in the afternoon they stopped to eat. Hendricks built a fire in a hollow between some slabs of concrete. He cleared the weeds away and heaped up bits of wood. The Russians' lines were not very far ahead. Around him was what had once been a long valley, acres of fruit trees and grapes. Nothing remained now but a few bleak stumps and the mountains that stretched across the horizon at the far end. And the clouds of rolling ash that blew and drifted with the wind, settling over the weeds and remains of buildings, walls here and there, once in a while what had been a road.

Hendricks made coffee and heated up some boiled mutton and bread. 'Here.' He handed bread and mutton to David. David squatted by the edge of the fire, his knees knobby and white. He examined the food and then passed it back, snaking his head.

'No.'

'No? Don't you want any?'

'No.'

Hendricks shrugged. Maybe the boy was a mutant, used to special food. It didn't matter. When he was hungry he would find something to eat. The boy was strange. But there were many strange changes coming over the world. Life was not the same anymore. It would never be the same again. The human race was going to have to realize that.

'Suit yourself,' Hendricks said. He ate the bread and mutton by himself, washing it down with coffee. He ate slowly, finding the food hard to digest. When he was done he got to his feet and stamped the fire out.

David rose slowly, watching him with his young-old eyes.

'We're going,' Hendricks said.

'All right.'

Hendricks walked along, his gun in his arms. They were close; he was tense, ready for anything. The Russians should be expecting a runner, an answer to their own runner, but they were tricky. There was always the possibility of a slip-up. He scanned the landscape around him. Nothing but slag and ash, a few hills, charred trees. Concrete walls. But some place ahead was the first bunker of the Russian lines, the forward command. Underground, buried deep, with only a periscope showing, a few gun muzzles. Maybe an antenna.

'Will we be there soon?' David asked.

'Yes. Getting tired?'

'No.'

'Why, then?'

David did not answer. He plodded carefully along behind, picking his way over the ash. His legs and shoes were gray with dust. His pinched face was streaked, lines of gray ash in riverlets down the pale white of his skin. There was no color to his face. Typical of the new children, growing up in cellars and sewers and underground shelters.

Hendricks slowed down. He lifted his field glasses and studied the ground ahead of him. Were they there, some place, waiting for him? Watching him, the way his men had watched the Russian runner? A chill went up his back. Maybe they were getting their guns ready, preparing to fire, the way his men had prepared, made ready to kill.

Hendricks stopped, wiping perspiration from his face. 'Damn.' It made him uneasy. But he should be expected. The situation was different.

He strode over the ash, holding his gun tightly with both hands. Behind him came David. Hendricks peered around, tight-lipped. Any second it might happen. A burst of white light, a blast, carefully aimed from inside a deep concrete bunker.

He raised his arm and waved it around in a circle.

Nothing moved. To the right a long ridge ran, topped with dead tree trunks. A few wild vines had grown up around the trees, remains of arbors. And the eternal dark weeds. Hendricks studied the ridge. Was anything up there? Perfect place for a lookout. He approached the ridge warily, David coming silently behind. If it were his command he'd have a sentry up there, watching for troops trying to infiltrate into the command area. Of course, if it were his command there would be the claws around the area for full protection.

He stopped, feet apart, hands on his hips.

'Are we there?' David said.

'Almost.'

'Why have we stopped?'

'I don't want to take any chances.' Hendricks advanced slowly. Now the ridge lay directly beside him, along his right. Overlooking him. His uneasy feeling increased. If an Ivan were up there he wouldn't have a chance. He waved his arm again. They should be expecting someone in the UN uniform, in response to the note capsule. Unless the whole thing was a trap.

'Keep up with me.' He turned toward David. 'Don't drop behind.'

'With you?'

'Up beside me. We're close. We can't take any chances. Come on.'

'I'll be all right.' David remained behind him, in the rear, a few paces away, still clutching his teddy bear.

'Have it your way.' Hendricks raised his glasses again, suddenly tense. For a moment – had something moved? He scanned the ridge carefully. Everything was silent. Dead. No life up there, only tree trunks and ash. Maybe a few rats. The big black rats that had survived the claws. Mutants – built their own shelters out of saliva and ash. Some kind of plaster. Adaptation. He started forward again.

A tall figure came out on the ridge above him, cloak flapping. Gray-green. A Russian. Behind him a second soldier appeared, another Russian. Both lifted their guns, aiming.

Hendricks froze. He opened his mouth. The soldiers were kneeling, sighting down the side of the slope. A third figure had joined them on the ridge top, a smaller figure in gray-green. A woman. She stood behind the other two.

Hendricks found his voice. 'Stop!' He waved up at them frantically. 'I'm—'

The two Russians fired. Behind Hendricks there was a faint *pop*. Waves of heat lapped against him, throwing him to the ground. Ash tore at his face, grinding into his eyes and nose. Choking, he pulled himself to his knees. It was all a trap. He was finished. He had come to be killed, like a steer. The soldiers and the woman were coming down the side of the ridge toward him, sliding down through the soft ash. Hendricks was numb. His head throbbed. Awkwardly, he got his rifle up and took aim. It weighed a thousand tons; he could hardly hold it. His nose and cheeks stung. The air was full of the blast smell, a bitter acrid stench.

'Don't fire,' the first Russian said, in heavily accented English.

The three of them came up to him, surrounding him. 'Put down your rifle, Yank,' the other said.

Hendricks was dazed. Everything had happened so fast. He had been caught. And they had blasted the boy. He turned his head. David was gone. What remained of him was strewn across the ground.

The three Russians studied him curiously. Hendricks sat, wiping blood from his nose, picking out bits of ash. He shook his head, trying to clear it. 'Why did you do it?' he murmured thickly. 'The boy.'

'Why?' One of the soldiers helped him roughly to his feet. He turned Hendricks around. 'Look.'

Hendricks closed his eyes.

'Look!' The two Russians pulled him forward. 'See. Hurry up. There isn't much time to spare, Yank!'

Hendricks looked. And gasped.

'See now? Now do you understand?'

From the remains of David a metal wheel rolled. Relays, glinting metal. Parts, wiring. One of the Russians kicked at the heap of remains. Parts popped out, rolling away, wheels and springs and rods. A plastic section fell in, half charred. Hendricks bent shakily down. The front of the head had come off. He could make out the intricate brain, wires and relays, tiny tubes and switches, thousands of minute studs—

'A robot,' the soldier holding his arm said. 'We watched it tagging you.'

'Tagging me?'

'That's their way. They tag along with you. Into the bunker. That's how they get in.'

Hendricks blinked, dazed. 'But—'

'Come on.' They led him toward the ridge. 'We can't stay here. It isn't safe. There must be hundreds of them all around here.'

The three of them pulled him up the side of the ridge, sliding and slipping on the ash. The woman reached the top and stood waiting for them.

'The forward command,' Hendricks muttered. 'I came to negotiate with the Soviet—'

'There is no more forward command. *They* got in. We'll explain.' They reached the top of the ridge. 'We're all that's left. The three of us. The rest were down in the bunker.'

'This way. Down this way.' The woman unscrewed a lid, a gray manhole cover set in the ground. 'Get in.'

Hendricks lowered himself. The two soldiers and the woman came behind him, following him down the ladder. The woman closed the lid after them, bolting it tightly into place.

'Good thing we saw you,' one of the two soldiers grunted. 'It had tagged you about as far as it was going to.'

'Give me one of your cigarettes,' the woman said. 'I haven't had an American cigarette for weeks.'

Hendricks pushed the pack to her. She took a cigarette and passed the pack to the two soldiers. In the corner of the small room the lamp gleamed fitfully. The room was low-ceilinged, cramped. The four of them sat around a small wood table. A few dirty dishes were stacked to one side. Behind a ragged curtain a second room was partly visible. Hendricks saw the corner of a coat, some blankets, clothes hung on a hook.

'We were here,' the soldier beside him said. He took off his helmet, pushing his blond hair back. 'I'm Corporal Rudi Maxer. Polish. Impressed in the Soviet Army two years ago.' He held out his hand.

Hendricks hesitated and then shook. 'Major Joseph Hendricks.'

'Klaus Epstein.' The other soldier shook with him, a small dark man with thinning hair. Epstein plucked nervously at his ear. 'Austrian. Impressed God knows when. I don't remember. The three of us were here, Rudi and I, with Tasso.' He indicated the woman. 'That's how we escaped. All the rest were down in the bunker.'

'And – and *they* got in?'

Epstein lit a cigarette. 'First just one of them. The kind that tagged you. Then it let others in.'

Hendricks became alert. 'The *kind*? Are there more than one kind?'

'The little boy. David. David holding his teddy bear. That's Variety Three. The most effective.'

'What are the other types?'

Epstein reached into his coat. 'Here.' He tossed a packet of photographs onto the table, tied with a string. 'Look for yourself.'

Hendricks untied the string.

'You see,' Rudi Maxer said, 'that was why we wanted to talk terms. The Russians, I mean. We found out about a week ago. Found out that your claws were beginning to make up new designs on their own. New types of their own. Better types. Down in your underground factories behind our lines. You let them stamp themselves, repair themselves. Made them more and more intricate. It's your fault this happened.'

Hendricks examined the photos. They had been snapped hurriedly; they were blurred and indistinct. The first few showed – David. David walking along a road, by himself. David and another David. Three Davids. All exactly alike. Each with a ragged teddy bear.

All pathetic.

'Look at the others,' Tasso said.

The next pictures, taken at a great distance, showed a towering wounded soldier sitting by the side of a path, his arm in a sling, the stump of one leg extended, a crude crutch on his lap. Then two wounded soldiers, both the same, standing side by side.

'That's Variety One. The Wounded Soldier.' Klaus reached out and took the pictures. 'You see, the claws were designed to get to human beings. To find them. Each kind was better than the last. They got farther, closer, past most of our defenses, into our lines. But as long as they were merely *machines*, metal spheres with claws and horns, feelers, they could be picked off like any other object. They could be detected as lethal robots as soon as they were seen. Once we caught sight of them—'

'Variety One subverted our whole north wing,' Rudi said. 'It was a long time before anyone caught on. Then it was too late. They came in, wounded soldiers, knocking and begging to be let in. So we let them in. And as soon as they were in they took over. We were watching out for machines . . .'

'At that time it was thought there was only the one type,' Klaus Epstein said. 'No one suspected there were other types. The pictures were flashed to us. When the runner was sent to you, we knew of just one type. Variety One. The Wounded Soldier. We thought that was all.'

'Your line fell to—'

'To Variety Three. David and his bear. That worked even better.' Klaus smiled bitterly. 'Soldiers are suckers for children. We brought them in and tried to feed them. We found out the hard way what they were after. At least, those who were in the bunker.'

'The three of us were lucky,' Rudi said. 'Klaus and I were — were visiting Tasso when it happened. This is her place.' He waved a big hand around. 'This little cellar. We finished and climbed the ladder to start back. From the ridge we saw that they were all around the bunker. Fighting was going on. David and his bear. Hundreds of them. Klaus took the pictures.'

Klaus tied up the photographs again.

'And it's going on all along your line?' Hendricks said.

'Yes.'

'How about *our* lines?' Without thinking, he touched the tab on his arm. 'Can they—'

'They're not bothered by your radiation tabs. It makes no difference to them, Russian, American, Pole, German. It's all the same. They're doing what they were designed to do. Carrying out the original idea. They track down life, wherever they find it.'

'They go by warmth,' Klaus said. 'That was the way you constructed them from the very start. Of course, those you designed were kept back by the radiation tabs you wear. Now they've got around that. These new varieties are lead-lined.'

'What's the other variety?' Hendricks asked. 'The David type, the Wounded Soldier — what's the other?'

'We don't know.' Klaus pointed up at the wall. On the wall were two metal plates, ragged at the edges. Hendricks got up and studied them. They were bent and dented.

'The one on the left came off a Wounded Soldier,' Rudi said. 'We

51

got one of them. It was going along toward our old bunker. We got it from the ridge, the same way we got the David tagging you.'

The plate was stamped: *I-V*. Hendricks touched the other plate. 'And this came from the David type?'

'Yes.' The plate was stamped; *III-V*.

Klaus took a look at them, leaning over Hendrick's broad shoulder. 'You can see what we're up against. There's another type. Maybe it was abandoned. Maybe it didn't work. But there must be a Second Variety. There's One and Three.'

'You were lucky,' Rudi said, 'The David tagged you all the way here and never touched you. Probably thought you'd get it into a bunker, somewhere.'

'One gets in and it's all over,' Klaus said. 'They move fast. One lets all the rest inside. They're inflexible. Machines with one purpose. They were built for only one thing.' He rubbed sweat from his lip. 'We saw.'

They were silent.

'Let me have another cigarette, Yank,' Tasso said. 'They are good. I almost forgot how they were.'

It was night. The sky was black. No stars were visible through the rolling clouds of ash. Klaus lifted the lid cautiously so that Hendricks could look out.

Rudi pointed into the darkness. 'Over that way are the bunkers. Where we used to be. Not over half a mile from us. It was just chance that Klaus and I were not there when it happened. Weakness. Saved by our lusts.'

'All the rest must be dead,' Klaus said in a low voice. 'It came quickly. This morning the Politburo reached their decision. They notified us – forward command. Our runner was sent out at once. We saw him start toward the direction of your lines. We covered him until he was out of sight.'

'Alex Radrivsky. We both knew him. He disappeared about six o'clock. The sun had just come up. About noon Klaus and I had an hour relief. We crept off, away from the bunkers. No one was watch-ing. We came here. This used to be a town here, a few houses, a street. This cellar was part of a big farmhouse. We knew Tasso would be here, hiding down in her little place. We had come here before. Others from the bunkers came here. Today happened to be our turn.'

'So we were saved,' Klaus said. 'Chance. It might have been others.

We – we finished, and then we came up to the surface and started back along the ridge. That was when we saw them, the Davids. We understood right away. We had seen the photos of the First Variety, the Wounded Soldier. Our Commissar distributed them to us with an explanation. If we had gone another step they would have seen us. As it was we had to blast two Davids before we got back. There were hundreds of them, all around. Like ants. We took pictures and slipped back here, bolting the lid tight.'

'They're not so much when you catch them alone. We moved faster than they did. But they're inexorable. Not like living things. They came right at us. And we blasted them.'

Major Hendricks rested against the edge of the lid, adjusting his eyes to the darkness. 'Is it safe to have the lid up at all?'

'If we're careful. How else can you operate your transmitter?'

Hendricks lifted the small belt transmitter slowly. He pressed it against his ear. The metal was cold and damp. He blew against the mike, raising up the short antenna. A faint hum sounded in his ear. 'That's true, I suppose.'

But he still hesitated.

'We'll pull you under if anything happens,' Klaus said.

'Thanks.' Hendricks waited a moment, resting the transmitter against his shoulder. 'Interesting, isn't it?'

'What?'

'This, the new types. The new varieties of claws. We're completely at their mercy, aren't we? By now they've probably gotten into the UN lines, too. It makes me wonder if we're not seeing the beginning of a new species. *The* new species. Evolution. The race to come after man.'

Rudi grunted. 'There is no race after man.'

'No? Why not? Maybe we're seeing it now, the end of human beings, the beginning of a new society.'

'They're not a race. They're mechanical killers. You made them to destroy. That's all they can do. They're machines with a job.'

'So it seems now. But how about later on? After the war is over. Maybe, when there aren't any humans to destroy, their real potentialities will begin to show.'

'You talk as if they were alive!'

'Aren't they?'

There was silence. 'They're machines,' Rudi said. 'They look like people, but they're machines.'

53

'Use your transmitter, Major,' Klaus said. 'We can't stay up here forever.'

Holding the transmitter tightly, Hendricks called the code of the command bunker. He waited, listening. No response. Only silence. He checked the leads carefully. Everything was in place.

'Scott!' he said into the mike. 'Can you hear me?'

Silence. He raised the gain up full and tried again. Only static.

'I don't get anything. They may hear me but they may not want to answer.'

'Tell them it's an emergency.'

'They'll think I'm being forced to call. Under your direction.' He tried again, outlining briefly what he had learned. But still the phone was silent, except for the faint static.

'Radiation pools kill most transmission,' Klaus said, after a while. 'Maybe that's it.'

Hendricks shut the transmitter up. 'No use. No answer. Radiation pools? Maybe. Or they hear me, but won't answer. Frankly, that's what I would do, if a runner tried to call from the Soviet lines. They have no reason to believe such a story. They may hear everything I say—'

'Or maybe it's too late.'

Hendricks nodded.

'We better get the lid down,' Rudi said nervously. 'We don't want to take unnecessary chances.'

They climbed slowly back down the tunnel. Klaus bolted the lid carefully into place. They descended into the kitchen. The air was heavy and close around them.

'Could they work that fast?' Hendricks said. 'I left the bunker this noon. Ten hours ago. How could they move so quickly?'

'It doesn't take them long. Not after the first one gets in. It goes wild. You know what the little claws can do. Even *one* of these is beyond belief. Razors, each finger. Maniacal.'

'All right.' Hendricks moved away impatiently. He stood with his back to them.

'What's the matter?' Rudi said.

'The Moon Base. God, if they've gotten there—'

'The Moon Base?'

Hendricks turned around. 'They couldn't have got to the Moon Base. How would they get there? It isn't possible. I can't believe it.'

'What is this Moon Base? We've heard rumors, but nothing definite. What is the actual situation? You seem concerned.'

'We're supplied from the Moon. The governments are there, under the lunar surface. All our people and industries. That's what keeps us going. If they should find some way of getting off Terra, onto the Moon—'

'It only takes one of them. Once the first one gets in it admits the others. Hundreds of them, all alike. You should have seen them. Identical. Like ants.'

'Perfect socialism,' Tasso said. 'The ideal of the communist state. All citizens interchangeable.'

Klaus grunted angrily. 'That's enough. Well? What next?'

Hendricks paced back and forth, around the small room. The air was full of smells of food and perspiration. The others watched him. Presently Tasso pushed through the curtain, into the other room. 'I'm going to take a nap.'

The curtain closed behind her. Rudi and Klaus sat down at the table, still watching Hendricks. 'It's up to you,' Klaus said. 'We don't know your situation.'

Hendricks nodded.

'It's a problem.' Rudi drank some coffee, filling his cup from a rusty pot. 'We're safe here for a while, but we can't stay here forever. Not enough food or supplies.'

'But if we go outside—'

'If we go outside they'll get us. Or probably they'll get us. We couldn't go very far. How far is your command bunker, Major?'

'Three or four miles.'

'We might make it. The four of us. Four of us could watch all sides. They couldn't slip up behind us and start tagging us. We have three rifles, three blast rifles. Tasso can have my pistol.' Rudi tapped his belt. 'In the Soviet army we didn't have shoes always, but we had guns. With all four of us armed one of us might get to your command bunker. Preferably you, Major.'

'What if they're already there?' Klaus said.

Rudi shrugged. 'Well, then we come back here.'

Hendricks stopped pacing. 'What do you think the chances are they're already in the American lines?'

'Hard to say. Fairly good. They're organized. They know exactly what they're doing. Once they start they go like a horde of locusts.

55

They have to keep moving, and fast. It's secrecy and speed they depend on. Surprise. They push their way in before anyone has any idea.'

'I see,' Hendricks murmured.

From the other room Tasso stirred. 'Major?'

Hendricks pushed the curtain back. 'What?'

Tasso looked up at him lazily from the cot. 'Have you any more American cigarettes left?'

Hendricks went into the room and sat down across from her, on a wood stool. He felt in his pockets, 'No. All gone.'

'Too bad.'

'What nationality are you?' Hendricks asked after a while.

'Russian.'

'How did you get here?'

'Here?'

'This used to be France. This was part of Normandy. Did you come with the Soviet army?'

'Why?'

'Just curious.' He studied her. She had taken off her coat, tossing it over the end of the cot. She was young, about twenty. Slim. Her long hair stretched out over the pillow. She was staring at him silently, her eyes dark and large.

'What's on your mind?' Tasso said.

'Nothing. How old are you?'

'Eighteen.' She continued to watch him, unblinking, her arms behind her head. She had on Russian army pants and shirt. Gray-green. Thick leather belt with counter and cartridges. Medicine kit.

'You're in the Soviet army?'

'No.'

'Where did you get the uniform?'

She shrugged. 'It was given to me,' she told him.

'How – how old were you when you came here?'

'Sixteen.'

'That young?'

Her eyes narrowed. 'What do you mean?

Hendricks rubbed his jaw. 'Your life would have been a lot different if there had been no war. Sixteen. You came here at sixteen. To live this way.'

'I had to survive.'

'I'm not moralizing.'

'Your life would have been different, too,' Tasso murmured. She reached down and unfastened one of her boots. She kicked the boot off, onto the floor. 'Major, do you want to go in the other room? I'm sleepy.'

'It's going to be a problem, the four of us here. It's going to be hard to live in these quarters. Are there just the two rooms?'

'Yes.'

'How big was the cellar originally? Was it larger than this? Are there other rooms filled up with debris? We might be able to open one of them.'

'Perhaps. I really don't know.' Tasso loosened her belt. She made herself comfortable on the cot, unbuttoning her shirt. 'You're sure you have no more cigarettes?'

'I had only the one pack.'

'Too bad. Maybe if we get back to your bunker we can find some.' The other boot fell. Tasso reached up for the light cord. 'Good night.'

'You're going to sleep?'

'That's right.'

The room plunged into darkness. Hendricks got up and made his way past the curtain, into the kitchen. And stopped, rigid.

Rudi stood against the wall, his face white and gleaming. His mouth opened and closed but no sounds came. Klaus stood in front of him, the muzzle of his pistol in Rudi's stomach. Neither of them moved. Klaus, his hand tight around the gun, his features set. Rudi, pale and silent, spreadeagled against the wall.

'What—' Hendricks muttered, but Klaus cut him off.

'Be quiet, Major. Come over here. Your gun. Get out your gun.'

Hendricks drew his pistol. 'What is it?'

'Cover him.' Klaus motioned him forward. 'Beside me. Hurry!'

Rudi moved a little, lowering his arms. He turned to Hendricks, licking his lips. The whites of his eyes shone wildly. Sweat dripped from his forehead, down his cheeks. He fixed his gaze on Hendricks. 'Major, he's gone insane. Stop him.' Rudi's voice was thin and hoarse, almost inaudible.

'What's going on?' Hendricks demanded.

Without lowering his pistol Klaus answered. 'Major, remember our discussion? The Three Varieties? We knew about One and Three. But we didn't know about Two. At least, we didn't know before.' Klaus's fingers tightened around the gun butt. 'We didn't know before, but we know now.'

He pressed the trigger. A burst of white heat rolled out of the gun, licking around Rudi.

'Major, this is the Second Variety.'

Tasso swept the curtain aside. 'Klaus! What did you do?'

Klaus turned from the charred form, gradually sinking down the wall onto the floor. 'The Second Variety, Tasso. Now we know. We have all three types identified. The danger is less. I—'

Tasso stared past him at the remains of Rudi, at the blackened, smoldering fragments and bits of cloth. 'You killed him.'

'Him? *It*, you mean. I was watching. I had a feeling, but I wasn't sure. At least, I wasn't sure before. But this evening I was certain.' Klaus rubbed his pistol butt nervously. 'We're lucky. Don't you understand? Another hour and it might—'

'You were *certain?*' Tasso pushed past him and bent down, over the steaming remains on the floor. Her face became hard. 'Major, see for yourself. Bones. Flesh.'

Hendricks bent down beside her. The remains were human remains. Seared flesh, charred bone fragments, part of a skull. Ligaments, viscera, blood. Blood forming a pool against the wall.

'No wheels,' Tasso said calmly. She straightened up. 'No wheels, no parts, no relays. Not a claw. Not the Second Variety.' She folded her arms. 'You're going to have to be able to explain this.'

Klaus sat down at the table, all the color drained suddenly from his face. He put his head in his hands and rocked back and forth.

'Snap out of it.' Tasso's fingers closed over his shoulder. 'Why did you do it? Why did you kill him?'

'He was frightened,' Hendricks said. 'All this, the whole thing, building up around us.'

'Maybe.'

'What, then. What do you think?'

'I think he may have had a reason for killing Rudi. A good reason.'

'What reason?'

'Maybe Rudi learned something.'

Hendricks studied her bleak face. 'About what?' he asked.

'About him. About Klaus.'

Klaus looked up quickly. 'You can see what she's trying to say. She thinks I'm the Second Variety. Don't you see, Major? Now she wants you to believe I killed him on purpose. That I'm—'

'Why did you kill him, then?' Tasso said.

'I told you.' Klaus shook his head wearily. 'I thought he was a claw. I thought I knew.'

'Why?'

'I had been watching him. I was suspicious.'

'Why?'

'I thought I had seen something. Heard something. I thought I—' He stopped.

'Go on.'

'We were sitting at the table. Playing cards. You two were in the other room. It was silent. I thought I heard him – *whirr.*'

There was silence.

'Do you believe that?' Tasso said to Hendricks.

'Yes. I believe what he says.'

'I don't. I think he killed Rudi for a good purpose.' Tasso touched the rifle, resting in the corner of the room. 'Major—'

'No.' Hendricks shook his head. 'Let's stop it right now. One is enough. We're afraid, the way he was. If we kill him we'll be doing what he did to Rudi.'

Klaus looked gratefully up at him. 'Thanks. I was afraid. You understand, don't you? Now she's afraid, the way I was. She wants to kill me.'

'No more killing.' Hendricks moved toward the end of the ladder. 'I'm going above and try the transmitter one more. If I can't get them we're moving back toward my lines tomorrow morning.'

Klaus rose quickly. 'I'll come up with you and give you a hand.'

The night air was cold. The earth was cooling off. Klaus took a deep breath, filling his lungs. He and Hendricks stepped onto the ground, out of the tunnel. Klaus planted his feet wide apart, the rifle up, watching and listening. Hendricks crouched by the tunnel mouth, tuning the small transmitter.

'Any luck?' Klaus asked presently.

'Not yet.'

'Keep trying. Tell them what happened.'

Hendricks kept trying. Without success. Finally he lowered the antenna. 'It's useless. They can't hear me. Or they hear me and won't answer. Or—'

'Or they don't exist.'

'I'll try once more.' Hendricks raised the antenna. 'Scott, can you hear me? Come in!'

He listened. There was only static. Then, still very faintly—

'This is Scott.'

His fingers tightened. 'Scott! Is it you?'

'This is Scott.'

Klaus squatted down. 'Is it your command?'

'Scott, listen. Do you understand? About them, the claws. Did you get my message? Did you hear me?'

'Yes.' Faintly. Almost inaudible. He could hardly make out the word.

'You got my message? Is everything all right at the bunker? None of them got in?'

'Everything is all right.'

'Have they tried to get in?'

The voice was weaker.

'No.'

Hendricks turned to Klaus. 'They're all right.'

'Have they been attacked?'

'No.' Hendricks pressed the phone tighter to his ear. 'Scott I can hardly hear you. Have you notified the Moon Base? Do they know? Are they alerted?'

No answer.

'Scott! Can you hear me?'

Silence.

Hendricks relaxed, sagging. 'Faded out. Must be radiation pools.'

Hendricks and Klaus looked at each other. Neither of them said anything. After a time Klaus said, 'Did it sound like any of your men? Could you identify the voice?'

'It was too faint.'

'You couldn't be certain?'

'No.'

'Then it could have been—'

'I don't know. Now I'm not sure. Let's go back down and get the lid closed.'

They climbed back down the ladder slowly, into the warm cellar. Klaus bolted the lid behind them. Tasso waited for them, her face expressionless.

'Any luck?' she asked.

Neither of them answered. 'Well?' Klaus said at last. 'What do you think, Major? Was it your officer, or was it one of *them?*'

'I don't know.'

'Then we're just where we were before.'

Hendricks stared down at the floor, his jaw set. 'We'll have to go. To be sure.'

'Anyhow, we have food here for only a few weeks. We'd have to go up after that, in any case.'

'Apparently so.'

'What's wrong?' Tasso demanded. 'Did you get across to your bunker? What's the matter?'

'It may have been one of my men,' Hendricks said slowly. 'Or it may have been one of *them*. But we'll never know standing here.' He examined his watch. 'Let's turn in and get some sleep. We want to be up early tomorrow.'

'Early?'

'Our best chance to get through the claws should be early in the morning,' Hendricks said.

The morning was crisp and clear. Major Hendricks studied the countryside through his field glasses.

'See anything?' Klaus said.

'No.'

'Can you make out our bunkers?'

'Which way?'

'Here.' Klaus took the glasses and adjusted them. 'I know where to look.' He looked a long time, silently.

Tasso came to the top of the tunnel and stepped up onto the ground. 'Anything?'

'No.' Klaus passed the glasses back to Hendricks. 'They're out of sight. Come on. Let's not stay here.'

The three of them made their way down the side of the ridge, sliding in the soft ash. Across a flat rock a lizard scuttled. They stopped instantly, rigid.

'What was it?' Klaus muttered.

'A lizard.'

The lizard ran on, hurrying through the ash. It was exactly the same color as the ash.

'Perfect adaptation,' Klaus said. 'Proves we were right. Lysenko, I mean.'

They reached the bottom of the ridge and stopped, standing close together, looking around them.

'Let's go.' Hendricks started off. 'It's a good long trip, on foot.'

Klaus fell in beside him, Tasso walked behind, her pistol held alertly. 'Major, I've been meaning to ask you something,' Klaus said. 'How did you run across the David? The one that was tagging you.'

'I met it along the way. In some ruins.'

'What did it say?'

'Not much. It said it was alone. By itself.'

'You couldn't tell it was a machine? It talked like a living person? You never suspected?'

'It didn't say much. I noticed nothing unusual.'

'It's strange, machines so much like people that you can be fooled. Almost alive. I wonder where it'll end.'

'They're doing what you Yanks designed them to do,' Tasso said. 'You designed them to hunt out life and destroy. Human life. Wherever they find it.'

Hendricks was watching Klaus intently. 'Why did you ask me? What's on your mind?'

'Nothing,' Klaus answered.

'Klaus thinks you're the Second Variety,' Tasso said calmly, from behind them. 'Now he's got his eye on you.'

Klaus flushed. 'Why not? We sent a runner to the Yank lines and *he* comes back. Maybe he thought he'd find some good game here.'

Hendricks laughed harshly. 'I came from the UN bunkers. There were human beings all around me.'

'Maybe you saw an opportunity to get into the Soviet lines. Maybe you saw your chance. Maybe you—'

'The Soviet lines had already been taken over. Your lines had been invaded before I left my command bunker. Don't forget that.'

Tasso came up beside him. 'That proves nothing at all, Major.'

'Why not?'

'There appears to be little communication between the varieties. Each is made in a different factory. They don't seem to work together. You might have started for the Soviet lines without knowing anything about the work of the other varieties. Or even what the other varieties were like.'

'How do you know so much about the claws?' Hendricks said.

'I've seen them. I've observed them take over the Soviet bunkers.'

'You know quite a lot,' Klaus said. 'Actually, you saw very little. Strange that you should have been such an acute observer.'

Tasso laughed. 'Do you suspect me, now?'

'Forget it,' Hendricks said. They walked on in silence.

'Are we going the whole way on foot?' Tasso said, after a while. 'I'm not used to walking.' She gazed around at the plain of ash, stretching out on all sides of them, as far as they could see. 'How dreary.'

'It's like this all the way,' Klaus said.

'In a way I wish you had been in your bunker when the attack came.'

'Somebody else would have been with you, if not me,' Klaus muttered.

Tasso laughed, putting her hands in her pockets. 'I suppose so.'

They walked on, keeping their eyes on the vast plain of silent ash around them.

The sun was setting. Hendricks made his way forward slowly, waving Tasso and Klaus back. Klaus squatted down, resting his gun butt against the ground.

Tasso found a concrete slab and sat down with a sigh. 'It's good to rest.'

'Be quiet,' Klaus said sharply.

Hendricks pushed up to the top of the rise ahead of them. The same rise the Russian runner had come up, the day before. Hendricks dropped down, stretching himself out, peering through his glasses at what lay beyond.

Nothing was visible. Only ash and occasional trees. But there, not more than fifty yards ahead, was the entrance of the forward command bunker. The bunker from which he had come. Hendricks watched silently. No motion. No sign of life. Nothing stirred.

Klaus slithered up beside him. 'Where is it?'

'Down there.' Hendricks passed him the glasses. Clouds of ash rolled across the evening sky. The world was darkening. They had a couple of hours of light left, at the most. Probably not that much.

'I don't see anything,' Klaus said.

'That tree there. The stump. By the pile of bricks. The entrance is to the right of the bricks.'

'I'll have to take your word for it.'

'You and Tasso cover me from here. You'll be able to sight all the way to the bunker entrance.'

'You're going down alone?'

'With my wrist tab I'll be safe. The ground around the bunker is a living field of claws. They collect down in the ash. Like crabs. Without tabs you wouldn't have a chance.'

'Maybe you're right.'

'I'll walk slowly all the way. As soon as I know for certain—'

'If they're down inside the bunker you won't be able to get back up here. They go fast. You don't realize.'

'What do you suggest?'

Klaus considered. 'I don't know. Get them to come to the surface. So you can see.'

Hendricks brought out his transmitter from his belt, raising the antenna. 'Let's get started.'

Klaus signaled to Tasso. She crawled expertly up the side of the rise to where they were sitting.

'He's going down alone,' Klaus said. 'We'll cover him from here. As soon as you see him start back, fire past him at once. They come quick.'

'You're not very optimistic,' Tasso said.

'No, I'm not.'

Hendricks opened the breech of his gun, checking it carefully. 'Maybe things are all right.'

'You didn't see them. Hundreds of them. All the same. Pouring out like ants.'

'I should be able to find out without going down all the way.' Hendricks locked his gun, gripping it in one hand, the transmitter in the other. 'Well, wish me luck.'

Klaus put out his hand. 'Don't go down until you're sure. Talk to them from here. Make them show themselves.'

Hendricks stood up. He stepped down the side of the rise.

A moment later he was walking slowly toward the pile of bricks and debris beside the dead tree stump. Toward the entrance of the forward command bunker.

Nothing stirred. He raised the transmitter, clicking it on. 'Scott? Can you hear me?'

Silence.

'Scott! This is Hendricks. Can you hear me? I'm standing outside the bunker. You should be able to see me in the view sight.'

He listened, the transmitter gripped tightly. No sound. Only static. He walked forward. A claw burrowed out of the ash and raced toward him. It halted a few feet away and then slunk off. A second claw appeared, one of the big ones with feelers. It moved toward him, studied him intently, and then fell in behind him, dogging respectfully after him, a few paces away. A moment later a second big claw joined it. Silently, the claws trailed him as he walked slowly toward the bunker.

Hendricks stopped, and behind him, the claws came to a halt. He was close now. Almost to the bunker steps.

'Scott! Can you hear me? I'm standing right above you. Outside. On the surface. Are you picking me up?'

He waited, holding his gun against his side, the transmitter tightly to his ear. Time passed. He strained to hear, but there was only silence. Silence, and faint static.

Then, distantly, metallically—

'This is Scott.'

The voice was neutral. Cold. He could not identify it. But the earphone was minute.

'Scott! Listen. I'm standing right above you. I'm on the surface, looking down into the bunker entrance.'

'Yes.'

'Can you see me?'

'Yes.'

'Through the view sight? You have the sight trained on me?'

'Yes.'

Hendricks pondered. A circle of claws waited quietly around him, gray-metal bodies on all sides of him. 'Is everything all right in the bunker? Nothing unusual has happened?'

'Everything is all right.'

'Will you come up to the surface? I want to see you for a moment.' Hendricks took a deep breath. 'Come up here with me. I want to talk to you.'

'Come down.'

'I'm giving you an order.'

Silence.

'Are you coming?' Hendricks listened. There was no response. 'I order you to come to the surface.'

'Come down.'

Hendricks set his jaw. 'Let me talk to Leone.'

There was a long pause. He listened to the static. Then a voice came, hard, thin, metallic. The same as the other. 'This is Leone.'

'Hendricks. I'm on the surface. At the bunker entrance. I want one of you to come up here.'

'Come down.'

'Why come down? I'm giving you an order!'

Silence. Hendricks lowered the transmitter. He looked carefully around him. The entrance was just ahead. Almost at his feet. He lowered the antenna and fastened the transmitter to his belt. Carefully, he gripped his gun with both hands. He moved forward, a step at a time. If they could see him they knew he was starting toward the entrance. He closed his eyes a moment.

Then he put his foot on the first step that led downward.

Two Davids came up at him, their faces identical and expressionless. He blasted them into particles. More came rushing silently up, a whole pack of them. All exactly the same.

Hendricks turned and raced back, away from the bunker, back toward the rise.

At the top of the rise Tasso and Klaus were firing down. The small claws were already streaking up toward them, shining metal spheres going fast, racing frantically through the ash. But he had no time to think about that. He knelt down, aiming at the bunker entrance, gun against his cheek. The Davids were coming out in groups, clutching their teddy bears, their thin knobby legs pumping as they ran up the steps to the surface. Hendricks fired into the main body of them. They burst apart, wheels and springs flying in all directions. He fired again, through the mist of particles.

A giant lumbering figure rose up in the bunker entrance, tall and swaying. Hendricks paused, amazed. A man, a soldier. With one leg, supporting himself with a crutch.

'Major!' Tasso's voice came. More firing. The huge figure moved forward, Davids swarming around it. Hendricks broke out of his freeze. The First Variety. The Wounded Soldier. He aimed and fired. The soldier burst into bits, parts and relays flying. Now many Davids were out on the flat ground, away from the bunker. He fired again and again, moving slowly back, half-crouching and aiming.

From the rise, Klaus fired down. The side of the rise was alive with claws making their way up. Hendricks retreated toward the rise, running and crouching. Tasso had left Klaus and was circling slowly to the right, moving away from the rise.

A David slipped up toward him its small white face expressionless, brown hair hanging down in its eyes. It bent over suddenly, opening its arms. Its teddy bear hurtled down and leaped across the ground, bounding toward him. Hendricks fired. The bear and the David both dissolved. He grinned, blinking. It was like a dream.

'Up here!' Tasso's voice. Hendricks made his way toward her. She was over by some columns of concrete, walls of a ruined building. She was firing past him, with the hand pistol Klaus had given her.

'Thanks.' He joined her, gasping for breath. She pulled him back, behind the concrete, fumbling at her belt.

'Close your eyes!' She unfastened a globe from her waist. Rapidly, she unscrewed the cap, locking it into place. 'Close your eyes and get down.'

She threw the bomb. It sailed in an arc, an expert, rolling and bouncing to the entrance of the bunker. Two Wounded Soldiers stood uncertainly by the brick pile. More Davids poured from behind them, out onto the plain. One of the Wounded Soldiers moved toward the bomb, stooping awkwardly down to pick it up.

The bomb went off. The concussion whirled Hendricks around, throwing him on his face. A hot wind rolled over him. Dimly he saw Tasso standing behind the columns, firing slowly and methodically at the Davids coming out of the raging clouds of white fire.

Back along the rise Klaus struggled with a ring of claws circling around him. He retreated, blasting at them and moving back, trying to break through the ring.

Hendricks struggled to his feet. His head ached. He could hardly see. Everything was licking at him, raging and whirling. His right arm would not move.

Tasso pulled back toward him. 'Come on. Let's go.'

'Klaus – he's still up there.'

'Come on!' Tasso dragged Hendricks back, away from the columns. Hendricks shook his head, trying to clear it. Tasso led him rapidly away, her eyes intense and bright, watching for claws that had escaped the blast.

One David came out of the rolling clouds of flame. Tasso blasted it. No more appeared.

'But Klaus. What about him?' Hendricks stopped, standing unsteadily. 'He—'

'Come on!'

They retreated, moving farther and farther away from the bunker. A few small claws followed them for a little while and then gave up, turning back and going off.

At last Tasso stopped. 'We can stop here and get our breaths.'

Hendricks sat down on some heaps of debris. He wiped his neck, gasping. 'We left Klaus back there.'

Tasso said nothing. She opened her gun, sliding a fresh round of blast cartridges into place.

Hendricks stared at her, dazed. 'You left him back there on purpose.'

Tasso snapped the gun together. She studied the heaps of rubble around them, her face expressionless. As if she were watching for something.

'What is it?' Hendricks demanded. 'What are you looking for? Is something coming?' He shook his head, trying to understand. What was she doing? What was she waiting for? He could see nothing. Ash lay all around them, ash and ruins. Occasional stark tree trunks, without leaves or branches. 'What—'

Tasso cut him off. 'Be still.' Her eyes narrowed. Suddenly her gun came up. Hendricks turned, following her gaze.

Back the way they had come a figure appeared. The figure walked unsteadily toward them. Its clothes were torn. It limped as it made its way along, going very slowly and carefully. Stopping now and then, resting and getting its strength. Once it almost fell. It stood for a moment, trying to steady itself. Then it came on.

Klaus.

Hendricks stood up. 'Klaus!' He started toward him. 'How the hell did you—'

Tasso fired. Hendricks swung back. She fired again, the blast passing him, a searing line of heat. The beam caught Klaus in the chest. He exploded, gears and wheels flying. For a moment he continued to walk. Then he swayed back and forth. He crashed to the ground, his arms flung out. A few more wheels rolled away.

Silence.

Tasso turned to Hendricks. 'Now you understand why he killed Rudi.'

Hendricks sat down again slowly. He shook his head. He was numb. He could not think.

'Do you see?' Tasso said. 'Do you understand?'

Hendricks said nothing. Everything was slipping away from him, faster and faster. Darkness, rolling and plucking at him.

He closed his eyes.

Hendricks opened his eyes slowly. His body ached all over. He tried to sit up but needles of pain shot through his arm and shoulder. He gasped.

'Don't try to get up,' Tasso said. She bent down, putting her cold hand against his forehead.

It was night. A few stars glinted above, shining through the drifting clouds of ash. Hendricks lay back, his teeth locked. Tasso watched him impassively. She had built a fire with some wood and weeds. The fire licked feebly, hissing at a metal cup suspended over it. Everything was silent. Unmoving darkness, beyond the fire.

'So he was the Second Variety,' Hendricks murmured.

'I had always thought so.'

'Why didn't you destroy him sooner?' He wanted to know.

'You held me back.' Tasso crossed to the fire to look into the metal cup. 'Coffee. It'll be ready to drink in a while.'

She came back and sat down beside him. Presently she opened her pistol and began to disassemble the firing mechanism, studying it intently.

'This is a beautiful gun,' Tasso said, half aloud. 'The construction is superb.'

'What about them? The claws.'

'The concussion from the bomb put most of them out of action. They're delicate. Highly organized, I suppose.'

'The Davids, too?'

'Yes.'

'How did you happen to have a bomb like that?'

Tasso shrugged. 'We designed it. You shouldn't underestimate our technology, Major. Without such a bomb you and I would no longer exist.'

'Very useful.'

Tasso stretched out her legs, warming her feet in the heat of the fire. 'It surprised me that you did not seem to understand, after he killed Rudi. Why did you think he—'

'I told you. I thought he was afraid.'

'Really? You know, Major, for a little while I suspected you. Because you wouldn't let me kill him. I thought you might be protecting him.' She laughed.

'Are we safe here?' Hendricks asked presently.

'For a while. Until they get reinforcements from some other area.' Tasso began to clean the interior of the gun with a bit of rag. She finished and pushed the mechanism back into place. She closed the gun, running her finger along the barrel.

'We were lucky,' Hendricks murmured.

'Yes. Very lucky.'

'Thanks for pulling me away.'

Tasso did not answer. She glanced up at him, her eyes bright in the firelight. Hendricks examined his arm. He could not move his fingers. His whole side seemed numb. Down inside him was a dull steady ache.

'How do you feel?' Tasso asked.

'My arm is damaged.'

'Anything else?'

'Internal injuries.'

'You didn't get down when the bomb went off.'

Hendricks said nothing. He watched Tasso pour the coffee from the cup into a flat metal pan. She brought it over to him.

'Thanks.' He struggled up enough to drink. It was hard to swallow. His insides turned over and he pushed the pan away. 'That's all I can drink now.'

Tasso drank the rest. Time passed. The clouds of ash moved across the dark sky above them. Hendricks rested, his mind blank. After a while he became aware that Tasso was standing over him, gazing down at him.

'What is it?' he murmured.

'Do you feel any better?'

'Some.'

'You know, Major, if I hadn't dragged you away they would have got you. You would be dead. Like Rudi.'

'I know.'

'Do you want to know why I brought you out? I could have left you. I could have left you there.'

'Why did you bring me out?'

'Because we have to get away from here.' Tasso stirred the fire with

70

a stick, peering calmly down into it. 'No human being can live here. When their reinforcements come we won't have a chance. I've pondered about it while you were unconscious. We have perhaps three hours before they come.'

'And you expect me to get us away?'

'That's right. I expect you to get us out of here.'

'Why me?'

'Because I don't know any way.' Her eyes shone at him in the half light, bright and steady. 'If you can't get us out of here they'll kill us within three hours. I see nothing else ahead. Well, Major? What are you going to do? I've been waiting all night. While you were unconscious I sat here, waiting and listening. It's almost dawn. The night is almost over.'

Hendricks considered. 'It's curious,' he said at last.

'Curious?'

'That you should think I can get us out of here. I wonder what you think I can do.'

'Can you get us to the Moon Base?'

'The Moon Base? How?'

'There must be some way.'

Hendricks shook his head. 'No. There's no way that I know of.'

Tasso said nothing. For a moment her steady gaze wavered. She ducked her head, turning abruptly away. She scrambled to her feet. 'More coffee?'

'No.'

'Suit yourself,' Tasso drank silently. He could not see her face. He lay back against the ground, deep in thought, trying to concentrate. It was hard to think. His head still hurt. And the numbing daze still hung over him.

'There might be one way,' he said suddenly.

'Oh?'

'How soon is dawn?'

'Two hours. The sun will be coming up shortly.'

'There's supposed to be a ship near here. I've never seen it. But I know it exists.'

'What kind of a ship?' Her voice was sharp.

'A rocket cruiser.'

'Will it take us off? To the Moon Base?'

'It's supposed to. In case of emergency.' He rubbed his forehead.

71

'What's wrong?'

'My head. It's hard to think. I can hardly – hardly concentrate. The bomb.'

'Is the ship near here?' Tasso slid over beside him, settling down on her haunches. 'How far is it? Where is it?'

'I'm trying to think.'

Her fingers dug into his arm. 'Nearby?' Her voice was like iron. 'Where would it be? Would they store it underground? Hidden underground?'

'Yes. In a storage locker.'

'How do we find it? Is it marked? Is there a code marker to identify it?'

Hendricks concentrated. 'No. No markings. No code symbol.'

'What then?'

'A sign.'

'What sort of sign?'

Hendricks did not answer. In the flickering light his eyes were glazed, two sightless orbs. Tasso's fingers dug into his arm.

'What sort of sign? What is it?'

'I – I can't think. Let me rest.'

'All right.' She let go and stood up. Hendricks lay back against the ground, his eyes closed. Tasso walked away from him, her hands in her pockets. She kicked a rock out of her way and stood staring up at the sky. The night blackness was already beginning to fade into gray. Morning was coming.

Tasso gripped her pistol and walked around the fire in a circle, back and forth. On the ground Major Hendricks lay, his eyes closed, unmoving. The grayness rose in the sky, higher and higher. The landscape became visible, fields of ash stretching out in all directions. Ash and ruins of buildings, a wall here and there, heaps of concrete, the naked trunk of a tree.

The air was cold and sharp. Somewhere a long way off a bird made a few bleak sounds.

Hendricks stirred. He opened his eyes. 'Is it dawn? Already?'

'Yes.'

Hendricks sat up a little. 'You wanted to know something. You were asking me.'

'Do you remember now?'

'Yes.'

'What is it?' She tensed. 'What?' she repeated sharply.

'A well. A ruined well. It's in a storage locker under a well.'

'A well.' Tasso relaxed. 'Then we'll find a well.' She looked at her watch. 'We have about an hour, Major. Do you think we can find it in an hour?'

'Give me a hand,' Hendricks said.

Tasso put her pistol away and helped him to his feet. 'This is going to be difficult.'

'Yes it is.' Hendricks set his lips tightly. 'I don't think we're going to go very far.'

They began to walk. The early sun cast a little warmth down on them. The land was flat and barren, stretching out gray and lifeless as far as they could see. A few birds sailed silently, far above them, circling slowly.

'See anything?' Hendricks said. 'Any claws?'

'No. Not yet.'

They passed through some ruins, upright concrete and bricks. A cement foundation. Rats scuttled away. Tasso jumped back warily.

'This used to be a town,' Hendricks said. 'A village. Provincial village. This was all grape country, once. Where we are now.'

They came onto a ruined street, weeds and cracks crisscrossing it. Over to the right a stone chimney stuck up.

'Be careful,' he warned her.

A pit yawned, an open basement. Ragged ends of pipes jutted up, twisted and bent. They passed part of a house, a bathtub turned on its side. A broken chair. A few spoons and bits of china dishes. In the center of the street the ground had sunk away. The depression was filled with weeds and debris and bones.

'Over here,' Hendricks murmured.

'This way?'

'To the right.'

They passed the remains of a heavy-duty tank. Hendricks's belt counter clicked ominously. The tank had been radiation-blasted. A few feet from the tank a mummified body lay sprawled out, mouth open. Beyond the road was a flat field. Stones and weeds, and bits of broken glass.

'There,' Hendricks said.

A stone well jutted up, sagging and broken. A few boards lay across it. Most of the well had sunk into rubble. Hendricks walked unsteadily toward it, Tasso beside him.

'Are you certain about this?' Tasso said. 'This doesn't look like anything.'

'I'm sure.' Hendricks sat down at the edge of the well, his teeth locked. His breath came quickly. He wiped perspiration from his face. 'This was arranged so the senior command officer could get away. If anything happened. If the bunker fell.'

'That was you?'

'Yes.'

'Where is the ship? Is it here?'

'We're standing on it.' Hendricks ran his hands over the surface of the well stones. 'The eye-lock responds to me, not to anybody else. It's my ship. Or it was supposed to be.'

There was a sharp click. Presently they heard a low grating sound from below them.

'Step back,' Hendricks said. He and Tasso moved away from the well.

A section of the ground slid back. A metal frame pushed slowly up through the ash, shoving bricks and weeds out of the way. The action ceased as the ship nosed into view.

'There it is,' Hendricks said.

The ship was small. It rested quietly, suspended in its mesh frame like a blunt needle. A rain of ash sifted down into the dark cavity from which the ship had been raised. Hendricks made his way over to it. He mounted the mesh and unscrewed the hatch, pulling it back. Inside the ship the control banks and the pressure seat were visible.

Tasso came and stood beside him, gazing into the ship. 'I'm not accustomed to rocket piloting,' she said after a while.

Hendricks glanced at her. 'I'll do the piloting.'

'Will you? There's only one seat, Major. I can see it's built to carry only a single person.'

Hendricks' breathing changed. He studied the interior of the ship intently. Tasso was right. There was only one seat. The ship was built to carry only one person. 'I see,' he said slowly. 'And the one person is you.'

She nodded.

'Of course.'

'Why?'

'*You* can't go. You might not live through the trip. You're injured. You probably wouldn't get there.'

'An interesting point. But you see, I know where the Moon Base is. And you don't. You might fly around for months and not find it. It's well hidden. Without knowing what to look for—'

'I'll have to take my chances. Maybe I won't find it. Not by myself. But I think you'll give me all the information I need. Your life depends on it.'

'How?'

'If I find the Moon Base in time, perhaps I can get them to send a ship back to pick you up. *If* I find the Base in time. If not, then you haven't a chance. I imagine there are supplies on the ship. They will last me long enough—'

Hendricks moved quickly. But his injured arm betrayed him. Tasso ducked, sliding lithely aside. Her hand came up, lightning fast. Hendricks saw the gun butt coming. He tried to ward off the blow, but she was too fast. The metal butt struck against the side of his head, just above his ear. Numbing pain rushed through him. Pain and rolling clouds of blackness. He sank down, sliding to the ground.

Dimly, he was aware that Tasso was standing over him, kicking him with her toe.

'Major! Wake up!'

He opened his eyes, groaning.

'Listen to me.' She bent down, the gun pointed at his face. 'I have to hurry. There isn't much time left. The ship is ready to go, but you must give me the information I need before I leave.'

Hendricks shook his head, trying to clear it.

'Hurry up! Where is the Moon Base? How do I find it? What do I look for?'

Hendricks said nothing.

'Answer me!'

'Sorry.'

'Major, the ship is loaded with provisions. I can coast for weeks. I'll find the Base eventually. And in a half-hour you'll be dead. Your only chance of survival—' She broke off.

Along the slope, by some crumbling ruins, something moved. Something in the ash. Tasso turned quickly, aiming. She fired. A puff of flame leaped. Something scuttled away, rolling across the ash. She fired again. The claw burst apart, wheels flying.

'See?' Tasso said. 'A scout. It won't be long.'

'You'll bring them back here to get me?'

'Yes. As soon as possible.'

Hendricks looked up at her. He studied her intently. 'You're telling the truth?' A strange expression had come over his face, an avid hunger. 'You will come back for me? You'll get me to the Moon Base?'

'I'll get you to the Moon Base. But tell me where it is! There's only a little time left.'

'All right.' Hendricks picked up a piece of rock, pulling himself to a sitting position. 'Watch.'

Hendricks began to scratch in the ash. Tasso stood by him, watching the motion of the rock. Hendricks was sketching a crude lunar map.

'This is the Appenine range. Here is the Crater of Archimedes. The Moon Base is beyond the end of the Appenine, about two hundred miles. I don't know exactly where. No one on Terra knows. But when you're over the Appenine, signal with one red flare and a green flare, followed by two red flares in quick succession. The Base monitor will record your signal. The Base is under the surface, of course. They'll guide you down with magnetic controls.'

'And the controls? Can I operate them?'

'The controls are virtually automatic. All you have to do is give the right signal at the right time.'

'I will.'

'The seat absorbs most of the takeoff shock. Air and temperature are automatically controlled. The ship will leave Terra and pass out into free space. It'll line itself up with the Moon, falling into an orbit around it, about a hundred miles above the surface. The orbit will carry you over the Base. When you're in the region of the Appenine, release the signal rockets.'

Tasso slid into the ship and lowered herself into the pressure seat. The arm locks folded automatically around her. She fingered the controls. 'Too bad you're not going, Major. All this put here for you, and you can't make the trip.'

'Leave me the pistol.'

Tasso pulled the pistol from her belt. She held it in her hand, weighing it thoughtfully. 'Don't go too far from this location. It'll be hard to find you, as it is.'

'No, I'll stay here by the well.'

Tasso gripped the takeoff switch, running her fingers over the smooth metal. 'A beautiful ship, Major. Well built. I admire your workmanship. You people have always done good work. You build fine things. Your work, your creations, are your greatest achievement.'

'Give me the pistol,' Hendricks said impatiently, holding out his hand. He struggled to his feet.

'Good-bye, Major!' Tasso tossed the pistol past Hendricks. The pistol clattered against the ground, bouncing and rolling away. Hendricks hurried after it. He bent down, snatching it up.

The hatch of the ship clanged shut. The bolts fell into place. Hendricks made his way back. The inner door was being sealed. He raised the pistol unsteadily.

There was a shattering roar. The ship burst up from its metal cage, fusing the mesh behind it. Hendricks cringed, pulling back. The ship shot up into the rolling clouds of ash, disappearing into the sky.

Hendricks stood watching a long time, until even the streamer had dissipated. Nothing stirred. The morning air was chill and silent. He began to walk aimlessly back the way they had come. Better to keep moving around. It would be a long time before help came – if it came at all.

He searched his pockets until he found a package of cigarettes. He lit one grimly. They had all wanted cigarettes from him. But cigarettes were scarce.

A lizard slithered by him, through the ash. He halted, rigid. The lizard disappeared. Above, the sun rose higher in the sky. Some flies landed on a flat rock to one side of him. Hendricks kicked at them with his foot.

It was getting hot. Sweat trickled down his face, into his collar. His mouth was dry.

Presently he stopped walking and sat down on some debris. He unfastened his medicine kit and swallowed a few narcotic capsules. He looked around him. Where was he?

Something lay ahead. Stretched out on the ground. Silent and unmoving.

Hendricks drew his gun quickly. It looked like a man. Then he remembered. It was the remains of Klaus. The Second Variety. Where Tasso had blasted him. He could see wheels and relays and metal parts, strewn around on the ash. Glittering and sparkling in the sunlight.

Hendricks got to his feet and walked over. He nudged the inert form with his foot, turning it over a little. He could see the metal hull,

77

the aluminum ribs and struts. More wiring fell out. Like viscera. Heaps of wiring, switches and relays. Endless motors and rods.

He bent down. The brain cage had been smashed by the fall. The artificial brain was visible. He gazed at it. A maze of circuits. Miniature tubes. Wires as fine as hair. He touched the brain cage. It swung aside. The type plate was visible. Hendricks studied the plate.

And blanched.

IV – V.

For a long time he stared at the plate. Fourth Variety. Not the Second. They had been wrong. There were more types. Not just three. Many more, perhaps. At least four. And Klaus wasn't the Second Variety.

But if Klaus wasn't the Second Variety—

Suddenly he tensed. Something was coming, walking through the ash beyond the hill. What was it? He strained to see. Figures. Figures coming slowly along, making their way through the ash.

Coming toward him.

Hendricks crouched quickly, raising his gun. Sweat dripped down into his eyes. He fought down rising panic, as the figures neared.

The first was a David. The David saw him and increased its pace. The others hurried behind it. A second David. A third. Three Davids, all alike, coming toward him silently, without expression, their thin legs rising and falling. Clutching their teddy bears.

He aimed and fired. The first two Davids dissolved into particles. The third came on. And the figure behind it. Climbing silently toward him across the gray ash. A Wounded Soldier, towering over the David. And—

And behind the Wounded Soldier came two Tassos, walking side by side. Heavy belt, Russian army pants, shirt, long hair. The familiar figure, as he had seen her only a little while before. Sitting in the pressure seat of the ship. Two slim, silent figures, both identical.

They were very near. The David bent down suddenly, dropping its teddy bear. The bear raced across the ground. Automatically Hendricks' fingers tightened around the trigger. The bear was gone, dissolved into mist. The two Tasso Types moved on, expressionless, walking side by side, through the gray ash.

When they were almost to him, Hendricks raised the pistol waist high and fired.

The two Tassos dissolved. But already a new group was starting up the rise, five or six Tassos, all identical, a line of them coming rapidly toward him.

And he had given her the ship and the signal code. Because of him she was on her way to the moon, to the Moon Base. He had made it possible.

He had been right about the bomb, after all. It had been designed with knowledge of other types, the David Type and the Wounded Soldier Type. And the Klaus Type. Not designed by human beings. It had been designed by one of the underground factories, apart from all human contact.

The line of Tassos came up to him. Hendricks braced himself, watching them calmly. The familiar face, the belt, the heavy shirt, the bomb carefully in place.

The bomb—

As the Tassos reached for him, a last ironic thought drifted through Hendrick's mind. He felt a little better, thinking about it. The bomb. Made by the Second Variety to destroy the other varieties. Made for that end alone.

They were already beginning to design weapons to use against each other.

Impostor

'One of these days I'm going to take time off,' Spence Olham said at first-meal. He looked around at his wife. 'I think I've earned a rest. Ten years is a long time.'

'And the Project?'

'The war will be won without me. This ball of clay of ours isn't really in much danger.' Olham sat down at the table and lit a cigarette. 'The news-machines alter dispatches to make it appear the Outspacers are right on top of us. You know what I'd like to do on my vacation? I'd like to take a camping trip to those mountains outside of town, where we went that time. Remember? I got poison oak and you almost stepped on a gopher snake.'

'Sutton Wood?' Mary began to clear away the food dishes. 'The Wood was burned a few weeks ago. I thought you knew. Some kind of a flash fire.'

Olham sagged. 'Didn't they even try to find the cause?' His lips twisted. 'No one cares anymore. All they can think of is the war.' He clamped his jaws together, the whole picture coming up in his mind, the Outspacers, the war, the needle-ships.

'How can we think about anything else?'

Olham nodded. She was right, of course. The dark little ships out of Alpha Centauri had bypassed the Earth cruisers easily, leaving them like helpless turtles. It had been one-way fights, all the way back to Terra.

All the way, until the protec-bubble was demonstrated by Westinghouse Labs. Thrown around the major Earth cities and finally the planet itself, the bubble was the first real defense, the first legitimate answer to the Outspacers – as the news-machines labeled them.

But to win the war, that was another thing. Every lab, every project was working night and day, endlessly, to find something more: a weapon for positive combat. His own project, for example. All day long, year after year.

Olham stood up, putting out his cigarette. 'Like the Sword of

Damocles. Always hanging over us. I'm getting tired. All I want to do is take a long rest. But I guess everybody feels that way.'

He got his jacket from the closet and went out on the front porch. The shoot would be along any moment, the fast little bug that would carry him to the Project.

'I hope Nelson isn't late.' He looked at his watch. 'It's almost seven.'

'Here the bug comes,' Mary said, gazing between the rows of houses. The sun glittered behind the roofs, reflecting against the heavy lead plates. The settlement was quiet; only a few people were stirring. 'I'll see you later. Try not to work beyond your shift, Spence.'

Olham opened the car door and slid inside, leaning back against the seat with a sigh. There was an older man with Nelson.

'Well?' Olham said, as the bug shot ahead. 'Heard any interesting news?'

'The usual,' Nelson said. 'A few Outspace ships hit, another asteroid abandoned for strategic reasons.'

'It'll be good when we get the Project into final stage. Maybe it's just the propaganda from the news-machines, but in the last month I've gotten weary of all this. Everything seems so grim and serious, no color to life.'

'Do you think the war is in vain?' the older man said suddenly. 'You are an integral part of it, yourself.'

'This is Major Peters,' Nelson said. Olham and Peters shook hands. Olham studied the older man.

'What brings you along so early?' he said. 'I don't remember seeing you at the Project before.'

'No, I'm not with the Project,' Peters said, 'but I know something about what you're doing. My own work is altogether different.'

A look passed between him and Nelson. Olham noticed it and he frowned. The bug was gaining speed, flashing across the barren, lifeless ground toward the distant rim of the Project building.

'What is your business?' Olham said. 'Or aren't you permitted to talk about it?'

'I'm with the government,' Peters said. 'With FSA, the security organ.'

'Oh?' Olham raised an eyebrow. 'Is there any enemy infiltration in this region?'

'As a matter of fact I'm here to see you, Mr Olham.'

Olham was puzzled. He considered Peters' words, but he could make nothing of them. 'To see me? Why?'

'I'm here to arrest you as an Outspace spy. That's why I'm up so early this morning. *Grab him, Nelson—*'

The gun drove into Olham's ribs. Nelson's hands were shaking, trembling with released emotion, his face pale. He took a deep breath and let it out again.

'Shall we kill him now?' he whispered to Peters. 'I think we should kill him now. We can't wait.'

Olham stared into his friend's face. He opened his mouth to speak, but no words came. Both men were staring at him steadily, rigid and grim with fright. Olham felt dizzy. His head ached and spun.

'I don't understand,' he murmured.

At that moment the shoot car left the ground and rushed up, heading into space. Below them the Project fell away, smaller and smaller, disappearing. Olham shut his mouth.

'We can wait a little,' Peters said. 'I want to ask him some questions first.'

Olham gazed dully ahead as the bug rushed through space.

'The arrest was made all right,' Peters said into the vidscreen. On the screen the features of the security chief showed. 'It should be a load off everyone's mind.'

'Any complications?'

'None. He entered the bug without suspicion. He didn't seem to think my presence was too unusual.'

'Where are you now?'

'On our way out, just inside the protec-bubble. We're moving at a maximum speed. You can assume that the critical period is past. I'm glad the takeoff jets in this craft were in good working order. If there had been any failure at that point—'

'Let me see him,' the security chief said. He gazed directly at Olham where he sat, his hands in his lap, staring ahead.

'So that's the man.' He looked at Olham for a time. Olham said nothing. At last the chief nodded to Peters. 'All right. That's enough.' A faint trace of disgust wrinkled his features. 'I've seen all I want. You've done something that will be remembered for a long time. They're preparing some sort of citation for both of you.'

'That's not necessary,' Peters said.

'How much danger is there now? Is there still much chance that—'

'There is some chance, but not too much. According to my understanding it requires a verbal key phrase. In any case we'll have to take the risk.'

'I'll have the Moon base notified you're coming.'

'No.' Peters shook his head. 'I'll land the ship outside, beyond the base. I don't want it in jeopardy.'

'Just as you like.' The chief's eyes flickered as he glanced again at Olham. Then his image faded. The screen blanked.

Olham shifted his gaze to the window. The ship was already through the protec-bubble, rushing with greater and greater speed all the time. Peters was in a hurry; below him, rumbling under the floor, the jets were wide open. They were afraid, hurrying frantically, because of him.

Next to him on the seat, Nelson shifted uneasily. 'I think we should do it now,' he said. 'I'd give anything if we could get it over with.'

'Take it easy,' Peters said. 'I want you to guide the ship for a while so I can talk to him.'

He slid over beside Olham, looking into his face. Presently he reached out and touched him gingerly, on the arm and then on the cheek.

Olham said nothing. *If I could let Mary know*, he thought again. *If I could find some way of letting her know.* He looked around the ship. How? The vidscreen? Nelson was sitting by the board, holding the gun. There was nothing he could do. He was caught, trapped.

But why?

'Listen,' Peters said, 'I want to ask you some questions. You know where we're going. We're moving Moonward. In an hour we'll land on the far side, on the desolate side. After we land you'll be turned over immediately to a team of men waiting there. Your body will be destroyed at once. Do you understand that?' He looked at his watch. 'Within two hours your parts will be strewn over the landscape. There won't be anything left of you.'

Olham struggled out of his lethargy. 'Can't you tell me—'

'Certainly, I'll tell you.' Peters nodded. 'Two days ago we received a report that an Outspace ship had penetrated the protec-bubble. The ship let off a spy in the form of a humanoid robot. The robot was to destroy a particular human being and take his place.'

Peters looked calmly at Olham.

'Inside the robot was a U–Bomb. Our agent did not know how the

83

bomb was to be detonated, but he conjectured that it might be by a particular spoken phrase, a certain group of works. The robot would live the life of the person he killed, entering into his usual activities, his job, his social life. He had been constructed to resemble that person. No one would know the difference.'

Olham's face went sickly chalk.

'The person whom the robot was to impersonate was Spence Olham, a high-ranking official at one of the research Projects. Because this particular Project was approaching crucial stage, the presence of an animate bomb, moving toward the center of the Project—'

Olham stared down at his hands. '*But I'm Olham!*'

'Once the robot had located and killed Olham it was a simple matter to take over his life. The robot was probably released from the ship eight days ago. The substitution was probably accomplished over the last weekend, when Olham went for a short walk in the hills.'

'But I'm Olham.' He turned to Nelson, sitting at the controls. 'Don't you recognize me? You've known me for twenty years. Don't you remember how we went to college together?' He stood up. 'You and I were at the University. We had the same room.' He went toward Nelson.

'Stay away from me!' Nelson snarled.

'Listen. Remember our second year? Remember that girl? What was her name—' He rubbed his forehead. 'The one with the dark hair. The one we met over at Ted's place.'

'Stop!' Nelson waved the gun frantically. 'I don't want to hear any more. You killed him! You . . . machine.'

Olham looked at Nelson. 'You're wrong. I don't know what happened, but the robot never reached me. Something must have gone wrong. Maybe the ship crashed.' He turned to Peters. 'I'm Olham. I know it. No transfer was made. I'm the same as I've always been.'

He touched himself, running his hands over his body. 'There must be some way to prove it. Take me back to Earth. An X-ray examination, a neurological study, anything like that will show you. Or maybe we can find the crashed ship.'

Neither Peters nor Nelson spoke.

'I am Olham,' he said again. 'I know I am. But I can't prove it.'

'The robot,' Peters said, 'would be unaware that he was not the real Spence Olham. He would become Olham in mind as well as body. He was given an artificial memory system, false recall. He would look like him, have his memories, his thoughts and interests, perform his job.

'But there would be one difference. Inside the robot is a U–Bomb, ready to explode at the trigger phrase.' Peters moved a little away. 'That's the one difference. That's why we're taking you to the Moon. They'll disassemble you and remove the bomb. Maybe it will explode, but it won't matter, not there.'

Olham sat down slowly.

'We'll be there soon,' Nelson said.

He lay back, thinking frantically, as the ship dropped slowly down. Under them was the pitted surface of the Moon, the endless expanse of ruin. What could he do? What would save him?

'Get ready,' Peters said.

In a few minutes he would be dead. Down below he could see a tiny dot, a building of some kind. There were men in the building, the demolition team, waiting to tear him to bits. They would rip him open, pull off his arms and legs, break him apart. When they found no bomb they would be surprised; they would know, but it would be too late.

Olham looked around the small cabin. Nelson was still holding the gun. There was no chance there. If he could get to a doctor, have an examination made – that was the only way. Mary could help him. He thought frantically, his mind racing. Only a few minutes, just a little time left. If he could contact her, get word to her some way.

'Easy,' Peters said. The ship came down slowly, bumping on the rough ground. There was silence.

'Listen,' Olham said thickly. 'I can prove I'm Spence Olham. Get a doctor. Bring him here—'

'There's the squad,' Nelson pointed. 'They're coming.' He glanced nervously at Olham. 'I hope nothing happens.'

'We'll be gone before they start work,' Peters said. 'We'll be out of here in a moment.' He put on his pressure suit. When he had finished he took the gun from Nelson. 'I'll watch him for a moment.'

Nelson put on his pressure suit, hurrying awkwardly. 'How about him?' He indicated Olham. 'Will he need one?'

'No.' Peters shook his head. 'Robots probably don't require oxygen.'

The group of men were almost to the ship. They halted, waiting. Peters signaled to them.

'Come on!' He waved his hand and the men approached warily; stiff, grotesque figures in their inflated suits.

'If you open the door,' Olham said, 'it means my death. It will be murder.'

'Open the door,' Nelson said. He reached for the handle.

Olham watched him. He saw the man's hand tighten around the metal rod. In a moment the door would swing back, the air in the ship would rush out. He would die, and presently they would realize their mistake. Perhaps at some other time, when there was no war, men might not act this way, hurrying an individual to his death because they were afraid. Everyone was frightened, everyone was willing to sacrifice the individual because of the group fear.

He was being killed because they could not wait to be sure of his guilt. There was not enough time.

He looked at Nelson. Nelson had been his friend for years. They had gone to school together. He had been best man at his wedding. Now Nelson was going to kill him. But Nelson was not wicked; it was not his fault. It was the times. Perhaps it had been the same way during the plagues. When men had shown a spot they probably had been killed, too, without a moment's hesitation, without proof, on suspicion alone. In times of danger there was no other way.

He did not blame them. But he had to live. His life was too precious to be sacrificed. Olham thought quickly. What could he do? Was there anything? He looked around.

'Here goes,' Nelson said.

'You're right,' Olham said. The sound of his own voice surprised him. It was the strength of desperation. 'I have no need of air. Open the door.'

They paused, looking at him in curious alarm.

'Go ahead. Open it. It makes no difference.' Olham's hand disappeared inside his jacket. 'I wonder how far you two can run?'

'Run?'

'You have fifteen seconds to live.' Inside his jacket his fingers twisted, his arm suddenly rigid. He relaxed, smiling a little. 'You were wrong about the trigger phrase. In that respect you were mistaken. Fourteen seconds, now.'

Two shocked faces stared at him from the pressure suits. Then they were struggling, running, tearing the door open. The air shrieked out, spilling into the void. Peters and Nelson bolted out of the ship.

Olham came after them. He grasped the door and dragged it shut. The automatic pressure system chugged furiously, restoring the air. Olham let his breath out with a shudder.

One more second—

Beyond the window the two men had joined the group. The group scattered, running in all directions. One by one they threw themselves down, prone on the ground. Olham seated himself at the control board. He moved the dials into place. As the ship rose up into the air the men below scrambled to their feet and stared up, their mouths open.

'Sorry,' Olham murmured, 'but I've got to get back to Earth.'

He headed the ship back the way it had come.

It was night. All around the ship crickets chirped, disturbing the chill darkness. Olham bent over the vidscreen. Gradually the image formed; the call had gone through without trouble. He breathed a sigh of relief.

'Mary,' he said. The woman stared at him. She gasped.

'Spence! Where are you? What's happened?'

'I can't tell you. Listen, I have to talk fast. They may break this call off any minute. Go to the Project grounds and get Dr Chamberlain. If he isn't there, get any doctor. Bring him to the house and have him stay there. Have him bring equipment, X-ray, fluoroscope, everything.'

'But—'

'Do as I say. Hurry. Have him get it ready in an hour.' Olham leaned toward the screen. 'Is everything all right? Are you alone?'

'Alone?'

'Is anyone with you? Has . . . has Nelson or anyone contacted you?'

'No. Spence, I don't understand.'

'All right. I'll see you at the house in an hour. And don't tell anyone anything. Get Chamberlain there on any pretext. Say you're very ill.'

He broke the connection and looked at his watch. A moment later he left the ship, stepping down into the darkness. He had a half mile to go. He began to walk.

One light showed in the window, the study light. He watched it, kneeling against the fence. There was no sound, no movement of any kind. He held his watch up and read it by starlight. Almost an hour had passed.

Along the street a shoot bug came. It went on.

Olham looked toward the house. The doctor should have already come. He should be inside, waiting with Mary. A thought struck him. Had she been able to leave the house? Perhaps they had intercepted her. Maybe he was moving into a trap.

But what else could he do?

With a doctor's records, photographs and reports, there was a chance, a chance of proof. If he could be examined, if he could remain alive long enough for them to study him—

He could prove it that way. It was probably the only way. His one hope lay inside the house. Dr Chamberlain was a respected man. He was the staff doctor for the Project. He would know, his word on the matter would have meaning. He could overcome their hysteria, their madness, with facts.

Madness – that was what it was. If only they would wait, act slowly, take their time. But they could not wait. He had to die, die at once, without proof, without any kind of trial or examination. The simplest test would tell, but they had no time for the simplest test. They could think only of the danger. Danger, and nothing more.

He stood up and moved toward the house. He came up on the porch. At the door he paused, listening. Still no sound. The house was absolutely still.

Too still.

Olham stood on the porch, unmoving. They were trying to be silent inside. Why? It was a small house; only a few feet away, beyond the door, Mary and Dr Chamberlain should be standing. Yet he could hear nothing, no sound of voices, nothing at all. He looked at the door. It was a door he had opened and closed a thousand times, every morning and every night.

He put his hand on the knob. Then, all at once, he reached out and touched the bell instead. The bell pealed, off some place in the back of the house. Olham smiled. He could hear movement.

Mary opened the door. As soon as he saw her face he knew.

He ran, throwing himself into the bushes. A security officer shoved Mary out of the way, firing past her. The bushes burst apart. Olham wriggled around the side of the house. He leaped up and ran, racing frantically into the darkness. A searchlight snapped on, a beam of light circling past him.

He crossed the road and squeezed over a fence. He jumped down and made his way across a backyard. Behind him men were coming, security officers, shouting to each other as they came. Olham gasped for breath, his chest rising and falling.

Her face— He had known at once. The set lips, the terrified, wretched eyes. Suppose he had gone ahead, pushed open the door and entered! They had tapped the call and come at once, as soon as he had broken off. Probably she believed their account. No doubt she thought he was the robot, too.

Olham ran on and on. He was losing the officers, dropping them behind. Apparently they were not much good at running. He climbed a hill and made his way down the other side. In a moment he would be back at the ship. But where to, this time? He slowed down, stopping. He could see the ship already, outlined against the sky, where he had parked it. The settlement was behind him; he was on the outskirts of the wilderness between the inhabited places, where the forests and desolation began. He crossed a barren field and entered the trees.

As he came toward it, the door of the ship opened.

Peters stepped out, framed against the light. In his arms was a heavy Boris gun. Olham stopped, rigid. Peters stared around him, into the darkness. 'I know you're there, some place,' he said. 'Come on up here, Olham. There are security men all around you.'

Olham did not move.

'Listen to me. We will catch you very shortly. Apparently you still do not believe you're the robot. Your call to the woman indicates that you are still under the illusion created by your artificial memories.

'But you *are* the robot. You are the robot, and inside you is the bomb. Any moment the trigger phrase may be spoken, by you, by someone else, by anyone. When that happens the bomb will destroy everything for miles around. The Project, the woman, all of us will be killed. Do you understand?'

Olham said nothing. He was listening. Men were moving toward him, slipping through the woods.

'If you don't come out, we'll catch you. It will be only a matter of time. We no longer plan to remove you to the Moon base. You will be destroyed on sight, and we will have to take the chance that the bomb will detonate. I have ordered every available security officer into the area. The whole county is being searched, inch by inch. There is no place you can go. Around this wood is a cordon of armed men. You have about six hours left before the last inch is covered.'

Olham moved away. Peters went on speaking; he had not seen him at all. It was too dark to see anyone. But Peters was right. There was no place he could go. He was beyond the settlement, on the outskirts where the woods began. He could hide for a time, but eventually they would catch him.

Only a matter of time.

Olham walked quietly through the wood. Mile by mile, each part of the county was being measured off, laid bare, searched, studied, examined. The cordon was coming all the time, squeezing him into a smaller and smaller space.

What was there left? He had lost the ship, the one hope of escape. They were at his home; his wife was with them, believing, no doubt, that the real Olham had been killed. He clenched his fists. Some place there was a wrecked Outspace needle-ship, and in it the remains of the robot. Somewhere nearby the ship had crashed and broken up.

And the robot lay inside, destroyed.

A faint hope stirred him. What if he could find the remains? If he could show them the wreckage, the remains of the ship, the robot—

But where? Where would he find it?

He walked on, lost in thought. Some place, not too far off, probably. The ship would have landed close to the Project; the robot would have expected to go the rest of the way on foot. He went up the side of a hill and looked around. Crashed and burned. Was there some clue, some hint? Had he read anything, heard anything? Some place close by, within walking distance. Some wild place, a remote spot where there would be no people.

Suddenly Olham smiled. Crashed and burned—

Sutton Wood.

He increased his pace.

It was morning. Sunlight filtered down through the broken trees, onto the man crouching at the edge of the clearing. Olham glanced up from time to time, listening. They were not far off, only a few minutes away. He smiled.

Down below him, strewn across the clearing and into the charred stumps that had been Sutton Wood, lay a tangled mass of wreckage. In the sunlight it glittered a little, gleaming darkly. He had not had too much trouble finding it. Sutton Wood was a place he knew well; he had climbed around it many times in his life, when he was younger. He had known where he would find the remains. There was one peak that jutted up suddenly, without a warning.

A descending ship, unfamiliar with the Wood, had little chance of missing it. And now he squatted, looking down at the ship, or what remained of it.

Olham stood up. He could hear them, only a little distance away, coming together, talking in low tones. He tensed himself. Everything depended on who first saw him. If it was Nelson, he had no chance. Nelson would fire at once. He would be dead before they saw the ship. But if he had time to call out, hold them off for a moment— That was all he needed. Once they saw the ship he would be safe.

But if they fired first—

A charred branch cracked. A figure appeared, coming forward uncertainly. Olham took a deep breath. Only a few seconds remained, perhaps the last seconds of his life. He raised his arms, peering intently.

It was Peters.

'Peters!' Olham waved his arms. Peters lifted his gun, aiming. 'Don't fire!' His voice shook. 'Wait a minute. Look past me, across the clearing.'

'I've found him,' Peters shouted. Security men came pouring out of the burned woods around him.

'Don't shoot. Look past me. The ship, the needle-ship. The Outspace ship. Look!'

Peters hesitated. The gun wavered.

'It's down there,' Olham said rapidly. 'I knew I'd find it here. The burned wood. Now you believe me. You'll find the remains of the robot in the ship. Look, will you?'

'There is something down there,' one of the men said nervously.

'Shoot him!' a voice said. It was Nelson.

'Wait.' Peters turned sharply. 'I'm in charge. Don't anyone fire. Maybe he's telling the truth.'

'Shoot him,' Nelson said. 'He killed Olham. Any minute he may kill us all. If the bomb goes off—'

'Shut up.' Peters advanced toward the slope. He stared down. 'Look at that.' He waved two men up to him. 'Go down there and see what that is.'

The men raced down the slope, across the clearing. They bent down, poking in the ruins of the ship.

'Well?' Peters called.

Olham held his breath. He smiled a little. It must be there; he had not had time to look, himself, but it had to be there. Suddenly doubt assailed him. Suppose the robot had lived long enough to wander away? Suppose his body had been completely destroyed, burned to ashes by the fire?

He licked his lips. Perspiration came out on his forehead. Nelson was staring at him, his face still livid. His chest rose and fell.

'Kill him,' Nelson said. 'Before he kills us.'

The two men stood up.

'What have you found?' Peters said. He held the gun steady. 'Is there anything there?'

'Looks like something. It's a needle-ship, all right. There's something beside it.'

'I'll look.' Peters strode past Olham. Olham watched him go down the hill and up to the men. The others were following after him, peering to see.

'It's a body of some sort,' Peters said. 'Look at it!'

Olham came along with them. They stood around in a circle, staring down.

On the ground, bent and twisted in a strange shape, was a grotesque form. It looked human, perhaps; except that it was bent so strangely, the arms and legs flung off in all directions. The mouth was open; the eyes stared glassily.

'Like a machine that's run down,' Peters murmured.

Olham smiled feebly. 'Well?' he said.

Peters looked at him. 'I can't believe it. You were telling the truth all the time.'

'The robot never reached me,' Olham said. He took out a cigarette and lit it. 'It was destroyed when the ship crashed. You were all too busy with the war to wonder why an out-of-the-way woods would suddenly catch fire and burn. Now you know.'

He stood smoking, watching the men. They were dragging the grotesque remains from the ship. The body was stiff, the arms and legs rigid.

'You'll find the bomb now,' Olham said. The men laid the body on the ground. Peters bent down.

'I think I see the corner of it.' He reached out, touching the body.

The chest of the corpse had been laid open. Within the gaping tear something glinted, something metal. The men stared at the metal without speaking.

'That would have destroyed us all, if it had lived,' Peters said. 'That metal box there.'

There was silence.

'I think we owe you something,' Peters said to Olham. 'This must have been a nightmare to you. If you hadn't escaped, we would have—' He broke off.

Olham put out his cigarette. 'I knew, of course, that the robot had never reached me. But I had no way of proving it. Sometimes it isn't possible to prove a thing right away. That was the whole trouble. There wasn't any way I could demonstrate that I was myself.'

'How about a vacation?' Peters said. 'I think we might work out a month's vacation for you. You could take it easy, relax.'

'I think right now I want to go home,' Olham said.

'All right, then,' Peters said. 'Whatever you say.'

Nelson had squatted down on the ground, beside the corpse. He reached out toward the glint of metal visible within the chest.

'Don't touch it,' Olham said. 'It might still go off. We better let the demolition squad take care of it later on.'

Nelson said nothing. Suddenly he grabbed hold of the metal, reaching his hand inside the chest. He pulled.

'What are you doing?' Olham cried.

Nelson stood up. He was holding on to the metal object. His face was blank with terror. It was a metal knife, an Outspace needle-knife, covered with blood.

'This killed him,' Nelson whispered. 'My friend was killed with this.' He looked at Olham. 'You killed him with this and left him beside the ship.'

Olham was trembling. His teeth chattered. He looked from the knife to the body. 'This can't be Olham,' he said. His mind spun, everything was whirling. 'Was I wrong?'

He gaped.

'But if that's Olham, than I must be—'

He did not complete the sentence, only the first phrase. The blast was visible all the way to Alpha Centauri.

The Preserving Machine

Doc Labyrinth leaned back in his lawn chair, closing his eyes gloomily. He pulled his blanket up around his knees.

'Well?' I said. I was standing by the barbecue pit, warming my hands. It was a clear cold day. The sunny Los Angeles sky was almost cloud-free. Beyond Labyrinth's modest house a gently undulating expanse of green stretched off until it reached the mountains – a small forest that gave the illusion of wilderness within the very limits of the city. 'Well?' I said. 'Then the Machine did work the way you expected?'

Labyrinth did not answer. I turned around. The old man was staring moodily ahead, watching an enormous dun-colored beetle that was slowly climbing the side of his blanket. The beetle rose methodically, its face blank with dignity. It passed over the top and disappeared down the far side. We were alone again.

Labyrinth sighed and looked up at me. 'Oh, it worked well enough.'

I looked after the beetle, but it was nowhere to be seen. A faint breeze eddied around me, chill and thin in the fading afternoon twilight. I moved nearer the barbecue pit.

'Tell me about it,' I said.

Doctor Labyrinth, like most people who read a great deal and who have too much time on their hands, had become convinced that our civilization was going the way of Rome. He saw, I think, the same cracks forming that had sundered the ancient world, the world of Greece and Rome; and it was his conviction that presently our world, our society, would pass away as theirs did, and a period of darkness would follow.

Now Labyrinth, having thought this, began to brood over all the fine and lovely things that would be lost in the reshuffling of societies. He thought of the art, the literature, the manners, the music, every-thing that would be lost. And it seemed to him that of all these grand and noble things, music would probably be the most lost, the quickest forgotten.

Music is the most perishable of things, fragile and delicate, easily destroyed.

Labyrinth worried about this, because he loved music, because he hated the idea that some day there would be no more Brahms and Mozart, no more gentle chamber music that he could dreamily associate with powdered wigs and resined bows, with long, slender candles, melting away in the gloom.

What a dry and unfortunate world it would be, without music! How dusty and unbearable.

This is how he came to think of the Preserving Machine. One evening as he sat in his living room in his deep chair, the gramophone on low, a vision came to him. He perceived in his mind a strange sight, the last score of a Schubert trio, the last copy, dog-eared, well-thumbed, lying on the floor of some gutted place, probably a museum.

A bomber moved overhead. Bombs fell, bursting the museum to fragments, bringing the walls down in a roar of rubble and plaster. In the debris the last score disappeared, lost in the rubbish, to rot and mold.

And then, in Doc Labyrinth's vision, he saw the score come burrowing out, like some buried mole. Quick like a mole, in fact, with claws and sharp teeth and a furious energy.

If music had that faculty, the ordinary, everyday instinct of survival which every worm and mole has, how different it would be! If music could be transformed into living creatures, animals with claws and teeth, then music might survive. If only a Machine could be built, a Machine to process musical scores into living forms.

But Doc Labyrinth was no mechanic. He made a few tentative sketches and sent them hopefully around to the research laboratories. Most of them were much too busy with war contracts, of course. But at last he found the people he wanted. A small midwestern university was delighted with his plans, and they were happy to start work on the Machine at once.

Weeks passed. At last Labyrinth received a postcard from the university. The Machine was coming along fine; in fact, it was almost finished. They had given it a trial run, feeding a couple of popular songs into it. The results? Two small mouse-like animals had come scampering out, rushing around the laboratory until the cat caught and ate them. But the Machine was a success.

It came to him shortly after, packed carefully in a wood crate, wired together and fully insured. He was quite excited as he set to work, taking the slats from it. Many fleeting notions must have coursed through his mind as he adjusted the controls and made ready for the first transformation. He had selected a priceless score to begin with, the score of the Mozart G Minor Quintet. For a time he turned the pages, lost in thought, his mind far away. At last he carried it to the Machine and dropped it in.

Time passed. Labyrinth stood before it, waiting nervously, apprehensive and not really certain what would greet him when he opened the compartment. He was doing a fine and tragic work, it seemed to him, preserving the music of the great composers for all eternity. What would his thanks be? What would he find? What form would this all take, before it was over?

There were many questions unanswered. The red light of the Machine was glinting, even as he meditated. The process was over, the transformation had already taken place. He opened the door.

'Good Lord!' he said. 'This is very odd.'

A bird, not an animal, stepped out. The mozart bird was pretty, small and slender, with the flowing plumage of a peacock. It ran a little way across the room and then walked back to him, curious and friendly. Trembling, Doc Labyrinth bent down, his hand out. The mozart bird came near. Then, all at once, it swooped up into the air.

'Amazing,' he murmured. He coaxed the bird gently, patiently, and at last it fluttered down to him. Labyrinth stroked it for a long time, thinking. What would the rest of them be like? He could not guess. He carefully gathered up the mozart bird and put it into a box.

He was even more surprised the next day when the beethoven beetle came out, stern and dignified. That was the beetle I saw myself, climbing along his red blanket, intent and withdrawn, on some business of its own.

After that came the schubert animal. The schubert animal was silly, an adolescent sheep-creature that ran this way and that, foolish and wanting to play. Labyrinth sat down right then and there and did some heavy thinking.

Just what *were* survival factors? Was a flowing plume better than claws, better than sharp teeth? Labyrinth was stumped. He had expected an army of stout badger creatures, equipped with claws and scales, digging, fighting, ready to gnaw and kick. Was he getting the right thing? Yet who could say what was good for survival? – the dinosaurs had been well armed, but there were none of them left. In any case the Machine was built; it was too late to turn back, now.

Labyrinth went ahead, feeding the music of many composers into the Preserving Machine, one after another, until the woods behind his house was filled with creeping, bleating things that screamed and crashed in the night. There were many oddities that came out, creations that startled and astonished him. The brahms insect had many legs sticking in all directions, a vast, platter-shaped centipede. It was low and flat, with a coating of uniform fur. The brahms insect liked to be by itself, and it went off promptly, taking great pains to avoid the wagner animal who had come just before.

The wagner animal was large and splashed with deep colors. It seemed to have quite a temper, and Doc Labyrinth was a little afraid of it, as were the bach bugs, the round ball-like creatures, a whole flock of them, some large, some small, that had been obtained for the Forty-Eight Preludes and Fugues. And there was the stravinsky bird, made up of curious fragments and bits, and many others besides.

So he let them go, off into the woods, and away they went, hopping and rolling and jumping as best they could. But already a sense of failure hung over him. Each time a creature came out he was astonished; he did not seem to have control over the results at all. It was out of his hands, subject to some strong, invisible law that had subtly taken over, and this worried him greatly. The creatures were bending, changing before a deep, impersonal force, a force that Labyrinth could neither see nor understand. And it made him afraid.

Labyrinth stopped talking. I waited for a while but he did not seem to be going on. I looked around at him. The old man was staring at me in a strange, plaintive way.

'I don't really know much more,' he said. 'I haven't been back there for a long time, back in the woods. I'm afraid to. I know something is going on, but—'

'Why don't we both go and take a look?'

He smiled with relief. 'You wouldn't mind, would you? I was hoping you might suggest that. This business is beginning to get me down.' He pushed his blanket aside and stood up, brushing himself off. 'Let's go then.'

We walked around the side of the house and along a narrow path, into the woods. Everything was wild and chaotic, overgrown and matted, an unkempt, unattended sea of green. Doc Labyrinth went first, pushing the branches off the path, stooping and wriggling to get through.

'Quite a place,' I observed. We made our way for a time. The woods were dark and damp; it was almost sunset now, and a light mist was descending on us, drifting down through the leaves above.

'No one comes here.' Then Doc stopped suddenly, looking around. 'Maybe we'd better go and find my gun. I don't want anything to happen.'

'You seem certain that things have got out of hand.' I came up beside him and we stood together. 'Maybe it's not as bad as you think.'

Labyrinth looked around. He pushed some shrubbery back with his foot. 'They're all around us, everywhere, watching us. Can't you feel it?'

I nodded absently. 'What's this?' I lifted up a heavy, moldering branch, particles of fungus breaking from it. I pushed it out of the way. A mound lay outstretched, shapeless and indistinct, half buried in the soft ground.

'What is it?' I said again. Labyrinth stared down, his face tight and forlorn. He began to kick at the mound aimlessly. I felt uncomfortable. 'What is it, for heaven's sake?' I said. 'Do you know?'

Labyrinth looked slowly up at me. 'It's the schubert animal,' he murmured. 'Or it was, once. There isn't much left of it, any more.'

The schubert animal – that was the one that had run and leaped like a puppy, silly and wanting to play. I bent down, staring at the mound, pushing a few leaves and twigs from it. It was dead all right. Its mouth was open, its body had been ripped wide. Ants and vermin were already working on it, toiling endlessly away. It had begun to stink.

'But what happened?' Labyrinth said. He shook his head. 'What could have done it?'

There was a sound. We turned quickly.

For a moment we saw nothing. Then a bush moved, and for the first time we made out its form. It must have been standing there watching us all the time. The creature was immense, thin and extended, with bright, intense eyes. To me, it looked something like a coyote, but much heavier. Its coat was matted and thick, its muzzle hung partly open as it gazed at us silently, studying us as if astonished to find us there.

'The wagner animal,' Labyrinth said thickly. 'But it's changed. It's changed. I hardly recognize it.'

The creature sniffed the air, its hackles up. Suddenly it moved back, into the shadows, and a moment later it was gone.

We stood for a while, not saying anything. At last Labyrinth stirred. 'So, that's what it was,' he said. 'I can hardly believe it. But why? What—'

'Adaptation,' I said. 'When you toss an ordinary house cat out it becomes wild. Or a dog.'

'Yes.' He nodded. 'A dog becomes a wolf again, to stay alive. The law of the forest. I should have expected it. It happens to everything.'

I looked down at the corpse on the ground, and then around at the silent bushes. Adaptation – or maybe something worse. An idea was forming in my mind, but I said nothing, not right away.

'I'd like to see some more of them,' I said. 'Some of the others. Let's look around some more.'

He agreed. We began to poke slowly through the grass and weeds, pushing branches and foliage out of the way. I found a stick, but Labyrinth got down on his hands and knees, reaching and feeling, staring near-sightedly down.

'Even children turn into beasts,' I said. 'You remember the wolf children of India? No one could believe they had been ordinary children.'

Labyrinth nodded. He was unhappy, and it was not hard to understand why. He had been wrong, mistaken in his original idea, and the consequences of it were just now beginning to become apparent to him. Music would survive as living creatures, but he had forgotten the lesson of the Garden of Eden: that once a thing has been fashioned it begins to exist on its own, and thus ceases to be the property of its creator to mold and direct as he wishes. God, watching man's development, must have felt the same sadness – and the same humiliation – as Labyrinth, to see His creatures alter and change to meet the needs of survival.

That his musical creatures should survive could mean nothing to him any more, for the very thing he had created them to prevent, the brutalization of beautiful things, was happening in *them*, before his own eyes. Doc Labyrinth looked up at me suddenly, his face full of misery. He had ensured their survival, all right, but in so doing he had erased any meaning, any value in it. I tried to smile a little at him, but he promptly looked away again.

'Don't worry so much about it,' I said. 'It wasn't much of a change for the wagner animal. Wasn't it pretty much that way anyhow, rough and temperamental? Didn't it have a proclivity towards violence—'

I broke off. Doc Labyrinth had leaped back, jerking his hand out of the grass. He clutched his wrist, shuddering with pain.

'What is it?' I hurried over. Trembling, he held his little old hand out to me. 'What is it? What happened?'

I turned the hand over. All across the back of it were marks, red cuts that swelled even as I watched. He had been stung, stung or bitten by something in the grass. I looked down, kicking the grass with my foot.

There was a stir. A little golden ball rolled quickly away, back toward the bushes. It was covered with spines like a nettle.

'Catch it!' Labyrinth cried. 'Quick!'

I went after it, holding out my handkerchief, trying to avoid the spines. The sphere rolled frantically, trying to get away, but finally I got it into the handkerchief.

Labyrinth stared at the struggling handkerchief as I stood up. 'I can hardly believe it,' he said. 'We'd better go back to the house.'

'What is it?'

'One of the bach bugs. But it's changed . . .'

We made our way back along the path, toward the house, feeling our way through the darkness. I went first, pushing the branches aside, and Labyrinth followed behind, moody and withdrawn, rubbing his hand from time to time.

We entered the yard and went up to the back steps of the house, onto the porch. Labyrinth unlocked the door and we went into the kitchen. He snapped on the light and hurried to the sink to bathe his hand.

I took an empty fruit jar from the cupboard and carefully dropped the bach bug into it. The golden ball rolled testily around as I clamped the lid on. I sat down at the table. Neither of us spoke, Labyrinth at the sink, running cold water over his stung hand, I at the table, uncomfortably watching the golden ball in the fruit jar trying to find some way to escape.

'Well?' I said at last.

'There's no doubt.' Labyrinth came over and sat down opposite me. 'It's undergone some metamorphosis. It certainly didn't have poisoned spines to start with. You know, it's a good thing that I played my Noah role carefully.'

'What do you mean?'

'I made them all neuter. They can't reproduce. There will be no second generation. When these die, that will be the end of it.'

'I must say I'm glad you thought of that.'

'I wonder,' Labyrinth murmured. 'I wonder how it would sound, now, this way.'

'What?'

'The sphere, the bach bug. That's the real test, isn't it? I could put it back through the Machine. We could see. Do you want to find out?'

'Whatever you say, Doc,' I said. 'It's up to you. But don't get your hopes up too far.'

He picked up the fruit jar carefully and we walked downstairs, down the steep flights of steps to the cellar. I made out an immense column of dull metal rising up in the corner, by the laundry tubs. A strange feeling went through me. It was the Preserving Machine.

'So this is it,' I said.

'Yes, this is it.' Labyrinth turned the controls on and worked with them for a time. At last he took the jar and held it over the hopper. He removed the lid carefully, and the bach bug dropped reluctantly from the jar, into the Machine. Labyrinth closed the hopper after it.

'Here we go,' he said. He threw the control and the Machine began to operate. Labyrinth folded his arms and we waited. Outside the night came on, shutting out the light, squeezing it out of existence. At last an indicator on the face of the Machine blinked red. The Doc turned the control to OFF and we stood in silence, neither of us wanting to be the one who opened it.

'Well?' I said finally. 'Which one of us is going to look?'

Labyrinth stirred. He pushed the slot-piece aside and reached into the Machine. His fingers came out grasping a slim sheet, a score of music. He handed it to me. 'This is the result,' he said. 'We can go upstairs and play it.'

We went back up to the music room. Labyrinth sat down before the grand piano and I passed him back the score. He opened it and studied it for a moment, his face blank, without expression. Then he began to play.

I listened to the music. It was hideous. I have never heard anything like it. It was distorted, diabolical, without sense or meaning, except, perhaps, an alien, disconcerting meaning that should never have been there. I could believe only with the greatest effort that it had once been a Bach Fugue, part of a most orderly and respected work.

'That settles it,' Labyrinth said. He stood up, took the score in his hands, and tore it to shreds.

As we made our way down the path to my car I said, 'I guess the struggle for survival is a force bigger than any human ethos. It makes our precious morals and manners look a little thin.'

Labyrinth agreed. 'Perhaps nothing can be done, then, to save those manners and morals.'

'Only time will tell,' I said. 'Even though this method failed, some other may work; something that we can't foresee or predict now may come along, some day.'

I said good night and got into my car. It was pitch dark; night had fallen completely. I switched on my headlights and moved off down the road, driving into the utter darkness. There were no other cars in sight anywhere. I was alone, and very cold.

At the corner I stopped, slowing down to change gears. Something moved suddenly at the curb, something by the base of a huge sycamore tree, in the darkness. I peered out, trying to see what it was.

At the base of the sycamore tree a huge dun-colored beetle was building something, putting a bit of mud into place on a strange, awkward structure. I watched the beetle for a time, puzzled and curious, until at last it noticed me and stopped. The beetle turned abruptly and entered its building, snapping the door firmly shut behind it.

I drove away.

The Variable Man

I

Security Commissioner Reinhart rapidly climbed the front steps and entered the Council building. Council guards stepped quickly aside and he entered the familiar place of great whirring machines. His thin face rapt, eyes alight with emotion, Reinhart gazed intently up at the central SRB computer, studying its reading.

'Straight gain for the last quarter,' observed Kaplan, the lab organizer. He grinned proudly as if personally responsible. 'Not bad, Commissioner.'

'We're catching up to them,' Reinhart retorted. 'But too damn slowly. We must finally go over – and soon.'

Kaplan was in a talkative mood. 'We design new offensive weapons, they counter with improved defenses. And nothing is actually made! Continual improvement, but neither we nor Centaurus can stop designing long enough to stabilize for production.'

'It will end,' Reinhart stated coldly, 'as soon as Terra turns out a weapon for which Centaurus can build no defense.'

'Every weapon has a defense. Design and discord. Immediate obsolescence. Nothing lasts long enough to—'

'What we count on is the *lag*,' Reinhart broke in, annoyed. His hard gray eyes bored into the lab organizer and Kaplan slunk back. 'The time lag between our offensive design and their counter development. The lag varies.' He waved impatiently toward the massed banks of SRB machines. 'As you well know.'

At this moment, 9:30 AM, May 7, 2136, the statistical ratio on the SRB machines stood at 21–17 on the Centauran side of the ledger. All facts considered, the odds favored a successful repulsion by Proxima Centaurus of a Terran military attack. The ratio was based on the total information known to the SRB machines, on a gestalt of the vast flow of data that poured in endlessly from all sectors of the Sol and Centaurus systems.

21–17 on the Centauran side. But a month ago it had been 24–18 in the enemy's favor. Things were improving, slowly but steadily. Centaurus, older and less virile than Terra, was unable to match Terra's rate of technocratic advance. Terra was pulling ahead.

'If we went to war now,' Reinhart said thoughtfully, 'we would lose. We're not far enough along to risk an overt attack.' A harsh, ruthless glow twisted across his handsome features, distorting them into a stern mask. 'But the odds are moving in our favor. Our offensive designs are gradually gaining on their defenses.'

'Let's hope the war comes soon,' Kaplan agreed. 'We're all on edge. This damn waiting . . .'

The war would come soon. Reinhart knew it intuitively. The air was full of tension, the *élan*. He left the SRB rooms and hurried down the corridor to his own elaborately guarded office in the Security wing. It wouldn't be long. He could practically feel the hot breath of destiny on his neck – for him a pleasant feeling. His thin lips set in a humorless smile, showing an even line of white teeth against his tanned skin. It made him feel good, all right. He'd been working at it a long time.

First contact, a hundred years earlier, had ignited instant conflict between Proxima Centauran outposts and exploring Terran raiders. Flash fights, sudden eruptions of fire and energy beams.

And then the long, dreary years of inaction between enemies where contact required years of travel, even at nearly the speed of light. The two systems were evenly matched. Screen against screen. Warship against power station. The Centauran Empire surrounded Terra, an iron ring that couldn't be broken, rusty and corroded as it was. New weapons had to be conceived, if Terra was to break out.

Through the windows of his office, Reinhart could see endless buildings and streets. Terrans hurrying back and forth. Bright specks that were commute ships, little eggs that carried businessmen and white-collar workers around. The huge transport tubes that shot masses of workmen to factories and labor camps from their housing units. All these people, waiting to break out. Waiting for the day.

Reinhart snapped on his vidscreen, the confidential channel. 'Give me Military Designs,' he ordered sharply.

He sat tense, his wiry body taut, as the vidscreen warmed into life. Abruptly he was facing the hulking image of Peter Sherikov, director of the vast network of labs under the Ural Mountains.

Sherikov's great bearded features hardened as he recognized Reinhart. His bushy black eyebrows pulled up in a sullen line. 'What do you want? You know I'm busy. We have too much work to do, as it is. Without being bothered by – politicians.'

'I'm dropping over your way,' Reinhart answered lazily. He adjusted the cuff of his immaculate gray cloak. 'I want a full description of your work and whatever progress you've made.'

'You'll find a regular departmental report plate filed in the usual way, around your office someplace. If you'll refer to that you'll know exactly what we—'

'I'm not interested in that. I want to *see* what you're doing. And I expect you to be prepared to describe your work fully. I'll be there shortly. Half an hour.'

Reinhart cut the circuit. Sherikov's heavy features dwindled and faded. Reinhart relaxed, letting his breath out. Too bad he had to work with Sherikov. He had never liked the man. The big Polish scientist was an individualist, refusing to integrate himself with society. Independent, atomistic in outlook. He held concepts of the individual as an end, diametrically contrary to the accepted organic state Weltansicht.

But Sherikov was the leading research scientist, in charge of the Military Designs Department. And on Designs the whole future of Terra depended. Victory over Centaurus – or more waiting, bottled up in the Sol system, surrounded by a rotting, hostile Empire, now sinking into ruin and decay, yet still strong.

Reinhart got quickly to his feet and left the office. He hurried down the hall and out of the Council building.

A few minutes later he was heading across the mid-morning sky in his highspeed cruiser, toward the Asiatic landmass, the vast Ural mountain range. Toward the Military Designs labs.

Sherikov met him at the entrance. 'Look here, Reinhart. Don't think you're going to order me around. I'm not going to—'

'Take it easy.' Reinhart fell into step beside the bigger man. They passed through the check and into the auxiliary labs. 'No immediate coercion will be exerted over you or your staff. You're free to continue your work as you see fit – for the present. Let's get this straight. My concern is to integrate your work with our total social needs. As long as your work is sufficiently productive—'

Reinhart stopped in his tracks.

'Pretty, isn't he?' Sherikov said ironically.

'What the hell is it?'

'Icarus, we call him. Remember the Greek myth? The legend of Icarus. Icarus flew . . . This Icarus is going to fly, one of these days.' Sherikov shrugged. 'You can examine him, if you want. I suppose this is what you came here to see.'

Reinhart advanced slowly. 'This is the weapon you've been working on?'

'How does he look?'

Rising up in the center of the chamber was a squat metal cylinder, a great ugly cone of dark gray. Technicians circled around it, wiring up the exposed relay banks. Reinhart caught a glimpse of endless tubes and filaments, a maze of wires and terminals and parts criss-crossing each other, layer on layer.

'What is it?' Reinhart perched on the edge of a workbench, leaning his big shoulders against the wall.

'An idea of Jamison Hedge – the same man who developed our instantaneous interstellar vidcasts forty years ago. He was trying to find a method of faster than light travel when he was killed, destroyed along with most of his work. After that ftl research was abandoned. It looked as if there were no future in it.'

'Wasn't it shown that nothing could travel faster than light?'

'The interstellar vidcasts do! No, Hedge developed a valid ftl drive. He managed to propel an object at fifty times the speed of light. But as the object gained speed, its length began to diminish and its mass increased. This was in line with familiar twentieth-century concepts of mass-energy transformation. We conjectured that as Hedge's object gained velocity it would continue to lose length and gain mass until its length became nil and its mass infinite. Nobody can imagine such an object.'

'Go on.'

'But what actually occurred is this. Hedge's object continued to lose length and gain mass until it reached the theoretical limit of velocity, the speed of light. At that point the object, still gaining speed, simply ceased to exist. Having no length, it ceased to occupy space. It disappeared. However, the object had not been *destroyed*. It continued on its way, gaining momentum each moment, moving in an arc across the galaxy, away from the Sol system. Hedge's object entered some other realm of being, beyond our powers of conception. The next phase of Hedge's experiment consisted in a search for some way to slow the ftl object down, back to a sub-ftl speed, hence back into our universe. This counterprinciple was eventually worked out.'

'With what result?'

'The death of Hedge and destruction of most of his equipment. His experimental object, in re-entering the space–time universe, came into being in space already occupied by matter. Possessing an incredible mass, just below infinity level, Hedge's object exploded in a titanic cataclysm. It was obvious that no space travel was possible with such a drive. Virtually all space contains *some* matter. To re-enter space would bring automatic destruction. Hedge had found his ftl drive and his counterprinciple, but no one before this has been able to put them to any use.'

Reinhart walked over toward the great metal cylinder. Sherikov jumped down and followed him. 'I don't get it,' Reinhart said. 'You said the principle is no good for space travel.'

'That's right.'

'What's this for, then? If the ship explodes as soon as it returns to our universe—'

'This is not a ship.' Sherikov grinned slyly. 'Icarus is the first practical application of Hedge's principles. Icarus is a bomb.'

'So this is our weapon,' Reinhart said. 'A bomb. An immense bomb.'

'A bomb, moving at a velocity greater than light. A bomb which will not exist in our universe. The Centaurans won't be able to detect or stop it. How could they? As soon as it passes the speed of light it will cease to exist – beyond all detection.'

'But—'

'Icarus will be launched outside the lab, on the surface. He will align himself with Proxima Centaurus, gaining speed rapidly. By the time he reaches his destination he will be traveling at ftl-100. Icarus will be brought back to this universe within Centaurus itself. The explosion should destroy the star and wash away most of its planets – including their central hub-planet, Armun. There is no way they can halt Icarus, once he has been launched. No defense is possible. Nothing can stop him. It is a real fact.'

'When will it be ready?'

Sherikov's eyes flickered. 'Soon.'

'Exactly how soon?'

The big Pole hesitated. 'As a matter of fact, there's only one thing holding us back.'

Sherikov led Reinhart around to the other side of the lab. He pushed a lab guard out of the way.

'See this?' He tapped a round globe, open at one end, the size of a grapefruit. 'This is holding us up.'

'What is it?'

'The central control turret. This thing brings Icarus back to sub-ftl flight at the correct moment. It must be absolutely accurate. Icarus will be within the star only a matter of a microsecond. If the turret does not function exactly, Icarus will pass out the other side and shoot beyond the Centauran system.'

'How near completed is this turret?'

Sherikov hedged uncertainly, spreading out his big hands. 'Who can say? It must be wired with infinitely minute equipment – microscope grapples and wires invisible to the naked eye.'

'Can you name any completion date?'

Sherikov reached into his coat and brought out a manila folder. 'I've drawn up the data for the SRB machines, giving a date of completion. You can go ahead and feed it. I entered ten days as the maximum period. The machines can work from that.'

Reinhart accepted the folder cautiously. 'You're sure about the date? I'm not convinced I can trust you, Sherikov.'

Sherikov's features darkened. 'You'll have to take a chance, Commissioner. I don't trust you any more than you trust me. I know how much you'd like an excuse to get me out of here and one of your puppets in.'

Reinhart studied the huge scientist thoughtfully. Sherikov was going to be a hard nut to crack. Designs was responsible to Security, not the Council. Sherikov was losing ground – but he was still a potential danger. Stubborn, individualistic, refusing to subordinate his welfare to the general good.

'All right.' Reinhart put the folder slowly away in his coat. 'I'll feed it. But you better be able to come through. There can't be any slip-ups. Too much hangs on the next few days.'

'If the odds change in our favor are you going to give the mobilization order?'

'Yes,' Reinhart stated. 'I'll give the order the moment I see the odds change.'

Standing in front of the machines, Reinhart waited nervously for the results. It was two o'clock in the afternoon. The day was warm, a pleasant May afternoon. Outside the building the daily life of the planet went on as usual.

As usual? Not exactly. The feeling was in the air, an expanding excitement growing every day. Terra had waited a long time. The attack on Proxima Centaurus had to come – and the sooner the better. The ancient Centauran Empire hemmed in Terra, bottled the human race up in its one system. A vast, suffocating net draped across the heavens, cutting Terra off from the bright diamonds beyond . . . And it had to end.

The SRB machines whirred, the visible combination disappearing. For a time no ratio showed. Reinhart tensed, his body rigid. He waited.

The new ratio appeared.

Reinhart gasped. 7–6. Toward Terra!

Within five minutes the emergency mobilization alert had been flashed to all Government departments. The Council and President Duffe had been called to immediate session. Everything was happening fast.

But there was no doubt. 7–6. In Terra's favor. Reinhart hurried frantically to get his papers in order, in time for the Council session.

At histo-research the message plate was quickly pulled from the confidential slot and rushed across the central lab to the chief official.

'Look at this!' Fredman dropped the plate on his superior's desk. 'Look at it!'

Harper picked up the plate, scanning it rapidly. 'Sounds like the real thing. I didn't think we'd live to see it.'

Fredman left the room, hurrying down the hall. He entered the time bubble office. 'Where's the bubble?' he demanded, looking around.

One of the technicians looked slowly up. 'Back about two hundred years. We're coming up with interesting data on the War of 1914. According to material the bubble has already brought up—'

'Cut it. We're through with routine work. Get the bubble back to the present. From now on all equipment has to be free for Military work.'

'But – the bubble is regulated automatically.'

'You can bring it back manually.'

'It's risky.' The technician hedged. 'If the emergency requires it, I suppose we could take a chance and cut the automatic.'

'The emergency requires *everything*,' Fredman said feelingly.

'But the odds might change back,' Margaret Duffe, President of the Council, said nervously. 'Any minute they can revert.'

'This is our chance!' Reinhart snapped, his temper rising. 'What the hell's the matter with you? We've waited years for this.'

The Council buzzed with excitement. Margaret Duffe hesitated uncertainly, her blue eyes clouded with worry. 'I realize the opportunity is here. At least, statistically. But the new odds have just appeared. How do we know they'll last? They stand on the basis of a single weapon.'

'You're wrong. You don't grasp the situation.' Reinhart held himself in check with great effort. 'Sherikov's weapon tipped the ratio in our favor. But the odds have been moving in our direction for months. It was only a question of time. The new balance was inevitable, sooner or later. It's not just Sherikov. He's only one factor in this. It's all nine planets of the Sol system – not a single man.'

One of the Councilmen stood up. 'The President must be aware the entire planet is eager to end this waiting. All our activities for the past eighty years have been directed toward—'

Reinhart moved close to the slender President of the Council. 'If you don't approve the war, there probably will be mass rioting. Public reaction will be strong. Damn strong. And you know it.'

Margaret Duffe shot him a cold glance. 'You sent out the emergency order to force my hand. You were fully aware of what you were doing. You knew once the order was out there'd be no stopping things.'

A murmur rushed through the Council, gaining volume. 'We have to approve the war! . . . We're committed! . . . It's too late to turn back!'

Shouts, angry voices, insistent waves of sound lapped around Margaret Duffe. 'I'm as much for the war as anybody,' she said sharply. 'I'm only urging moderation. An inter-system war is a big thing. We're going to war because a machine says we have a statistical chance of winning.'

'There's no use starting the war unless we can win it,' Reinhart said. 'The SRB machines tell us whether we can win.'

'They tell us our *chance* of winning. They don't guarantee anything.'

'What more can we ask, besides a good chance of winning?'

Margaret Duffe clamped her jaw together tightly. 'All right. I hear all the clamor. I won't stand in the way of Council approval. The vote can go ahead.' Her cold, alert eyes appraised Reinhart. 'Especially since the emergency order has already been sent out to all Government departments.'

'Good.' Reinhart stepped away with relief. 'Then it's settled. We can finally go ahead with full mobilization.'

Mobilization proceeded rapidly. The next forty-eight hours were alive with activity.

Reinhart attended a policy-level Military briefing in the Council rooms, conducted by Fleet Commander Carleton.

'You can see our strategy,' Carleton said. He traced a diagram on the blackboard with a wave of his hand. 'Sherikov states it'll take eight more days to complete the ftl bomb. During that time the fleet we have near the Centauran system will take up positions. As the bomb goes off the fleet will begin operations against the remaining Centauran ships. Many will no doubt survive the blast, but with Armun gone we should be able to handle them.'

Reinhart took Commander Carleton's place. 'I can report on the economic situation. Every factory on Terra is converted to arms production. With Armun out of the way we should be able to promote mass insurrection among the Centauran colonies. An inter-system Empire is hard to maintain, even with ships that approach light speed. Local war-lords should pop up all over the place. We want to have weapons available for them and ships starting *now* to reach them in time. Eventually we hope to provide a unifying principle around which the colonies can all collect. Our interest is more economic than political. They can have any kind of government they want, as long as they act as supply areas for us. As our eight system planets act now.'

Carleton resumed his report. 'Once the Centauran fleet has been scattered we can begin the crucial stage of the war. The landing of men and supplies from the ships we have waiting in all key areas throughout the Centauran system. In this stage—'

Reinhart moved away. It was hard to believe only two days had passed since the mobilization order had been sent out. The whole system was alive, functioning with feverish activity. Countless problems were being solved – but much remained.

He entered the lift and ascended to the SRB room, curious to see if there had been any change in the machines' reading. He found it the same. So far so good. Did the Centaurans know about Icarus? No doubt; but there wasn't anything they could do about it. At least, not in eight days.

Kaplan came over to Reinhart, sorting a new batch of data that had come in. The lab organizer searched through his data. 'An amusing item came in. It might interest you.' He handed a message plate to Reinhart.

It was from histo-research:

> May 9, 2136
>
> This is to report that in bringing the research time bubble up to the present the manual return was used for the first time. Therefore a clean break was not made and a quantity of material from the past was brought forward. This material included an individual from the early twentieth century who escaped from the lab immediately. He has not yet been taken into protective custody. Histo-research regrets this incident, but attributes it to the emergency.
>
> E. Fredman

Reinhart handed the plate back to Kaplan. 'Interesting. A man from the past – hauled into the middle of the biggest war the universe has seen.'

'Strange things happen. I wonder what the machines will think.'

'Hard to say. Probably nothing.' Reinhart left the room and hurried along the corridor to his own office.

As soon as he was inside he called Sherikov on the vidscreen, using the confidential line.

The Pole's heavy features appeared. 'Good day, Commissioner. How's the war effort?'

'Fine. How's the turret wiring proceeding?'

A faint frown flickered across Sherikov's face. 'As a matter of fact, Commissioner—'

'What's the matter?' Reinhart said sharply.

Sherikov floundered. 'You know how these things are. I've taken my crew off it and tried robot workers. They have greater dexterity, but they can't make decisions. This calls for more than mere dexterity. This calls for—' He searched for the word. '—for an *artist*.'

Reinhart's face hardened. 'Listen, Sherikov. You have eight days left to complete the bomb. The data given to the SRB machines contained that information. The 7—6 ratio is based on that estimate. If you don't come through—'

Sherikov twisted in embarrassment. 'Don't get excited, Commissioner. We'll complete it.'

'I hope so. Call me as soon as it's done.' Reinhart snapped off the connection. If Sherikov let them down he'd have him taken out and shot. The whole war depended on the ftl bomb.

The vidscreen glowed again. Reinhart snapped it on. Kaplan's face formed on it. The lab organizer's face was pale and frozen. 'Commissioner, you better come up to the SRB office. Something's happened.'

'What is it?'

'I'll show you.'

Alarmed, Reinhart hurried out of his office and down the corridor. He found Kaplan standing in front of the SRB machines. 'What's the story?' Reinhart demanded. He glanced down at the reading. It was unchanged.

Kaplan held up a message plate nervously. 'A moment ago I fed this into the machines. After I saw the results I quickly removed it. It's that item I showed you. From histo-research. About the man from the past.'

'What happened when you fed it?'

Kaplan swallowed unhappily. 'I'll show you. I'll do it again. Exactly as before.' He fed the plate into a moving intake belt. 'Watch the visible figures,' Kaplan muttered.

Reinhart watched, tense and rigid. For a moment nothing happened. 7—6 continued to show. Then— The figures disappeared. The machines faltered. New figures showed briefly. 4—24 for Centaurus. Reinhart gasped, suddenly sick with apprehension. But the figures vanished. New figures appeared. 16—38 for Centaurus. Then 48—86. 79—15 in Terra's favor. Then nothing. The machines whirred, but nothing happened.

Nothing at all. No figures. Only a blank.

'What's it mean?' Reinhart muttered, dazed.

'It's fantastic. We didn't think this could—'

'*What's happened?*'

'The machines aren't able to handle the item. No reading can come.

It's data they can't integrate. They can't use it for prediction material, and it throws off all their other figures.'

'Why?'

'It's – it's a variable.' Kaplan was shaking, white-lipped and pale. 'Something from which no inference can be made. The man from the past. The machines can't deal with him. The variable man!'

II

Thomas Cole was sharpening a knife with his whetstone when the tornado hit.

The knife belonged to the lady in the big green house. Every time Cole came by with his Fixit cart the lady had something to be sharpened. Once in a while she gave him a cup of coffee, hot black coffee from an old bent pot. He liked that fine; he enjoyed good coffee.

The day was drizzly and overcast. Business had been bad. An automobile had scared his two horses. On bad days less people were outside and he had to get down from the cart and go to ring doorbells.

But the man in the yellow house had given him a dollar for fixing his electric refrigerator. Nobody else had been able to fix it, not even the factory man. The dollar would go a long way. A dollar was a lot.

He knew it was a tornado even before it hit him. Everything was silent. He was bent over his whetstone, the reins between his knees, absorbed in his work.

He had done a good job on the knife; he was almost finished. He spat on the blade and was holding it up to see – and then the tornado came.

All at once it was there, completely around him. Nothing but grayness. He and the cart and horses seemed to be in a calm spot in the center of the tornado. They were moving in a great silence, gray mist everywhere.

And while he was wondering what to do, and how to get the old lady's knife back to her, all at once there was a bump and the tornado tipped him over, sprawled out on the ground. The horses screamed in fear, struggling to pick themselves up. Cole got quickly to his feet.

Where was he?

The grayness was gone. White walls stuck up on all sides. A deep light gleamed down, not daylight but something like it. The team was pulling the cart on its side, dragging it along, tools and equipment falling out. Cole righted the cart, leaping up onto the seat.

And for the first time saw the people.

Men, with astonished white faces, in some sort of uniforms. And a feeling of danger!

Cole headed the team toward the door. Hoofs thundered steel against steel as they pounded through the doorway, scattering the astonished men in all directions. He was out in a wide hall. A building, like a hospital.

The hall divided. More men were coming, spilling from all sides.

Shouting and milling in excitement, like white ants. Something cut past him, a beam of dark violet. It seared off a corner of the cart, leaving the wood smoking.

Cole felt fear. He kicked at the terrified horses. They reached a big door, crashing wildly against it. The door gave – and they were outside, bright sunlight blinking down on them. For a sickening second the cart tilted, almost turning over. Then the horses gained speed, racing across an open field, toward a distant line of green, Cole holding tightly to the reins.

Behind him the little white-faced men had come out and were standing in a group, gesturing frantically. He could hear their faint shrill shouts.

But he had got away. He was safe. He slowed the horses down and began to breathe again.

The woods were artificial. Some kind of park. But the park was wild and overgrown. A dense jungle of twisted plants. Everything growing in confusion.

The park was empty. No one was there. By the position of the sun he could tell it was either early morning or late afternoon. The smell of the flowers and grass, the dampness of the leaves, indicated morning. It had been late afternoon when the tornado had picked him up. And the sky had been overcast and cloudy.

Cole considered. Clearly, he had been carried a long way. The hospital, the men with white faces, the odd lighting, the accented words he had caught – everything indicated he was no longer in Nebraska – maybe not even in the United States.

Some of his tools had fallen out and gotten lost along the way. Cole collected everything that remained, sorting them, running his fingers over each tool with affection. Some of the little chisels and wood gouges were gone. The bit box had opened, and most of the smaller bits had been lost. He gathered up those that remained and replaced them tenderly in the box. He took a keyhole saw down, and with an oil rag wiped it carefully and replaced it.

Above the cart the sun rose slowly in the sky. Cole peered up, his horny hand over his eyes. A big man, stoop-shouldered, his chin gray and stubbled. His clothes wrinkled and dirty. But his eyes were clear, a pale blue, and his hands were finely made.

He could not stay in the park. They had seen him ride that way; they would be looking for him.

Far above something shot rapidly across the sky. A tiny black dot moving with incredible haste. A second dot followed. The two dots were gone almost before he saw them. They were utterly silent.

Cole frowned, perturbed. The dots made him uneasy. He would have to keep moving – and looking for food. His stomach was already beginning to rumble and groan.

Work. There was plenty he could do: gardening, sharpening, grinding, repair work on machines and clocks, fixing all kinds of household things. Even painting and odd jobs and carpentry and chores.

He could do anything. Anything people wanted done. For a meal and pocket money.

Thomas Cole urged the team into life, moving forward. He sat hunched over in the seat, watching intently, as the Fixit cart rolled slowly across the tangled grass, through the jungle of trees and flowers.

Reinhart hurried, racing his cruiser at top speed, followed by a second ship, a military escort. The ground sped by below him, a blur of gray and green.

The remains of New York lay spread out, a twisted, blunted ruin overgrown with weeds and grass. The great atomic wars of the twentieth century had turned virtually the whole seaboard area into an endless waste of slag.

Slag and weeds below him. And then the sudden tangle that had been Central Park.

Histo-research came into sight. Reinhart swooped down, bringing his cruiser to rest at the small supply field behind the main buildings.

Harper, the chief official of the department, came over quickly as soon as Reinhart's ship landed.

'Frankly, we don't understand why you consider this matter important,' Harper said uneasily.

Reinhart shot him a cold glance. 'I'll be the judge of what's important. Are you the one who gave the order to bring the bubble back manually?'

'Fredman gave the actual order. In line with your directive to have all facilities ready for—'

Reinhart headed toward the entrance of the research building. 'Where is Fredman?'

'Inside.'

'I want to see him. Let's go.'

Fredman met them inside. He greeted Reinhart calmly, showing no emotion. 'Sorry to cause you trouble, Commissioner. We were trying to get the station in order for the war. We wanted the bubble back as quickly as possible.' He eyed Reinhart curiously. 'No doubt the man and his cart will soon be picked up by your police.'

'I want to know everything that happened, in exact detail.'

Fredman shifted uncomfortably. 'There's not much to tell. I gave the order to have the automatic setting canceled and the bubble brought back manually. At the moment the signal reached it, the bubble was passing through the spring of 1913. As it broke loose, it tore off a piece of ground on which this person and his cart were located. The person naturally was brought up to the present, inside the bubble.'

'Didn't any of your instruments tell you the bubble was loaded?'

'We were too excited to take any readings. Half an hour after the manual control was thrown, the bubble materialized in the observation room. It was de-energized before anyone noticed what was inside. We tried to stop him but he drove the cart out into the hall, bowling us out of the way. The horses were in a panic.'

'What kind of cart was it?'

'There was some kind of sign on it. Painted in black letters on both sides. No one saw what it was.'

'Go ahead. What happened then?'

'Somebody fired a Slem-ray after him, but it missed. The horses carried him out of the building and onto the grounds. By the time we reached the exit the cart was halfway to the park.'

Reinhart reflected. 'If he's still in the park we should have him shortly. But we must be careful.' He was already starting back toward his ship, leaving Fredman behind. Harper fell in beside him.

Reinhart halted by his ship. He beckoned some Government guards over. 'Put the executive staff of this department under arrest. I'll have them tried on a treason count, later on.' He smiled ironically as Harper's face blanched sickly pale. 'There's a war going on. You'll be lucky if you get off alive.'

Reinhart entered his ship and left the surface, rising rapidly into the sky. A second ship followed after him, a military escort. Reinhart flew high above the sea of gray slag, the unrecovered waste area. He passed over a sudden square of green set in the ocean of gray. Reinhart gazed back at it until it was gone.

Central Park. He could see police ships racing through the sky, ships and transports loaded with troops, heading toward the square of green. On the ground some heavy guns and surface cars rumbled along, lines of black approaching the park from all sides.

They would have the man soon. But meanwhile, the SRB machines were blank. And on the SRB machines' readings the whole war depended.

About noon the cart reached the edge of the park. Cole rested for a moment, allowing the horses time to crop at the thick grass. The silent expanse of slag amazed him. What had happened? Nothing stirred. No buildings, no sign of life. Grass and weeds poked up occasionally through it, breaking the flat surface here and there, but even so, the sight gave him an uneasy chill.

Cole drove the cart slowly out onto the slag, studying the sky above him. There was nothing to hide him, now that he was out of the park. The slag was bare and uniform, like the ocean. If he were spotted—

A horde of tiny black dots raced across the sky, coming rapidly closer. Presently they veered to the right and disappeared. More planes, wingless metal planes. He watched them go, driving slowly on.

Half an hour later something appeared ahead. Cole slowed the cart down, peering to see. The slag came to an end. He had reached its limits. Ground appeared, dark soil and grass. Weeds grew everywhere. Ahead of him, beyond the end of the slag, was a line of buildings, houses of some sort. Or sheds.

Houses, probably. But not like any he had ever seen.

The houses were uniform, all exactly the same. Like little green shells, rows of them, several hundred. There was a little lawn in front of each. Lawn, a path, a front porch, bushes in a meager row around each house. But the houses were all alike and very small.

Little green shells in precise, even rows. He urged the cart cautiously forward, toward the houses.

No one seemed to be around. He entered a street between two rows of houses, the hoofs of his two horses sounding loudly in the silence. He was in some kind of town. But there were no dogs or children. Everything was neat and silent. Like a model. An exhibit. It made him uncomfortable.

A young man walking along the pavement gaped at him in wonder. An oddly-dressed youth, in a toga-like cloak that hung down to his knees. A single piece of fabric. And sandals.

Or what looked like sandals. Both the cloak and the sandals were of some strange half-luminous material. It glowed faintly in the sunlight. Metallic, rather than cloth.

A woman was watering flowers at the edge of a lawn. She straightened up as his team of horses came near. Her eyes widened in astonishment – and then fear. Her mouth fell open in a soundless O and her sprinkling can slipped from her fingers and rolled silently onto the lawn.

Cole blushed and turned his head quickly away. The woman was scarcely dressed! He flicked the reins and urged the horses to hurry.

Behind him, the woman still stood. He stole a brief, hasty look back – and then shouted hoarsely to his team, ears scarlet. He had seen right. She wore only a pair of translucent shorts. Nothing else. A mere fragment of the same half-luminous material that glowed and sparkled. The rest of her small body was utterly naked.

He slowed the team down. She had been pretty. Brown hair and eyes, deep red lips. Quite a good figure. Slender waist, downy legs, bare and supple, full breasts— He clamped the thought furiously off. He had to get to work. Business.

Cole halted the Fixit cart and leaped down onto the pavement. He selected a house at random and approached it cautiously. The house was attractive. It had a certain simple beauty. But it looked frail – and exactly like the others.

He stepped up on the porch. There was no bell. He searched for it, running his hand uneasily over the surface of the door. All at once there was a click, a sharp snap on a level with his eyes. Cole glanced up, startled. A lens was vanishing as the door section slid over it. He had been photographed.

While he was wondering what it meant, the door swung suddenly open. A man filled up the entrance, a big man in a tan uniform, blocking the way ominously.

'What do you want?' the man demanded.

'I'm looking for work,' Cole murmured. 'Any kind of work. I can do anything, fix any kind of thing. I repair broken objects. Things that need mending.' His voice trailed off uncertainly. 'Anything at all.'

'Apply to the Placement Department of the Federal Activities Control Board,' the man said crisply. 'You know all occupational therapy is handled through them.' He eyed Cole curiously. 'Why have you got on those ancient clothes?'

'Ancient? Why, I—'

The man gazed past him at the Fixit cart and the two dozing horses. 'What's that? What are those two animals? *Horses?*' The man rubbed his jaw, studying Cole intently. 'That's strange,' he said.

'Strange?' Cole murmured uneasily. 'Why?'

'There haven't been any horses for over a century. All the horses were wiped out during the Fifth Atomic War. That's why it's strange.'

Cole tensed, suddenly alert. There was something in the man's eyes, a hardness, a piercing look. Cole moved back off the porch, onto the path. He had to be careful. Something was wrong.

'I'll be going,' he murmured.

'There haven't been any horses for over a hundred years.' The man came toward Cole. 'Who are you? Why are you dressed up like that? Where did you get that vehicle and pair of horses?'

'I'll be going,' Cole repeated, moving away.

The man whipped something from his belt, a thin metal tube. He stuck it toward Cole.

It was a rolled-up paper, a thin sheet of metal in the form of a tube. Words, some kind of script. He could not make any of them out. The man's picture, rows of numbers, figures—

'I'm Director Winslow,' the man said. 'Federal Stockpile Conservation. You better talk fast, or there'll be a Security car here in five minutes.'

Cole moved – fast. He raced, head down, back along the path to the cart, toward the street.

Something hit him. A wall of force, throwing him down on his face. He sprawled in a heap, numb and dazed. His body ached, vibrating wildly, out of control. Waves of shock rolled over him, gradually diminishing.

He got shakily to his feet. His head spun. He was weak, shattered, trembling violently. The man was coming down the walk after him. Cole pulled himself onto the cart, gasping and retching. The horses jumped into life. Cole rolled over against the seat, sick with the motion of the swaying cart.

He caught hold of the reins and managed to drag himself up in a sitting position. The cart gained speed, turning a corner. Houses flew past. Cole urged the team weakly, drawing great shuddering breaths. Houses and streets, a blur of motion, as the cart flew faster and faster along.

Then he was leaving the town, leaving the neat little houses behind. He was on some sort of highway. Big buildings, factories, on both sides of the highway. Figures, men watching in astonishment.

After a while the factories fell behind. Cole slowed the team down. What had the man meant? Fifth Atomic War. Horses destroyed. It didn't make sense. And they had things he knew nothing about. Force fields. Planes without wings – soundless.

Cole reached around in his pockets. He found the identification tube the man had handed him. In the excitement he had carried it off. He unrolled the tube slowly and began to study it. The writing was strange to him.

For a long time he studied the tube. Then, gradually, he became aware of something. Something in the top right-hand corner.

A date. October 6, 2128.

Cole's vision blurred. Everything spun and wavered around him. October, 2128. Could it be?

But he held the paper in his hand. Thin, metal paper. Like foil. And it had to be. It said so, right in the corner, printed on the paper itself.

Cole rolled the tube up slowly, numbed with shock. Two hundred years. It didn't seem possible. But things were beginning to make sense. He was in the future, two hundred years in the future.

While he was mulling this over, the swift black Security ship appeared overhead, diving rapidly toward the horse-drawn cart, as it moved slowly along the road.

Reinhart's vidscreen buzzed. He snapped it quickly on. 'Yes?'

'Report from Security.'

'Put it through.' Reinhart waited tensely as the lines locked in place. The screen re-lit.

'This is Dixon. Western Regional Command.' The officer cleared his throat, shuffling his message plates. 'The man from the past has been reported, moving away from the New York area.'

'Which side of your net?'

'Outside. He evaded the net around Central Park by entering one of the small towns at the rim of the slag area.'

'*Evaded?*'

'We assumed he would avoid the towns. Naturally the net failed to encompass any of the towns.'

Reinhart's jaw stiffened. 'Go on.'

'He entered the town of Petersville a few minutes before the net closed around the park. We burned the park level, but naturally found nothing. He had already gone. An hour later we received a report from a resident in Petersville, an official of the Stockpile Conservation Department. The man from the past had come to his door, looking for work. Winslow, the official, engaged him in conversation, trying to hold onto him, but he escaped, driving his cart off. Winslow called Security right away, but by then it was too late.'

'Report to me as soon as anything more comes in. We must have him — and damn soon.' Reinhart snapped the screen off. It died quickly.

He sat back in his chair, waiting.

Cole saw the shadow of the Security ship. He reacted at once. A second after the shadow passed over him, Cole was out of the cart, running and falling. He rolled, twisting and turning, pulling his body as far away from the cart as possible.

There was a blinding roar and flash of white light. A hot wind rolled over Cole, picking him up and tossing him like a leaf. He shut his eyes, letting his body relax. He bounced, falling and striking the ground. Gravel and stones tore into his face, his knees, the palms of his hands.

Cole cried out, shrieking in pain. His body was on fire. He was being consumed, incinerated by the blinding white orb of fire. The orb expanded, growing in size, swelling like some monstrous sun, twisted and bloated. The end had come. There was no hope. He gritted his teeth—

The greedy orb faded, dying down. It sputtered and winked out, blackening into ash. The air reeked, a bitter acrid smell. His clothes were burning and smoking. The ground under him was hot, baked dry, seared by the blast. But he was alive. At least, for a while.

Cole opened his eyes slowly. The cart was gone. A great hole gaped where it had been, a shattered sore in the center of the highway. An ugly cloud hung above the hole, black and ominous. Far above, the wingless plane circled, watching for any signs of life.

Cole lay, breathing shallowly, slowly. Time passed. The sun moved across the sky with agonizing slowness. It was perhaps four in the afternoon. Cole calculated mentally. In three hours it would be dark. If he could stay alive until then—

Had the plane seen him leap from the cart?

He lay without moving. The late afternoon sun beat down on him. He felt sick, nauseated and feverish. His mouth was dry.

Some ants ran over his outstretched hand. Gradually, the immense black cloud was beginning to drift away, dispersing into a formless blob.

The cart was gone. The thought lashed against him, pounding at his brain, mixing with his labored pulsebeat. *Gone.* Destroyed. Nothing but ashes and debris remained. The realization dazed him.

Finally the plane finished its circling, winging its way toward the horizon. At last it vanished. The sky was clear.

Cole got unsteadily to his feet. He wiped his face shakily. His body ached and trembled. He spat a couple of times, trying to clear his mouth. The plane would probably send in a report. People would be coming to look for him. Where could he go?

To his right a line of hills rose up, a distant green mass. Maybe he could reach them. He began to walk slowly. He had to be very careful. They were looking for him – and they had weapons. Incredible weapons.

He would be lucky to still be alive when the sun set. His team and Fixit cart were gone – and all his tools. Cole reached into his pockets, searching through them hopefully. He brought out some small screwdrivers, a little pair of cutting pliers, some wire, some solder, the whetstone, and finally the lady's knife.

Only a few small tools remained. He had lost everything else. But without the cart he was safer, harder to spot. They would have more trouble finding him, on foot.

Cole hurried along, crossing the level fields toward the distant range of hills.

The call came through to Reinhart almost at once. Dixon's features formed on the vidscreen. 'I have a further report, Commissioner.' Dixon scanned the plate. 'Good news. The man from the past was sighted moving away from Petersville, along highway 13, at about ten miles an hour, on his horse-drawn cart. Our ship bombed him immediately.'

'Did – did you get him?'

'The pilot reports no sign of life after the blast.'

Reinhart's pulse almost stopped. He sank back in his chair. 'Then he's dead!'

'Actually, we won't know for certain until we can examine the debris. A surface car is speeding toward the spot. We should have the complete report in a short time. We'll notify you as soon as the information comes in.'

Reinhart reached out and cut the screen. It faded into darkness. Had they got the man from the past? Or had he escaped again? Weren't they ever going to get him? Couldn't he be captured? And meanwhile, the SRB machines were silent, showing nothing at all.

Reinhart sat brooding, waiting impatiently for the report of the surface car to come.

It was evening.

'Come on!' Steven shouted, running frantically after his brother. 'Come on back!'

'Catch me.' Earl ran and ran, down the side of the hill, over behind a military storage depot, along a neotex fence, jumping finally down into Mrs Norris' back yard.

Steven hurried after his brother, sobbing for breath, shouting and gasping as he ran. 'Come back! You come back with that!'

'What's he got?' Sally Tate demanded, stepping out suddenly to block Steven's way.

Steven halted, his chest rising and falling. 'He's got my inter-system vidsender.' His small face twisted with rage and misery. 'He better give it back!'

Earl came circling around from the right. In the warm gloom of evening he was almost invisible. 'Here I am,' he announced. 'What are you going to do?'

Steven glared at him hotly. His eyes made out the square box in Earl's hands. 'You give that back! Or – or I'll tell Dad.'

Earl laughed. 'Make me.'

'Dad'll make you.'

'You better give it to him,' Sally said.

'Catch me.' Earl started off. Steven pushed Sally out of the way, lashing wildly at his brother. He collided with him, throwing him sprawling. The box fell from Earl's hands. It skidded to the pavement, crashing into the side of a guide-light post.

Earl and Steven picked themselves up slowly. They gazed down at the broken box.

'See?' Steven shrilled, tears filling his eyes. 'See what you did?'

'You did it. You pushed into me.'

'You did it!' Steven bent down and picked up the box. He carried it over to the guide-light, sitting down on the curb to examine it.

Earl came slowly over. 'If you hadn't pushed me it wouldn't have got broken.'

Night was descending rapidly. The line of hills rising above the town were already lost in darkness. A few lights had come on here and there. The evening was warm. A surface car slammed its doors, some place off in the distance. In the sky ships droned back and forth, weary commuters coming home from work in the big underground factory units.

Thomas Cole came slowly toward the three children grouped around the guide-light. He moved with difficulty, his body sore and bent with fatigue. Night had come, but he was not safe yet.

He was tired, exhausted and hungry. He had walked a long way. And he had to have something to eat – soon.

A few feet from the children Cole stopped. They were all intent and absorbed by the box on Steven's knees. Suddenly a hush fell over the children. Earl looked up slowly.

In the dim light the big stooped figure of Thomas Cole seemed extra menacing. His long arms hung down loosely at his sides. His face was lost in shadow. His body was shapeless, indistinct. A big unformed statue, standing silently a few feet away, unmoving in the half-darkness.

'Who are you?' Earl demanded, his voice low.

'What do you want?' Sally said. The children edged away nervously. 'Get away.'

Cole came toward them. He bent down a little. The beam from the guide-light crossed his features. Lean, prominent nose, beak-like, faded blue eyes—

Steven scrambled to his feet, clutching the vidsender box. 'You get out of here!'

'Wait.' Cole smiled crookedly at them. His voice was dry and raspy. 'What do you have there?' He pointed with his long, slender fingers. 'The box you're holding.'

The children were silent. Finally Steven stirred. 'It's my inter-system vidsender.'

'Only it doesn't work,' Sally said.

'Earl broke it.' Steven glared at his brother bitterly. 'Earl threw it down and broke it.'

Cole smiled a little. He sank down wearily on the edge of the curb, sighing with relief. He had been walking too long. His body ached with fatigue. He was hungry and tired. For a long time he sat, wiping perspiration from his neck and face, too exhausted to speak.

'Who are you?' Sally demanded, at last. 'Why do you have on those funny clothes? Where did you come from?'

'Where?' Cole looked around at the children. 'From a long way off. A long way.' He shook his head slowly from side to side, trying to clear it.

'What's your therapy?' Earl said.

'My therapy?'

'What do you do? Where do you work?'

Cole took a deep breath and let it out again slowly. 'I fix things. All kinds of things. Any kind.'

Earl sneered. 'Nobody fixes things. When they break you throw them away.'

Cole didn't hear him. Sudden need had roused him, getting him suddenly to his feet. 'You know any work I can find?' he demanded. 'Things I could do? I can fix anything. Clocks, typewriters, refrigerators, pots and pans. Leaks in the roof. I can fix anything there is.'

Steven held out his inter-system vidsender. 'Fix this.'

There was silence. Slowly, Cole's eyes focused on the box. 'That?'

'My sender. Earl broke it.'

Cole took the box slowly. He turned it over, holding it up to the light. He frowned, concentrating on it. His long, slender fingers moved carefully over the surface, exploring it.

'He'll steal it!' Earl said suddenly.

'No.' Cole shook his head vaguely. 'I'm reliable.' His sensitive fingers found the studs that held the box together. He depressed the studs, pushing them expertly in. The box opened, revealing its complex interior.

'He got it open,' Sally whispered.

'Give it back!' Steven demanded, a little frightened. He held out his hand. 'I want it back.'

The three children watched Cole apprehensively. Cole fumbled in his pocket. Slowly he brought out his tiny screwdrivers and pliers. He laid them in a row beside him. He made no move to return the box.

'I want it back,' Steven said feebly.

Cole looked up. His faded blue eyes took in the sight of the three children standing before him in the gloom. 'I'll fix it for you. You said you wanted it fixed.'

'I want it back.' Steven stood on one foot, then the other, torn by doubt and indecision. 'Can you really fix it? Can you make it work again?'

'Yes.'

'All right. Fix it for me, then.'

A sly smile flickered across Cole's tired face. 'Now, wait a minute. If I fix it, will you bring me something to eat? I'm not fixing it for nothing.'

'Something to eat?'

'Food. I need hot food. Maybe some coffee.'

Steven nodded. 'Yes. I'll get it for you.'

Cole relaxed. 'Fine. That's fine.' He turned his attention back to the box resting between his knees. 'Then I'll fix it for you. I'll fix it for you good.'

His fingers flew, working and twisting, tracing down wires and relays, exploring and examining. Finding out about the inter-system vidsender. Discovering how it worked.

Steven slipped into the house through the emergency door. He made his way to the kitchen with great care, walking on tip-toe. He punched the kitchen controls at random his heart beating excitedly. The stove began to whirr, purring into life. Meter readings came on, crossing toward the completion marks.

Presently the stove opened; sliding out a tray of steaming dishes. The mechanism clicked off, dying into silence. Steven grabbed up the contents of the tray, filling his arms. He carried everything down the hall, out the emergency door and into the yard. The yard was dark. Steven felt his way carefully along.

He managed to reach the guide-light without dropping anything at all.

Thomas Cole got slowly to his feet as Steven came into view. 'Here,' Steven said. He dumped the food onto the curb, gasping for breath. 'Here's the food. Is it finished?'

Cole held out the inter-system vidsender. 'It's finished. It was pretty badly smashed.'

Earl and Sally gazed up, wide-eyed. 'Does it work?' Sally asked.

'Of course not,' Earl stated. 'How could it work? He couldn't—'

'Turn it on!' Sally nudged Steven eagerly. 'See if it works.'

Steven was holding the box under the light, examining the switches. He flicked the main switch on. The indicator light gleamed. 'It lights up,' Steven said.

'Say something into it.'

Steven spoke into the box. 'Hello! Hello! This is operator 6–Z75 calling. Can you hear me? This is operator 6–Z75. Can you hear me?'

In the darkness, away from the beam of the guide-light, Thomas Cole sat crouched over the food. He ate gratefully, silently. It was good food, well cooked and seasoned. He drank a container of orange juice and then a sweet drink he didn't recognize. Most of the food was strange to him, but he didn't care. He had walked a long way and he still had a long way to go, before morning. He had to be deep in the hills before the sun came up. Instinct told him that he would be safe among the trees and tangled growth – at least, as safe as he could hope for.

He ate rapidly, intent on the food. He did not look up until he was finished. Then he got slowly to his feet, wiping his mouth with the back of his hand.

The three children were standing around in a circle, operating the inter-system vidsender. He watched them for a few minutes. None of them looked up from the small box. They were intent, absorbed in what they were doing.

'Well?' Cole said, at last. 'Does it work all right?'

After a moment Steven looked up at him. There was a strange expression on his face. He nodded slowly. 'Yes. Yes, it works. It works fine.'

Cole grunted. 'All right.' He turned and moved away from the light. 'That's fine.'

The children watched silently until the figure of Thomas Cole had completely disappeared. Slowly, they turned and looked at each other. Then down at the box in Steven's hands. They gazed at the box in growing awe. Awe mixed with dawning fear.

Steven turned and edged toward his house. 'I've got to show it to my Dad,' he murmured, dazed. 'He's got to know. *Somebody's* got to know!'

III

Eric Reinhart examined the vidsender box carefully, turning it around and around.

'Then he did escape from the blast,' Dixon admitted reluctantly. 'He must have leaped from the cart just before the concussion.'

Reinhart nodded. 'He escaped. He got away from you – twice.' He pushed the vidsender box away and leaned abruptly toward the man standing uneasily in front of his desk. 'What's your name again?'

'Elliot. Richard Elliot.'

'And your son's name?'

'Steven.'

'It was last night this happened?'

'About eight o'clock.'

'Go on.'

'Steven came into the house. He acted queerly. He was carrying his inter-system vidsender.' Elliot pointed at the box on Reinhart's desk. 'That. He was nervous and excited. I asked what was wrong. For a while he couldn't tell me. He was quite upset. Then he showed me the vidsender.' Elliot took a deep, shaky breath. 'I could see right away it was different. You see I'm an electrical engineer. I had opened it once before, to put in a new battery. I had a fairly good idea how it should look.' Elliot hesitated. 'Commissioner, it had been *changed*. A lot of the wiring was different. Moved around. Relays connected differently. Some parts were missing. New parts had been jury rigged out of old. Then I discovered the thing that made me call Security. The vidsender – it really *worked*.'

'Worked?'

'You see, it never was anything more than a toy. With a range of a few city blocks. So the kids could call back and forth from their rooms. Like a sort of portable vidscreen. Commissioner, I tried out the vidsender, pushing the call button and speaking into the microphone. I

– I got a ship of the line. A battleship operating beyond Proxima Centaurus – over eight light years away. As far out as the actual vidsenders operate. Then I called Security. Right away.'

For a time Reinhart was silent. Finally he tapped the box lying on the desk. 'You got a ship of the line – with *this*?'

'That's right.'

'How big are the regular vidsenders?'

Dixon supplied the information. 'As big as a twenty-ton safe.'

'That's what I thought.' Reinhart waved his hand impatiently. 'All right, Elliot. Thanks for turning the information over to us. That's all.'

Security police led Elliot outside the office.

Reinhart and Dixon looked at each other. 'This is bad,' Reinhart said harshly. 'He has some ability, some kind of mechanical ability. Genius, perhaps, to do a thing like this. Look at the period he came from, Dixon. The early part of the twentieth century. Before the wars began. That was a unique period. There was a certain vitality, a certain ability. It was a period of incredible growth and discovery. Edison. Pasteur. Burbank. The Wright brothers. Inventions and machines. People had an uncanny ability with machines. A kind of intuition about machines – which we don't have.'

'You mean—'

'I mean a person like this coming into our own time is bad in itself, war or no war. He's too different. He's oriented along different lines. He has abilities we lack. This fixing skill of his. It throws us off, out of kilter. And with the war . . .

'Now I'm beginning to understand why the SRB machines couldn't factor him. It's impossible for us to understand this kind of person. Winslow says he asked for work, any kind of work. The man said he could do anything, fix anything. Do you understand what that means?'

'No,' Dixon said. 'What does it mean?'

'Can any of us fix anything? No. None of us can do that. We're specialized. Each of us has his own line, his own work. I understand my work, you understand yours. The tendency in evolution is toward greater and greater specialization. Man's society is an ecology that forces adaptation to it. Continual complexity makes it impossible for any of us to know anything outside our own personal field – I can't follow the work of the man sitting at the next desk over from me. Too much knowledge has piled up in each field. And there are too many fields.

'This man is different. He can fix anything, do anything. He doesn't work with knowledge, with science – the classified accumulation of facts. He *knows* nothing. It's not in his head, a form of learning. He works by intuition – his power is in his hands, not his head. Jack-of-all-trades. His hands! Like a painter, an artist. In his hands – and he cuts across our lives like a knife-blade.'

'And the other problem?'

'The other problem is that this man, this variable man, has escaped into the Albertine Mountain Range. Now we'll have one hell of a time finding him. He's clever – in a strange kind of way. Like some sort of animal. He's going to be hard to catch.'

Reinhart sent Dixon out. After a moment he gathered up the handful of reports on his desk and carried them up to the SRB room. The SRB room was closed up, sealed off by a ring of armed Security police. Standing angrily before the ring of police was Peter Sherikov, his beard waggling angrily, his immense hands on his hips.

'What's going on?' Sherikov demanded. 'Why can't I go in and peep at the odds?'

'Sorry.' Reinhart cleared the police aside. 'Come inside with me. I'll explain.' The doors opened for them and they entered. Behind them the doors shut and the ring of police formed outside. 'What brings you away from your lab?' Reinhart asked.

Sherikov shrugged. 'Several things. I wanted to see you. I called you on the vidphone and they said you weren't available. I thought maybe something had happened. What's up?'

'I'll tell you in a few minutes.' Reinhart called Kaplan over. 'Here are some new items. Feed them in right away. I want to see if the machines can total them.'

'Certainly, Commissioner.' Kaplan took the message plates and placed them on an intake belt. The machines hummed into life.

'We'll know soon,' Reinhart said, half aloud.

Sherikov shot him a keen glance. 'We'll know what? Let me in on it. What's taking place?'

'We're in trouble. For twenty-four hours the machines haven't given any reading at all. Nothing but a blank. A total blank.'

Sherikov's features registered disbelief. 'But that isn't possible. *Some* odds exist at all times.'

'The odds exist, but the machines aren't able to calculate them.'

'Why not?'

'Because a variable factor has been introduced. A factor which the machines can't handle. They can't make any predictions from it.'

'Can't they reject it?' Sherikov said slyly. 'Can't they just – just *ignore* it?'

'No. It exists, as real data. Therefore it affects the balance of the material, the sum total of all other available data. To reject it would be to give a false reading. The machines can't reject any data that's known to be true.'

Sherikov pulled moodily at his black beard. 'I would be interested in knowing what sort of factor the machines can't handle. I thought they could take in all data pertaining to contemporary reality.'

'They can. This factor has nothing to do with contemporary reality. That's the trouble. Histo-research in bringing its time bubble back from the past got overzealous and cut the circuit too quickly. The bubble came back loaded – with a man from the twentieth century. A man from the past.'

'I see. A man from two centuries ago.' The big Pole frowned. 'And with a radically different Weltanschauung. No connection with our present society. Not integrated along our lines at all. Therefore the SRB machines are perplexed.'

Reinhart grinned. 'Perplexed? I suppose so. In any case, they can't do anything with the data about this man. The variable man. No statistics at all have been thrown up – no predictions have been made. And it knocks everything else out of phase. We're dependent on the constant showing of these odds. The whole war effort is geared around them.'

'The horse-shoe nail. Remember the old poem? "For want of a nail the shoe was lost. For want of the shoe the horse was lost. For want of the horse the rider was lost. For want—" '

'Exactly. A single factor coming along like this, one single individual, can throw everything off. It doesn't seem possible that one person could knock an entire society out of balance – but apparently it is.'

'What are you doing about this man?'

'The Security police are organized in a mass search for him.'

'Results?'

'He escaped into the Albertine Mountain Range last night. It'll be hard to find him. We must expect him to be loose for another forty-eight hours. It'll take that long for us to arrange the annihilation of the range area. Perhaps a trifle longer. And meanwhile—'

'Ready, Commissioner,' Kaplan interrupted. 'The new totals.'

The SRB machines had finished factoring the new data. Reinhart and Sherikov hurried to take their places before the view windows.

For a moment nothing happened. Then odds were put up, locking in place.

Sherikov gasped. 99–2. In favor of Terra. 'That's wonderful! Now we—'

The odds vanished. New odds took their places. 97–4. In favor of Centaurus. Sherikov groaned in astonished dismay. 'Wait,' Reinhart said to him. 'I don't think they'll last.'

The odds vanished. A rapid series of odds shot across the screen, a violent stream of numbers, changing almost instantly. At last the machines became silent.

Nothing showed. No odds. No totals at all. The view windows were blank.

'You see?' Reinhart murmured. 'The same damn thing!'

Sherikov pondered. 'Reinhart, you're too Anglo-Saxon, too impulsive. Be more Slavic. This man will be captured and destroyed within two days. You said so yourself. Meanwhile, we're all working night and day on the war effort. The warfleet is waiting near Proxima, taking up positions for the attack on the Centaurans. All our war plants are going full blast. By the time the attack date comes we'll have a full-sized invasion army ready to take off for the long trip to the Centauran colonies. The whole Terran population has been mobilized. The eight supply planets are pouring in material. All this is going on day and night, even without odds showing. Long before the attack comes this man will certainly be dead, and the machines will be able to show odds again.'

Reinhart considered. 'But it worries me, a man like that out in the open. Loose. A man who can't be predicted. It goes against science. We've been making statistical reports on society for two centuries. We have immense files of data. The machines are able to predict what each person and group will do at a given time, in a given situation. But this man is beyond all prediction. He's a variable. It's contrary to science.'

'The indeterminate particle.'

'What's that?'

'The particle that moves in such a way that we can't predict what position it will occupy at a given second. Random. The random particle.'

'Exactly. It's – it's *unnatural*.'

Sherikov laughed sarcastically. 'Don't worry about it, Commissioner. The man will be captured and things will return to their natural state. You'll be able to predict people again, like laboratory rats in a maze. By the way – why is this room guarded?'

'I don't want anyone to know the machines show no totals. It's dangerous to the war effort.'

'Margaret Duffe, for example?'

Reinhart nodded reluctantly. 'They're too timid, these parliamentarians. If they discover we have no SRB odds they'll want to shut down the war planning and go back to waiting.'

'Too slow for you, Commissioner? Laws, debates, council meetings, discussions . . . Saves a lot of time if one man has all the power. One man to tell people what to do, think for them, lead them around.'

Reinhart eyed the big Pole critically. 'That reminds me. How is Icarus coming? Have you continued to make progress on the control turret?'

A scowl crossed Sherikov's broad features. 'The control turret?' He waved his big hand vaguely. 'I would say it's coming along all right. We'll catch up in time.'

Instantly Reinhart became alert. 'Catch up? You mean you're still behind?'

'Somewhat. A little. But we'll catch up.' Sherikov retreated toward the door. 'Let's go down to the cafeteria and have a cup of coffee. You worry too much, Commissioner. Take things more in your stride.'

'I suppose you're right.' The two men walked out into the hall. 'I'm on edge. This variable man. I can't get him out of my mind.'

'Has he done anything yet?'

'Nothing important. Rewired a child's toy. A toy vidsender.'

'Oh?' Sherikov showed interest. 'What do you mean? What did he do?'

'I'll show you.' Reinhart led Sherikov down the hall to his office. They entered and Reinhart locked the door. He handed Sherikov the toy and roughed in what Cole had done. A strange look crossed Sherikov's face. He found the studs on the box and depressed them. The box opened. The big Pole sat down at the desk and began to study the interior of the box. 'You're sure it was the man from the past who rewired this?'

'Of course. On the spot. The boy damaged it playing. The variable man came along and the boy asked him to fix it. He fixed it, all right.'

'Incredible.' Sherikov's eyes were only an inch from the wiring. 'Such tiny relays. How could he—'

'What?'

'Nothing.' Sherikov got abruptly to his feet, closing the box carefully. 'Can I take this along? To my lab? I'd like to analyze it more fully.'

'Of course. But why?'

'No special reason. Let's go get our coffee.' Sherikov headed toward the door. 'You say you expect to capture this man in a day or so?'

'*Kill* him, not capture him. We've got to eliminate him as a piece of data. We're assembling the attack formations right now. No slip-ups, this time. We're in the process of setting up a cross-bombing pattern to level the entire Albertine Range. He must be destroyed, within the next forty-eight hours.'

Sherikov nodded absently. 'Of course,' he murmured. A preoccupied expression still remained on his broad features. 'I understand perfectly.'

Thomas Cole crouched over the fire he had built, warming his hands. It was almost morning. The sky was turning violet gray. The mountain air was crisp and chilly. Cole shivered and pulled himself closer to the fire.

The heat felt good against his hands. *His hands.* He gazed down at them, glowing yellow-red in the firelight. The nails were black and chipped. Warts and endless calluses on each finger, and the palms. But they were good hands, the fingers were long and tapered. He respected them, although in some ways he didn't understand them.

Cole was deep in thought, meditating over his situation.

He had been in the mountains two nights and a day. The first night had been the worst. Stumbling and falling, making his way uncertainly up the steep slopes, through the tangled brush and undergrowth—

But when the sun came up he was safe, deep in the mountains, between two great peaks. And by the time the sun had set again he had fixed himself a shelter and a means of making a fire. Now he had a neat little box trap, operated by a plaited grass rope and pit, a notched stake.

One rabbit already hung by his hind legs and the trap was waiting for another.

The sky turned from violet gray to a deep cold gray, a metallic color. The mountains were silent and empty. Far off someplace a bird sang, its voice echoing across the vast slopes and ravines. Other birds began to sing. Off to his right something crashed through the brush, an animal pushing its way along.

Day was coming. His second day. Cole got to his feet and began to unfasten the rabbit. Time to eat. And then? After that he had no plans. He knew instinctively that he could keep himself alive indefinitely with the tools he had retained, and the genius of his hands. He could kill game and skin it. Eventually he could build himself a permanent shelter, even make clothes out of hides. In winter—

But he was not thinking that far ahead. Cole stood by the fire, staring up at the sky, his hands on his hips. He squinted, suddenly tense. Something was moving. Something in the sky, drifting slowly through the grayness. A black dot.

He stamped out the fire quickly. What was it? He strained, trying to see. A bird?

A second dot joined the first. Two dots. Then three. Four. Five. A fleet of them, moving rapidly across the early morning sky. Toward the mountains.

Toward him.

Cole hurried away from the fire. He snatched up the rabbit and carried it along with him, into the tangled shelter he had built. He was invisible, inside the shelter. No one could find him. But if they had seen the fire—

He crouched in the shelter, watching the dots grow larger. They were planes, all right. Black wingless planes, coming closer each moment. Now he could hear them, a faint dull buzz, increasing until the ground shook under him.

The first plane dived. It dropped like a stone, swelling into a great black shape. Cole gasped, sinking down. The plane roared in an arch, swooping low over the ground. Suddenly bundles tumbled out, white bundles falling and scattering like seeds.

The bundles drifted rapidly to the ground. They landed. They were men. Men in uniform.

Now the second plane was diving. It roared overhead, releasing its load. More bundles tumbled out, filling the sky. The third plane dived, then the fourth. The air was thick with drifting bundles of white, a blanket of descending weed spores, settling to earth.

On the ground the soldiers were forming into groups. Their shouts carried to Cole, crouched in his shelter. Fear leaped through him. They were landing on all sides of him. He was cut off. The last two planes had dropped men behind him.

He got to his feet, pushing out of the shelter. Some of the soldiers had found the fire, the ashes and coals. One dropped down, feeling the coals with his hand. He waved to the others. They were circling all around, shouting and gesturing. One of them began to set up some kind of gun. Others were unrolling coils of tubing, locking a collection of strange pipes and machinery in place.

Cole ran. He rolled down a slope, sliding and falling. At the bottom he leaped to his feet and plunged into the brush. Vines and leaves tore at his face, slashing and cutting him. He fell again, tangled in a mass of twisted shrubbery. He fought desperately, trying to free himself. If he could reach the knife in his pocket—

Voices. Footsteps. Men were behind him, running down the slope. Cole struggled frantically, gasping and twisting, trying to pull loose. He strained, breaking the vines, clawing at them with his hands.

A soldier dropped to his knee, leveling his gun. More soldiers arrived, bringing their rifles and aiming.

Cole cried out. He closed his eyes, his body suddenly went limp. He waited, his teeth locked together, sweat dripping down his neck, into his shirt, sagging against the mesh of vines and branches coiled around him.

Silence.

Cole opened his eyes slowly. The soldiers had regrouped. A huge man was striding down the slope toward them, barking orders as he came.

Two soldiers stepped into the brush. One of them grabbed Cole by the shoulder.

'Don't let go of him.' The huge man came over, his black beard jutting out. 'Hold on.'

Cole gasped for breath. He was caught. There was nothing he couid do. More soldiers were pouring down into the gully, surrounding him on all sides. They studied him curiously, murmuring together. Cole shook his head wearily and said nothing.

The huge man with the beard stood directly in front of him, his hands on his hips, looking him up and down. 'Don't try to get away,' the man said. 'You can't get away. Do you understood?'

Cole nodded.

'All right. Good.' The man waved. Soldiers clamped metal bands around Cole's arms and wrists. The metal dug into his flesh, making him gasp with pain. More clamps locked around his legs. 'Those stay there until we're out of here. A long way out.'

'Where – where are you taking me?'

Peter Sherikov studied the variable man for a moment before he answered. 'Where? I'm taking you to my labs. Under the Urals.' He glanced suddenly up at the sky. 'We better hurry. The Security police will be starting their demolition attack in a few hours. We want to be a long way from here when that begins.'

Sherikov settled down in his comfortable reinforced chair with a sigh. 'It's good to be back.' He signaled to one of his guards. 'All right. You can unfasten him.'

The metal clamps were removed from Cole's arms and legs. He sagged, sinking down in a heap. Sherikov watched him silently.

Cole sat on the floor, rubbing his wrists and legs, saying nothing.

'What do you want?' Sherikov demanded. 'Food? Are you hungry?'

'No.'

'Medicine? Are you sick? Injured?'

'No.'

Sherikov wrinkled his nose. 'A bath wouldn't hurt you any. We'll arrange that later.' He lit a cigar, blowing a cloud of gray smoke around him. At the door of the room two lab guards stood with guns ready. No one else was in the room beside Sherikov and Cole.

Thomas Cole sat huddled in a heap on the floor, his head sunk down against his chest. He did not stir. His bent body seemed more elongated and stooped than ever, his hair tousled and unkempt, his chin and jowls a rough stubbled gray. His clothes were dirty and torn from crawling through the brush. His skin was cut and scratched; open sores dotted his neck and cheeks and forehead. He said nothing. His chest rose and fell. His faded blue eyes were almost closed. He looked quite old, a withered, dried-up old man.

Sherikov waved one of the guards over. 'Have a doctor brought up here. I want this man checked over. He may need intravenous injections. He may not have had anything to eat for awhile.'

The guard departed.

'I don't want anything to happen to you,' Sherikov said. 'Before we go on I'll have you checked over. And deloused at the same time.'

Cole said nothing.

Sherikov laughed. 'Buck up! You have no reason to feel bad.' He leaned toward Cole, jabbing an immense finger at him. 'Another two hours and you'd have been dead, out there in the mountains. You know that?'

Cole nodded.

'You don't believe me. Look.' Sherikov leaned over and snapped on the vidscreen mounted in the wall. 'Watch this. The operation should still be going on.'

The screen lit up. A scene gained form.

'This is a confidential Security channel. I had it tapped several years ago – for my own protection. What we're seeing now is being piped in to Eric Reinhart.' Sherikov grinned. 'Reinhart arranged what you're seeing on the screen. Pay close attention. You were there, two hours ago.'

Cole turned toward the screen. At first he could not make out what was happening. The screen showed a vast foaming cloud, a vortex of motion. From the speaker came a low rumble, a deep-throated roar. After a time the screen shifted, showing a slightly different view. Suddenly Cole stiffened.

He was seeing the destruction of a whole mountain range.

The picture was coming from a ship, flying above what had once been the Albertine Mountain Range. Now there was nothing but swirling clouds of gray and columns of particles and debris, a surging tide of restless material gradually sweeping off and dissipating in all directions.

The Albertine Mountains had been disintegrated. Nothing remained but these vast clouds of debris. Below, on the ground, a ragged plain stretched out, swept by fire and rain. Gaping wounds yawned, immense holes without bottoms, craters side by side as far as the eye could see. Craters and debris. Like the blasted, pitted surface of the moon. Two hours ago it had been rolling peaks and gulleys, brush and green bushes and trees.

Cole turned away.

'You see?' Sherikov snapped the screen off. 'You were down there, not so long ago. All that noise and smoke – all for you. All for you,

Mr Variable Man from the past. Reinhart arranged that, to finish you off. I want you to understand that. It's very important that you realize that.'

Cole said nothing.

Sherikov reached into a drawer of the table before him. He carefully brought out a small square box and held it out to Cole. 'You wired this, didn't you?'

Cole took the box in his hands and held it. For a time his tired mind failed to focus. What did he have? He concentrated on it. The box was the children's toy. The inter-system vidsender, they had called it.

'Yes. I fixed this.' He passed it back to Sherikov. 'I repaired that. It was broken.'

Sherikov gazed down at him intently, his large eyes bright. He nodded, his black beard and cigar rising and falling. 'Good. That's all I wanted to know.' He got suddenly to his feet, pushing his chair back. 'I see the doctor's here. He'll fix you up. Everything you need. Later on I'll talk to you again.'

Unprotesting, Cole got to his feet, allowing the doctor to take hold of his arm and help him up.

After Cole had been released by the medical department, Sherikov joined him in his private dining room, a floor above the actual laboratory.

The Pole gulped down a hasty meal, talking as he ate. Cole sat silently across from him, not eating or speaking. His old clothing had been taken away and new clothing given to him. He was shaved and rubbed down. His sores and cuts were healed, his body and hair washed. He looked much healthier and younger, now. But he was still stooped and tired, his blue eyes worn and faded. He listened to Sherikov's account of the world of 2136 AD without comment.

'You can see,' Sherikov said finally, waving a chicken leg, 'that your appearance here has been very upsetting to our program. Now that you know more about us you can see why Commissioner Reinhart was so interested in destroying you.'

Cole nodded.

'Reinhart, you realize, believes that the failure of the SRB machines is the chief danger to the war effort. But that is nothing!' Sherikov pushed his plate away noisily, draining his coffee mug. 'After all, wars *can* be fought without statistical forecasts. The SRB machines only describe. They're nothing more than mechanical onlookers. In themselves, they don't affect the course of the war. *We* make the war. They only analyze.'

Cole nodded.

'More coffee?' Sherikov asked. He pushed the plastic container toward Cole. 'Have some.'

Cole accepted another cupful. 'Thank you.'

'You can see that our real problem is another thing entirely. The machines only do figuring for us in a few minutes that eventually we could do for our own selves. They're our servants, tools. Not some sort of gods in a temple which we go and pray to. Not oracles who can see into the future for us. They don't see into the future. They only make statistical predictions – not prophecies. There's a big difference there, but Reinhart and his kind have made such things as the SRB machines into gods. But I have no gods. At least, not any I can see.'

Cole nodded, sipping his coffee.

'I'm telling you all these things because you must understand what we're up against. Terra is hemmed in on all sides by the ancient Centauran Empire. It's been out there for centuries, thousands of years. No one knows how long. It's old – crumbling and rotting. Corrupt and venal. But it holds most of the galaxy around us, and we can't break out of the Sol system. I told you about Icarus, and Hedge's work in ftl flight. We must win the war against Centaurus. We've waited and worked a long time for this, the moment when we can break out and get room among the stars for ourselves. Icarus is the deciding weapon. The data on Icarus tipped the SRB odds in our favor – for the first time in history. Success in the war against Centaurus will depend on Icarus, not on the SRB machines. You see?'

Cole nodded.

'However, there is a problem. The data on Icarus which I turned over to the machines specified that Icarus would be completed in ten days. More than half that time has already passed. Yet, we are no closer to wiring up the control turret than we were then. The turret baffles us.' Sherikov grinned ironically. 'Even *I* have tried my hand on the wiring, but with no success. It's intricate – and small. Too many technical buts not worked out. We are building only once, you understand. If we had many experimental models worked out before—'

'But this is the experimental model,' Cole said.

'And built from the designs of a man dead four years – who isn't here to correct us. We've made Icarus with our own hands down here in the labs. And he's giving us plenty of trouble.' All at once Sherikov got to his feet. 'Let's go down to the lab and look at him.'

They descended to the floor below, Sherikov leading the way. Cole stopped short at the lab door.

'Quite a sight,' Sherikov agreed. 'We keep him down here at the bottom for safety's sake. He's well protected. Come on in. We have work to do.'

In the center of the lab Icarus rose up, the gray squat cylinder that someday would flash through space at a speed of thousands of times that of light, toward the heart of Proxima Centaurus, over four light years away. Around the cylinder groups of men in uniform were laboring feverishly to finish the remaining work.

'Over here. The turret.' Sherikov led Cole over to one side of the room. 'It's guarded. Centauran spies are swarming everywhere on Terra. They see into everything. But so do we. That's how we get information for the SRB machines. Spies in both systems.'

The translucent globe that was the control turret reposed in the center of a metal stand, an armed guard standing at each side. They lowered their guns as Sherikov approached.

'We don't want anything to happen to this,' Sherikov said. 'Everything depends on it.' He put out his hand for the globe. Halfway to it his hand stopped, striking against an invisible presence in the air.

Sherikov laughed. 'The wall. Shut it off. It's still on.'

One of the guards pressed a stud at his wrist. Around the globe the air shimmered and faded.

'Now.' Sherikov's hand closed over the globe. He lifted it carefully from its mount and brought it out for Cole to see. 'This is the control turret for our enormous friend here. This is what will slow him down when he's inside Centaurus. He slows down and re-enters this universe. Right in the heart of the star. Then – no more Centaurus.' Sherikov beamed. 'And no more Armun.'

But Cole was not listening. He had taken the globe from Sherikov and was turning it over and over, running his hands over it, his face close to its surface. He peered down into its interior, his face rapt and intent.

'You can't see the wiring. Not without lenses.' Sherikov signalled for a pair of micro-lenses to be brought. He fitted them on Cole's nose, hooking them behind his ears. 'Now try it. You can control the magnification. It's set for 1000X right now. You can increase or decrease it.'

Cole gasped, swaying back and forth. Sherikov caught hold of him. Cole gazed down into the globe, moving his head slightly, focusing the glasses.

'It takes practice. But you can do a lot with them. Permits you to do microscopic wiring. There are tools to go along, you understand.' Sherikov paused, licking his lip. 'We can't get it done correctly. Only a few men can wire circuits using the micro-lenses and the little tools. We've tried robots, but there are too many decisions to be made. Robots can't make decisions. They just react.'

Cole said nothing. He continued to gaze into the interior of the globe, his lips tight, his body taut and rigid. It made Sherikov feel strangely uneasy.

'You look like one of those old fortunetellers,' Sherikov said jokingly, but a cold shiver crawled up his spine. 'Better hand it back to me.' He held out his hand.

Slowly, Cole returned the globe. After a time he removed the micro-lenses, still deep in thought.

'Well?' Sherikov demanded. 'You know what I want. I want you to wire this damn thing up.' Sherikov came close to Cole, his big face hard. 'You can do it, I think. I could tell by the way you held it – and the job you did on the children's toy, of course. You could wire it up right, and in five days. Nobody else can. And if it's not wired up Centaurus will keep on running the galaxy and Terra will have to sweat it out here in the Sol system. One tiny mediocre sun, one dust mote out of a whole galaxy.'

Cole did not answer.

Sherikov became impatient. 'Well? What do you say?'

'What happens if I don't wire this control for you? I mean, what happens to *me*?'

'Then I turn you over to Reinhart. Reinhart will kill you instantly. He thinks you're dead, killed when the Albertine Range was annihilated. If he had any idea I had saved you—'

'I see.'

'I brought you down here for one thing. If you wire it up I'll have you sent back to your own time continuum. If you don't—'

Cole considered, his face dark and brooding.

'What do you have to lose? You'd already be dead, if we hadn't pulled you out of those hills.'

'Can you really return me to my own time?'

'Of course!'

'Reinhart won't interfere?'

Sherikov laughed. 'What can he do? How can he stop me? I have my own men. You saw them. They landed all around you. You'll be returned.'

'Yes. I saw your men.'

'Then you agree?'

'I agree,' Thomas Cole said. 'I'll wire it for you. I'll complete the control turret – within the next five days.'

IV

Three days later Joseph Dixon slid a closed-circuit message plate across the desk to his boss.

'Here. You might be interested in this.'

Reinhart picked the plate up slowly. 'What is it? You came all the way here to show me this?'

'That's right.'

'Why didn't you vidscreen it?'

Dixon smiled grimly. 'You'll understand when you decode it. It's from Proxima Centaurus.'

'Centaurus!'

'Our counter-intelligence service. They sent it direct to me. Here, I'll decode it for you. Save you the trouble.'

Dixon came around behind Reinhart's desk. He leaned over the Commissioner's shoulder, taking hold of the plate and breaking the seal with his thumb nail.

'Hang on,' Dixon said. 'This is going to hit you hard. According to our agents on Armun, the Centauran High Council has called an emergency session to deal with the problem of Terra's impending attack. Centauran replay couriers have reported to the High Council that the Terran bomb Icarus is virtually complete. Work on the bomb has been rushed through final stages in the underground laboratories under the Ural Range, directed by the Terran physicist Peter Sherikov.'

'So I understand from Sherikov himself. Are you surprised the

Centaurans know about the bomb? They have spies swarming over Terra. That's no news.'

'There's more.' Dixon traced the message plate grimly, with an unsteady finger. 'The Centauran replay couriers reported that Peter Sherikov brought an expert mechanic out of a previous time continuum to complete the wiring of the turret!'

Reinhart staggered, holding on tight to the desk. He closed his eyes, gasping.

'The variable man is still alive,' Dixon murmured. 'I don't know how. Or why. There's nothing left of the Albertines. And how the hell did the man get halfway around the world?'

Reinhart opened his eyes slowly, his face twisting. 'Sherikov! He must have removed him before the attack was forthcoming. I gave him the exact hour. He had to get help – from the variable man. He couldn't meet his promise otherwise.'

Reinhart leaped up and began to pace back and forth. 'I've already informed the SRB machines that the variable man has been destroyed. The machines now show the original 7–6 ratio in our favor. But the ratio is based on false information.'

'Then you'll have to withdraw the false data and restore the original situation.'

'No.' Reinhart shook his head. 'I can't do that. The machines must be kept functioning. We can't allow them to jam again. It's too dangerous. If Duffe should become aware that—'

'What are you going to do, then?' Dixon picked up the message plate. 'You can't leave the machines with false data. That's treason.'

'The data can't be withdrawn! Not unless equivalent data exists to take its place.' Reinhart paced angrily back and forth. 'Damn it, I was *certain* the man was dead. This is an incredible situation. He must be eliminated – at any cost.'

Suddenly Reinhart stopped pacing. 'The turret. It's probably finished by this time. Correct?'

Dixon nodded slowly in agreement. 'With the variable man helping, Sherikov has undoubtedly completed work well ahead of schedule.'

Reinhart's gray eyes flickered. 'Then he's no longer of any use – even to Sherikov. We could take a chance . . . Even if there were active opposition . . .'

'What's this?' Dixon demanded. 'What are you thinking about?'

145

'How many units are ready for immediate action? How large a force can we raise without notice?'

'Because of the war we're mobilized on a twenty-four hour basis. There are seventy air units and about two hundred surface units. The balance of the Security forces have been transferred to the line, under military control.'

'Men?'

'We have about five thousand men ready to go, still on Terra. Most of them in the process of being transferred to military transports. I can hold it up at any time.'

'Missiles?'

'Fortunately, the launching tubes have not yet been disassembled. They're still here on Terra. In another few days they'll be moving out for the Colonial fracas.'

'Then they're available for immediate use?'

'Yes.'

'Good.' Reinhart locked his hands, knotting his fingers harshly together in sudden decision. 'That will do exactly. Unless I am completely wrong, Sherikov has only a half-dozen air units and no surface cars. And only about two hundred men. Some defense shields, of course—'

'What are you planning?'

Reinhart's face was gray and hard, like stone. 'Send out orders for all available Security units to be unified under your immediate command. Have them ready to move by four o'clock this afternoon. We're going to pay a visit,' Reinhart stated grimly. 'A surprise visit. On Peter Sherikov.'

'Stop here,' Reinhart ordered.

The surface car slowed to a halt. Reinhart peered cautiously out, studying the horizon ahead.

On all sides a desert of scrub grass and sand stretched out. Nothing moved or stirred. To the right the grass and sand rose up to form immense peaks, a range of mountains without end, disappearing finally into the distance. The Urals.

'Over there,' Reinhart said to Dixon, pointing. 'See?'

'No.'

'Look hard. It's difficult to spot unless you know what to look for. Vertical pipes. Some kind of vent. Or periscopes.'

Dixon saw them finally. 'I would have driven past without noticing.'

'It's well concealed. The main labs are a mile down. Under the range itself. It's virtually impregnable. Sherikov had it built years ago, to withstand any attack. From the air, by surface cars, bombs, missiles—'

'He must feel safe down there.'

'No doubt.' Reinhart gazed up at the sky. A few faint black dots could be seen, moving lazily about, in broad circles. 'Those aren't ours, are they? I gave orders—'

'No. They're not ours. All our units are out of sight. Those belong to Sherikov. His patrol.'

Reinhart relaxed. 'Good.' He reached over and flicked on the vidscreen over the board of the car. 'This screen is shielded? It can't be traced?'

'There's no way they can spot it back to us. It's nondirectional.'

The screen glowed into life. Reinhart punched the combination keys and sat back to wait.

After a time an image formed on the screen. A heavy face, bushy black beard and large eyes.

Peter Sherikov gazed at Reinhart with surprised curiosity. 'Commissioner! Where are you calling from? What—'

'How's the work progressing?' Reinhart broke in coldly. 'Is Icarus almost complete?'

Sherikov beamed with expansive pride. 'He's done, Commissioner. Two days ahead of time. Icarus is ready to be launched into space. I tried to call your office, but they told me—'

'I'm not at my office.' Reinhart leaned toward the screen. 'Open your entrance tunnel at the surface. You're about to receive visitors.'

Sherikov blinked. 'Visitors?'

'I'm coming down to see you. About Icarus. Have the tunnel opened for me at once.'

'Exactly where are you, Commissioner?'

'On the surface.'

Sherikov's eyes flickered. 'Oh? But—'

'Open up!' Reinhart snapped. He glanced at his wristwatch. 'I'll be at the entrance in five minutes. I expect to find it ready for me.'

'Of course.' Sherikov nodded in bewilderment. 'I'm always glad to see you, Commissioner. But I—'

'Five minutes, then.' Reinhart cut the circuit. The screen died. He turned quickly to Dixon. 'You stay up here, as we arranged. I'll go down with one company of police. You understand the necessity of exact timing on this?'

'We won't slip up. Everything's ready. All units are in their places.'

'Good.' Reinhart pushed the door open for him. 'You join your directional staff. I'll proceed toward the entrance tunnel.'

'Good luck.' Dixon leaped out of the car, onto the sandy ground. A gust of dry air swirled into the car around Reinhart. 'I'll see you later.'

Reinhart slammed the door. He turned to the group of police crouched in the rear of the car, their guns held tightly. 'Here we go,' Reinhart murmured. 'Hold on.'

The car raced across the sandy ground, toward the entrance tunnel to Sherikov's underground fortress.

Sherikov met Reinhart at the bottom end of the tunnel, where the tunnel opened up onto the main floor of the lab.

The big Pole approached, his hand out, beaming with pride and satisfaction. 'It's a pleasure to see you, Commissioner.'

Reinhart got out of the car, with his group of armed Security police. 'Calls for a celebration, doesn't it?' he said.

'That's a good idea! We're two days ahead, Commissioner. The SRB machines will be interested. The odds should change abruptly at the news.'

'Let's go down to the lab. I want to see the control turret myself.'

A shadow crossed Sherikov's face. 'I'd rather not bother the workmen right now, Commissioner. They've been under a great load, trying to complete the turret in time. I believe they're putting a few last finishes on it at this moment.'

'We can view them by vidscreen. I'm curious to see them at work. It must be difficult to wire such minute relays.'

Sherikov shook his head. 'Sorry, Commissioner. No vidscreen on them. I won't allow it. This is too important. Our whole future depends on it.'

Reinhart snapped a signal to his company of police. 'Put this man under arrest.'

Sherikov blanched. His mouth fell open. The police moved quickly around him, their gun-tubes up, jabbing into him. He was searched rapidly, efficiently. His gun belt and concealed energy screen were yanked off.

'What's going on?' Sherikov demanded, some color returning to his face. 'What are you doing?'

'You're under arrest for the duration of the war. You're relieved of all authority. From now on one of my men will operate Designs. When the war is over you'll be tried before the Council and President Duffe.'

Sherikov shook his head, dazed. 'I don't understand. What's this all about? Explain it to me, Commissioner. What's happened?'

Reinhart signalled to his police. 'Get ready. We're going into the lab. We may have to shoot our way in. The variable man should be in the area of the bomb, working on the control turret.'

Instantly Sherikov's face hardened. His black eyes glittered, alert and hostile.

Reinhart laughed harshly. 'We received a counter-intelligence report from Centaurus. I'm surprised at you, Sherikov. You know the Centaurans are everywhere with their relay couriers. You should have known—'

Sherikov moved. Fast. All at once he broke away from the police, throwing his massive body against them. They fell, scattering. Sherikov ran – directly at the wall. The police fired wildly. Reinhart fumbled frantically for his gun tube, pulling it up.

Sherikov reached the wall, running head down, energy beams flashing around him. He struck against the wall – and vanished.

'Down!' Reinhart shouted. He dropped to his hands and knees. All around him his police dived for the floor. Reinhart cursed wildly, dragging himself quickly toward the door. They had to get out, and right away. Sherikov had escaped. A false wall, an energy barrier set to respond to his pressure. He had dashed through it to safety. He—

From all sides an inferno burst, a flaming roar of death surging over them, around them, on every side. The room was alive with blazing masses of destruction, bouncing from wall to wall. They were caught between four banks of power, all of them open to full discharge. A trap – a death trap.

Reinhart reached the hall gasping for breath. He leaped to his feet. A few Security police followed him. Behind them, in the flaming room, the rest of the company screamed and struggled, blasted out of existence by the leaping bursts of power.

Reinhart assembled his remaining men. Already, Sherikov's guards were forming. At one end of the corridor a snub-barreled robot gun was maneuvering into position. A siren wailed. Guards were running on all sides, hurrying to battle stations.

The robot gun opened fire. Part of the corridor exploded, bursting into fragments. Clouds of choking debris and particles swept around them. Reinhart and his police retched, moving back along the corridor.

They reached a junction. A second robot gun was rumbling toward them, hurrying to get within range. Reinhart fired carefully, aiming at its delicate control. Abruptly the gun spun convulsively. It lashed against the wall, smashing itself into the unyielding metal. Then it collapsed in a heap, gears still whining and spinning.

'Come on.' Reinhart moved away, crouching and running. He glanced at his watch. *Almost time*. A few more minutes. A group of lab guards appeared ahead of them. Reinhart fired. Behind him his police fired past him, violet shafts of energy catching the group of guards as they entered the corridor. The guards spilled apart, falling and twisting. Part of them settled into dust, drifting down the corridor. Reinhart made his way toward the lab, crouching and leaping, pushing past heaps of debris and remains, followed by his men. 'Come on! Don't stop!'

Suddenly from around them the booming, enlarged voice of Sherikov thundered, magnified by rows of wall speakers along the corridor. Reinhart halted, glancing around.

'Reinhart! You haven't got a chance. You'll never get back to the surface. Throw down your guns and give up. You're surrounded on all sides. You're a mile under the surface.'

Reinhart threw himself into motion, pushing into billowing clouds of particles drifting along the corridor. 'Are you sure, Sherikov?' he grunted.

Sherikov laughed, his harsh, metallic peals rolling in waves against Reinhart's eardrums. 'I don't want to have to kill you, Commissioner. You're vital to the war. I'm sorry you found out about the variable man. I admit we overlooked the Centauran espionage as a factor in this. But now that you know about him—'

Suddenly Sherikov's voice broke off. A deep rumble had shaken the floor, a lapping vibration that shuddered through the corridor.

Reinhart sagged with relief. He peered through the clouds of debris, making out the figures on his watch. Right on time. Not a second late.

The first of the hydrogen missiles, launched from the Council buildings on the other side of the world, were beginning to arrive. The attack had begun.

At exactly six o'clock Joseph Dixon, standing on the surface four miles from the entrance tunnel, gave the sign to the waiting units.

The first job was to break down Sherikov's defense screens. The missiles had to penetrate without interference. At Dixon's signal a fleet of thirty Security ships dived from a height of ten miles, swooping above the mountains, directly over the underground laboratories. Within five minutes the defense screens had been smashed, and all the tower projectors leveled flat. Now the mountains were virtually unprotected.

'So far so good,' Dixon murmured, as he watched from his secure position. The fleet of Security ships roared back, their work done. Across the face of the desert the police surface cars were crawling rapidly toward the entrance tunnel, snaking from side to side.

Meanwhile, Sherikov's counter-attack had begun to go into operation.

Guns mounted among the hills opened fire. Vast columns of flames burst up in the path of the advancing cars. The cars hesitated and retreated, as the plain was churned up by a howling vortex, a thundering chaos of explosions. Here and there a car vanished in a cloud of particles. A group of cars moving away suddenly scattered, caught up by a giant wind that lashed across them and swept them up into the air.

Dixon gave orders to have the cannon silenced. The police air arm again swept overhead, a sullen roar of jets that shook the ground below. The police ships divided expertly and hurtled down on the cannon protecting the hills.

The cannon forgot the surface cars and lifted their snouts to meet the attack. Again and again the airships came, rocking the mountains with titanic blasts.

The guns became silent. Their echoing boom diminished, died away reluctantly, as bombs took critical toll of them.

Dixon watched with satisfaction as the bombing came to an end. The airships rose in a thick swarm, black gnats shooting up in triumph from a dead carcass. They hurried back as emergency anti-aircraft robot guns swung into position and saturated the sky with blazing puffs of energy.

Dixon checked his wristwatch. The missiles were already on the way from North America. Only a few minutes remained.

The surface cars, freed by the successful bombing, began to regroup for a new frontal attack. Again they crawled forward, across the burning plain, bearing down cautiously on the battered wall of mountains, heading toward the twisted wrecks that had been the ring of defense guns. Toward the entrance tunnel.

An occasional cannon fired feebly at them. The cars came grimly on. Now, in the hollows of the hills, Sherikov's troops were hurrying to the surface to meet the attack. The first car reached the shadow of the mountains . . .

A deafening hail of fire burst loose. Small robot guns appeared everywhere, needle barrels emerging from behind hidden screens, trees, shrubs, rocks, and stones. The police cars were caught in a withering cross-fire, trapped at the base of the hills.

Down the slopes Sherikov's guards raced, toward the stalled cars. Clouds of heat rose up and boiled across the plain as the cars fired up at the running men. A robot gun dropped like a slug onto the plain and screamed toward the cars, firing as it came.

Dixon twisted nervously. Only a few minutes. Any time, now. He shaded his eyes and peered up at the sky. No sign of them yet. He wondered about Reinhart. No signal had come from below. Clearly, Reinhart had run into trouble. No doubt there was desperate fighting going on in the maze of underground tunnels, the intricate web of passages that honeycombed the earth below the mountains.

In the air, Sherikov's few defense ships darted rapidly, wildly, putting up a futile fight.

Sherikov's guards streamed out onto the plain. Crouching and running, they advanced toward the stalled cars. The police airships screeched down at them, guns thundering.

Dixon held his breath. When the missiles arrived—

The first missile struck. A section of the mountain vanished, turned to smoke and foaming gases. The wave of heat slapped Dixon across the face, spinning him around. Quickly he re-entered his ship and took off, shooting rapidly away from the scene. He glanced back. A second and third missile had arrived. Great gaping pits yawned among the mountains, vast sections missing like broken teeth. Now the missiles could penetrate to the underground laboratories below.

On the ground, the surface cars halted beyond the danger area, waiting for the missile attack to finish. When the eighth missile had struck, the cars again moved forward. No more missiles fell.

Dixon swung his ship around, heading back toward the scene. The laboratory was exposed. The top sections of it had been ripped open.

The laboratory lay like a tin can, torn apart by mighty explosions, its first floors visible from the air. Men and cars were pouring down into it, fighting with the guards swarming to the surface.

Dixon watched intently. Sherikov's men were bringing up heavy guns, big robot artillery. But the police ships were diving again. Sherikov's defensive patrols had been cleaned from the sky. The police ships whined down, arcing over the exposed laboratory. Small bombs fell, whistling down, pinpointing the artillery rising to the surface on the remaining lift stages.

Abruptly Dixon's vidscreen clicked. Dixon turned toward it.

Reinhart's features formed. 'Call off the attack.' His uniform was torn. A deep bloody gash crossed his cheek. He grinned sourly at Dixon, pushing his tangled hair back out of his face. 'Quite a fight.'

'Sherikov—'

'He's called off his guards. We've agreed to a truce. It's all over. No more needed.' Reinhart gasped for breath, wiping grime and sweat from his neck. 'Land your ship and come down here at once.'

'The variable man?'

'That comes next,' Reinhart said grimly. He adjusted his gun tube. 'I want you down here, for that part. I want you to be in on the kill.'

Reinhart turned away from the vidscreen. In the corner of the room Sherikov stood silently, saying nothing. 'Well?' Reinhart barked. 'Where is he? Where will I find him?'

Sherikov licked his lips nervously, glancing up at Reinhart. 'Commissioner, are you sure—'

'The attack has been called off. Your labs are safe. So is your life. Now it's your turn to come through.' Reinhart gripped his gun, moving toward Sherikov. '*Where is he?*'

For a moment Sherikov hesitated. Then slowly his huge body sagged, defeated. He shook his head wearily. 'All right. I'll show you where he is.' His voice was hardly audible, a dry whisper. 'Down this way. Come on.'

Reinhart followed Sherikov out of the room, into the corridor. Police and guards were working rapidly, clearing the debris and ruins away, putting out the hydrogen fires that burned everywhere. 'No tricks, Sherikov.'

'No tricks.' Sherikov nodded resignedly. 'Thomas Cole is by himself. In a wing lab off the main rooms.'

'Cole?'

'The variable man. That's his name.' The Pole turned his massive head a little. 'He has a name.'

Reinhart waved his gun. 'Hurry up. I don't want anything to go wrong. This is the part I came for.'

'You must remember something, Commissioner.'

'What is it?'

Sherikov stopped walking. 'Commissioner, nothing must happen to the globe. The control turret. Everything depends on it, the war, our whole—'

'I know. Nothing will happen to the damn thing. Let's go.'

'If it should get damaged—'

'I'm not after the globe. I'm interested only in – in Thomas Cole.'

They came to the end of the corridor and stopped before a metal door. Sherikov nodded at the door. 'In there.'

Reinhart moved back. 'Open the door.'

'Open it yourself. I don't want to have anything to do with it.'

Reinhart shrugged. He stepped up to the door. Holding his gun level he raised his hand, passing it in front of the eye circuit. Nothing happened.

Reinhart frowned. He pushed the door with his hand. The door slid open. Reinhart was looking into a small laboratory. He glimpsed a workbench, tools, heaps of equipment, measuring devices, and in the center of the bench the transparent globe, the control turret.

'Cole?' Reinhart advanced quickly into the room. He glanced around him, suddenly alarmed. 'Where—'

The room was empty. Thomas Cole was gone.

When the first missile struck, Cole stopped work and sat listening.

Far off, a distant rumble rolled through the earth, shaking the floor under him. On the bench, tools and equipment danced up and down. A pair of pliers fell crashing to the floor. A box of screws tipped over, spilling its minute contents out.

Cole listened for a time. Presently he lifted the transparent globe from the bench. With carefully controlled hands he held the globe up, running his fingers gently over the surface, his faded blue eyes thoughtful. Then, after a time, he placed the globe back on the bench, in its mount.

The globe was finished. A faint glow of pride moved through the variable man. The globe was the finest job he had ever done.

The deep rumblings ceased. Cole became instantly alert. He jumped down from his stool, hurrying across the room to the door. For a moment he stood by the door listening intently. He could hear noise on the other side, shouts, guards rushing past, dragging heavy equipment, working frantically.

A rolling crash echoed down the corridor and lapped against his door. The concussion spun him around. Again a tide of energy shook the walls and floor and sent him down on his knees.

The lights flickered and winked out.

Cole fumbled in the dark until he found a flashlight. Power failure. He could hear crackling flames. Abruptly the lights came on again, an ugly yellow, then faded back out. Cole bent down and examined the door with his flashlight. A magnetic lock. Dependent on an externally induced electric flux. He grabbed a screwdriver and pried at the door. For a moment it held. Then it fell open.

Cole stepped warily out into the corridor. Everything was in shambles. Guards wandered everywhere, burned and half blinded. Two lay groaning under a pile of wrecked equipment. Fused guns, reeking metal. The air was heavy with the smell of burning wiring and plastic. A thick cloud that choked him and made him bend double as he advanced.

'Halt,' a guard gasped feebly, struggling to rise. Cole pushed past him and down the corridor. Two small robot guns, still functioning, glided past him hurriedly toward the drumming chaos of battle. He followed.

At a major intersection the fight was in full swing. Sherikov's guards fought Security police, crouched behind pillars and barricades, firing wildly, desperately. Again the whole structure shuddered as a great booming blast ignited some place above. Bombs? Shells?

Cole threw himself down as a violet beam cut past his ear and disintegrated the wall behind him. A Security policeman, wild-eyed, firing erratically. One of Sherikov's guards winged him and his gun skidded to the floor.

A robot cannon turned toward him as he made his way past the intersection. He began to run. The cannon rolled along behind him, aiming itself uncertainly. Cole hunched over as he shambled rapidly along, gasping for breath. In the flickering yellow tight he saw a handful of Security police advancing, firing expertly, intent on a line of defense Sherikov's guards had hastily set up.

The robot cannon altered its course to take them on, and Cole escaped around a corner.

He was in the main lab, the big chamber where Icarus himself rose, the vast squat column.

Icarus! A solid wall of guards surrounded him, grim-faced, hugging guns and protection shields. But the Security police were leaving Icarus alone. Nobody wanted to damage him. Cole evaded a lone guard tracking him and reached the far side of the lab.

It took him only a few seconds to find the force field generator. There was no switch. For a moment that puzzled him – and then he remembered. The guard had controlled it from his wrist.

Too late to worry about that. With his screwdriver he unfastened the plate over the generator and ripped out the wiring in handfuls. The generator came loose and he dragged it away from the wall. The screen was off, thank God. He managed to carry the generator into a side corridor.

Crouched in a heap, Cole bent over the generator, deft fingers flying. He pulled the wiring to him and laid it out on the floor, tracing the circuits with feverish haste.

The adaptation was easier than he had expected. The screen flowed at right angles to the wiring, for a distance of six feet. Each lead was shielded on one side; the field radiated outward, leaving a hollow cone in the center. He ran the wiring through his belt, down his trouser legs, under his shirt, all the way to his wrists and ankles.

He was just snatching up the heavy generator when two Security police appeared. They raised their blasters and fired point-blank.

Cole clicked on the screen. A vibration leaped through him that snapped his jaw and danced up his body. He staggered away, half-stupefied by the surging force that radiated out from him. The violet rays struck the field and deflected harmlessly.

He was safe.

He hurried on down the corridor, past a ruined gun and sprawled bodies still clutching blasters. Great drifting clouds of radioactive particles billowed around him. He edged by one cloud nervously. Guards lay everywhere, dying and dead, partly destroyed, eaten and corroded by the hot metallic salts in the air. He had to get out – and fast.

At the end of the corridor a whole section of the fortress was in ruins. Towering flames leaped on all sides. One of the missiles had penetrated below ground level.

Cole found a lift that still functioned. A load of wounded guards was being raised to the surface. None of them paid any attention to him. Flames surged around the lift, licking at the wounded. Workmen were desperately trying to get the lift into action. Cole leaped onto the lift. A moment later it began to rise, leaving the shouts and the flames behind.

The lift emerged on the surface and Cole jumped off. A guard spotted him and gave chase. Crouching, Cole dodged into a tangled mass of twisted metal, still white-hot and smoking. He ran for a distance, leaping from the side of a ruined defense-screen tower, onto the fused ground and down the side of a hill. The ground was hot underfoot. He hurried as fast as he could, gasping for breath. He came to a long slope and scrambled up the side.

The guard who had followed was gone, lost behind in the rolling clouds of ash that drifted from the ruins of Sherikov's underground fortress.

Cole reached the top of the hill. For a brief moment he halted to get his breath and figure where he was. It was almost evening. The sun was beginning to set. In the darkening sky a few dots still twisted and rolled, black specks that abruptly burst into flame and fused out again.

Cole stood up cautiously, peering around him. Ruins stretched out below, on all sides, the furnace from which he had escaped. A chaos of incandescent metal and debris, gutted and wrecked beyond repair. Miles of tangled rubbish and half-vaporized equipment.

He considered. Everyone was busy putting out the fires and pulling the wounded to safety. It would be a while before he was missed. But as soon as they realized he was gone they'd be after him. Most of the laboratory had been destroyed. Nothing lay back that way.

Beyond the ruins lay the great Ural peaks, the endless mountains, stretching out as far as the eye could see.

Mountains and green forests. A wilderness. They'd never find him there.

Cole started along the side of the hill, walking slowly and carefully, his screen generator under his arm. Probably in the confusion he could find enough food and equipment to last him indefinitely. He could wait until early morning then circle back toward the ruins and load up. With a few tools and his own innate skill he would get along fine. A screwdriver, hammer, nails, odds and ends—

A great hum sounded in his ears. It swelled to a deafening roar. Startled, Cole whirled around. A vast shape filled the sky behind him, growing each moment. Cole stood frozen, utterly transfixed. The shape thundered over him, above his head, as he stood stupidly, rooted to the spot.

Then, awkwardly, uncertainly, he began to run. He stumbled and fell and rolled a short distance down the side of the hill. Desperately, he struggled to hold onto the ground. His hands dug wildly, futilely, into the soft soil, trying to keep the generator under his arm at the same time.

A flash, and a blinding spark of light around him.

The spark picked him up and tossed him like a dry leaf. He grunted in agony as searing fire crackled about him, a blazing inferno that gnawed and ate hungrily through his screen. He spun dizzily and fell through the cloud of fire, down into a pit of darkness, a vast gulf between two hills. His wiring ripped off. The generator tore out of his grip and was lost behind. Abruptly, his force field ceased.

Cole lay in the darkness at the bottom of the hill. His whole body shrieked in agony as the unholy fire played over him. He was a blazing cinder, a half-consumed ash flaming in a universe of darkness. The pain made him twist and crawl like an insect, trying to burrow into the ground. He screamed and shrieked and struggled to escape, to get away from the hideous fire. To reach the curtain of darkness beyond, where it was cool and silent, where the flames couldn't crackle and eat at him.

He reached imploringly out, into the darkness, groping feebly toward it, trying to pull himself into it. Gradually, the glowing orb that was his own body faded. The impenetrable chaos of night descended. He allowed the tide to sweep over him, to extinguish the searing fire.

Dixon landed his ship expertly, bringing it to a halt in front of an overturned defense tower. He leaped out and hurried across the smoking ground.

From a lift Reinhart appeared, surrounded by his Security police. 'He got away from us! He escaped!'

'He didn't escape,' Dixon answered. 'I got him myself.'

Reinhart quivered violently. 'What do you mean?'

'Come along with me. Over in this direction.' He and Reinhart climbed the side of a demolished hill, both of them panting for breath. 'I was landing. I saw a figure emerge from a lift and run toward the mountains, like some sort of animal. When he came out in the open I dived on him and released a phosphorous bomb.'

'Then he's – *dead*?'

'I don't see how anyone could have lived through a phosphorous bomb.' They reached the top of the hill. Dixon halted, then pointed excitedly down into the pit beyond the hill. 'There!'

They descended cautiously. The ground was singed and burned clean. Clouds of smoke hung heavily in the air. Occasional fires still flickered here and there. Reinhart coughed and bent over to see. Dixon flashed on a pocket flare and set it beside the body.

The body was charred, half destroyed by the burning phosphorous. It lay motionless, one arm over its face, mouth open, legs sprawled grotesquely. Like some abandoned rag doll, tossed in an incinerator and consumed almost beyond recognition.

'He's alive!' Dixon muttered. He felt around curiously. 'Must have had some kind of protection screen. Amazing that a man could—'

'It's him? It's really him?'

'Fits the description.' Dixon tore away a handful of burned clothing. 'This is the variable man. What's left of him, at least.'

Reinhart sagged with relief. 'Then we've finally got him. The data is accurate. He's no longer a factor.'

Dixon got out his blaster and released the safety catch thoughtfully. 'If you want, I can finish the job right now.'

At that moment Sherikov appeared, accompanied by two armed Security police. He strode grimly down the hillside, black eyes snapping. 'Did Cole—' He broke off. 'Good God.'

'Dixon got him with a phosphorous bomb,' Reinhart said non-committally. 'He had reached the surface and was trying to get into the mountains.'

Sherikov turned wearily away. 'He was an amazing person. During the attack he managed to force the lock on his door and escape. The guards fired at him, but nothing happened. He had rigged up some kind of force field around him. Something he adapted.'

'Anyhow, it's over with,' Reinhart answered. 'Did you have SRB plates made up on him?'

Sherikov reached slowly into his coat. He drew out a manila envelope. 'Here's all the information I collected about him, while he was with me.'

'Is it complete? Everything previous has been merely fragmentary.'

'As near complete as I could make it. It includes photographs and diagrams of the interior of the globe. The turret wiring he did for me. I haven't had a chance even to look at them.' Sherikov fingered the envelope. 'What are you going to do with Cole?'

'Have him loaded up, taken back to the city – and officially put to sleep by the Euthanasia Ministry.'

'Legal murder?' Sherikov's lips twisted. 'Why don't you simply do it right here and get it over with?'

Reinhart grabbed the envelope and stuck it in his right pocket. 'I'll turn this right over to the machines.' He motioned to Dixon. 'Let's go. Now we can notify the fleet to prepare for the attack on Centaurus.' He turned briefly back to Sherikov. 'When can Icarus be launched?'

'In an hour or so, I suppose. They're locking the control turret in place. Assuming it functions correctly, that's all that's needed.'

'Good. I'll notify Duffe to send out the signal to the warfleet.' Reinhart nodded to the police to take Sherikov to the waiting Security ship. Sherikov moved off dully, his face gray and haggard. Cole's inert body was picked up and tossed onto a freight cart. The cart rumbled into the hold of the Security ship and the lock slid shut after it.

'It'll be interesting to see how the machines respond to the additional data,' Dixon said.

'It should make quite an improvement in the odds,' Reinhart agreed. He patted the envelope bulging in his inside pocket. 'We're two days ahead of time.'

Margaret Duffe got up slowly from her desk. She pushed her chair automatically back. 'Let me get all this straight. You mean the bomb is finished? Ready to go?'

Reinhart nodded impatiently. 'That's what I said. The Technicians are checking the turret locks to make sure it's properly attached. The launching will take place in half an hour.'

'Thirty minutes! Then—'

'Then the attack can begin at once. I assume the fleet is ready for action.'

'Of course. It's been ready for several days. But I can't believe the bomb is ready so soon.' Margaret Duffe moved numbly toward the door of her office. 'This is a great day, Commissioner. An old era lies behind us. This time tomorrow Centaurus will be gone. And eventually the colonies will be ours.'

'It's been a long climb,' Reinhart murmured.

'One thing. Your charge against Sherikov. It seems incredible that a person of his caliber could ever—'

'We'll discuss that later,' Reinhart interrupted coldly. He pulled the manila envelope from his coat. 'I haven't had an opportunity to feed the additional data to the SRB machines. If you'll excuse me, I'll do that now.'

For a moment Margaret Duffe stood at the door. The two of them faced each other silently, neither speaking, a faint smile on Reinhart's thin lips, hostility in the woman's blue eyes.

'Reinhart, sometimes I think perhaps you'll go too far. And sometimes I think you've *already* gone too far . . .'

'I'll inform you of any change in the odds showing.' Reinhart strode past her, out of the office and down the hall. He headed toward the SRB room, an intense thalamic excitement rising up inside him.

A few moments later he entered the SRB room. He made his way to the machines. The odds 7–6 showed in the view windows. Reinhart smiled a little. 7–6. False odds, based on incorrect information. Now they could be removed.

Kaplan hurried over. Reinhart handed him the envelope, and moved over to the window, gazing down at the scene below. Men and cars scurried frantically everywhere. Officials coming and going like ants, hurrying in all directions.

The war was on. The signal had been sent out to the warfleet that had waited so long near Proxima Centaurus. A feeling of triumph raced through Reinhart. He had won. He had destroyed the man from the past and broken Peter Sherikov. The war had begun as planned. Terra was breaking out. Reinhart smiled thinly. He had been completely successful.

'Commissioner.'

Reinhart turned slowly. 'All right.'

Kaplan was standing in front of the machines, gazing down at the reading. 'Commissioner—'

Sudden alarm plucked at Reinhart. There was something in Kaplan's voice. He hurried quickly over. 'What is it?'

Kaplan looked up at him, his face white, his eyes wide with terror. His mouth opened and closed, but no sound came.

'*What is it?*' Reinhart demanded, chilled. He bent toward the machines, studying the reading.

And sickened with horror.

100–1. *Against* Terra!

He could not tear his gaze away from the figures. He was numb, shocked with disbelief. 100–1. *What had happened?* What had gone wrong? The turret was finished, Icarus was ready, the fleet had been notified—

There was a sudden deep buzz from outside the building. Shouts drifted up from below. Reinhart turned his head slowly toward the window, his heart frozen with fear.

Across the evening sky a trail moved, rising each moment. A thin line of white. Something climbed, gaining speed each moment. On the ground, all eyes were turned toward it, awed faces peering up.

The object gained speed. Faster and faster. Then it vanished. Icarus was on his way. The attack had begun; it was too late to stop, now.

And on the machines the odds read a hundred to one – for failure.

At eight o'clock in the evening of May 15, 2136, Icarus was launched toward the star Centaurus. A day later, while all Terra waited, Icarus entered the star, traveling at thousands of times the speed of light.

Nothing happened. Icarus disappeared into the star. There was no explosion. The bomb failed to go off.

At the same time the Terran warfleet engaged the Centauran outer fleet, sweeping down in a concentrated attack. Twenty major ships were seized. A good part of the Centauran fleet was destroyed. Many of the captive systems began to revolt, in the hope of throwing off the Imperial bonds.

Two hours later the massed Centauran warfleet from Armun abruptly appeared and joined battle. The great struggle illuminated half the Centauran system. Ship after ship flashed briefly and then faded to ash. For a whole day the two fleets fought, strung out over millions of miles of space. Innumerable fighting men died – on both sides.

At last the remains of the battered Terran fleet turned and limped toward Armun – defeated. Little of the once impressive armada remained. A few blackened hulks, making their way uncertainly toward captivity.

Icarus had not functioned. Centaurus had not exploded. The attack was a failure.

The war was over.

'We've lost the war,' Margaret Duffe said in a small voice, wondering and awed. 'It's over. Finished.'

The Council members sat in their places around the conference table, gray-haired elderly men, none of them speaking or moving. All gazed up mutely at the great stellar maps that covered two walls of the chamber.

'I have already empowered negotiators to arrange a truce,' Margaret Duffe murmured. 'Orders have been sent out to Vice-Commander Jessup to give up the battle. There's no hope. Fleet Commander Carleton destroyed himself and his flagship a few minutes ago. The Centauran High Council has agreed to end the fighting. Their whole Empire is rotten to the core. Ready to topple of its own weight.'

Reinhart was slumped over at the table, his head in his hands. 'I don't understand . . . *Why?* Why didn't the bomb explode?' He mopped his forehead shakily. All his poise was gone. He was trembling and broken. '*What went wrong?*'

Gray-faced, Dixon mumbled an answer. 'The variable man must have sabotaged the turret. The SRB machines knew . . . They analyzed the data. *They knew!* But it was too late.'

Reinhart's eyes were bleak with despair as he raised his head a little. 'I knew he'd destroy us. We're finished. A century of work and planning.' His body knotted in a spasm of furious agony. 'All because of Sherikov!'

Margaret Duffe eyed Reinhart coldly. 'Why because of Sherikov?'

'He kept Cole alive! I wanted him killed from the start.' Suddenly Reinhart jumped from his chair. His hand clutched convulsively at his gun. 'And he's *still* alive! Even if we've lost I'm going to have the pleasure of putting a blast beam through Cole's chest!'

'Sit down!' Margaret Duffe ordered.

Reinhart was halfway to the door. 'He's still at the Euthanasia Ministry, waiting for the official—'

'No, he's not ' Margaret Duffe said.

Reinhart froze. He turned slowly, as if unable to believe his sense. '*What?*'

'Cole isn't at the Ministry. I ordered him transferred and your instructions cancelled.'

'Where – where is he?'

There was unusual hardness in Margaret Duffe's voice as she answered. 'With Peter Sherikov. In the Urals. I had Sherikov's full authority restored. I then had Cole transferred there, put in Sherikov's safekeeping. I want to make sure Cole recovers, so we can keep our promise to him – our promise to return him to his own time.'

Reinhart's mouth opened and closed. All the color had drained from his face. His cheek muscles twitched spasmodically. At last he managed to speak. 'You've gone insane! The traitor responsible for Earth's greatest defeat—'

'We have lost the war,' Margaret Duffe stated quietly. 'But this is not a day of defeat. It is a day of victory. The most incredible victory Terra has ever had.'

Reinhart and Dixon were dumbfounded. 'What—' Reinhart gasped. 'What do you—' The whole room was in an uproar. All the Council members were on their feet. Reinhart's words were drowned out.

'Sherikov will explain when he gets here,' Margaret Duffe's calm voice came. 'He's the one who discovered it.' She looked around the chamber at the incredulous Council members. 'Everyone stay in his seat. You are all to remain here until Sherikov arrives. It's vital you hear what he has to say. His news transforms this whole situation.'

Peter Sherikov accepted the briefcase of papers from his armed technician. 'Thanks.' He pushed his chair back and glanced thoughtfully around the Council chamber. 'Is everybody ready to hear what I have to say?'

'We're ready,' Margaret Duffe answered. The Council members sat alertly around the table. At the far end, Reinhart and Dixon watched uneasily as the big Pole removed papers from his briefcase and carefully examined them.

'To begin, I recall to you the original work behind the ftl bomb. Jamison Hedge was the first human to propel an object at a speed greater than light. As you know, that object diminished in length and gained in mass as it moved toward light speed. When it reached that speed it vanished. It ceased to exist in our terms. Having no length it could not occupy space. It rose to a different order of existence.

'When Hedge tried to bring the object back, an explosion occurred. Hedge was killed, and all his equipment was destroyed. The force of the blast was beyond calculation. Hedge had placed his observation ship many millions of miles away. It was not far enough, however. Originally, he had hoped his drive might be used for space travel. But after his death the principle was abandoned.

'That is – until Icarus. I saw the possibilities of a bomb, an incredibly powerful bomb to destroy Centaurus and all the Empire's forces. The reappearance of Icarus would mean the annihilation of their System. As Hedge had shown, the object would re-enter space already occupied by matter, and the cataclysm would be beyond belief.'

'But Icarus never came back,' Reinhart cried. 'Cole altered the wiring so the bomb kept on going. It's probably still going.'

'Wrong,' Sherikov boomed. 'The bomb *did* reappear. But it didn't explode.'

Reinhart reacted violently. 'You mean—'

'The bomb came back, dropping below the ftl speed as soon as it entered the star Proxima. But it did not explode. There was no cataclysm. It reappeared and was absorbed by the sun, turned into gas at once.'

'Why didn't it explode?' Dixon demanded.

'Because Thomas Cole solved Hedge's problem. He found a way to bring the ftl object back into this universe without collision. Without an explosion. The variable man found what Hedge was after . . .'

The whole Council was on its feet. A growing murmur filled the chamber, a rising pandemonium breaking out on all sides.

'I don't believe it!' Reinhart gasped. 'It isn't possible. If Cole solved Hedge's problem that would mean—' He broke off, staggered.

'Faster than light drive can now be used for space travel,' Sherikov continued, waving the noise down. 'As Hedge intended. My men have studied the photographs of the control turret. They don't know *how* or *why*, yet. But we have complete records of the turret. We can duplicate the wiring, as soon as the laboratories have been repaired.'

Comprehension was gradually beginning to settle over the room. 'Then it'll be possible to build ftl ships,' Margaret Duffe murmured, dazed. 'And if we can do that—'

'When I showed him the control turret, Cole understood its purpose. Not *my* purpose, but the original purpose Hedge had been working toward. Cole realized Icarus was actually an incomplete spaceship, not a bomb at all. He saw what Hedge had seen, an ftl space drive. He set out to make Icarus work.'

'We can go *beyond* Centaurus,' Dixon murmured. His lips twisted. 'Then the war was trivial. We can leave the Empire completely behind. We can go beyond the galaxy.'

'The whole universe is open to us,' Sherikov agreed. 'Instead of taking over an antiquated Empire, we have the entire cosmos to map and explore, God's total creation.'

Margaret Duffe got to her feet and moved slowly toward the great stellar maps that towered above them at the far end of the chamber. She stood for a long time, gazing up at the myriad suns, the legions of systems, awed by what she saw.

'Do you suppose he realized all this?' she asked suddenly. 'What we can see, here on these maps?'

'Thomas Cole is a strange person,' Sherikov said, half to himself. 'Apparently he has a kind of intuition about machines, the way things are supposed to work. An intuition more in his hands than in his head. A kind of genius, such as a painter or a pianist has. Not a scientist. He has no verbal knowledge about things, no semantic references. He deals with the things themselves. Directly.

'I doubt very much if Thomas Cole understood what would come about. He looked into the globe, the control turret. He saw unfinished wiring and relays. He saw a job half done. An incomplete machine.'

'Something to be fixed,' Margaret Duffe put in.

'Something to be fixed. Like an artist, he saw his work ahead of him. He was interested in only one thing: turning out the best job he could, with the skill he possessed. For us, that skill has opened up a whole universe, endless galaxies and systems to explore. Worlds without end. Unlimited, *untouched* worlds.'

Reinhart got unsteadily to his feet. 'We better get to work. Start organizing construction teams. Exploration crews. We'll have to re-convert from war production to ship designing. Begin the manufacture of mining and scientific instruments for survey work.'

'That's right,' Margaret Duffe said. She looked reflectively up at him. 'But you're not going to have anything to do with it.'

Reinhart saw the expression on her face. His hands flew to his gun and he backed quickly toward the door. Dixon leaped up and joined him. 'Get back!' Reinhart shouted.

Margaret Duffe signaled and a phalanx of Government troops closed in around the two men. Grim-faced, efficient soldiers with magnetic grapples ready.

Reinhart's blaster wavered – toward the Council members sitting shocked in their seats, and toward Margaret Duffe, straight at her blue eyes. Reinhart's features were distorted with insane fear. 'Get back! Don't anybody come near me or she'll be the first to get it!'

Peter Sherikov slid from the table and with one great stride swept his immense bulk in front of Reinhart. His huge black-furred fist rose in a smashing arc. Reinhart sailed against the wall, struck with ringing force and then slid slowly to the floor.

The Government troops threw their grapples quickly around him and jerked him to his feet. His body was frozen rigid. Blood dripped from his mouth. He spat bits of tooth, his eyes glazed over. Dixon stood dazed, mouth open, uncomprehending, as the grapples closed around his arms and legs.

Reinhart's gun skidded to the floor as he was yanked toward the door. One of the elderly Council members picked the gun up and examined it curiously. He laid it carefully on the table. 'Fully loaded,' he murmured. 'Ready to fire.'

Reinhart's battered face was dark with hate. 'I should have killed all of you. *All* of you!' An ugly sneer twisted across his shredded lips. 'If I could get my hands loose—'

'You won't,' Margaret Duffe said. 'You might as well not even bother to think about it.' She signaled to the troops and they pulled Reinhart and Dixon roughly out of the room, two dazed figures, snarling and resentful.

For a moment the room was silent. Then the Council members shuffled nervously in their seats, beginning to breathe again.

Sherikov came over and put his big paw on Margaret Duffe's shoulder. 'Are you all right, Margaret?'

She smiled faintly. 'I'm fine. Thanks . . .'

Sherikov touched her soft hair briefly. Then he broke away and began to pack up his briefcase busily. 'I have to go. I'll get in touch with you later.'

'Where are you going?' she asked hesitantly. 'Can't you stay and—'

'I have to get back to the Urals.' Sherikov grinned at her over his bushy black beard as he headed out of the room. 'Some very important business to attend to.'

Thomas Cole was sitting up in bed when Sherikov came to the door. Most of his awkward, hunched-over body was sealed in a thin envelope of transparent air-proof plastic. Two robot attendants whirred ceaselessly at his side, their leads contacting his pulse, blood-pressure, respiration, and body temperature.

Cole turned a little as the huge Pole tossed down his briefcase and seated himself on the window ledge.

'How are you feeling?' Sherikov asked him.

'Better.'

'You see we've quite advanced therapy. Your burns should be healed in a few months.'

'How is the war coming?'

'The war is over.'

Cole's lips moved. 'Icarus—'

'Icarus went as expected. As *you* expected.' Sherikov leaned toward the bed. 'Cole, I promised you something, I mean to keep my promise – as soon as you're well enough.'

'To return me to my own time?'

'That's right. It's a relatively simple matter, now that Reinhart has been removed from power. You'll be back home again, back in your own time, your own world. We can supply you with some discs of platinum or something of the kind to finance your business. You need a new Fixit truck. Tools. And clothes. A few thousand dollars ought to do it.'

Cole was silent.

'I've already contacted histo-research,' Sherikov continued. 'The time bubble is ready as soon as you are. We're somewhat beholden to you, as you probably realize. You've made it possible for us to actualize our greatest dream. The whole planet is seething with excitement. We're changing our economy over from war to—'

'They don't resent what happened? The dud must have made an awful lot of people feel downright bad.'

'At first. But they got over it – as soon as they understood what was ahead. Too bad you won't be here to see it, Cole. A whole world breaking loose. Bursting out into the universe. They want me to have an ftl ship ready by the end of the week! Thousands of applications are already on file, men and women wanting to get in on the initial flight.'

Cole smiled a little. 'There won't be any band, there. No parade or welcoming committee waiting for them.'

'Maybe not. Maybe the first ship will wind up on some dead world, nothing but sand and dried salt. But everyone wants to go. It's almost like a holiday. People running around and shouting and throwing things in the streets.

'Afraid I must get back to the labs. Lots of reconstruction work being started.' Sherikov dug into his bulging briefcase. 'By the way . . . One little thing. While you're recovering here, you might like to look at these.' He tossed a handful of schematics on the bed.

Cole picked them up slowly. 'What's this?'

'Just a little thing I designed.' Sherikov arose and lumbered toward the door. 'We're realigning our political structure to eliminate any recurrence of the Reinhart affair. This will block any more one-man power grabs.' He jabbed a thick finger at the schematics. 'It'll turn power over to all of us, not to just a limited number one person could dominate – the way Reinhart dominated the Council.

'This gimmick makes it possible for citizens to raise and decide issues directly. They won't have to wait for the Council to verbalize a measure. Any citizen can transmit his will with one of these, make his needs register on a central control that automatically responds. When a large enough segment of the population wants a certain thing done, these little gadgets set up an active field that touches all the others. An issue won't have to go through a formal Council. The citizens can express their will long before any bunch of gray-haired old men could get around to it.'

Sherikov broke off, frowning. 'Of course,' he continued slowly, 'there's one little detail . . .'

'What's that?'

'I haven't been able to get a model to function. A few bugs . . . Such intricate work never was in my line.' He paused at the door. 'Well, I hope I'll see you again before you go. Maybe if you feel well enough later on we could get together for one last talk. Maybe have dinner sometime. Eh?'

But Thomas Cole wasn't listening. He was bent over the schematics, an intense frown on his weathered face. His long fingers moved restlessly over the schematics, tracing wiring and terminals. His lips moved as he calculated.

Sherikov waited a moment. Then he stepped out into the hall and softly closed the door after him.

He whistled merrily as he strode off down the corridor.

Paycheck

All at once he was in motion. Around him smooth jets hummed. He was on a small private rocket cruiser, moving leisurely across the afternoon sky, between cities.

'Ugh!' he said, sitting up in his seat and rubbing his head. Beside him Earl Rethrick was staring keenly at him, his eyes bright.

'Coming around?'

'Where are we?' Jennings shook his head, trying to clear the dull ache. 'Or maybe I should ask that a different way.' Already, he could see that it was not late fall. It was spring. Below the cruiser the fields were green. The last thing he remembered was stepping into an elevator with Rethrick. And it was late fall. And in New York.

'Yes,' Rethrick said. 'It's almost two years later. You'll find a lot of things have changed. The Government fell a few months ago. The new Government is even stronger. The SP, Security Police, have almost unlimited power. They're teaching the schoolchildren to inform, now. But we all saw that coming. Let's see, what else? New York is larger. I understand they've finished filling in San Francisco Bay.'

'What I want to know is what the hell I've been doing the last two years!' Jennings lit a cigarette nervously, pressing the strike end. 'Will you tell me that?'

'No. Of course I won't tell you that.'

'Where are we going?'

'Back to the New York Office. Where you first met me. Remember? You probably remember it better than I. After all, it was just a day or so ago for you.'

Jennings nodded. Two years! Two years out of his life, gone forever. It didn't seem possible. He had still been considering, debating, when he stepped into the elevator. Should he change his mind? Even if he were getting that much money – and it was a lot, even for him – it didn't really seem worth it. He would always wonder what work he had been doing. Was it legal? Was it— But that was past speculation, now. Even while he was trying to make up his mind the curtain had fallen. He looked ruefully out the window at the afternoon sky. Below, the earth was moist and alive. Spring, spring two years later. And what did he have to show for the two years?

'Have I been paid?' he asked. He slipped his wallet out and glanced into it. 'Apparently not.'

'No. You'll be paid at the Office. Kelly will pay you.'

'The whole works at once?'

'Fifty thousand credits.'

Jennings smiled. He felt a little better, now that the sum had been spoken aloud. Maybe it wasn't so bad, after all. Almost like being paid to sleep. But he was two years older; he had just that much less to live. It was like selling part of himself, part of his life. And life was worth plenty, these days. He shrugged. Anyhow, it was in the past.

'We're almost there,' the older man said. The robot pilot dropped the cruiser down, sinking toward the ground. The edge of New York City became visible below them. 'Well, Jennings, I may never see you again.' He held out his hand. 'It's been a pleasure working with you. We did work together, you know. Side by side. You're one of the best mechanics I've ever seen. We were right in hiring you, even at that salary. You paid us back many times – although you don't realize it.'

'I'm glad you got your money's worth.'

'You sound angry.'

'No. I'm just trying to get used to the idea of being two years older.'

Rethrick laughed. 'You're still a very young man. And you'll feel better when she gives you your pay.'

They stepped out onto the tiny rooftop field of the New York office building. Rethrick led him over to an elevator. As the doors slid shut Jennings got a mental shock. This was the last thing he remembered, this elevator. After that he had blacked out.

'Kelly will be glad to see you,' Rethrick said, as they came out into a lighted hall. 'She asks about you, once in a while.'

'Why?'

'She says you're good-looking.' Rethrick pushed a code key against a door. The door responded, swinging wide. They entered the luxurious office of Rethrick Construction. Behind a long mahogany desk a young woman was sitting, studying a report.

'Kelly,' Rethrick said, 'look whose time finally expired.'

The girl looked up, smiling. 'Hello, Mr Jennings. How does it feel to be back in the world?'

'Fine.' Jennings walked over to her. 'Rethrick says you're the paymaster.'

Rethrick clapped Jennings on the back. 'So long, my friend. I'll go back to the plant. If you ever need a lot of money in a hurry come around and we'll work out another contract with you.'

Jennings nodded. As Rethrick went back out he sat down beside the desk, crossing his legs. Kelly slid a drawer open, moving her chair back. 'All right. Your time is up, so Rethrick Construction is ready to pay. Do you have your copy of the contract?'

Jennings took an envelope from his pocket and tossed it on the desk. 'There it is.'

Kelly removed a small cloth sack and some sheets of handwritten paper from the desk drawer. For a time she read over the sheets, her small face intent.

'What is it?'

'I think you're going to be surprised.' Kelly handed him his contract back. 'Read that over again.'

'Why?' Jennings unfastened the envelope.

'There's an alternate clause. "If the party of the second part so desires, at any time during his time of contract to the aforesaid Rethrick Construction Company—"'

'"If he so desires, instead of the monetary sum specified, he may choose instead, according to his own wish, articles or products which, in his own opinion, are of sufficient value to stand in lieu of the sum—"'

Jennings snatched up the cloth sack, pulling it open. He poured the contents into his palm. Kelly watched.

'Where's Rethrick?' Jennings stood up. 'If he has an idea that this—'

'Rethrick has nothing to do with it. It was your own request. Here, look at this.' Kelly passed him the sheets of paper. 'In your own hand. Read them. It was your idea, not ours. Honest.' She smiled up at him. 'This happens every once in a while with people we take on contract. During their time they decide to take something else instead of money. Why, I don't know. But they come out with their minds clean, having agreed—'

Jennings scanned the pages. It was his own writing. There was no doubt of it. His hands shook. 'I can't believe it. Even if it is my own writing.' He folded up the paper, his jaw set. 'Something was done to me while I was back there. I never would have agreed to this.'

'You must have had a reason. I admit it doesn't make sense. But you don't know what factors might have persuaded you, before your mind was cleaned. You aren't the first. There have been several others before you.'

Jennings stared down at what he held in his palm. From the cloth sack he had spilled a little assortment of items. A code key. A ticket stub. A parcel receipt. A length of fine wire. Half a poker chip, broken across. A green strip of cloth. A bus token.

'This, instead of fifty thousand credits,' he murmured. 'Two years . . .'

He went out of the building, onto the busy afternoon street. He was still dazed, dazed and confused. Had he been swindled? He felt in his pocket for the little trinkets, the wire, the ticket stub, all the rest. *That*, for two years of work! But he had seen his own handwriting, the statement of waiver, the request for the substitution. Like Jack and the Beanstalk. Why? What for? What had made him do it?

He turned, starting down the sidewalk. At the corner he stopped for a surface cruiser that was turning.

'All right, Jennings. Get in.'

His head jerked up. The door of the cruiser was open. A man was kneeling, pointing a heat–rifle straight at his face. A man in blue–green. The Security Police.

Jennings got in. The door closed, magnetic locks slipping into place behind him. Like a vault. The cruiser glided off down the street. Jennings sank back against the seat. Beside him the SP man lowered his gun. On the other side a second officer ran his hands expertly over him, searching for weapons. He brought out Jennings' wallet and the handful of trinkets. The envelope and contract.

'What does he have?' the driver said.

'Wallet, money. Contract with Rethrick Construction. No weapons.' He gave Jennings back his things.

'What's this all about?' Jennings said.

'We want to ask you a few questions. That's all. You've been working for Rethrick?'

'Yes.'

'Two years?'

'Almost two years.'

'At the Plant?'

Jennings nodded. 'I suppose so.'

The officer leaned toward him. 'Where is that Plant, Mr Jennings. Where is it located?'

'I don't know.'

The two officers looked at each other. The first one moistened his lips, his face sharp and alert. 'You don't know? The next question. The last. In those two years, what kind of work did you do? What was your job?'

'Mechanic. I repaired electronic machinery.'

'What *kind* of electronic machinery?'

'I don't know.' Jennings looked up at him. He could not help smiling, his lips twisting ironically. 'I'm sorry, but I don't know. It's the truth.'

There was silence.

'What do you mean, you don't know? You mean you worked on machinery for two years without knowing what it was? Without even knowing where you were?'

Jennings roused himself. 'What is all this? What did you pick me up for? I haven't done anything. I've been—'

'We know. We're not arresting you. We only want to get information for our records. About Rethrick Construction. You've been working for them, in their Plant. In an important capacity. You're an electronic mechanic?'

'Yes.'

'You repair high-quality computers and allied equipment?' The officer consulted his notebook. 'You're considered one of the best in the country, according to this.'

Jennings said nothing.

'Tell us the two things we want to know, and you'll be released at once. Where is Rethrick's Plant? What kind of work are they doing? You serviced their machines for them, didn't you? Isn't that right? For two years.'

'I don't know. I suppose so. I don't have any idea what I did during the two years. You can believe me or not.' Jennings stared wearily down at the floor.

'What'll we do?' the driver said finally. 'We have no instructions past this.'

'Take him to the station. We can't do any more questioning here.' Beyond the cruiser, men and women hurried along the sidewalk. The streets were choked with cruisers, workers going to their homes in the country.

'Jennings, why don't you answer us? What's the matter with you? There's no reason why you can't tell us a couple of simple things like that. Don't you want to cooperate with your Government? Why should you conceal information from us?'

'I'd tell you if I knew.'

The officer grunted. No one spoke. Presently the cruiser drew up before a great stone building. The driver turned the motor off, removing the control cap and putting it in his pocket. He touched the door with a code key, releasing the magnetic lock.

'What shall we do, take him in? Actually, we don't—'

'Wait.' The driver stepped out. The other two went with him, closing and locking the doors behind them. They stood on the pavement before the Security Station, talking.

Jennings sat silently, staring down at the floor. The SP wanted to know about Rethrick Construction. Well, there was nothing he could tell them. They had come to the wrong person, but how could he prove that? The whole thing was impossible. Two years wiped clean from his mind. Who would believe him? It seemed unbelievable to him, too.

His mind wandered, back to when he had first read the ad. It had hit home, hit him direct. *Mechanic wanted*, and a general outline of the work, vague, indirect, but enough to tell him that it was right up his line. And the pay! Interviews at the Office. Tests, forms. And then the gradual realization that Rethrick Construction was finding all about him while he knew nothing about them. What kind of work did they do? Construction, but what kind? What sort of machines did they have? Fifty thousand credits for two years . . .

And he had come out with his mind washed clean. Two years, and he remembered nothing. It took him a long time to agree to that part of the contract. But he *had* agreed.

Jennings looked out the window. The three officers were still talking on the sidewalk, trying to decide what to do with him. He was in a tough spot. They wanted information he couldn't give, information he didn't know. But how could he prove it? How could he prove that he had worked two years and come out knowing no more than when he had gone in! The SP would work him over. It would be a long time before they'd believe him, and by that time—

He glanced quickly around. Was there any escape? In a second they would be back. He touched the door. Locked, the triple-ring magnetic locks. He had worked on magnetic locks many times. He had even designed part of a trigger core. There was no way to open the doors without the right code key. No way, unless by some chance he could short out the lock. But with what?

He felt in his pockets. What could he use? If he could short the locks, blow them out, there was a faint chance. Outside, men and women were swarming by, on their way home from work. It was past five; the great office buildings were shutting down, the streets were alive with traffic. If he once got out they wouldn't dare fire. – If he could get out.

The three officers separated. One went up the steps into the Station building. In a second the others would reenter the cruiser. Jennings dug into his pocket, bringing out the code key, the ticket stub, the wire. The wire! Thin wire, thin as human hair. Was it insulated? He unwound it quickly. No.

He knelt down, running his fingers expertly across the surface of the door. At the edge of the lock was a thin line, a groove between the lock and the door. He brought the end of the wire up to it, delicately maneuvering the wire into the almost invisible space. The wire disappeared an inch or so. Sweat rolled down Jennings' forehead. He moved the wire a fraction of an inch, twisting it. He held his breath. The relay should be—

A flash.

Half blinded, he threw his weight against the door. The door fell open, the lock fused and smoking. Jennings tumbled into the street and leaped to his feet. Cruisers were all around him, honking and sweeping past. He ducked behind a lumbering truck, entering the middle lane of traffic. On the sidewalk he caught a momentary glimpse of the SP men starting after him.

A bus came along, swaying from side to side, loaded with shoppers and workers. Jennings caught hold of the back rail, pulling himself up onto the platform. Astonished faces loomed up, pale moons thrust suddenly at him. The robot conductor was coming toward him, whirring angrily.

'Sir—' the conductor began. The bus was slowing down. 'Sir, it is not allowed—'

'It's all right,' Jennings said. He was filled, all at once, with a strange elation. A moment ago he had been trapped, with no way to escape. Two years of his life had been lost for nothing. The Security Police had arrested him, demanding information he couldn't give. A hopeless situation! But now things were beginning to click in his mind.

He reached into his pocket and brought out the bus token. He put it calmly into the conductor's coin slot.

'Okay?' he said. Under his feet the bus wavered, the driver hesitating. Then the bus resumed pace, going on. The conductor turned away, its whirrs subsiding. Everything was all right. Jennings smiled. He eased past the standing people, looking for a seat, some place to sit down. Where he could think.

He had plenty to think about. His mind was racing.

The bus moved on, flowing with the restless stream of urban traffic. Jennings only half saw the people sitting around him. There was no doubt of it: he had not been swindled. It was on the level. The decision had actually been his. Amazingly, after two years of work he had preferred a handful of trinkets instead of fifty thousand credits. But more amazingly, the handful of trinkets were turning out to be worth more than the money.

With a piece of wire and a bus token he had escaped from the Security Police. That was worth plenty. Money would have been useless to him once he disappeared inside the great stone Station. Even fifty thousand credits wouldn't have helped him. And there were five trinkets left. He felt around in his pocket. Five more things. He had used two. The others – what were they for? Something as important?

But the big puzzle: how had *he* – his earlier self – known that a piece of wire and a bus token would save his life?' *He* had known, all right. Known in advance. But how? And the other five. Probably they were just as precious, or would be.

The *he* of those two years had known things that he did not know now, things that had been washed away when the company cleaned his mind. Like an adding machine which had been cleared. Everything was slate-clean. What *he* had known was gone, now. Gone, except for seven trinkets, five of which were still in his pocket.

But the real problem right now was not a problem of speculation. It was very concrete. The Security Police were looking for him. They had his name and description. There was no use thinking of going to his apartment – if he even still had an apartment. But where, then? Hotels? The SP combed them daily. Friends? That would mean putting them in jeopardy, along with him. It was only a question of time before the SP found him, walking along the street, eating in a restaurant, in a show, sleeping in some rooming house. The SP were everywhere.

Everywhere? Not quite. When an individual person was defenseless, a business was not. The big economic forces had managed to remain free, although virtually everything else had been absorbed by the Government. Laws that had been eased away from the private person still protected property and industry. The SP could pick up any given person, but they could not enter and seize a company, a business. That had been clearly established in the middle of the twentieth century.

Business, industry, corporations, were safe from the Security Police. Due process was required. Rethrick Construction was a target of SP interest, but they could do nothing until some statute was violated. If he could get back to the Company, get inside its doors, he would be safe. Jennings smiled grimly. The modern church, sanctuary. It was the Government against the corporation, rather than the State against the Church. The new Notre Dame of the world. Where the law could not follow.

Would Rethrick take him back? Yes, on the old basis. He had already said so. Another two years sliced from him, and then back onto the streets. Would that help him? He felt suddenly in his pocket. And there were the remaining trinkets. Surely *he* had intended them to be used! No, he could not go back to Rethrick and work another contract time. Something else was indicated. Something more permanent. Jennings pondered. Rethrick Construction. What did it construct? What had *he* known, found out, during those two years? And why were the SP so interested?

He brought out the five objects and studied them. The green strip of cloth. The code key. The ticket stub. The parcel receipt. The half poker chip. Strange, that little things like that could be important.

And Rethrick Construction was involved.

There was no doubt. The answer, all the answers, lay at Rethrick. But where *was* Rethrick? He had no idea where the plant was, no idea at all. He knew where the Office was, the big, luxurious room with the young woman and her desk. But that was not Rethrick Construction. Did anyone know, beside Rethrick? Kelly didn't know. Did the SP know?

It was out of town. That was certain. He had gone there by rocket.

It was probably in the United States, maybe in the farmlands, the country, between cities. What a hell of a situation! Any moment the SP might pick him up. The next time he might not get away. His only chance, his own real chance for safety, lay in reaching Rethrick. And his only chance to find out the things he had to know. The plant – a place where he had been, but which he could not recall. He looked down at the five trinkets. Would any of them help?

A burst of despair swept through him. Maybe it was just coincidence, the wire and the token. Maybe—

He examined the parcel receipt, turning it over and holding it up to the light. Suddenly his stomach muscles knotted. His pulse changed. He had been right. No, it was not a coincidence, the wire and the token. The parcel receipt was dated two days hence. The parcel, whatever it might be, had not even been deposited yet. Not for forty-eight more hours.

He looked at the other things. The ticket stub. What good was a ticket stub? It was creased and bent, folded over, again and again. He couldn't go anyplace with that. A stub didn't take you anywhere. It only told you where you had been.

Where you had been!

He bent down, peering at it, smoothing the creases. The printing had been torn through the middle. Only part of each word could be made out.

> PORTOLA T
> STUARTSVI
> IOW

He smiled. That was it. Where he had been. He could fill in the missing letters. It was enough. There was no doubt: *he* had foreseen this, too. Three of the seven trinkets used. Four left. Stuartsville, Iowa. Was there such a place? He looked out the window of the bus. The Intercity rocket station was only a block or so away. He could be there in a second. A quick sprint from the bus, hoping the Police wouldn't be there to stop him—

But somehow he knew they wouldn't. Not with the other four things in his pocket. And once he was on the rocket he would be safe. Intercity was big, big enough to keep free of the SP. Jennings put the remaining trinkets back into his pocket and stood up, pulling the bellcord.

A moment later he stepped gingerly out onto the sidewalk.

The rocket let him off at the edge of town, at a tiny brown field. A few disinterested porters moved about, stacking luggage, resting from the heat of the sun.

Jennings crossed the field to the waiting room, studying the people around him. Ordinary people, workmen, businessmen, housewives. Stuartsville was a small middle Western town. Truck drivers. High school kids.

He went through the waiting room, out onto the street. So this was where Rethrick's Plant was located – perhaps. If he had used the stub correctly. Anyhow, *something* was here, or *he* wouldn't have included the stub with the other trinkets.

Stuartsville, Iowa. A faint plan was beginning to form in the back of his mind, still vague and nebulous. He began to walk, his hands in his pockets, looking around him. A newspaper office, lunch counters, hotels, poolrooms, a barber shop, a television repair shop. A rocket sales store with huge showrooms of gleaming rockets. Family size. And at the end of the block the Portola Theater.

The town thinned out. Farms, fields. Miles of green country. In the sky above a few transport rockets lumbered, carrying farm supplies and equipment back and forth. A small, unimportant town. Just right for Rethrick Construction. The Plant would be lost here, away from the city, away from the SP.

Jennings walked back. He entered a lunchroom, BOB'S PLACE. A young man with glasses came over as he sat down at the counter, wiping his hands on his white apron.

'Coffee,' Jennings said.

'Coffee.' The man brought the cup. There were only a few people in the lunchroom. A couple of flies buzzed, against the window.

Outside in the street shoppers and farmers moved leisurely by.

'Say,' Jennings said, stirring his coffee. 'Where can a man get work around here? Do you know?'

'What kind of work?' The young man came back, leaning against the counter.

'Electrical wiring. I'm an electrician. Television, rockets, computers. That sort of stuff?'

'Why don't you try the big industrial areas? Detroit. Chicago. New York.'

Jennings shook his head. 'Can't stand the big cities. I never liked cities.'

The young man laughed. 'A lot of people here would be glad to work in Detroit. You're an electrician?'

'Are there any plants around here? Any repair shops or plants?'

'None that I know of.' The young man went off to wait on some men that had come in. Jennings sipped his coffee. Had he made a mistake? Maybe he should go back and forget about Stuartsville, Iowa. Maybe he had made the wrong inference from the ticket stub. But the ticket meant something, unless he was completely wrong about everything. It was a little late to decide that, though.

The young man came back. 'Is there *any* kind of work I can get here?' Jennings said. 'Just to tide me over.'

'There's always farm work.'

'How about the retail repair shops? Garages. TV.'

'There's a TV repair shop down the street. Maybe you might get something there. You could try. Farm work pays good. They can't get many men, anymore. Most men in the military. You want to pitch hay?'

Jennings laughed. He paid for his coffee. 'Not very much. Thanks.'

'Once in a while some of the men go up the road and work. There's some sort of Government station.'

Jennings nodded. He pushed the screen door open, stepping outside onto the hot sidewalk. He walked aimlessly for a time, deep in thought, turning his nebulous plan over and over. It was a good plan; it would solve everything, all his problems at once. But right now it hinged on one thing: finding Rethrick Construction. And he had only one clue, if it really was a clue. The ticket stub, folded and creased, in his pocket. And a faith that *he* had known what he was doing.

A Government station. Jennings paused, looking around him. Across the street was a taxi stand, a couple of cabbies sitting in their cabs, smoking and reading the newspaper. It was worth a try, at least. There wasn't much else to do. Rethrick would be something else, on the surface. If it posed as a Government project no one would ask any questions. They were all too accustomed to Government projects working without explanation, in secrecy.

He went over to the first cab. 'Mister,' he said, 'can you tell me something?'

The cabbie looked up. 'What do you want?'

'They tell me there's work to be had, out at the Government station. Is that right?'

The cabbie studied him. He nodded.

'What kind of work is it?'

'I don't know.'

'Where do they do the hiring?'

'I don't know.' The cabbie lifted his paper.

'Thanks.' Jennings turned away.

'They don't do any hiring. Maybe once in a long while. They don't take many on. You better go someplace else if you're looking for work.'

'All right.'

The other cabbie leaned out of his cab. 'They use only a few day laborers, buddy. That's all. And they're very choosy. They don't hardly let anybody in. Some kind of war work.'

Jennings pricked up his ears. 'Secret?'

'They come into town and pick up a load of construction workers. Maybe a truck full. That's all. They're real careful who they pick.'

Jennings walked back toward the cabbie. 'That right?'

'It's a big place. Steel wall. Charged. Guards. Work going on day and night. But nobody gets in. Set up on top of a hill, out the old Henderson Road. About two miles and a half.' The cabbie poked at his shoulder. 'You can't get in unless you're identified. They identify their laborers, after they pick them out. You know.'

Jennings stared at him. The cabbie was tracing a line on his shoulder. Suddenly Jennings understood. A flood of relief rushed over him.

'Sure,' he said. 'I understand what you mean. At least, I think so.' He reached into his pocket, bringing out the four trinkets. Carefully, he unfolded the strip of green cloth, holding it up. 'Like this?'

The cabbies stared at the cloth. 'That's right,' one of them said slowly, staring at the cloth. 'Where did you get it?'

Jennings laughed. 'A friend.' He put the cloth back in his pocket. 'A friend gave it to me.'

He went off, toward the Intercity field. He had plenty to do, now that the first step was over. Rethrick was here, all right. And apparently the trinkets were going to see him through. One for every crisis. A pocketful of miracles, from someone who knew the future!

But the next step couldn't be done alone. He needed help. Somebody else was needed for this part. But who? He pondered, entering the Intercity waiting room. There was only one person he could possibly go to. It was a long chance, but he had to take it. He couldn't work alone, here on out. If the Rethrick plant was here then Kelly would be too . . .

The street was dark. At the corner a lamppost cast a fitful beam. A few cruisers moved by.

From the apartment building entrance a slim shape came, a young woman in a coat, a purse in her hand. Jennings watched as she passed under the streetlamp. Kelly McVane was going someplace, probably to a party. Smartly dressed, high heels tap-tapping on the pavement, a little coat and hat.

He stepped out behind her. 'Kelly.'

She turned quickly, her mouth open. 'Oh!'

Jennings took her arm. 'Don't worry. It's just me. Where are you going, all dressed up?'

'No place.' She blinked. 'My golly, you scared me. What is it? What's going on?'

'Nothing. Can you spare a few minutes? I want to talk to you.'

Kelly nodded. 'I guess so.' She looked around. 'Where'll we go?'

'Where's a place we can talk? I don't want anyone to overhear us.'

'Can't we just walk along?'

'No. The Police.'

'The Police?'

'They're looking for me.'

'For you? But why?'

'Let's not stand here,' Jennings said grimly. 'Where can we go?'

Kelly hesitated. 'We can go up to my apartment. No one's there.'

They went up to the elevator. Kelly unlocked the door, pressing the code key against it. The door swung open and they went inside, the heater and lights coming on automatically at her step. She closed the door and took off her coat.

'I won't stay long.' Jennings said.

'That's all right. I'll fix you a drink.' She went into the kitchen. Jennings sat down on the couch, looking around at the neat little apartment. Presently the girl came back. She sat down beside him and Jennings took his drink. Scotch and water, cold.

'Thanks.'

Kelly smiled. 'Not at all.' The two of them sat silently for a time.

'Well?' she said at last. 'What's this all about? Why are the Police looking for you?'

'They want to find out about Rethrick Construction. I'm only a pawn in this. They think I know something because I worked two years at Rethrick's Plant.'

'But you don't!'

'I can't prove that.'

Kelly reached out, touching Jennings' head, just above the ear. 'Feel there. That spot.'

Jennings reached up. Above his ear, under the hair, was a tiny hard spot. 'What is it?'

'They burned through the skull there. Cut a tiny wedge from the brain. All your memories of the two years. They located them and burned them out. The SP couldn't possibly make you remember. It's gone. You don't have it.'

'By the time they realize that there won't be much left of me.'

Kelly said nothing.

'You can see the spot I'm in. It would be better for me if I did remember. Then I could tell them and they'd—'

'And destroy Rethrick!'

Jennings shrugged. 'Why not? Rethrick means nothing to me. I don't even know what they're doing. And why are the Police so interested? From the very start, all the secrecy, cleaning my mind—'

'There's reason. Good reason.'

'Do you know why?'

'No.' Kelly shook her head. 'But I'm sure there's a reason. If the SP are interested, there's reason.' She set down her drink, turning toward him. 'I hate the Police. We all do, every one of us. They're after us all the time. I don't know anything about Rethrick. If I did my life wouldn't be safe. There's not much standing between Rethrick and them. A few laws, a handful of laws. Nothing more.'

'I have the feeling Rethrick is a great deal more than just another construction company the SP wants to control.'

'I suppose it is. I really don't know. I'm just a receptionist. I've never been to the Plant. I don't even know where it is.'

'But you wouldn't want anything to happen to it.'

'Of course not! They're fighting the Police. Anyone that's fighting the Police is on our side.'

'Really? I've heard that kind of logic before. Anyone fighting communism was automatically good, a few decades ago. Well, time will tell. As far as I'm concerned I'm an individual caught between two ruthless forces. Government and business. The Government has men and wealth. Rethrick Construction has its technocracy. What they've done with it, I don't know. I did, a few weeks ago. All I have now is a faint glimmer, a few references. A theory.'

Kelly glanced at him. 'A theory?'

'And my pocketful of trinkets. Seven. Three or four now. I've used some. They're the basis of my theory. If Rethrick is doing what I think it's doing, I can understand the SP's interest. As a matter of fact, I'm beginning to share their interest.'

'What is Rethrick doing?'

'It's developed a time scoop.'

'What?'

'A time scoop. It's been theoretically possible for several years. But it's illegal to experiment with time scoops and mirrors. It's a felony, and if you're caught, all your equipment and data becomes the property of the Government.' Jennings smiled crookedly. 'No wonder the Government's interested. If they can catch Rethrick with the goods—'

'A time scoop. It's hard to believe.'

'Don't you think I'm right?'

'I don't know. Perhaps. Your trinkets. You're not the first to come out with a little cloth sack of odds and ends. You've used some? How?'

'First, the wire and the bus token. Getting away from the Police. It seems funny, but if I hadn't had them, I'd be there yet. A piece of wire and a ten-cent token. But I don't usually carry such things. That's the point.'

'Time travel.'

'No. Not time travel. Berkowsky demonstrated that time travel is impossible. This is a time scoop, a mirror to see and a scoop to pick up things. These trinkets. At least one of them is from the future. Scooped up. Brought back.'

'How do you know?'

'It's dated. The others, perhaps not. Things like tokens and wire belong to classes of things. Any one token is as good as another. There, *he* must have used a mirror.'

'*He?*'

'When I was working with Rethrick. I must have used the mirror. I looked into my own future. If I was repairing their equipment I could hardly keep from it! I must have looked ahead, seen what was coming. The SP picking me up. I must have seen that, and seen what a piece of thin wire and a bus token would do – if I had them with me at the exact moment.'

Kelly considered. 'Well? What do you want me for?'

'I'm not sure, now. Do you really look on Rethrick as a benevolent institution, waging war against the Police? A sort of Roland at Roncesvalles—'

'What does it matter how I feel about the Company?'

'It matters a lot.' Jennings finished his drink, pushing the glass aside. 'It matters a lot, because I want you to help me. I'm going to blackmail Rethrick Construction.'

Kelly stared at him.

'It's my one chance to stay alive, I've got to get a hold over Rethrick, a big hold. Enough of a hold so they'll let me in, on my own terms. There's no other place I can go. Sooner or later the Police are going to pick me up. If I'm not inside the Plant, and soon—'

'Help you blackmail the Company? Destroy Rethrick?'

'No. Not destroy. I don't want to destroy it – my life depends on the Company. My life depends on Rethrick being strong enough to defy the SP. But if I'm on the *outside* it doesn't much matter how strong Rethrick is. Do you see? I want to get in. I want to get inside before it's too late. And I want in on my own terms, not as a two-year worker who gets pushed out again afterward.'

'For the Police to pick up.'

Jennings nodded. 'Exactly.'

'How are you going to blackmail the Company?'

'I'm going to enter the Plant and carry out enough material to prove Rethrick is operating a time scoop.'

Kelly laughed. 'Enter the Plant? Let's see you *find* the Plant. The SP have been looking for it for years.'

'I've already found it.' Jennings leaned back, lighting a cigarette. 'I've located it with my trinkets. And I have four left, enough to get me inside, I think. And to get me what I want. I'll be able to carry out enough papers and photographs to hang Rethrick. But I don't want to hang Rethrick. I only want to bargain. That's where you come in.'

'I?'

'You can be trusted not to go to the Police. I need someone I can turn the material over to. I don't dare keep it myself. As soon as I have it I must turn it over to someone else, someone who'll hide it where I won't be able to find it.'

'Why?'

'Because,' Jennings said calmly, 'any minute the SP may pick me up. I have no love for Rethrick, but I don't want to scuttle it. That's why you've got to help me. I'm going to turn the information over to you, to hold, while I bargain with Rethrick. Otherwise I'll have to hold it myself. And if I have it on me—'

He glanced at her. Kelly was staring at the floor, her face tense. Set.

'Well? What do you say? Will you help me, or shall I take the chance the SP won't pick me up with the material? Data enough to destroy Rethrick. Well? Which will it be? Do you want to see Rethrick destroyed? What's your answer?'

The two of them crouched, looking across the fields at the hill beyond. The hill rose up, naked and brown, burned clean of vegetation. Nothing grew on its sides. Halfway up a long steel fence twisted, topped with charged barbed wire. On the other side a guard walked slowly, a tiny figure patrolling with a rifle and helmet.

At the top of the hill lay an enormous concrete block, a towering structure without windows or doors. Mounted guns caught the early morning sunlight, glinting in a row along the roof of the building.

'So that's the Plant,' Kelly said softly.

'That's it. It would take an army to get up there, up that hill and over the fence. Unless they were allowed in.' Jennings got to his feet, helping Kelly up. They walked back along the path, through the trees, to where Kelly had parked the cruiser.

'Do you really think your green cloth band will get you in?' Kelly said, sliding behind the wheel.

'According to the people in the town, a truckload of laborers will be brought in to the Plant sometime this morning. The truck is unloaded at the entrance and the men examined. If everything's in order they're let inside the grounds, past the fence. For construction work, manual labor. At the end of the day they're let out again and driven back to town.'

'Will that get you close enough?'

'I'll be on the other side of the fence, at least.'

'How will you get to the time scoop? That must be inside the building, some place.'

Jennings brought out a small code key. 'This will get me in. I hope. I assume it will.'

Kelly took the key, examining it. 'So that's one of your trinkets. We should have taken a better look inside your little cloth bag.'

'We?'

'The Company. I saw several little bags of trinkets pass out, through my hands. Rethrick never said anything.'

'Probably the Company assumed no one would ever want to get back inside again.' Jennings took the code key from her. 'Now, do you know what you're supposed to do?'

'I'm supposed to stay here with the cruiser until you get back. You're to give me the material. Then I'm to carry it back to New York and wait for you to contact me.'

'That's right.' Jennings studied the distant road, leading through the trees to the Plant gate. 'I better get down there. The truck may be along any time.'

'What if they decide to count the number of workers?'

'I'll have to take the chance. But I'm not worried. I'm sure *he* foresaw everything.'

Kelly smiled. 'You and your friend, your helpful friend. I hope *he* left you enough things to get you out again, after you have the photographs.'

'Do you?'

'Why not?' Kelly said easily. 'I always liked you. You know that. You knew when you came to me.'

Jennings stepped out of the cruiser. He had on overalls and work-shoes, and a gray sweatshirt. 'I'll see you later. If everything goes all right. I think it will.' He patted his pocket. 'With my charms here, my good-luck charms.'

He went off through the trees, walking swiftly.

The trees led to the very edge of the road. He stayed with them, not coming out into the open. The Plant guards were certainly scanning the hillside. They had burned it clean, so that anyone trying to creep up to the fence would be spotted at once. And he had seen infrared searchlights.

Jennings crouched low, resting against his heels, watching the road. A few yards up the road was a roadblock, just ahead of the gate. He examined his watch. Ten thirty. He might have a wait, a long wait. He tried to relax.

It was after eleven when the great truck came down the road, rumbling and wheezing.

Jennings came to life. He took out the strip of green cloth and fastened it around his arm. The truck came closer. He could see its load now. The back was full of workmen, men in jeans and workshirts, bounced and jolted as the truck moved along. Sure enough, each had an arm band like his own, a swathe of green around his upper arm. So far so good.

The truck came slowly to a halt, stopping at the roadblock. The men got down slowly onto the road, sending up a cloud of dust into the hot midday sun. They slapped the dust from their jeans, some of them lighting cigarettes. Two guards came leisurely from behind the roadblock. Jennings tensed. In a moment it would be time. The guards moved among the men, examining them, their arm bands, their faces, looking at the identification tabs of a few.

The roadblock slid back. The gate opened. The guards returned to their positions.

Jennings slid forward, slithering through the brush, toward the road. The men were stamping out their cigarettes, climbing back up into the truck. The truck was gunning its motor, the driver releasing the brakes. Jennings dropped onto the road, behind the truck. A rattle of leaves and dirt showered after him. Where he had landed, the view of the guards was cut off by the truck. Jennings held his breath. He ran toward the back of the truck.

The men stared at him curiously as he pulled himself up among them, his chest rising and falling. Their faces were weathered, gray and lined. Men of the soil. Jennings took his place between two burly farmers as the truck started up. They did not seem to notice him. He had rubbed dirt into his skin, and let his beard grow for a day. A quick glance he didn't look much different from the others. But if anyone made a count—

The truck passed through the gate, into the grounds. The gate slid shut behind. Now they were going up, up the steep side of the hill, the truck rattling and swaying from side to side. The vast concrete structure loomed nearer. Were they going to enter it? Jennings watched, fascinated. A thin high door was sliding back, revealing a dark interior. A row of artificial lights gleamed.

The truck stopped. The workmen began to get down again. Some mechanics came around them.

'What's this crew for?' one of them asked.

'Digging. Inside.' Another jerked a thumb. 'They're digging again. Send them inside.'

Jennings's heart thudded. He was going inside! He felt at his neck. There, inside the gray sweater, a flatplate camera hung like a bib around his neck. He could scarcely feel it, even knowing it was there. Maybe this would be less difficult than he had thought.

The workmen pushed through the door on foot, Jennings with them. They were in an immense workroom, long benches with half-completed machinery, booms and cranes, and the constant roar of work. The door closed after them, cutting them off from outside. He was in the Plant. But where was the time scoop, and the mirror?

'This way,' a foreman said. The workmen plodded over to the right. A freight lift rose to meet them from the bowels of the building. 'You're going down below. How many of you have experience with drills?'

A few hands went up.

'You can show the others. We are moving earth with drills and eaters. Any of you work eaters?'

No hands. Jennings glanced at the worktables. Had he worked here, not so long ago? A sudden chill went through him. Suppose he were recognized? Maybe he had worked with these very mechanics.

'Come on,' the foreman said impatiently. 'Hurry up.'

Jennings got into the freight lift with the others. A moment later they began to descend, down the black tube. Down, down, into the lower levels of the Plant. Rethrick Construction was *big*, a lot bigger than it looked above ground. A lot bigger than he had imagined. Floors, underground levels, flashing past one after the other.

The elevator stopped. The doors opened. He was looking down a long corridor. The floor was thick with stone dust. The air was moist. Around him, the workmen began to crowd out. Suddenly Jennings stiffened, pulling back.

At the end of the corridor before a steel door, was Earl Rethrick. Talking to a group of technicians.

'All out,' the foreman said. 'Let's go.'

Jennings left the elevator, keeping behind the others. Rethrick! His heart beat dully. If Rethrick saw him he was finished. He felt in his pockets. He had a miniature Boris gun, but it wouldn't be much use if he was discovered. Once Rethrick saw him it would be all over.

'Down this way.' The foreman led them toward what seemed to be an underground railway, to one side of the corridor. The men were getting into metal cars along a track. Jennings watched Rethrick. He saw him gesture angrily, his voice coming faintly down the hall. Suddenly Rethrick turned. He held up his hand and the great steel door behind him opened.

Jennings's heart almost stopped beating.

There, beyond the steel door, was the time scoop. He recognized it at once. The mirror. The long metal rods, ending in claws. Like Berkowsky's theoretical model – only this was real.

Rethrick went into the room, the technicians following behind him. Men were working at the scoop, standing all around it. Part of the shield was off. They were digging into the works. Jennings stared, hanging back.

'Say you—' the foreman said, coming toward him. The steel door shut. The view was cut off. Rethrick, the scoop, the technicians, were gone.

'Sorry,' Jennings murmured.

'You know you're not supposed to be curious around here.' The foreman was studying him intently. 'I don't remember you. Let me see your tab.'

'My tab?'

'Your identification tab.' The foreman turned away. 'Bill, bring me the board.' He looked Jennings up and down. 'I'm going to check you from the board, mister. I've never seen you in the crew before. Stay here.' A man was coming from a side door with a check board in his hands.

It was now or never.

Jennings sprinted, down the corridor, toward the great steel door. Behind there was a startled shout, the foreman and his helper. Jennings whipped out the code key, praying fervently as he ran. He came up to the door, holding out the key. With the other hand he brought out the Boris gun. Beyond the door was the time scoop. A few photographs, some schematics snatched up, and then, if he could get out—

The door did not move. Sweat leaped out on his face. He knocked he key against the door. Why didn't it open? Surely— He began to shake, panic rising up in him. Down the corridor people were coming, racing after him. Open—

But the door did not open. The key he held in his hand was the wrong key.

He was defeated. The door and the key did not match. Either *he* had been wrong, or the key was to be used someplace else. But where? Jennings looked frantically around. Where? Where could he go?

To one side a door was half open, a regular bolt-lock door. He crossed the corridor, pushing it open. He was in a storeroom of some sort. He slammed the door, throwing the bolt. He could hear them outside, confused, calling for guards. Soon armed guards would be along. Jennings held the Boris gun tightly, gazing around. Was he trapped? Was there a second way out?

He ran through the room, pushing among bales and boxes, towering stacks of silent cartons, end on end. At the rear was an emergency hatch. He opened it immediately. An impulse came to throw the code key away. What good had it been? But surely *he* had known what he was doing. *He* had already seen all this. Like God, it had already happened for *him*. Predetermined. *He* could not err. Or could he?

A chill went through him. Maybe the future was variable. Maybe this had been the right key, once. But not any more!

There were sounds behind him. They were melting the storeroom door. Jennings scrambled through the emergency hatch, into a low concrete passage, damp and ill lit. He ran quickly along it, turning corners. It was like a sewer. Other passages ran into it, from all sides.

He stopped. Which way? Where could he hide? The mouth of a major vent pipe gaped above his head. He caught hold and pulled himself up. Grimly, he eased his body onto it. They'd ignore a pipe, go on past. He crawled cautiously down the pipe. Warm air blew into his face. Why such a big vent? It implied an unusual chamber at the other end. He came to a metal grill and stopped.

And gasped.

He was looking into the great room, the room he had glimpsed beyond the steel door. Only now he was at the other end. There was the time scoop. And far down, beyond the scoop, was Rethrick, conferring at an active vidscreen. An alarm was sounding, whining shrilly, echoing everywhere. Technicians were running in all directions. Guards in uniform poured in and out of doors.

The scoop. Jennings examined the grill. It was slotted in place. He moved it laterally and it fell into his hands. No one was watching. He slid cautiously out, into the room, the Boris gun ready. He was fairly hidden behind the scoop, and the technicians and guards were all the way down at the other end of the room, where he had first seen them.

And there it was, all around him, the schematics, the mirror, papers, data, blueprints. He flicked his camera on. Against his chest the camera vibrated, film moving through it. He snatched up a handful of schematics. Perhaps *he* had used these very diagrams, a few weeks before!

He stuffed his pockets with papers. The film came to an end. But he was finished. He squeezed back into the vent, pushing through the mouth and down the tube. The sewerlike corridor was still empty, but there was an insistent drumming sound, the noise of voices and foot-steps. So many passages— They were looking for him in a maze of escape corridors.

Jennings ran swiftly. He ran on and on, without regard to direction, trying to keep along the main corridor. On all sides passages flocked off, one after another, countless passages. He was dropping down, lower and lower. Running downhill.

Suddenly he stopped, gasping. The sound behind him had died away for a moment. But there was a new sound, ahead. He went along slowly. The corridor twisted, turning to the right. He advanced slowly, the Boris gun ready.

Two guards were standing a little way ahead, lounging and talking together. Beyond them was a heavy code door. And behind him the sound of voices were coming again, growing louder. They had found the same passage he had taken. They were on the way.

Jennings stepped out, the Boris gun raised. 'Put up your hands. Let go of your guns.'

The guards gawked at him. Kids, boys with cropped blond hair and shiny uniforms. They moved back, pale and scared.

'The guns. Let them fall.'

The two rifles clattered down. Jennings smiled. Boys. Probably this was their first encounter with trouble. Their leather boots shone, brightly polished.

'Open the door,' Jennings said. 'I want through.'

They stared at him. Behind, the noise grew.

'Open it.' He became impatient. 'Come on.' He waved the pistol. 'Open it, damn it! Do you want me to—'

'We – we can't.'

'What?'

'We can't. It's a code door. We don't have the key. Honest, mister.

They don't let us have the key.' They were frightened. Jennings felt fear himself now. Behind him the drumming was louder. He was trapped, caught.

Or was he?

Suddenly he laughed. He walked quickly up to the door. 'Faith,' he murmured, raising his hand. 'That's something you should never lose.'

'What – what's that?'

'Faith in yourself. Self-confidence.'

The door slid back as he held the code key against it. Blinding sunlight streamed in, making him blink. He held the gun steady. He was outside, at the gate. Three guards gaped in amazement at the gun. He was at the gate – and beyond lay the woods.

'Get out of the way.' Jennings fired at the metal bars of the gate. The metal burst into flame, melting, a cloud of fire rising.

'Stop him!' From behind, men came pouring, guards, out of the corridor.

Jennings leaped through the smoking gate. The metal tore at him, searing him. He ran through the smoke, rolling and falling. He got to his feet and scurried on, into the trees.

He was outside. *He* had not let him down. The key had worked, all right. He had tried it first on the wrong door.

On and on he ran, sobbing for breath, pushing through the trees. Behind him the Plant and the voices fell away. He had the papers. And he was free.

He found Kelly and gave her the film and everything he had managed to stuff into his pockets. Then he changed back to his regular clothes. Kelly drove him to the edge of Stuartsville and left him off: Jennings watched the cruiser rise up into the air, heading toward New York. Then he went into town and boarded the Intercity rocket.

On the flight he slept, surrounded by dozing businessmen. When he awoke the rocket was settling down, landing at the huge New York spaceport.

Jennings got off, mixing with the flow of people. Now that he was back there was the danger of being picked up by the SP again. Two security officers in their green uniforms watched him impassively as he took a taxi at the field station. The taxi swept him into downtown traffic. Jennings wiped his brow. That was close. Now, to find Kelly.

He ate dinner at a small restaurant, sitting in the back away from the windows. When he emerged the sun was beginning to set. He walked slowly along the sidewalk, deep in thought.

So far so good. He had got the papers and film, and he had got away. The trinkets had worked every step along the way. Without them he would have been helpless. He felt in his pocket. Two left. The serrated half poker chip, and the parcel receipt. He took the receipt out, examining it in the fading evening light.

Suddenly he noticed something. The date on it was today's date. He had caught up with the slip.

He put it away, going on. What did it mean? What was it for? He shrugged. He would know, in time. And the half poker chip. What the hell was it for? No way to tell. In any case, he was certain to get through. *He* had got him by, up to now. Surely there wasn't much left.

He came to Kelly's apartment house and stopped, looking up. Her light was on. She was back; her fast little cruiser had beaten the Intercity rocket. He entered the elevator and rose to her floor.

'Hello,' he said, when she opened the door.

'You're all right?'

'Sure. Can I come in?'

He went inside. Kelly closed the door behind him. 'I'm glad to see you. The city's swarming with SP men. Almost every block. And the patrols—'

'I know. I saw a couple at the spaceport.' Jennings sat down on the couch. 'It's good to be back, though.'

'I was afraid they might stop all the Intercity flights and check through the passengers.'

'They have no reason to assume I'd be coming into the city.'

'I didn't think of that.' Kelly sat down across from him. 'Now, what comes next? Now that you have got away with the material, what are you going to do?'

'Next I meet Rethrick and spring the news on him. The news that the person who escaped from the Plant was myself. He knows that someone got away, but he doesn't know who it was. Undoubtedly, he assumes it was an SP man.'

'Couldn't he use the time mirror to find out?'

A shadow crossed Jennings' face. 'That's so. I didn't think of that.' He rubbed his jaw, frowning. 'In any case, I have the material. Or, you have the material.'

Kelly nodded.

'All right. We'll go ahead with our plans. Tomorrow we'll see Rethrick. We'll see him here, in New York. Can you get him down to the Office? Will he come if you send for him?'

'Yes. We have a code. If I ask him to come, he'll come.'

'Fine. I'll meet him there. When he realizes that we have the picture and schematics he'll have to agree to my demands. He'll have to let me into Rethrick Construction, on my own terms. It's either that, or face the possibility of having the material turned over to the Security Police.'

'And once you're in? Once Rethrick agrees to your demands?'

'I saw enough at the Plant to convince me that Rethrick is far bigger than I had realized. How big, I don't know. No wonder *he* was so interested!'

'You're going to demand equal control of the Company?'

Jennings nodded.

'You would never be satisfied to go back as a mechanic, would you? The way you were before.'

'No. To get booted out again?' Jennings smiled. 'Anyhow, I know *he* intended better things than that. *He* laid careful plans. The trinkets. He must have planned everything long in advance. No, I'm not going back as a mechanic. I saw a lot there, level after level of machines and men. They're doing something. And I want to be in on it.'

Kelly was silent.

'See?' Jennings said.

'I see.'

He left the apartment, hurrying along the dark street. He had stayed there too long. If the SP found the two of them together it would be all up with Rethrick Construction. He could take no chances, with the end almost in sight.

He looked at his watch. It was past midnight. He would meet Rethrick this morning, and present him with the proposition. His spirits rose as he walked. He would be safe. More than safe. Rethrick Construction was aiming at something far larger than mere industrial power. What he had seen had convinced him that a revolution was brewing. Down in the many levels below the ground, down under the fortress of concrete, guarded by guns and armed men, Rethrick was planning a war. Machines were being turned out. The time scoop and the mirror were hard at work, watching, dipping, extracting.

No wonder *he* had worked out such careful plans. *He* had seen all

196

this and understood, begun to ponder. The problem of the mind cleaning. His memory would be gone when he was released. Destruction of all the plans. Destruction? There was the alternate clause in the contract. Others had seen it, used it. But not the way *he* intended!

He was after much more than anyone who had come before. *He* was the first to understand, to plan. The seven trinkets were a bridge to something beyond anything that—

At the end of the block an SP cruiser pulled up to the curb. Its doors slid open.

Jennings stopped, his heart constricting. The night patrol, roaming through the city. It was after eleven, after curfew. He looked quickly around. Everything was dark. The stores and houses were shut up tight, locked for the night. Silent apartment houses, buildings. Even the bars were dark.

He looked back the way he had come. Behind him, a second SP cruiser had stopped. Two SP officers had stepped out onto the curb. They had seen him. They were coming toward him. He stood frozen, looking up and down the street.

Across from him was the entrance of a swank hotel, its neon sign glimmering. He began to walk toward it, his heels echoing against the pavement.

'Stop!' one of the SP men called. 'Come back here. What are you doing out? What's your—'

Jennings went up the stairs, into the hotel. He crossed the lobby. The clerk was staring at him. No one else was around. The lobby was deserted. His heart sank. He didn't have a chance. He began to run aimlessly, past the desk, along a carpeted hall. Maybe it led out some back way. Behind him, the SP men had already entered the lobby.

Jennings turned a corner. Two men stepped out, blocking his way.

'Where are you going?'

He stopped, wary. 'Let me by.' He reached into his coat for the Boris gun, At once the men moved.

'Get him.'

His arms were pinned to his sides. Professional hoods. Past them he could see light. Light and sound. Some kind of activity. People.

'All right,' one of the hoods said. They dragged him back along the corridor, toward the lobby. Jennings struggled futilely. He had entered a blind alley. Hoods, a joint. The city was dotted with them, hidden in the darkness. The swank hotel a front. They would toss him out, into the hands of the SP.

Some people came along the halls, a man and a woman. Older people. Well dressed. They gazed curiously at Jennings, suspended between the two men.

Suddenly Jennings understood. A wave of relief hit him, blinding him. 'Wait,' he said thickly. 'My pocket.'

'Come on.'

'Wait. Look. My right pocket. Look for yourselves.'

He relaxed, waiting. The hood on his right reached, dipping cautiously into the pocket. Jennings smiled. It was over. *He* had seen even this. There was no possibility of failure. This solved one problem: where to stay until it was time to meet Rethrick. He could stay here.

The hood brought out the half poker chip, examining the serrated edges. 'Just a second.' From his own coat he took a matching chip, fitting on a gold chain. He touched the edges together.

'All right?' Jennings said.

'Sure.' They let him go. He brushed off his coat automatically. 'Sure, mister. Sorry. Say, you should have—'

'Take me in the back,' Jennings said, wiping his face. 'Some people are looking for me. I don't particularly want them to find me.'

'Sure.' They led him back, into the gambling rooms. The half chip had turned what might have been a disaster into an asset. A gambling and girl joint. One of the few institutions the Police left alone. He was safe. No question of that. Only one thing remained. The struggle with Rethrick!

Rethrick's face was hard. He gazed at Jennings, swallowing rapidly.

'No,' he said. 'I didn't know it was you. We thought it was the SP.'

There was silence. Kelly sat at the chair by her desk, her legs crossed, a cigarette between her fingers. Jennings leaned against the door, his arms folded.

'Why didn't you use the mirror?' he said.

Rethrick's face flickered. 'The mirror? You did a good job, my friend. We *tried* to use the mirror.'

'Tried?'

'Before you finished your term with us you changed a few leads inside the mirror. When we tried to operate it nothing happened. I left the plant half an hour ago. They were still working on it.'

'I did that before I finished my two years?'

'Apparently you had worked out your plans in detail. You know that with the mirror we would have no trouble tracking you down. You're a good mechanic, Jennings. The best we ever had. We'd like to have you back, sometime. Working for us again. There's not one of us that can operate the mirror the way you could. And right now, we can't use it at all.'

Jennings smiled. 'I had no idea *he* did anything like that. I under-estimated him. *His* protection was even—'

'Who are you talking about?'

'Myself. During the two years. I use the objective. It's easier.'

'Well, Jennings. So the two of you worked out an elaborate plan to steal our schematics. Why? What's the purpose? You haven't turned them over to the Police.'

'No.'

'Then I can assume it's blackmail.'

'That's right.'

'What for? What do you want?' Rethrick seemed to have aged. He slumped, his eyes small and glassy, rubbing his chin nervously. 'You went to a lot of trouble to get us into this position. I'm curious why. While you were working for us you laid the groundwork. Now you've completed it, in spite of our precautions.'

'Precautions?'

'Erasing your mind. Concealing the Plant.'

'Tell him,' Kelly said. 'Tell him why you did it.'

Jennings took a deep breath. 'Rethrick, I did it to get back in. Back to the Company. That's the only reason. No other.'

Rethrick stared at him. 'To get back into the Company? You can come back in. I told you that.' His voice was thin and sharp, edged with strain. 'What's the matter with you? You can come back in. For as long as you want to stay.'

'As a mechanic.'

'Yes. As a mechanic. We employ many—'

'I don't want to come back as a mechanic. I'm not interested in working for you. Listen, Rethrick. The SP picked me up as soon as I left this Office. If it hadn't been for *him* I'd be dead.'

'They picked you up?'

'They wanted to know what Rethrick Construction does. They wanted me to tell them.'

Rethrick nodded. 'That's bad. We didn't know that.'

'No, Rethrick. I'm not coming in as an employee you can toss out any time it pleases you. I'm coming in with you, not for you.'

'With me?' Rethrick stared at him. Slowly a film settled over his face, an ugly hard film. 'I don't understand what you mean.'

'You and I are going to run Rethrick Construction together. That'll be the way, from now on. And no one will be burning my memory out, for their own safety.'

'That's what you want?'

'Yes.'

'And if we don't cut you in?'

'Then the schematics and films go to the SP. It's as simple as that. But I don't want to. I don't want to destroy the Company. I want to get into the Company! I want to be safe. You don't know what it's like, being out there, with no place to go. An individual has no place to turn to, anymore. No one to help him. He's caught between two ruthless forces, a pawn between political and economic powers. And I'm tired of being a pawn.'

For a long time Rethrick said nothing. He stared down at the floor, his face dull and blank. At last he looked up. 'I know it's that way. That's something I've known for a long time. Longer than you have. I'm a lot older than you. I've seen it come, grow that way, year after year. That's why Rethrick Construction exists. Someday, it'll be all different. Someday, when we have the scoop and the mirror finished. When the weapons are finished.'

Jennings said nothing.

'I know very well how it is! I'm an old man. I've been working a long time. When they told me someone had got out of the Plant with schematics, I thought the end had come. We already knew you had damaged the mirror. We knew there was a connection, but we had parts figured wrong.

'We thought, of course, that Security had planted you with us, to find out what we were doing. Then, when you realized you couldn't carry out your information, you damaged the mirror. With the mirror damaged, SP could go ahead and—'

He stopped, rubbing his cheek.

'Go on,' Jennings said.

'So you did this alone . . . Blackmail. To get into the Company. You don't know what the Company is for, Jennings! How dare you try to come in! We've been working and building for a long time. You'd wreck us, to save your hide. You'd destroy us, just to save yourself.'

'I'm not wrecking you. I can be a lot of help.'

'I run the Company alone. It's my Company. I made it, put it together. It's mine.'

Jennings laughed. 'And what happens when you die? Or is the revolution going to come in your own lifetime?'

Rethrick's head jerked up.

'You'll die, and there won't be anyone to go on. You know I'm a good mechanic. You said so yourself. You're a fool, Rethrick. You want to manage it all yourself. Do everything, decide everything. But you'll die, someday. And then what will happen?'

There was silence.

'You better let me in – for the Company's good, as well as my own. I can do a lot for you. When you're gone the Company will survive in my hands. And maybe the revolution will work.'

'You should be glad you're alive at all! If we hadn't allowed you to take your trinkets out with you—'

'What else could you do? How could you let men service your mirror, see their own futures, and not let them lift a finger to help themselves. It's easy to see why you were forced to insert the alternate-payment clause. You had no choice.'

'You don't even know what we are doing. Why we exist.'

'I have a good idea. After all, I worked for you two years.'

Time passed. Rethrick moistened his lips again and again, rubbing his cheek. Perspiration stood out on his forehead. At last he looked up.

'No,' he said. 'It's no deal. No one will ever run the Company but me. If I die, it dies with me. It's my property.'

Jennings became instantly alert. 'Then the papers go to the Police.'

Rethrick said nothing, but a peculiar expression moved across his face, an expression that gave Jennings a sudden chill.

'Kelly,' Jennings said. 'Do you have the papers with you?'

Kelly stirred, standing up. She put out her cigarette, her face pale. 'No.'

'Where are they? Where did you put them?'

'Sorry,' Kelly said softly. 'I'm not going to tell you.'

He stared at her. 'What?'

'I'm sorry,' Kelly said again. Her voice was small and faint. 'They're safe. The SP won't ever get them. But neither will you. When it's convenient, I'll turn them back to my father.'

'Your father!'

'Kelly is my daughter,' Rethrick said. 'That was one thing you didn't count on, Jennings. *He* didn't count on it, either. No one knew that but the two of us. I wanted to keep all positions of trust in the family. I see now that it was a good idea. But it had to be kept secret. If the SP had guessed they would have picked her up at once. Her life wouldn't have been safe.'

Jennings let his breath out slowly. 'I see.'

'It seemed like a good idea to go along with you,' Kelly said. 'Otherwise you'd have done it alone, anyhow. And you would have had the papers on you. As you said, if the SP caught you with the papers it would be the end of us. So I went along with you. As soon as you gave me the papers I put them in a good safe place.' She smiled a little. 'No one will find them but me. I'm sorry.'

'Jennings, you can come in with us,' Rethrick said. 'You can work for us forever, if you want. You can have anything you want. Anything except—'

'Except that no one runs the Company but you.'

'That's right. Jennings, the Company is old. Older than I am. I didn't bring it into existence. It was – you might say, *willed* to me. I took the burden on. The job of managing it, making it grow, moving it toward the day. The day of revolution, as you put it.

'My grandfather founded the Company, back in the twentieth century. The Company has always been in the family. And it will always be. Someday, when Kelly marries, there'll be an heir to carry it on after me. So that's taken care of. The Company was founded up in Maine, in a small New England town. My grandfather was a little old New Englander, frugal, honest, passionately independent. He had a little repair business of some sort, a little tool and fix-it place. And plenty of knack.

'When he saw government and big business closing in on everyone, he went underground. Rethrick Construction disappeared from the map. It took government quite a while to organize Maine, longer than most places. When the rest of the world had been divided up between international cartels and world-states, there was New England, still alive. Still free. And my grandfather and Rethrick Construction.

'He brought in a few men, mechanics, doctors, lawyers, little once-a–week newspapermen from the Middle West. The Company grew. Weapons appeared, weapons and knowledge. The time scoop and mirror! The Plant was built, secretly, at great cost, over a long period of time. The Plant is big. Big and deep. It goes down many more levels than you saw. *He* saw them, your alter ego. There's a lot of power there. Power, and men who've disappeared, purged all over the world, in fact. We got them first, the best of them.

'Someday, Jennings, we're going to break out. You see, conditions like this can't go on. People can't live this way, tossed back and forth by political and economic powers. Masses of people shoved this way and that according to the needs of this government or that cartel. There's going to be resistance, someday. A strong, desperate resistance. Not by big people, powerful people, but by little people. Bus drivers. Grocers. Vidscreen operators. Waiters. And that's where the Company comes in.

'We're going to provide them with the help they'll need, the tools, weapons, the knowledge. We're going to "sell" them our services. They'll be able to hire us. And they'll need someone they can hire. They'll have a lot lined up against them. A lot of wealth and power.'

There was silence.

'Do you see?' Kelly said. 'That's why you mustn't interfere. It's Dad's Company. It's always been that way. That's the way Maine people are. It's part of the family. The Company belongs to the family. It's ours.'

'Come in with us,' Rethrick said. 'As a mechanic. I'm sorry, but that's our limited outlook showing through. Maybe it's narrow, but we've always done things this way.'

Jennings said nothing. He walked slowly across the office, his hands in his pockets. After a time he raised the blind and stared out at the street, far below.

Down below, like a tiny black bug, a Security cruiser moved along, drifting silently with the traffic that flowed up and down the street. It joined a second cruiser, already parked. Four SP men were standing by it in their green uniforms, and even as he watched some more could be seen coming from across the street. He let the blind down.

'It's a hard decision to make,' he said.

'If you go out there they'll get you,' Rethrick said. 'They're out there all the time. You haven't got a chance.'

'Please—' Kelly said, looking up at him.

203

Suddenly Jennings smiled. 'So you won't tell me where the papers are. Where you put them.'

Kelly shook her head.

'Wait.' Jennings reached into his pocket. He brought out a small piece of paper. He unfolded it slowly, scanning it. 'By any chance did you deposit it with the Dunne National Bank, about three o'clock yesterday afternoon? For safekeeping in their storage vaults?'

Kelly gasped. She grabbed her handbag, unsnapping it. Jennings put the slip of paper, the parcel receipt, back in his pocket. 'So *he* saw even that,' he murmured. 'The last of the trinkets. I wondered what it was for.'

Kelly groped frantically in her purse, her face wild. She brought out a slip of paper, waving it.

'You're wrong! Here it is! It's still here.' She relaxed a little. 'I don't know what *you* have, but this is—'

In the air above them something moved. A dark space formed, a circle. The space stirred. Kelly and Rethrick stared up, frozen.

From the dark circle a claw appeared, a metal claw, joined to a shimmering rod. The claw dropped, swinging in a wide arc. The claw swept the paper from Kelly's fingers. It hesitated for a second. Then it drew itself up again, disappearing with the paper, into the circle of black. Then, silently, the claw and the rod and the circle blinked out. There was nothing. Nothing at all.

'Where — where did it go?' Kelly whispered. 'The paper. What was that?'

Jennings patted his pocket. 'It's safe. It's safe, right here. I wondered when *he* would show up. I was beginning to worry.'

Rethrick and his daughter stood, shocked into silence.

'Don't look so unhappy,' Jennings said. He folded his arms. 'The paper's safe — and the Company's safe. When the time comes it'll be there, strong and very glad to help out the revolution. We'll see to that, all of us, you, me and your daughter.'

He glanced at Kelly, his eyes twinkling. 'All three of us. And maybe by that time there'll be even *more* members to the family!'

Adjustment Team

It was bright morning. The sun shone down on the damp lawns and sidewalks, reflecting off the sparkling parked cars. The Clerk came walking hurriedly, leafing through his instructions, flipping pages and frowning. He stopped in front of the small green stucco house for a moment, and then turned up the walk, entering the back yard.

The dog was asleep inside his shed, his back turned to the world. Only his thick tail showed.

'For heaven's sake,' the Clerk exclaimed, hands on his hips. He tapped his mechanical pencil noisily against his clipboard. 'Wake up, you in there.'

The dog stirred. He came slowly out of his shed, head first, blinking and yawning in the morning sunlight 'Oh, it's you. Already?' He yawned again.

'Big doings.' The Clerk ran his expert finger down the traffic-control sheet. 'They're adjusting Sector T137 this morning. Starting at exactly nine o'clock.' He glanced at his pocket watch. 'Three hour alteration. Will finish by noon.'

'T137? That's not far from here.'

The Clerk's thin lips twisted with contempt. 'Indeed. You're showing astonishing perspicacity, my black-haired friend. Maybe you can divine why I'm here.'

'We overlap with T137.'

'Exactly. Elements from this Sector are involved. We must make sure they're properly placed when the adjustment begins.' The Clerk glanced toward the small green stucco house. 'Your particular task concerns the man in there. He is employed by a business establishment lying within Sector T137. It's essential that he be there before nine o'clock.'

The dog studied the house. The shades had been let up. The kitchen light was on. Beyond the lace curtains dim shapes could be seen, stirring around the table. A man and woman. They were drinking coffee.

'There they are,' the dog murmured. 'The man, you say? He's not going to be harmed, is he?'

'Of course not. But he must be at his office early. Usually he doesn't leave until after nine. Today he must leave at eight-thirty. He must be within Sector T137 before the process begins, or he won't be altered to coincide with the new adjustment.'

The dog sighed. 'That means I have to summon.'

'Correct.' The Clerk checked his instruction sheet. 'You're to summon at precisely eight-fifteen. You've got that? Eight-fifteen. No later.'

'What will an eight-fifteen summons bring?'

The Clerk flipped open his instruction book, examining the code columns. 'It will bring A Friend with a Car. To drive him to work early.' He closed the book and folded his arms, preparing to wait. 'That way he'll get to his office almost an hour ahead of time. Which is vital.'

'Vital,' the dog murmured. He lay down, half inside his shed. His eyes closed 'Vital.'

'Wake up! This must be done exactly on time. If you summon too soon or too late—'

The dog nodded sleepily. 'I know. I'll do it right. I *always* do it right.'

Ed Fletcher poured more cream in his coffee. He sighed, leaning back in his chair. Behind him the oven hissed softly, filling the kitchen with warm fumes. The yellow overhead light beamed down.

'Another roll?' Ruth asked.

'I'm full.' Ed sipped his coffee. 'You can have it.'

'Have to go.' Ruth got to her feet, unfastening her robe. 'Time to go to work.'

'Already?'

'Sure. You lucky bum! Wish I could sit around.' Ruth moved toward the bathroom, running her fingers through her long black hair. 'When you work for the Government you start early.'

'But you get off early,' Ed pointed out. He unfolded the *Chronicle*, examining the sporting green. 'Well, have a good time today. Don't type any wrong words, any double-entendres.'

The bathroom door closed, as Ruth shed her robe and began dressing.

Ed yawned and glanced up at the clock over the sink. Plenty of time. Not even eight. He sipped more coffee and then rubbed his stubbled chin. He would have to shave. He shrugged lazily. Ten minutes, maybe.

Ruth came bustling out in her nylon slip, hurrying into the bedroom. 'I'm late.' She rushed rapidly around, getting into her blouse and skirt, her stockings, her little white shoes. Finally she bent over and kissed him. 'Good-bye, honey. I'll do the shopping tonight.'

'Good-bye.' Ed lowered his newspaper and put his arm around his wife's trim waist, hugging her affectionately. 'You smell nice. Don't flirt with the boss.'

Ruth ran out the front door, clattering down the steps. He heard the click of her heels diminish down the sidewalk.

She was gone. The house was silent. He was alone.

Ed got to his feet, pushing his chair back. He wandered lazily into the bathroom, and got his razor down. Eight-ten. He washed his face, rubbing it down with shaving cream, and began to shave. He shaved leisurely. He had plenty of time.

The Clerk bent over his round pocket watch, licking his lips nervously. Sweat stood out on his forehead. The second hand ticked on. Eight-fourteen. Almost time.

'Get ready!' the Clerk snapped. He tensed, his small body rigid. 'Ten seconds to go!'

'*Time!*' the Clerk cried.

Nothing happened.

The Clerk turned, eyes wide with horror. From the little shed a thick black tail showed. The dog had gone back to sleep.

'TIME!' the Clerk shrieked. He kicked wildly at the furry rump. 'In the name of God—'

The dog stirred. He thumped around hastily, backing out of the shed. 'My goodness.' Embarrassed, he made his way quickly to the fence. Standing up on his hind paws, he opened his mouth wide. 'Woof!' he summoned. He glanced apologetically at the Clerk. 'I beg your pardon. I can't understand how—'

The Clerk gazed fixedly down at his watch. Cold terror knotted his stomach. The hands showed eight-sixteen. 'You failed,' he grated. 'You failed! You miserable flea-bitten rag-bag of a wornout old mutt! You failed!'

207

The dog dropped and came anxiously back. 'I failed, you say? You mean the summons time was—?'

'You summoned too late.' The Clerk put his watch away slowly, a glazed expression on his face. 'You summoned too late. We won't get A Friend with a Car. There's no telling what will come instead. I'm afraid to see what eight-sixteen brings.'

'I hope he'll be in Sector T137 in time.'

'He won't,' the Clerk wailed. 'He won't be there. We've made a mistake. We've made things go wrong!'

Ed was rinsing the shaving cream from his face when the muffled sound of the dog's bark echoed through the silent house.

'Damn,' Ed muttered. 'Wake up the whole block.' He dried his face, listening. Was somebody coming?

A vibration. Then—

The doorbell rang.

Ed came out of the bathroom. Who could it be? Had Ruth forgotten something? He tossed on a white shirt and opened the front door.

A bright young man, face bland and eager, beamed happily at him. 'Good morning, sir.' He tipped his hat. 'I'm sorry to bother you so early—'

'What do you want?'

'I'm from the Federal Life Insurance Company. I'm here to see you about—'

Ed pushed the door closed. 'Don't want any. I'm in a rush. Have to get to work.'

'Your wife said this was the only time I could catch you.' The young man picked up his briefcase, easing the door open again. 'She especially asked me to come this early. We don't usually begin our work at this time, but since she asked me, I made a special note about it.'

'OK.' Sighing wearily, Ed admitted the young man. 'You can explain your policy while I get dressed.'

The young man opened his briefcase on the couch, laying out heaps of pamphlets and illustrated folders. 'I'd like to show you some of these figures, if I may. It's of great importance to you and your family to—'

Ed found himself sitting down, going over the pamphlets. He

purchased a ten-thousand-dollar policy on his own life and then eased the young man out. He looked at the clock. Practically nine-thirty!

'Damn.' He'd be late to work. He finished fastening his tie, grabbed his coat, turned off the oven and the lights, dumped the dishes in the sink, and ran out on the porch.

As he hurried toward the bus stop he was cursing inwardly. Life insurance salesmen. Why did the jerk have to come just as he was getting ready to leave?

Ed groaned. No telling what the consequences would be, getting to the office late. He wouldn't get there until almost ten. He set himself in anticipation. A sixth sense told him he was in for it. Something bad. It was the wrong day to be late.

If only the salesman hadn't come.

Ed hopped off the bus a block from his office. He began walking rapidly. The huge clock in front of Stein's Jewelry Store told him it was almost ten.

His heart sank. Old Douglas would give him hell for sure. He could see it now. Douglas puffing and blowing, red-faced, waving his thick finger at him; Miss Evans, smiling behind her typewriter; Jackie, the office boy, grinning and snickering; Earl Hendricks; Joe and Tom; Mary, dark-eyed, full bosom and long lashes. All of them, kidding him the whole rest of the day.

He came to the corner and stopped for the light. On the other side of the street rose a big white concrete building, the towering column of steel and cement girders and glass windows – the office building. Ed flinched. Maybe he could say the elevator got stuck. Somewhere between the second and third floor.

The street light changed. Nobody else was crossing. Ed crossed alone. He hopped up on the curb on the far side—

And stopped, rigid.

The sun had winked off. One moment it was beaming down. Then it was gone. Ed looked up sharply. Gray clouds swirled above him. Huge, formless clouds. Nothing more. An ominous, thick haze that made everything waver and dim. Uneasy chills plucked at him. *What was it?*

He advanced cautiously, feeling his way through the mist. Everything was silent. No sounds – not even the traffic sounds. Ed peered frantically around, trying to see through the rolling haze. No people. No cars. No sun. Nothing.

The office building loomed up ahead, ghostly. It was an indistinct gray. He put out his hand uncertainly—

A section of the building fell away. It rained down, a torrent of particles. Like sand. Ed gaped foolishly. A cascade of gray debris, spilling around his feet. And where he had touched the building, a jagged cavity yawned – an ugly pit marring the concrete.

Dazed, he made his way to the front steps. He mounted them. The steps gave way underfoot. His feet sank down. He was wading through shifting sand, weak, rotted stuff that broke under his weight.

He got into the lobby. The lobby was dim and obscure. The overhead lights flickered feebly in the gloom. An unearthly pall hung over everything.

He spied the cigar stand. The seller leaned silently, resting on the counter, toothpick between his teem, his face vacant. *And gray*. He was gray all over.

'Hey,' Ed croaked. 'What's going on?'

The seller did not answer. Ed reached out toward him. His hand touched the seller's gray arm – and passed right through.

'Good God,' Ed said.

The seller's arm came loose. It fell to the lobby floor, disintegrating into fragments. Bits of gray fiber. Like dust. Ed's senses reeled.

'Help!' he shouted, finding his voice.

No answer. He peered around. A few shapes stood here and there: a man reading a newspaper, two women waiting at the elevator.

Ed made his way over to the man. He reached out and touched him.

The man slowly collapsed. He settled into a heap, a loose pile of gray ash. Dust. Particles. The two women dissolved when he touched them. Silently. They made no sound as they broke apart.

Ed found the stairs. He grabbed hold of the banister and climbed. The stairs collapsed under him. He hurried faster. Behind him lay a broken path – his footprints clearly visible in the concrete. Clouds of ash blew around him as he reached the second floor.

He gazed down the silent corridor. He saw more clouds of ash. He heard no sound. There was just darkness – rolling darkness.

He climbed unsteadily to the third floor. Once, his shoe broke completely through the stair. For a sickening second he hung, poised over a yawning hole that looked down into a bottomless nothing.

Then he climbed on, and emerged in front of his own office: DOUGLAS AND BLAKE, REAL ESTATE.

The hall was dim, gloomy with clouds of ash. The overhead lights flickered fitfully. He reached for the door handle. The handle came off in his hand. He dropped it and dug his fingernails into the door. The plate glass crashed past him, breaking into bits. He tore the door open and stepped over it, into the office.

Miss Evans sat at her typewriter, fingers resting quietly on the keys. She did not move. She was gray, her hair, her skin, her clothing. She was without color. Ed touched her. His fingers went through her shoulder, into dry flakiness.

He drew back, sickened. Miss Evans did not stir.

He moved on. He pushed against a desk. The desk collapsed into rotting dust Earl Hendricks stood by the water cooler, a cup in his hand. He was a gray statue, unmoving. Nothing stirred. No sound. No life. The whole office was gray dust – without life or motion.

Ed found himself out in the corridor again. He shook his head, dazed. What did it mean? Was he going out of his mind? Was he—?

A sound.

Ed turned, peering into the gray mist. A creature was coming, hurrying rapidly. A man – a man in a white robe. Behind him others came. Men in white, with equipment. They were lugging complex machinery.

'Hey—' Ed gasped weakly.

The men stopped. Their mouths opened. Their eyes popped.

'Look!'

'Something's gone wrong!'

'One still charged.'

'Get the de-energizer.'

'We can't proceed until—'

The men came toward Ed, moving around him. One lugged a long hose with some sort of nozzle. A portable cart came wheeling up. Instructions were rapidly shouted.

Ed broke out of his paralysis. Fear swept over him. Panic. Something hideous was happening. He had to get out. Warn people. Get away.

He turned and ran, back down the stairs. The stairs collapsed under him. He fell half a flight, rolling in heaps of dry ash. He got to his feet and hurried on, down to the ground floor.

The lobby was lost in the clouds of gray ash. He pushed blindly through, toward the door. Behind him, the white-clad men were coming, dragging their equipment and shouting to each other, hurrying quickly after him.

He reached the sidewalk. Behind him the office building wavered and sagged, sinking to one side, torrents of ash raining down in heaps. He raced toward the corner, the men just behind him. Gray cloud swirled around him. He groped his way across the street, hands out-stretched. He gained the opposite curb—

The sun winked on. Warm yellow sunlight streamed down on him. Cars honked. Traffic lights changed. On all sides men and women in bright spring clothes hurried and pushed: shoppers, a blue-clad cop, salesmen with briefcases. Stores, windows, signs . . . noisy cars moving up and down the street—

And overhead was the bright sun and familiar blue sky.

Ed halted, gasping for breath. He turned and looked back the way he had come. Across the street was the office building – as it had always been. Firm and distinct. Concrete and glass and steel.

He stepped back a pace and collided with a hurrying citizen. 'Hey,' the man grunted. 'Watch it.'

'Sorry.' Ed shook his head, trying to clear it. From where he stood, the office building looked like always, big and solemn and substantial, rising up imposingly on the other side of the street.

But a minute ago—

Maybe he was out of his mind. He had seen the building crumbling into dust. Building – and people. They had fallen into gray clouds of dust. And the men in white – they had chased him. Men in white robes, shouting orders, wheeling complex equipment.

He was out of his mind. There was no other explanation. Weakly, Ed turned and stumbled along the sidewalk, his mind reel-ing. He moved blindly, without purpose, lost in a haze of confusion and terror.

The Clerk was brought into the top-level Administrative chambers and told to wait.

He paced back and forth nervously, clasping and wringing his hands in an agony of apprehension. He took off his glasses and wiped them shakily.

Lord. All the trouble and grief. And it wasn't his fault. But he would have to take the rap. It was his responsibility to get the Summoners routed out and their instructions followed. The miserable flea-infested

Summoner had gone back to sleep – and *he* would have to answer for it.

The doors opened. 'All right,' a voice murmured, preoccupied. It was a tired, care-worn voice. The Clerk trembled and entered slowly, sweat dripping down his neck into his celluloid collar.

The Old Man glanced up, laying aside his book. He studied the Clerk calmly, his faded blue eyes mild – a deep, ancient mildness that made the Clerk tremble even more. He took out his handkerchief and mopped his brow.

'I understand there was a mistake,' the Old Man murmured. 'In connection with Sector T137. Something to do with an element from an adjoining area.'

'That's right.' The Clerk's voice was faint and husky. 'Very unfortunate.'

'What exactly occurred?'

'I started out this morning with my instruction sheets. The material relating to T137 had top priority, of course. I served notice on the Summoner in my area that an eight-fifteen summons was required.'

'Did the Summoner understand the urgency?'

'Yes, sir.' The Clerk hesitated. 'But—'

'But what?'

The Clerk twisted miserably. 'While my back was turned the Summoner crawled back in his shed and went to sleep. I was occupied, checking the exact time with my watch. I called the moment – but there was no response.'

'You called at eight-fifteen exactly?'

'Yes, sir! Exactly eight-fifteen. But the Summoner was asleep. By the time I managed to arouse him it was eight-*sixteen*. He summoned, but instead of A Friend with a Car we got – A Life Insurance Salesman.' The Clerk's face screwed up with disgust. 'The Salesman kept the element there until almost nine-thirty. Therefore he was late to work instead of early.'

For a moment the Old Man was silent. 'Then the element was not within T137 when the adjustment began.'

'No. He arrived about ten o'clock.'

'During the middle of the adjustment.' The Old Man got to his feet and paced slowly back and forth, face grim, hands behind his back. His long robe flowed out behind him. 'A serious matter. During a Sector Adjustment all related elements from other Sectors must be included.

Otherwise, their orientations remain out of phase. When this element entered T137 the adjustment had been in progress fifty minutes. The element encountered the Sector at its most de-energized stage. He wandered about until one of the adjustment teams met him.'

'Did they catch him?'

'Unfortunately, no. He fled, out of the Sector. Into a nearby fully energized area.'

'What – what then?'

The Old Man stopped pacing, his lined face grim. He ran a heavy hand through his long white hair. 'We do not know. We lost contact with him. We will reestablish contact soon, of course. But for the moment he is out of control.'

'What are you going to do?'

'He must be contacted and contained. He must be brought up here. There's no other solution.'

'Up *here!*'

'It is too late to de-energize him. By the time he is regained he will have told others. To wipe his mind clean would only complicate matters. Usual methods will not suffice. I must deal with this problem myself.'

'I hope he's located quickly,' the Clerk said.

'He will be. Every Watcher is alerted. Every Watcher and every Summoner.' The Old Man's eyes twinkled. 'Even the Clerks, although we hesitate to count on them.'

The Clerk flushed. 'I'll be glad when this thing is over,' he muttered.

Ruth came tripping down the stairs and out of the building, into the hot noonday sun. She lit a cigarette and hurried along the walk, her small bosom rising and falling as she breathed in the spring air.

'Ruth.' Ed stepped up behind her.

'Ed!' She spun, gasping in astonishment. 'What are you doing away from—?'

'Come on.' Ed grabbed her arm, pulling her along. 'Let's keep moving.'

'But what—?'

'I'll tell you later.' Ed's face was pale and grim. 'Let's go where we can talk. In private.'

'I was going down to have lunch at Louie's. We can talk there.'

Ruth hurried along breathlessly. 'What is it? What's happened? You look so strange. And why aren't you at work? Did you— did you get fired?'

They crossed the street and entered a small restaurant. Men and women milled around, getting their lunch. Ed found a table in the back, secluded in a corner. 'Here.' He sat down abruptly. 'This will do.' She slid into the other chair.

Ed ordered a cup of coffee. Ruth had salad and creamed tuna on toast, coffee and peach pie. Silently, Ed watched her as she ate, his face dark and moody.

'Please tell me,' Ruth begged him.

'You really want to know?'

'Of course I want to know!' Ruth put her small hand anxiously on his. 'I'm your wife.'

'Something happened today. This morning. I was late to work. A damn insurance man came by and held me up. I was half an hour late.'

Ruth caught her breath. 'Douglas fired you.'

'No.' Ed ripped a paper napkin slowly into bits. He stuffed the bits in the half-empty water glass. 'I was worried as hell. I got off the bus and hurried down the street. I noticed it when I stepped up on the curb in front of the office.'

'Noticed what?'

Ed told her. The whole works. Everything.

When he had finished, Ruth sat back, her face white, hands trembling. 'I see,' she murmured. 'No wonder you're upset.' She drank a little cold coffee, the cup rattling against the saucer. 'What a terrible thing.'

Ed leaned intently toward his wife. 'Ruth. Do you think I'm going crazy?'

Ruth's red lips twisted. 'I don't know what to say. It's so strange . . .'

'Yeah. Strange is hardly the word for it. I poked my hands right through them. Like they were clay. Old dry clay. Dust. Dust figures.' Ed lit a cigarette from Ruth's pack. 'When I got out I looked back and there it was. The office building. Like always.'

'You were afraid Mr Douglas would bawl you out, weren't you?'

'Sure. I was afraid – and guilty.' Ed's eyes flickered. 'I know what you're thinking. I was late and I couldn't face him. So I had some sort of protective psychotic fit. Retreat from reality.' He stubbed the

215

cigarette out savagely. 'Ruth, I've been wandering around town since. Two and a half hours. Sure, I'm afraid. I'm afraid like hell to go back.'

'Of Douglas?'

'No! The men in white.' Ed shuddered. 'God. Chasing me. With their damn hoses and – and equipment.'

Ruth was silent. Finally she looked up at her husband, her dark eyes bright. 'You have to go back, Ed.'

'Back? Why?'

'To prove something.'

'Prove what?'

'Prove it's all right.' Ruth's hand pressed against his. 'You have to, Ed. You have to go back and face it. To show yourself there's nothing to be afraid of.'

'The hell with it! After what I saw? Listen, Ruth. I saw the fabric of reality split open. I saw – *behind*. Underneath. I saw what was really there. And I don't want to go back. I don't want to see dust people again. Ever.'

Ruth's eyes were fixed intently on him. 'I'll go back with you,' she said.

'For God's sake.'

'For *your* sake. For your sanity. So you'll know.' Ruth got abruptly to her feet, pulling her coat around her. 'Come on, Ed. I'll go with you. We'll go up there together. To the office of Douglas and Blake, Real Estate. I'll even go in with you to see Mr Douglas.'

Ed got up slowly, staring hard at his wife. 'You think I blacked out. Cold feet. Couldn't face the boss.' His voice was low and strained. 'Don't you?'

Ruth was already threading her way toward the cashier. 'Come on. You'll see. It'll all be there. Just like it always was.'

'OK,' Ed said. He followed her slowly. 'We'll go back there – and see which of us is right.'

They crossed the street together, Ruth holding on tight to Ed's arm. Ahead of them was the building, the towering structure of concrete and metal and glass.

'There it is,' Ruth said. 'See?'

There it was, all right. The big building rose up, firm and solid, glittering in the early afternoon sun, its windows sparkling brightly.

Ed and Ruth stepped up onto the curb. Ed tensed himself, his body rigid. He winced as his foot touched the pavement—

216

But nothing happened: the street noises continued; cars, people hurrying past; a kid selling papers. There were sounds, smells, the noise of a city in the middle of the day. And overhead was the sun and the bright blue sky.

'See?' Ruth said. 'I was right.'

They walked up the front steps, into the lobby. Behind the cigar stand the seller stood, arms folded, listening to the ball game. 'Hi, Mr Fletcher,' he called to Ed. His face lit up good-naturedly. 'Who's the dame? Your wife know about this?'

Ed laughed unsteadily. They passed on toward the elevator. Four or five businessmen stood waiting. They were middle-aged men, well dressed, waiting impatiently in a bunch. 'Hey, Fletcher,' one said. 'Where you been all day? Douglas is yelling his head off.'

'Hello, Earl,' Ed muttered. He gripped Ruth's arm. 'Been a little sick.'

The elevator came. They got in. The elevator rose. 'Hi, Ed,' the elevator operator said. 'Who's the good-looking gal? Why don't you introduce her around?'

Ed grinned mechanically. 'My wife.'

The elevator let them off at the third floor. Ed and Ruth got out, heading toward the glass door of Douglas and Blake, Real Estate.

Ed halted, breathing shallowly. 'Wait.' He licked his lips. 'I—'

Ruth waited calmly as Ed wiped his forehead and neck with his handkerchief. 'All right now?'

'Yeah.' Ed moved forward. He pulled open the glass door.

Miss Evans glanced up, ceasing her typing. 'Ed Fletcher! Where on earth have you been?'

'I've been sick. Hello, Tom.'

Tom glanced up from his work, 'Hi, Ed. Say, Douglas is yelling for your scalp. Where have you been?'

'I know.' Ed turned wearily to Ruth. 'I guess I better go in and face the music.'

Ruth squeezed his arm. 'You'll be all right. I know.' She smiled, a relieved flash of white teeth and red lips. 'OK? Call me if you need me.'

'Sure.' Ed kissed her briefly on the mouth. 'Thanks, honey. Thanks a lot. I don't know what the hell went wrong with me. I guess it's over.'

'Forget it. So long.' Ruth skipped back out of the office, the door closing after her. Ed listened to her race down the hall to the elevator.

217

'Nice little gal,' Jackie said appreciatively.

'Yeah.' Ed nodded, straightening his necktie. He moved unhappily toward the inner office, steeling himself. Well, he had to face it. Ruth was right. But he was going to have a hell of a time explaining it to the boss. He could see Douglas now, thick red wattles, big bull roar, face distorted with rage—

Ed stopped abruptly at the entrance to the inner office. He froze rigid. The inner office – it was *changed*.

The hackles of his neck rose. Cold fear gripped him, clutching at his windpipe. The inner office was different. He turned his head slowiy, taking in the sight: the desks, chairs, fixtures, file cabinets, pictures.

Changes. Little changes. Subtle. Ed closed his eyes and opened them slowly. He was alert, breathing rapidly, his pulse racing. It was changed, all right. No doubt about it.

'What's the matter, Ed?' Tom asked. The staff watched him curiously, pausing in their work.

Ed said nothing. He advanced slowly into the inner office. The office had been *gone over*. He could tell. Things had been altered. Rearranged. Nothing obvious – nothing he could put his finger on. But he could tell.

Joe Kent greeted him uneasily. 'What's the matter, Ed? You look like a wild dog. Is something—?'

Ed studied Joe. He was different. Not the same. What was it?

Joe's face. It was a little fuller. His shirt was blue-striped. Joe never wore blue stripes. Ed examined Joe's desk. He saw papers and accounts. The desk – it was too far to the right. And it was bigger. It wasn't the same desk.

The picture on the wall. It wasn't the same. It was a different picture entirely. And the things on top of the file cabinet – some were new, others were gone.

He looked back through the door. Now that he thought about it, Miss Evans' hair was different, done a different way. And it was lighter.

In here, Mary, filing her nails, over by the window – she was taller, fuller. Her purse, lying on the desk in front of her – a red purse, red knit.

'You always . . . have that purse?' Ed demanded.

Mary glanced up. 'What?'

'That purse. You always have that?'

Mary laughed. She smoothed her skirt coyly around her shapely thighs, her long lashes blinking modestly. 'Why, Mr Fletcher. What do you mean?'

Ed turned away. *He knew*. Even if she didn't. She had been redone – changed: her purse, her clothes, her figure, everything about her. None of them knew – but him. His mind spun dizzily. They were all changed. All of them were different. They had all been remolded, recast. Subtly – but it was there.

The wastebasket. It was smaller, not the same. The window shades – white, not ivory. The wallpaper was not the same pattern. The lighting fixtures . . .

Endless, subtle changes.

Ed made his way back to the inner office. He lifted his hand and knocked on Douglas's door.

'Come in.'

Ed pushed the door open. Nathan Douglas looked up impatiently. 'Mr Douglas—' Ed began. He came into the room unsteadily – and stopped.

Douglas was not the same. Not at all. His whole office was changed: the rugs, the drapes. The desk was oak, not mahogany. And Douglas himself . . .

Douglas was younger, thinner. His hair, brown. His skin not so red. His face smoother. No wrinkles. Chin reshaped. Eyes green, not black. He was a different man. But still Douglas – a different Douglas. A different version!

'What is it?' Douglas demanded impatiently. 'Oh, it's you, Fletcher. Where were you this morning?'

Ed backed out. Fast.

He slammed the door and hurried back through the inner office. Tom and Miss Evans glanced up, startled. Ed passed them by, grabbing the hall door open.

'Hey!' Tom called. 'What—?'

Ed hurried down the hall. Terror leaped through him. He had to hurry. He had *seen*. There wasn't much time. He came to the elevator and stabbed the button.

No time.

He ran to the stairs and started down. He reached the second floor. His terror grew. It was a matter of seconds.

Seconds!

The public phone. Ed ran into the phone booth. He dragged the door shut after him. Wildly, he dropped a dime in the slot and dialed. He had to call the police. He held the receiver to his ear, his heart pounding.

Warn them. Changes. Somebody tampering with reality. Altering it. He had been right. The white-clad men . . . their equipment . . . going through the building.

'Hello!' Ed shouted hoarsely. There was no answer. No hum. Nothing.

Ed peered frantically out the door.

And he sagged, defeated. Slowly he hung up the telephone receiver.

He was no longer on the second floor. The phone booth was rising, leaving the second floor behind, carrying him up, faster and faster. It rose floor by floor, moving silently, swiftly.

The phone booth passed through the ceiling of the building and out into the bright sunlight. It gained speed. The ground fell away below. Buildings and streets were getting smaller each moment. Tiny specks hurried along, far below, cars and people, dwindling rapidly.

Clouds drifted between him and the earth. Ed shut his eyes, dizzy with fright. He held on desperately to the door handles of the phone booth.

Faster and faster the phone booth climbed. The earth was rapidly being left behind, far below.

Ed peered up wildly. *Where?* Where was he going? Where was it taking him?

He stood gripping the door handles, waiting.

The Clerk nodded curtly. 'That's him, all right. The element in question.'

Ed Fletcher looked around him. He was in a huge chamber. The edges fell away into indistinct shadows. In front of him stood a man with notes and ledgers under his arm, peering at him through steel-rimmed glasses. He was a nervous little man, sharp-eyed, with celluloid collar, blue serge suit, vest, watch chain. He wore black shiny shoes.

And beyond him—

An old man sat quietly, in an immense modern chair. He watched Fletcher calmly, his blue eyes mild and tired. A strange thrill shot through Fletcher. It was not fear. Rather it was a vibration, rattling his bones – a deep sense of awe, tinged with fascination.

'Where – what is this place?' he asked faintly. He was still dazed from his quick ascent.

'Don't ask questions!' the nervous little man snapped angrily, tapping his pencil against his ledgers. 'You're here to answer, not ask.'

The Old Man moved a little. He raised his hand. 'I will speak to the element alone,' he murmured. His voice was low. It vibrated and rumbled through the chamber. Again the waver of fascinated awe swept Ed.

'Alone?' The little fellow backed away, gathering his books and papers in his arms. 'Of course.' He glanced hostilely at Ed Fletcher. 'I'm glad he's finally in custody. All the work and trouble just for—'

He disappeared through a door. The door closed softly behind him. Ed and the Old Man were alone.

'Please sit down,' the Old Man said.

Ed found a seat. He sat down awkwardly, nervously. He got out his cigarettes and then put them away again.

'What's wrong?' the Old Man asked.

'I'm just beginning to understand.'

'Understand what?'

'That I'm dead.'

The Old Man smiled briefly. 'Dead? No, you're not dead. You're . . . visiting. An unusual event, but necessitated by circumstances.' He leaned toward Ed. 'Mr Fletcher, you have got yourself involved with something.'

'Yeah,' Ed agreed. 'I wish I knew what it was. Or how it happened.'

'It was not your fault. You were a victim of a clerical error. A mistake was made – not by you. But involving you.'

'What mistake?' Ed rubbed his forehead wearily. 'I – I got in on something. I saw *through*. I saw something I wasn't supposed to see.'

The Old Man nodded. 'That's right. You saw something you were not supposed to see – something few elements have been aware of, let alone witnessed.'

'Elements?'

'An official term. Let it pass. A mistake was made, but we hope to rectify it. It is my hope that—'

'Those people,' Ed interrupted 'Heaps of dry ash. And gray. Like they were dead. Only it was everything: the stairs and walls and floor. No color or life.'

221

'That Sector had been temporarily de-energized. So the adjustment team could enter and effect changes.'

'Changes.' Ed nodded. 'That's right. When I went back later, everything was alive again. But not the same. It was all different.'

'The adjustment was complete by noon. The team finished its work and re-energized the Sector.'

'I see,' Ed muttered.

'You were supposed to have been in the Sector when the adjustment began. Because of an error you were not. You came into the Sector late – during the adjustment itself. You fled, and when you returned it was over. You saw, and you should not have seen. Instead of a witness you should have been part of the adjustment. Like the others, you should have undergone changes.'

Sweat came out on Ed Fletcher's head. He wiped it away. His stomach turned over. Weakly, he cleared his throat. 'I get the picture.' His voice was almost inaudible. A chilling premonition moved through him. 'I was supposed to be changed like the others. But I guess something went wrong.'

'Something went wrong. An error occurred. And now a serious problem exists. You have seen these things. You know a great deal. And you are not coordinated with the new configuration.'

'Gosh,' Ed muttered. 'Well, I won't tell anybody.' Cold sweat poured off him. 'You can count on that. I'm as good as changed.'

'You have already told someone,' the Old Man said coldly.

'Me?' Ed blinked. 'Who?'

'Your wife.'

Ed trembled. The color drained from his face, leaving it sickly white. 'That's right. I did.'

'Your wife knows.' The Old Man's face twisted angrily. 'A woman. Of all the things to tell—'

'I didn't know.' Ed retreated, panic leaping through him. 'But I know *now*. You can count on me. Consider me changed.'

The ancient blue eyes bored keenly into him, peering far into his depths. 'And you were going to call the police. You wanted to inform the authorities.'

'But I didn't know *who* was doing the changing.'

'Now you know. The natural process must be supplemented – adjusted here and there. Corrections must be made. We are fully licensed to make such corrections. Our adjustment teams perform vital work.'

Ed plucked up a measure of courage. 'This particular adjustment. Douglas. The office. What was it for? I'm sure it was some worthwhile purpose.'

The Old Man waved his hand. Behind him in the shadows an immense map glowed into existence. Ed caught his breath. The edges of the map faded off in obscurity. He saw an infinite web of detailed sections, a network of squares and ruled lines. Each square was marked. Some glowed with a blue light. The lights altered constantly.

'The Sector Board,' the Old Man said. He sighed wearily. 'A staggering job. Sometimes we wonder how we can go on another period. But it must be done. For the good of all. For *your* good.'

'The change. In our – our Sector.'

'Your office deals in real estate. The old Douglas was a shrewd man, but rapidly becoming infirm. His physical health was waning. In a few days Douglas will be offered a chance to purchase a large unimproved forest area in western Canada. It will require most of his assets. The older, less virile Douglas would have hesitated. It is imperative he not hesitate. He must purchase the area and clear the land at once. Only a younger man – a younger Douglas – would undertake this.

'When the land is cleared, certain anthropological remains will be discovered. They have already been placed there. Douglas will lease his land to the Canadian Government for scientific study. The remains found there will cause international excitement in learned circles.

'A chain of events will be set in motion. Men from numerous countries will come to Canada to examine the remains. Soviet, Polish, and Czech scientists will make the journey.

'The chain of events will draw these scientists together for the first time in years. National research will be temporarily forgotten in the excitement of these nonnational discoveries. One of the leading Soviet scientists will make friends with a Belgian scientist. Before they depart they will agree to correspond – without the knowledge of their governments, of course.

'The circle will widen. Other scientists on both sides will be drawn in. A society will be founded. More and more educated men will transfer an increasing amount of time to this international society. Purely national research will suffer a slight but extremely critical eclipse. The war tension will somewhat wane.

'This alteration is vital. And it is dependent on the purchase and clearing of the section of wilderness in Canada. The old Douglas would not have dared take the risk. But the altered Douglas, and his altered, more youthful staff, will pursue this work with wholehearted enthusiasm. And from this, the vital chain of widening events will come about. The beneficiaries will be *you*. Our methods may seem strange and indirect. Even incomprehensible. But I assure you we know what we're doing.'

'I know that now,' Ed said.

'So you do. You know a great deal. Much too much. No element should possess such knowledge. I should perhaps call an adjustment team in here . . .'

A picture formed in Ed's mind: swirling gray clouds, gray men and women. He shuddered. 'Look,' he croaked. 'I'll do anything. Anything at all. Only don't de-energize me.' Sweat ran down his face. 'OK?'

The Old Man pondered. 'Perhaps some alternative could be found. There is another possibility . . .'

'What?' Ed asked eagerly. 'What is it?'

The Old Man spoke slowly, thoughtfully. 'If I allow you to return, you will swear never to speak of the matter? Will you swear not to reveal to anyone the things you saw? The things you know?'

'Sure!' Ed gasped eagerly, blinding relief flooding over him. 'I swear!'

'Your wife. She must know nothing more. She must think it was only a passing psychological fit – retreat from reality.'

'She thinks that already.'

'She must continue to.'

Ed set his jaw firmly. 'I'll see that she continues to think it was a mental aberration. She'll never know what really happened.'

'You are certain you can keep the truth from her?'

'Sure,' Ed said confidently. 'I know I can.'

'All right.' The Old Man nodded slowly. 'I will send you back. But you must tell no one.' He swelled visibly. 'Remember: you will eventually come back to me – everyone does, in the end – and your fate will not be enviable.'

'I won't tell her,' Ed said, sweating. 'I promise. You have my word on that. I can handle Ruth. Don't give it a second throught.'

Ed arrived home at sunset.

He blinked, dazed from the rapid descent. For a moment he stood on the pavement, regaining his balance and catching his breath. Then he walked quickly up the path.

He pushed the door open and entered the little green stucco house.

'Ed!' Ruth came flying, face distorted with tears. She threw her arms around him, hugging him tight. 'Where the hell have you been?'

'Been?' Ed murmured. 'At the office, of course.'

Ruth pulled back abruptiy. 'No, you haven't.'

Vague tendrils of alarm plucked at Ed. 'Of course I have. Where else—?'

'I called Douglas about three. He said you left. You walked out, practically as soon as I turned my back. Eddie—'

Ed patted her nervously. 'Take it easy, honey.' He began unbuttoning his coat. 'Everything's OK. Understand? Things are perfectly all right.'

Ruth sat down on the arm of the couch. She blew her nose, dabbing at her eyes. 'If you knew how much I've worried.' She put her handkerchief away and folded her arms. 'I want to know where you were.'

Uneasily, Ed hung his coat in the closet. He came over and kissed her. Her lips were ice cold. 'I'll tell you all about it. But what do you say we have something to eat? I'm starved.'

Ruth studied him intently. She got down from the arm of the couch. 'I'll change and fix dinner.'

She hurried into the bedroom and slipped off her shoes and nylons. Ed followed her. 'I didn't mean to worry you,' he said carefully. 'After you left me today I realized you were right.'

'Oh?' Ruth unfastened her blouse and skirt, arranging them over a hanger. 'Right about what?'

'About me.' He manufactured a grin and made it glow across his face. 'About . . . what happened.'

Ruth hung her slip over the hanger. She studied her husband intently as she struggled into her tight-fitting jeans. 'Go on.'

The moment had come. It was now or never. Ed Fletcher braced himself and chose his words carefully. 'I realized,' he stated, 'that the whole darn thing was in my mind. You were right, Ruth. Completely right. And I even realize what caused it.'

Ruth rolled her cotton T-shirt down and tucked it in her jeans. 'What was the cause?'

'Overwork.'

'Overwork?'

'I need a vacation. I haven't had a vacation in years. My mind isn't

225

on the job. I've been daydreaming.' He said it firmly, but his heart was in his mouth. 'I need to get away. To the mountains. Bass fishing. Or—' He searched his mind frantically. 'Or—'

Ruth came toward him ominously. 'Ed!' she said sharply. 'Look at me!'

'What's the matter?' Panic shot through him. 'Why are you looking at me like that?'

'*Where were you this afternoon?*'

Ed's grin faded. 'I told you. I went for a walk. Didn't I tell you? A walk. To think things over.'

'Don't lie to me, Eddie Fletcher! I can tell when you're lying!' Fresh tears welled up in Ruth's eyes. Her breasts rose and fell excitedly under her cotton shirt. 'Admit it! You didn't go for a walk!'

Ed stammered weakly. Sweat poured off him. He sagged helplessly against the door. 'What do you mean?'

Ruth's black eyes flashed with anger. 'Come on! I want to know where you were! Tell me! I have a right to know. What really happened?'

Ed retreated in terror, his resolve melting like wax. It was going all wrong. 'Honest. I went out for a—'

'Tell me!' Ruth's sharp fingernails dug into his arm. 'I want to know where you were – and who you were with!'

Ed opened his mouth. He tried to grin, but his face failed to respond. 'I don't know what you mean.'

'You know what I mean. Who were you with? Where did you go? Tell me! I'll find out sooner or later.'

There was no way out. He was licked – and he knew it. He couldn't keep it from her. Desperately he stalled, praying for time. If he could only distract her, get her mind on something else. If she would only let up, even for a second. He could invent something – a better story. Time – he needed more time. 'Ruth, you've got to—'

Suddenly there was a sound: the bark of a dog, echoing through the dark house.

Ruth let go, cocking her head alertly. 'That was Dobbie. I think somebody's coming.'

The doorbell rang.

'You stay here. I'll be right back.' Ruth ran out of the room, to the front door. 'Darn it.' She pulled the front door open.

'Good evening!' The young man stepped quickly inside, loaded down with objects, grinning broadly at Ruth. 'I'm from the Sweep-Rite Vacuum Cleaner Company.'

Ruth scowled impatiently. 'Really, we're about to sit down at the table.'

'Oh, this will only take a moment.' The young man set down the vacuum cleaner and its attachments with a metallic crash. Rapidly, he unrolled a long illustrated banner, showing the vacuum cleaner in action. 'Now, if you'll just hold this while I plug in the cleaner—'

He bustled happily about, unplugging the TV set, plugging in the cleaner, pushing the chairs out of his way.

'I'll show you the drape scraper first.' He attached a hose and nozzle to the big gleaming tank. 'Now, if you'll just sit down I'll demonstrate each of these easy-to-use attachments.' His happy voice rose over the roar of the cleaner. 'You'll notice—'

Ed Fletcher sat down on the bed. He groped in his pocket until he found his cigarettes. Shakily he lit one and leaned back against the wall, weak with relief.

He gazed up, a look of gratitude on his face. 'Thanks,' he said softly. 'I think we'll make it – after all. Thanks a lot.'

The Father-Thing

'Dinner's ready,' commanded Mrs Walton. 'Go get your father and tell him to wash his hands. The same applies to you, young man.' She carried a steaming casserole to the neatly set table. 'You'll find him out in the garage.'

Charles hesitated. He was only eight years old, and the problem bothering him would have confounded Hillel. 'I—' he began uncertainly.

'What's wrong?' June Walton caught the uneasy tone in her son's voice and her matronly bosom fluttered with sudden alarm. 'Isn't Ted out in the garage? For heaven's sake, he was sharpening the hedge shears a minute ago. He didn't go over to the Andersons', did he? I told him dinner was practically on the table.'

'He's in the garage,' Charles said. 'But he's – talking to himself.'

'Talking to himself!' Mrs Walton removed her bright plastic apron and hung it over the doorknob. 'Ted? Why, he never talks to himself. Go tell him to come in here.' She poured boiling black coffee in the little blue-and-white china cups and began ladling out creamed corn. 'What's wrong with you? Go tell him!'

'I don't know which of them to tell,' Charles blurted out desperately. 'They both look alike.'

June Walton's fingers lost their hold on the aluminum pan; for a moment the creamed corn slushed dangerously. 'Young man—' she began angrily, but at that moment Ted Walton came striding into the kitchen, inhaling and sniffing and rubbing his hands together.

'Ah,' he cried happily. 'Lamb stew.'

'Beef stew,' June murmured. 'Ted, what were you doing out there?'

Ted threw himself down at his place and unfolded his napkin. 'I got the shears sharpened like a razor. Oiled and sharpened. Better not touch them – they'll cut your hand off.' He was a good-looking man in his early thirties; thick blond hair, strong arms, competent hands, square face and flashing brown eyes. 'Man, this stew looks good. Hard day at the office – Friday, you know. Stuff piles up and we have to get all the accounts out by five. Al McKinley claims the department could handle 20 per cent more stuff if we organized our lunch hours; staggered them so somebody was there all the time.' He beckoned Charles over. 'Sit down and let's go.'

Mrs Walton served the frozen peas. 'Ted,' she said, as she slowly took her seat, 'is there anything on your mind?'

'On my mind?' He blinked. 'No, nothing unusual. Just the regular stuff. Why?'

Uneasily, June Walton glanced over at her son. Charles was sitting bolt-upright at his place, face expressionless, white as chalk. He hadn't moved, hadn't unfolded his napkin or even touched his milk. A tension was in the air; she could feel it. Charles had pulled his chair away from his father's; he was huddled in a tense little bundle as far from his father as possible. His lips were moving, but she couldn't catch what he was saying.

'What is it?' she demanded, leaning toward him.

'*The other one*,' Charles was muttering under his breath. 'The other one came in.'

'What do you mean, dear?' June Walton asked out loud. 'What other one?'

Ted jerked. A strange expression flitted across his face. It vanished at once; but in the brief instant Ted Walton's face lost all familiarity. Something alien and cold gleamed out, a twisting, wriggling mass. The eyes blurred and receded, as an archaic sheen filmed over them. The ordinary look of a tired, middle-aged husband was gone.

And then it was back – or nearly back. Ted grinned and began to wolf down his stew and frozen peas and creamed corn. He laughed, stirred his coffee, kidded and ate. But something terrible was wrong.

'The other one,' Charles muttered, face white, hands beginning to tremble. Suddenly he leaped up and backed away from the table. 'Get away!' he shouted. 'Get out of here!'

'Hey,' Ted rumbled ominously. 'What's got into you?' He pointed sternly at the boy's chair. 'You sit down there and eat your dinner, young man. Your mother didn't fix it for nothing.'

Charles turned and ran out of the kitchen, upstairs to his room. June Walton gasped and fluttered in dismay. 'What in the world—'

Ted went on eating. His face was grim; his eyes were hard and dark. 'That kid,' he grated, 'is going to have to learn a few things. Maybe he and I need to have a little private conference together.'

Charles crouched and listened.

The father-thing was coming up the stairs, nearer and nearer. 'Charles!' it shouted angrily. 'Are you up there?'

He didn't answer. Soundlessly, he moved back into his room and pulled the door shut. His heart was pounding heavily. The father-thing had reached the landing; in a moment it would come in his room.

He hurried to the window. He was terrified; it was already fumbling in the dark hall for the knob. He lifted the window and climbed out on the roof. With a grunt he dropped into the flower garden that ran by the front door, staggered and gasped, then leaped to his feet and ran from the light that streamed out the window, a patch of yellow in the evening darkness.

He found the garage; it loomed up ahead, a black square against the skyline. Breathing quickly, he fumbled in his pocket for his flashlight, then cautiously slid the door up and entered.

The garage was empty. The car was parked out front. To the left was his father's workbench. Hammers and saws on the wooden walls. In the back were the lawnmower, rake, shovel, hoe. A drum of kerosene. License plates nailed up everywhere. Floor was concrete and dirt; a great oil slick stained the center, tufts of weeds greasy and black in the flickering beam of the flashlight.

Just inside the door was a big trash barrel. On top of the barrel were stacks of soggy newspapers and magazines, moldy and damp. A thick stench of decay issued from them as Charles began to move them around. Spiders dropped to the cement and scampered off; he crushed them with his foot and went on looking.

The sight made him shriek. He dropped the flashlight and leaped wildly back. The garage was plunged into instant gloom. He forced himself to kneel down, and for an ageless moment, he groped in the darkness for the light, among the spiders and greasy weeds. Finally he had it again. He managed to turn the beam down into the barrel, down the well he had made by pushing back the piles of magazines.

The father-thing had stuffed it down in the very bottom of the barrel. Among the old leaves and torn-up cardboard, the rotting remains of magazines and curtains, rubbish from the attic his mother had lugged down here with the idea of burning someday. It still looked a little like his father enough for him to recognize. He had found it – and the sight made him sick at his stomach. He hung onto the barrel and shut his eyes until finally he was able to look again. In the barrel were the remains of his father, his real father. Bits the father-thing had no use for. Bits it had discarded.

He got the rake and pushed it down to stir the remains. They were dry. They cracked and broke at the touch of the rake. They were like a discarded snake skin, flaky and crumbling, rustling at the touch. *An empty skin.* The insides were gone. The important part. This was all that remained, just the brittle, cracking skin, wadded down at the bottom of the trash barrel in a little heap. This was all the father-thing had left; it had eaten the rest. Taken the insides − and his father's place.

A sound.

He dropped the rake and hurried to the door. The father-thing was coming down the path, toward the garage. Its shoes crushed the gravel; it felt its way along uncertainly. 'Charles!' it called angrily. 'Are you in there? Wait'll I get my hands on you, young man!'

His mother's ample, nervous shape was outlined in the bright doorway of the house. 'Ted, please don't hurt him. He's all upset about something.'

'I'm not going to hurt him,' the father-thing rasped; it halted to strike a match. 'I'm just going to have a little talk with him. He needs to learn better manners. Leaving the table like that and running out at night, climbing down the roof—'

Charles slipped from the garage; the glare of the match caught his moving shape, and with a bellow the father-thing lunged forward.

'*Come here!*'

Charles ran. He knew the ground better than the father-thing; it knew a lot, had taken a lot when it got his father's insides, but nobody knew the way like *he* did. He reached the fence, climbed it, leaped into the Andersons' yard, raced past their clothesline, down the path around the side of their house, and out on Maple Street.

He listened, crouched down and not breathing. The father-thing hadn't come after him. It had gone back. Or it was coming around the sidewalk.

He took a deep, shuddering breath. He had to keep moving. Sooner or later it would find him. He glanced right and left, made sure it wasn't watching, and then started off at a rapid dog-trot.

'What do you want?' Tony Peretti demanded belligerently. Tony was fourteen. He was sitting at the table in the oak-panelled Peretti dining room, books and pencils scattered around him, half a ham-and-peanut butter sandwich and a coke beside him. 'You're Walton, aren't you?'

Tony Peretti had a job uncrating stoves and refrigerators after school at Johnson's Appliance Shop, downtown. He was big and blunt-faced. Black hair, olive skin, white teeth. A couple of times he had beaten up Charles; he had beaten up every kid in the neighborhood.

Charles twisted. 'Say, Peretti. Do me a favor?'

'What do you want?' Peretti was annoyed. 'You looking for a bruise?'

Gazing unhappily down, his fists clenched, Charles explained what had happened in short, mumbled words.

When he had finished, Peretti let out a low whistle. 'No kidding.'

'It's true.' He nodded quickly. 'I'll show you. Come on and I'll show you.'

Peretti got slowly to his feet. 'Yeah, show me. I want to see.'

He got his b.b. gun from his room, and the two of them walked silently up the dark street, toward Charles' house. Neither of them said much. Peretti was deep in thought, serious and solemn-faced. Charles was still dazed; his mind was completely blank.

They turned down the Anderson driveway, cut through the back yard, climbed the fence, and lowered themselves cautiously into Charles' back yard. There was no movement. The yard was silent. The front door of the house was closed.

They peered through the living room window. The shades were down, but a narrow crack of yellow streamed out. Sitting on the couch was Mrs Walton, sewing a cotton T-shirt. There was a sad, troubled look on her large face. She worked listlessly, without interest. Opposite her was the father-thing. Leaning back in his father's easy chair, its shoes off, reading the evening newspaper. The TV was on, playing to itself in the corner. A can of beer rested on the arm of the easy chair. The father-thing sat exactly as his own father had sat; it had learned a lot.

'Looks just like him,' Peretti whispered suspiciously. 'You sure you're not bulling me?'

Charles led him to the garage and showed him the trash barrel. Peretti reached his long tanned arms down and carefully pulled up the dry, flaking remains. They spread out, unfolded, until the whole figure of his father was outlined. Peretti laid the remains on the floor and pieced broken parts back into place. The remains were colorless.

Almost transparent. An amber yellow, thin as paper. Dry and utterly lifeless.

'That's all,' Charles said. Tears welled up in his eyes. 'That's all that's left of him. The thing has the insides.'

Peretti had turned pale. Shakily, he crammed the remains back in the trash barrel. 'This is really something,' he muttered. 'You say you saw the two of them together?'

'Talking. They looked exactly alike. I ran inside.' Charles wiped the tears away and sniveled; he couldn't hold it back any longer. 'It ate him while I was inside. Then it came in the house. It pretended it was him. But it isn't. It killed him and ate his insides.'

For a moment Peretti was silent. 'I'll tell you something,' he said suddenly. 'I've heard about this sort of thing. It's a bad business. You have to use your head and not get scared. You're not scared, are you?'

'No,' Charles managed to mutter.

'The first thing we have to do is figure out how to kill it.' He rattled his b.b. gun. 'I don't know if this'll work. It must be plenty tough to get hold of your father. He was a big man.' Peretti considered. 'Let's get out of here. It might come back. They say that's what a murderer does.'

They left the garage. Peretti crouched down and peeked through the window again. Mrs Walton had got to her feet. She was talking anxiously. Vague sounds filtered out. The father-thing threw down its newspaper. They were arguing.

'For God's sake!' the father-thing shouted. 'Don't do anything stupid like that.'

'Something's wrong,' Mrs Walton moaned. 'Something terrible. Just let me call the hospital and see.'

'Don't call anybody. He's all right. Probably up the street playing.'

'He's never out this late. He never disobeys. He was terribly upset – afraid of you! I don't blame him.' Her voice broke with misery. 'What's wrong with you? You're so strange.' She moved out of the room, into the hall. 'I'm going to call some of the neighbors.'

The father-thing glared after her until she had disappeared. Then a terrifying thing happened. Charles gasped; even Peretti grunted under his breath.

'Look,' Charles muttered. 'What—'

'Golly,' Peretti said, black eyes wide.

As soon as Mrs Walton was gone from the room, the father-thing

233

sagged in its chair. It became limp. Its mouth fell open. Its eyes peered vacantly. Its head fell forward, like a discarded rag doll.

Peretti moved away from the window. 'That's it,' he whispered. 'That's the whole thing.'

'What is it?' Charles demanded. He was shocked and bewildered. 'It looked like somebody turned off its power.'

'Exactly.' Peretti nodded slowly, grim and shaken. 'It's controlled from outside.'

Horror settled over Charles. 'You mean, something outside our world?'

Peretti shook his head with disgust. 'Outside the house! In the yard. You know how to find?'

'Not very well.' Charles pulled his mind together. 'But I know somebody who's good at finding.' He forced his mind to summon the name. 'Bobby Daniels.'

'That little black kid? Is he good at finding?'

'The best.'

'All right,' Peretti said. 'Let's go get him. We have to find the thing that's outside. That made *it* in there, and keeps it going . . .'

'It's near the garage,' Peretti said to the small, thin-faced Negro boy who crouched beside them in the darkness. 'When it got him, he was in the garage. So look there.'

'In the garage?' Daniels asked.

'*Around* the garage. Walton's already gone over the garage, inside. Look around outside. Nearby.'

There was a small bed of flowers growing by the garage, and a great tangle of bamboo and discarded debris between the garage and the back of the house. The moon had come out; a cold, misty light filtered down over everything. 'If we don't find it pretty soon,' Daniels said, 'I got to go back home. I can't stay up much later.' He wasn't any older than Charles. Perhaps nine.

'All right,' Peretti agreed. 'Then get looking.'

The three of them spread out and began to go over the ground with care. Daniels worked with incredible speed; his thin little body moved in a blur of motion as he crawled among the flowers, turned over rocks, peered under the house, separated stalks of plants, ran his expert hands over leaves and stems, in tangles of compost and weeds. No inch was missed.

Peretti halted after a short time. 'I'll guard. It might be dangerous. The father-thing might come and try to stop us.' He posted himself on the back step with his b.b. gun while Charles and Bobby Daniels searched. Charles worked slowly. He was tired, and his body was cold and numb. It seemed impossible, the father-thing and what had happened to his own father, his real father. But terror spurred him on; what if it happened to his mother, or to him? Or to everyone? Maybe the whole world.

'I found it!' Daniels called in a thin, high voice. 'You all come around here quick!'

Peretti raised his gun and got up cautiously. Charles hurried over; he turned the flickering yellow beam of his flashlight where Daniels stood.

The Negro boy had raised a concrete stone. In the moist, rotting soil the light gleamed on a metallic body. A thin, jointed thing with endless crooked legs was digging frantically. Plated, like an ant; a red-brown bug that rapidly disappeared before their eyes. Its rows of legs scabbed and clutched. The ground gave rapidly under it. Its wicked-looking tail twisted furiously as it struggled down the tunnel it had made.

Peretti ran into the garage and grabbed up the rake. He pinned down the tail of the bug with it. 'Quick! Shoot it with the b.b. gun!'

Daniels snatched the gun and took aim. The first shot tore the tail of the bug loose. It writhed and twisted frantically; its tail dragged uselessly and some of its legs broke off. It was a foot long, like a great millipede. It struggled desperately to escape down its hole.

'Shoot again,' Peretti ordered.

Daniels fumbled with the gun. The bug slithered and hissed. Its head jerked back and forth; it twisted and bit at the rake holding it down. Its wicked specks of eyes gleamed with hatred. For a moment it struck futilely at the rake; then abruptly, without warning, it thrashed in a frantic convulsion that made them all draw away in fear.

Something buzzed through Charles' brain. A loud humming, metallic and harsh, a billion metal wires dancing and vibrating at once. He was tossed about violently by the force; the banging crash of metal made him deaf and confused. He stumbled to his feet and backed off; the others were doing the same, white-faced and shaken.

'If we can't kill it with the gun,' Peretti gasped, 'we can drown it. Or burn it. Or stick a pin through its brain.' He fought to hold onto the rake, to keep the bug pinned down.

'I have a jar of formaldehyde,' Daniels muttered. His fingers fumbled nervously with the gun. 'How do this thing work? I can't seem to—'

Charles grabbed the gun from him. 'I'll kill it.' He squatted down, one eye to the sight, and gripped the trigger. The bug lashed and struggled. Its force-field hammered in his ears, but he hung onto the gun. His finger tightened . . .

'All right, Charles,' the father-thing said. Powerful fingers gripped him, a paralyzing pressure around his wrists. The gun fell to the ground as he struggled futilely. The father-thing shoved against Peretti. The boy leaped away and the bug, free of the rake, slithered triumphantly down its tunnel.

'You have a spanking coming, Charles,' the father-thing droned on. 'What got into you? Your poor mother's out of her mind with worry.'

It had been there, hiding in the shadows. Crouched in the darkness watching them. Its calm, emotionless voice, a dreadful parody of his father's, rumbled close to his ear as it pulled him relentlessly toward the garage. Its cold breath blew in his face, an icy-sweet odor, like decaying soil. Its strength was immense; there was nothing he could do.

'Don't fight me,' it said calmly. 'Come along, into the garage. This is for your own good. I know best, Charles.'

'Did you find him?' his mother called anxiously, opening the back door.

'Yes, I found him.'

'What are you going to do?'

'A little spanking.' The father-thing pushed up the garage door. 'In the garage.' In the half-light a faint smile, humorless and utterly without emotion, touched its lips. 'You go back in the living room, June. I'll take care of this. It's more in my line. You never did like punishing him.'

The back door reluctantly closed. As the light cut off, Peretti bent down and groped for the b.b. gun. The father-thing instantly froze.

'Go on home, boys,' it rasped.

Peretti stood undecided, gripping the b.b. gun.

'Get going,' the father-thing repeated. 'Put down that toy and get out of here.' It moved slowly toward Peretti, gripping Charles with one hand, reaching toward Peretti with the other. 'No b.b. guns allowed in town, sonny. Your father know you have that? There's a city ordinance. I think you better give me that before—'

Peretti shot it in the eye.

The father-thing grunted and pawed at its ruined eye. Abruptly it slashed out at Peretti. Peretti moved down the driveway, trying to cock the gun. The father-thing lunged. Its powerful fingers snatched the gun from Peretti's hands. Silently, the father-thing mashed the gun against the wall of the house.

Charles broke away and ran numbly off. Where could he hide? It was between him and the house. Already, it was coming back toward him, a black shape creeping carefully, peering into the darkness, trying to make him out. Charles retreated. If there were only some place he could hide . . .

The bamboo.

He crept quickly into the bamboo. The stalks were huge and old. They closed after him with a faint rustle. The father-thing was fumbling in its pocket; it lit a match, then the whole pack flared up. 'Charles,' it said. 'I know you're here, someplace. There's no use hiding. You're only making it more difficult.'

His heart hammering, Charles crouched among the bamboo. Here, debris and filth rotted. Weeds, garbage, papers, boxes, old clothing, boards, tin cans, bottles. Spiders and salamanders squirmed around him. The bamboo swayed with the night wind. Insects and filth.

And something else.

A shape, a silent, unmoving shape that grew up from the mound of filth like some nocturnal mushroom. A white column, a pulpy mass that glistened moistly in the moonlight. Webs covered it, a moldy cocoon. It had vague arms and legs. An indistinct half-shaped head. As yet, the features hadn't formed. But he could tell what it was.

A mother-thing. Growing here in the filth and dampness, between the garage and the house. Behind the towering bamboo.

It was almost ready. Another few days and it would reach maturity. It was still a larva, white and soft and pulpy. But the sun would dry and warm it. Harden its shell. Turn it dark and strong. It would emerge from its cocoon, and one day when his mother came by the garage . . . Behind the mother-thing were other pulpy white larvae, recently laid by the bug. Small. Just coming into existence. He could see where the father-thing had broken off; the place where it had grown. It had matured here. And in the garage, his father had met it.

Charles began to move numbly away, past the rotting boards, the filth and debris, the pulpy mushroom larvae. Weakly, he reached out to take hold of the fence – and scrambled back.

Another one. Another larvae. He hadn't seen this one, at first. It wasn't white. It had already turned dark. The web, the pulpy softness, the moistness, were gone. It was ready. It stirred a little, moved its arm feebly.

The Charles-thing.

The bamboo separated, and the father-thing's hand clamped firmly around the boy's wrist. 'You stay right here,' it said. 'This is exactly the place for you. Don't move.' With its other hand it tore at the remains of the cocoon binding the Charles-thing. 'I'll help it out – it's still a little weak.'

The last shred of moist gray was stripped back, and the Charles-thing tottered out. It floundered uncertainly, as the father-thing cleared a path for it toward Charles.

'This way,' the father-thing grunted. 'I'll hold him for you. When you've fed you'll be stronger.'

The Charles-thing's mouth opened and closed. It reached greedily toward Charles. The boy struggled wildly, but the father-thing's immense hand held him down.

'Stop that, young man,' the father-thing commanded. 'It'll be a lot easier for you if you—'

It screamed and convulsed. It let go of Charles and staggered back. Its body twitched violently. It crashed against the garage, limbs jerking. For a time it rolled and flopped in a dance of agony. It whimpered, moaned, tried to crawl away. Gradually it became quiet. The Charles-thing settled down in a silent heap. It lay stupidly among the bamboo and rotting debris, body slack, face empty and blank.

At last the father-thing ceased to stir. There was only the faint rustle of the bamboo in the night wind.

Charles got up awkwardly. He stepped down onto the cement driveway. Peretti and Daniels approached, wide-eyed and cautious. 'Don't go near it,' Daniels ordered sharply. 'It ain't dead yet. Takes a little while.'

'What did you do?' Charles muttered.

Daniels set down the drum of kerosene with a gasp of relief. 'Found this in the garage. We Daniels always used kerosene on our mosquitoes, back in Virginia.'

'Daniels poured the kerosene down the bug's tunnel,' Peretti explained, still awed. 'It was his idea.'

Daniels kicked cautiously at the contorted body of the father-thing. 'It's dead, now. Died as soon as the bug died.'

'I guess the other'll die, too,' Peretti said. He pushed aside the bamboo to examine the larvae growing here and there among the debris. The Charles-thing didn't move at all, as Peretti jabbed the end of a stick into its chest. 'This one's dead.'

'We better make sure,' Daniels said grimly. He picked up the heavy drum of kerosene and lugged it to the edge of the bamboo. 'It dropped some matches in the driveway. You get them, Peretti.'

They looked at each other.

'Sure,' Peretti said softly.

'We better turn on the hose,' Charles said. 'To make sure it doesn't spread.'

'Let's get going,' Peretti said impatiently. He was already moving off. Charles quickly followed him and they began searching for the matches, in the moonlit darkness.

Foster, You're Dead

School was agony, as always. Only today it was worse. Mike Foster finished weaving his two watertight baskets and sat rigid, while all around him the other children worked. Outside the concrete-and-steel building the late-afternoon sun shone cool. The hills sparkled green and brown in the crisp autumn air. In the overhead sky a few NATS circled lazily above the town.

The vast, ominous shape of Mrs Cummings, the teacher, silently approached his desk. 'Foster, are you finished?'

'Yes, ma'am,' he answered eagerly. He pushed the baskets up. 'Can I leave now?'

Mrs Cummings examined his baskets critically. 'What about your trap-making?' she demanded.

He fumbled in his desk and brought out his intricate small-animal trap. 'All finished, Mrs Cummings. And my knife, it's done, too.' He showed her the razor-edged blade of his knife, glittering metal he had shaped from a discarded gasoline drum. She picked up the knife and ran her expert ringer doubtfully along the blade.

'Not strong enough,' she stated. 'You've oversharpened it. It'll lose its edge the first time you use it. Go down to the main weapons-lab and examine the knives they've got there. Then hone it back some and get a thicker blade.'

'Mrs Cummings,' Mike Foster pleaded, 'could I fix it *tomorrow*? Could I leave right now, please?'

Everybody in the classroom was watching with interest. Mike Foster flushed; he hated to be singled out and made conspicuous, but he *had* to get away. He couldn't stay in school one minute more.

Inexorable, Mrs Cummings rumbled, 'Tomorrow is digging day. You won't have time to work on your knife.'

'I will,' he assured her quickly. 'After the digging.'

'No, you're not too good at digging.' The old woman was measuring the boy's spindly arms and legs. 'I think you better get your knife finished today. And spend all day tomorrow down at the field.'

'What's the use of digging?' Mike Foster demanded, in despair.

'Everybody has to know how to dig,' Mrs Cummings answered patiently. Children were snickering on all sides; she shushed them with a hostile glare. 'You all know the importance of digging. When the war begins the whole surface will be littered with debris and rubble. If we hope to survive we'll have to dig down, won't we? Have any of you ever watched a gopher digging around the roots of plants? The gopher knows he'll find something valuable down there under the surface of the ground. We're all going to be little brown gophers. We'll all have to learn to dig down in the rubble and find the good things, because that's where they'll be.'

Mike Foster sat miserably plucking his knife, as Mrs Cummings moved away from his desk and up the aisle. A few children grinned contemptuously at him, but nothing penetrated his haze of wretchedness. Digging wouldn't do him any good. When the bombs came he'd be killed instantly. All the vaccination shots up and down his arms, on his thighs and buttocks, would be of no use. He had wasted his allowance money: Mike Foster wouldn't be alive to catch any of the bacterial plagues. Not unless—

He sprang up and followed Mrs Cummings to her desk. In an agony of desperation he blurted, 'Please, I have to leave. I have to do something.'

Mrs Cumming's tired lips twisted angrily. But the boy's fearful eyes stopped her. 'What's wrong?' she demanded. 'Don't you feel well?'

The boy stood frozen, unable to answer her. Pleased by the tableau, the class murmured and giggled until Mrs Cummings rapped angrily on her desk with a writer. 'Be quiet,' she snapped. Her voice softened a shade. 'Michael, if you're not functioning properly, go downstairs to the psyche clinic. There's no point trying to work when your reactions are conflicted. Miss Groves will be glad to optimum you.'

'No,' Foster said.

'Then what is it?'

The class stirred. Voices answered for Foster, his tongue was stuck with misery and humiliation. 'His father's an anti-P,' the voices explained. 'They don't have a shelter and he isn't registered in Civic Defense. His father hasn't even contributed to the NATS. They haven't done anything.'

Mrs Cummings gazed up in amazement at the mute boy. 'You don't have a shelter?'

He shook his head.

A strange feeling filled the woman. 'But—' She had started to say, *But you'll die up here*. She changed it to 'But where'll you go?'

'Nowhere,' the mild voices answered for him. 'Everybody else'll be down in their shelters and he'll be up here. He even doesn't have a permit for the school shelter.'

Mrs Cummings was shocked. In her dull, scholastic way she had assumed every child in the school had a permit to the elaborate subsurface chambers under the building. But of course not. Only children whose parents were part of CD, who contributed to arming the community. And if Foster's father was an anti-P . . .

'He's afraid to sit here,' the voices chimed in calmly. 'He's afraid it'll come while he's sitting here, and everybody else will be safe down in the shelter.'

He wandered slowly along, hands deep in his pockets, kicking at dark stones on the sidewalk. The sun was setting. Snub-nosed commute rockets were unloading tired people, glad to be home from the factory strip a hundred miles to the west. On the distant hills something flashed: a radar tower revolving silently in the evening gloom. The circling NATS had increased in number. The twilight hours were the most dangerous; visual observers couldn't spot high-speed missiles coming in close to the ground. Assuming the missiles came.

A mechanical news-machine shouted at him excitedly as he passed. War, death, amazing new weapons developed at home and abroad. He hunched his shoulders and continued on, past the little concrete shells that served as houses, each exactly alike, sturdy reinforced pillboxes. Ahead of him bright neon signs glowed in the settling gloom: the business district, alive with traffic and milling people.

Half a block from the bright cluster of neons he halted. To his right was a public shelter, a dark tunnel-like entrance with a mechanical turnstile glowing dully. Fifty cents admission. If he was here, on the street, and he had fifty cents, he'd be all right. He had pushed down into public shelters many times, during the practice raids. But other times, hideous, nightmare times that never left his mind, he hadn't had the fifty cents. He had stood mute and terrified, while people pushed excitedly past him; and the shrill shrieks of the sirens thundered everywhere.

He continued slowiy, until he came to the brightest blotch of light, the great, gleaming showrooms of General Electronics, two blocks long, illuminated on all sides, a vast square of pure color and radiation. He halted and examined for the millionth time the fascinating shapes, the display that always drew him to a hypnotized stop whenever he passed.

In the center of the vast room was a single object. An elaborate pulsing blob of machinery and support struts, beams and walls and sealed locks. All spotlights were turned on it; huge signs announced its hundred and one advantages – as if there could be any doubt.

> THE NEW 1972 BOMBPROOF RADIATION–SEALED
> SUBSURFACE SHELTER IS HERE! CHECK THESE
> STAR–STUDDED FEATURES:
> * automatic descent-lift – jam-proof, self-powered, e-z locking
> * triple-layer hull guaranteed to withstand 5g pressure without buckling
> * A-powered heating and refrigeration system – self-servicing air-purification network
> * three decontamination stages for food and water
> * four hygienic stages for pre-burn exposure
> * complete antibiotic processing
> * e-z payment plan

He gazed at the shelter a long time. It was mostly a big tank, with a neck at one end that was the descent tube, and an emergency escape-hatch at the other. It was completely self-contained: a miniature world that supplied its own light, heat, air, water, medicines, and almost inexhaustible food. When fully stocked there were visual and audio tapes, entertainment, beds, chairs, vidscreen, everything that made up the above-surface home. It was, actually, a home below the ground. Nothing was missing that might be needed or enjoyed. A family would be safe, even comfortable, during the most severe H-bomb and bacterial-spray attack.

It cost twenty thousand dollars.

While he was gazing silently at the massive display, one of the salesmen stepped out onto the dark sidewalk, on his way to the cafeteria. 'Hi, sonny,' he said automatically, as he passed Mike Foster. 'Not bad, is it?'

'Can I go inside?' Foster asked quickly. 'Can I go down in it?'

The salesman stopped, as he recognized the boy. 'You're that kid,' he said slowly, 'that damn kid who's always pestering us.'

'I'd like to go down in it. Just for a couple minutes. I won't bust anything – I promise. I won't even touch anything.'

The salesman was young and blond, a good-looking man in his early twenties. He hesitated, his reactions divided. The kid was a pest. But he had a family, and that meant a reasonable prospect. Business was bad; it was late September and the seasonal slump was still on. There was no profit in telling the boy to go peddle his newstapes; but on the other hand it was bad business encouraging small fry to crawl around the merchandise. They wasted time; they broke things; they pilfered small stuff when nobody was looking.

'No dice,' the salesman said. 'Look, send your old man down here. Has he seen what we've got?'

'Yes,' Mike Foster said tightly.

'What's holding him back?' The salesman waved expansively up at the great gleaming display. 'We'll give him a good trade-in on his old one, allowing for depreciation and obsolescence. What model has he got?'

'We don't have any,' Mike Foster said.

The salesman blinked. 'Come again?'

'My father says it's a waste of money. He says they're trying to scare people into buying things they don't need. He says—'

'Your father's an anti-P?'

'Yes,' Mike Foster answered unhappily.

The salesman let out his breath. 'Okay, kid. Sorry we can't do business. It's not your fault.' He lingered. 'What the hell's wrong with him? Does he put on the NATS?'

'No.'

The salesman swore under his breath. A coaster, sliding along, safe because the rest of the community was putting up thirty per cent of its income to keep a constant-defense system going. There were always a few of them, in every town. 'How's your mother feel?' the salesman demanded. 'She go along with him?'

'She says—' Mike Foster broke off. 'Couldn't I go down in it for a little while? I won't bust anything. Just *once*.'

'How'd we ever sell it if we let kids run through it? We're not marking it down as a demonstration model – we've got roped into that too often.' The salesman's curiosity was aroused. 'How's a guy get to be anti-P? He always feel this way, or did he get stung with something?'

'He says they sold people as many cars and washing machine

and television sets as they could use. He says NATS and bomb shelters aren't good for anything, so people never get all they can use. He says factories can keep turning out guns and gas masks forever, and as long as people are afraid they'll keep paying for them because they think if they don't they might get killed, and maybe a man gets tired of paying for a new car every year and stops, but he's never going to stop buying shelters to protect his children.'

'You believe that?' the salesman asked.

'I wish we had that shelter,' Mike Foster answered. 'If we had a shelter like that I'd go down and sleep in it every night. It'd be there when we needed it.'

'Maybe there won't be a war,' the salesman said. He sensed the boy's misery and fear, and he grinned good-naturedly down at him. 'Don't worry all the time. You probably watch too many vidtapes – get out and play, for a change.'

'Nobody's safe on the surface,' Mike Foster said. 'We have to be down below. And there's no place I can go.'

'Send your old man around,' the salesman muttered uneasily. 'Maybe we can talk him into it. We've got a lot of time-payment plans. Tell him to ask for Bill O'Neill. Okay?'

Mike Foster wandered away, down the black evening street. He knew he was supposed to be home, but his feet dragged and his body was heavy and dull. His fatigue made him remember what the athletic coach had said the day before, during exercises. They were practicing breath suspension, holding a lungful of air and running. He hadn't done well; the others were still redfaced and racing when he halted, expelled his air, and stood gasping frantically for breath.

'Foster,' the coach said angrily, 'you're dead. You know that? If this had been a gas attack—' He shook his head wearily. 'Go over there and practice by yourself. You've got to do better, if you expect to survive.'

But he didn't expect to survive.

When he stepped up onto the porch of his home, he found the living room lights already on. He could hear his father's voice, and more faintly his mother's from the kitchen. He closed the door after him and began unpeeling his coat.

'Is that you?' his father demanded. Bob Foster sat sprawled out in his chair, his lap full of tapes and report sheets from his retail furniture store. 'Where have you been? Dinner's been ready half an hour.' He had taken off his coat and rolled up his sleeves. His arms were pale and thin, but muscular. He was tired; his eyes were large and dark, his hair thinning. Restlessly, he moved the tapes around, from one stack to another.

'I'm sorry,' Mike Foster said.

His father examined his pocket watch; he was surely the only man who still carried a watch. 'Go wash your hands. What have you been doing?' He scrutinized his son. 'You look odd. Do you feel all right?'

'I was downtown,' Mike Foster said.

'What were you doing?'

'Looking at the shelters.'

Wordless, his father grabbed up a handful of reports and stuffed them into a folder. His thin lips set; hard lines wrinkled his forehead. He snorted furiously as tapes spilled everywhere; he bent stiffly to pick them up. Mike Foster made no move to help him. He crossed to the closet and gave his coat to the hanger. When he turned away his mother was directing the table of food into the dining room.

They ate without speaking, intent on their food and not looking at each other. Finally his father said, 'What'd you see? Same old dogs, I suppose.'

'There's the new '72 models,' Mike Foster answered.

'They're the same as the '71 models.' His father threw down his fork savagely; the table caught and absorbed it. 'A few new gadgets, some more chrome. That's all.' Suddenly he was facing his son defiantly. 'Right?'

Mike Foster toyed wretchedly with his creamed chicken. 'The new ones have a jam-proof descent lift. You can't get stuck halfway down. All you have to do is get in it, and it does the rest.'

'There'll be one next year that'll pick you up and carry you down. This one'll be obsolete as soon as people buy it. That's what they want – they want you to keep buying. They keep putting out new ones as fast as they can. This isn't 1972, it's still 1971. What's that thing doing out already? Can't they wait?'

Mike Foster didn't answer. He had heard it all before, many times. There was never anything new, only chrome and gadgets; yet the old ones became obsolete, anyhow. His father's argument was loud, impassioned, almost frenzied, but it made no sense. 'Let's get an old one, then,' he blurted out. 'I don't care, any one'll do. Even a secondhand one.'

'No, you want the *new* one. Shiny and glittery to impress the neighbors. Lots of dials and knobs and machinery. How much do they want for it?'

'Twenty thousand dollars.'

His father let his breath out. 'Just like that.'

'They've easy time-payment plans.'

'Sure. You pay for it the rest of your life. Interest, carrying charges, and how long is it guaranteed for?'

'Three months.'

'What happens when it breaks down? It'll stop purifying and decontaminating. It'll fall apart as soon as the three months are over.'

Mike Foster shook his head. 'No. It's big and sturdy.'

His father flushed. He was a small man, slender and light, brittle-boned. He thought suddenly of his lifetime of lost battles, struggling up the hard way, carefully collecting and holding on to something, a job, money, his retail store, bookkeeper to manager, finally owner. 'They're scaring us to keep the wheels going,' he yelled desperately at his wife and son. 'They don't want another depression.'

'Bob,' his wife said, slowly and quietly, 'you have to stop this. I can't stand any more.'

Bob Foster blinked. 'What're you talking about?' he muttered. 'I'm tired. These goddamn taxes. It isn't possible for a little store to keep open, not with the big chains. There ought to be a law.' His voice trailed off. 'I guess I'm through eating.' He pushed away from the table and got to his feet. 'I'm going to lie down on the couch and take a nap.'

His wife's thin face blazed. 'You have to get one! I can't stand the way they talk about us. All the neighbors and the merchants, everybody who knows. I can't go anywhere or do anything without hearing about it. Ever since that day they put up the flag. *Anti-P*. The last in the whole town. Those things circling around up there, and everybody paying for them but us.'

'No,' Bob Foster said. 'I can't get one.'

'Why not?'

'Because,' he answered simply, 'I can't afford it.'

There was silence.

'You've put everything in that store,' Ruth said finally. 'And it's failing anyhow. You're just like a pack-rat, hoarding everything down at that ratty little hole-in-the-wall. Nobody wants wood furniture anymore. You're a relic – a curiosity.' She slammed at the table and it leaped wildly to gather the empty dishes, like a startled animal. It dashed furiously from the room and back into the kitchen, the dishes churning in its washtank as it raced.

Bob Foster sighed wearily. 'Let's not fight. I'll be in the living room. Let me take a nap for an hour or so. Maybe we can talk about it later.'

'Always later,' Ruth said bitterly.

Her husband disappeared into the living room, a small, hunched-over figure, hair scraggly and gray, shoulder blades like broken wings.

Mike got to his feet. 'I'll go study my homework,' he said. He followed after his father, a strange look on his face.

The living room was quiet; the vidset was off and the lamp was down low. Ruth was in the kitchen setting the controls on the stove for the next month's meals. Bob Foster lay stretched out on the couch, his shoes off, his head on a pillow. His face was gray with fatigue. Mike hesitated for a moment and then said, 'Can I ask you something?'

His father grunted and stirred, opened his eyes. 'What?'

Mike sat down facing him. 'Tell me again how you gave advice to the President.'

His father pulled himself up. 'I didn't give any advice to the President. I just talked to him.'

'Tell me about it.'

'I've told you a million times. Every once in a while, since you were a baby. You were with me.' His voice softened, as he remembered. 'You were just a toddler – we had to carry you.'

'What did he look like?'

'Well,' his father began, slipping into a routine he had worked out and petrified over the years, 'he looked about like he does in the vidscreen. Smaller, though.'

'Why was he here?' Mike demanded avidly, although he knew every detail. The President was his hero, the man he most admired in all the world. 'Why'd he come all the way out here to *our* town?'

'He was on a tour.' Bitterness crept into his father's voice. 'He happened to be passing through.'

'What kind of a tour?'

'Visiting towns all over the country.' The harshness increased. 'Seeing how we were getting along. Seeing if we had bought enough NATS and bomb shelters and plague shots and gas masks and radar networks to repel attack. The General Electronics Corporation was just beginning to put up its big showrooms and displays – everything bright and glittering and expensive. The first defense equipment available for home purchase.' His lips twisted. 'All on easy-payment plans. Ads, posters, searchlights, free gardenias and dishes for the ladies.'

Mike Foster's breath panted in his throat. 'That was the day we got our Preparedness Flag,' he said hungrily. 'That was the day he came to give us our flag. And they ran it up on the flagpole in the middle of the town, and everybody was there yelling and cheering.'

'You remember that?'

'I – think so. I remember people and sounds. And it was hot. It was June, wasn't it?'

'June 10, 1965. Quite an occasion. Not many towns had the big green flag, then. People were still buying cars and TV sets. They hadn't discovered those days were over. TV sets and cars are good for something – you can only manufacture and sell so many of them.'

'He gave *you* the flag, didn't he?'

'Well, he gave it to all us merchants. The Chamber of Commerce had it arranged. Competition between towns, see who can buy the most the soonest. Improve our town and at the same time stimulate business. Of course, the way they put it, the idea was if we had to *buy* our gas masks and bomb shelters we'd take better care of them. As if we ever damaged telephones and sidewalks. Or highways, because the whole state provided them. Or armies. Haven't there always been armies? Hasn't the government always organized its people for defense? I guess defense costs too much. I guess they save a lot of money, cut down the national debt by this.'

'Tell me what he said,' Mike Foster whispered.

His father fumbled for his pipe and lit it with trembling hands. 'He said, "*Here's your flag, boys. You've done a good job.*"' Bob Foster choked, as acrid pipe fumes guzzled up. 'He was red-faced, sunburned, not embarrassed. Perspiring and grinning. He knew how to handle himself. He knew a lot of first names. Told a funny joke.'

The boy's eyes were wide with awe. 'He came all the way out here, and you talked to him.'

'Yeah,' his father said. 'I talked to him. They were all yelling and cheering. The flag was going up, the big green Preparedness Flag.'

'You said—'

'I said to him, "*Is that all you brought us? A strip of green cloth?*"' Bob Foster dragged tensely on his pipe. 'That was when I became an anti-P.

Only I didn't know it at the time. All I knew was we were on our own, except for a strip of green cloth. We should have been a country, a whole nation, one hundred and seventy million people working together to defend ourselves. And instead, we're a lot of separate little towns, little walled forts. Sliding and slipping back to the Middle Ages. Raising our separate armies—'

'Will the President ever come back?' Mike asked.

'I doubt it. He was – just passing through.'

'If he comes back,' Mike whispered, tense and not daring to hope, 'can we go *see* him? Can we *look* at him?'

Bob Foster pulled himself up to a sitting position. His bony arms were bare and white; his lean face was drab with weariness. And resignation. 'How much was the damn thing you saw?' he demanded hoarsely. 'That bomb shelter?'

Mike's heart stopped beating. 'Twenty thousand dollars.'

'This is Thursday. I'll go down with you and your mother next Saturday.' Bob Foster knocked out his smoldering, half-lit pipe. 'I'll get it on the easy-payment plan. The fall buying season is coming up soon. I usually do good – people buy wood furniture for Christmas gifts.' He got up abruptly from the couch. 'Is it a deal?'

Mike couldn't answer; he could only nod.

'Fine,' his father said, with desperate cheerfulness. 'Now you won't have to go down and look at it in the window.'

The shelter was installed – for an additional two hundred dollars – by a fast-working team of laborers in brown coats with the words GENERAL ELECTRONICS stitched across their backs. The back yard was quickly restored, dirt and shrubs spaded in place, the surface smoothed over, and the bill respectfully slipped under the front door. The lumbering delivery truck, now empty, clattered off down the street and the neighborhood was again silent.

Mike Foster stood with his mother and a small group of admiring neighbors on the back porch of the house. 'Well,' Mrs Carlyle said finally, 'now you've got a shelter. The best there is.'

'That's right,' Ruth Foster agreed. She was conscious of the people around her; it had been some time since so many had shown up at once. Grim satisfaction filled her gaunt frame, almost resentment. 'It certainly makes a difference,' she said harshly.

'Yes,' Mr Douglas from down the street agreed. 'Now you have some place to go.' He had picked up the thick book of instructions the laborers had left. 'It says here you can stock it for a whole year. Live down there twelve months without coming up once.' He shook his head admiringly. 'Mine's an old '69 model. Good for only six months. I guess maybe—'

'It's still good enough for us,' his wife cut in, but there was a longing wistfulness in her voice. 'Can we go down and peek at it, Ruth? It's all ready, isn't it?'

Mike made a strangled noise and moved jerkily forward. His mother smiled understandingly. 'He has to go down there first. He gets first look at it – it's really for him, you know.'

Their arms folded against the chill September wind, the group of men and women stood waiting and watching, as the boy approached the neck of the shelter and halted a few steps in front of it.

He entered the shelter carefully, almost afraid to touch anything. The neck was big for him; it was built to admit a full grown man. As soon as his weight was on the descent lift it dropped beneath him. With a breathless *whoosh* it plummeted down the pitch-black tube to the body of the shelter. The lift slammed hard against its shock absorbers and the boy stumbled from it. The lift shot back to the surface, simultaneously sealing off the subsurface shelter, an impassable steel-and-plastic cork in the narrow neck.

Lights had come on around him automatically. The shelter was bare and empty; no supplies had yet been carried down. It smelled of varnish and motor grease: below him the generators were throbbing dully. His presence activated the purifying and decontamination systems; on the blank concrete wall meters and dials moved into sudden activity.

He sat down on the floor, knees drawn up, face solemn, eyes wide. There was no sound but that of the generators; the world above was completely cut off. He was in a little self-contained cosmos; everything needed was here – or would be here, soon: food, water, air, things to do. Nothing else was wanted. He could reach out and touch – whatever he needed. He could stay here forever, through all time, without stirring. Complete and entire. Not lacking, not fearing, with only the sound of the generators purring below him, and the sheer, ascetic walls around and above him on all sides, faintly warm, completely friendly, like a living container.

Suddenly he shouted, a loud jubilant shout that echoed and bounced from wall to wall. He was deafened by the reverberation. He shut his eyes tight and clenched his fists. Joy filled him. He shouted again – and let the roar of sound lap over him, his own voice reinforced by the near walls, close and hard and incredibly powerful.

The kids in school knew even before he showed up, the next morning. They greeted him as he approached, all of them grinning and nudging each other. 'Is it true your folks got a new General Electronics Model S-72ft?' Earl Peters demanded.

'That's right,' Mike answered. His heart swelled with a peaceful confidence he had never known. 'Drop around,' he said, as casually as he could. 'I'll show it to you.'

He passed on, conscious of their envious faces.

'Well, Mike,' Mrs Cummings said, as he was leaving the classroom at the end of the day. 'How does it feel?'

He halted by her desk, shy and full of quiet pride. 'It feels good,' he admitted.

'Is your father contributing to the NATS?'

'Yes.'

'And you've got a permit for our school shelter?'

He happily showed her the small blue seal clamped around his wrist. 'He mailed a check to the city for everything. He said, "As long as I've gone this far I might as well go the rest of the way." '

'Now you have everything everybody else has.' The elderly woman smiled across at him. 'I'm glad of that. You're now a pro-P, except there's no such term. You're just – like everyone else.'

The next day the news-machines shrilled out the news. The first revelation of the new Soviet bore-pellets.

Bob Foster stood in the middle of the living room, the newstape in his hands, his thin face flushed with fury and despair. 'Goddamn it, it's a plot!' His voice rose in baffled frenzy. 'We just bought the thing and now look. *Look!*' He shoved the tape at his wife. 'You see? I told you!'

'I've seen it,' Ruth said wildly. 'I suppose you think the whole world was just waiting with you in mind. They're always improving weapons, Bob. Last week it was those grain-impregnation flakes. This week it's bore-pellets. You don't expect them to stop the wheels of progress because you finally broke down and bought a shelter, do you?'

The man and woman faced each other. 'What the hell are we going to do?' Bob Foster asked quietly.

Ruth paced back into the kitchen. 'I heard they were going to turn out adaptors.'

'Adaptors! What do you mean?'

'So people won't have to buy new shelters. There was a commercial on the vidscreen. They're going to put some kind of metal grill on the market, as soon as the government approves it. They spread it over the ground and it intercepts the bore-pellets. It screens them, makes them explode on the surface, so they can't burrow down to the shelter.'

'How much?'

'They didn't say.'

Mike Foster sat crouched on the sofa, listening. He had heard the news at school. They were taking their test on berry-identification, examining encased samples of wild berries to distinguish the harmless ones from the toxic, when the bell had announced a general assembly. The principal read them the news about the bore-pellets and then gave a routine lecture on emergency treatment of a new variant of typhus, recently developed.

His parents were still arguing. 'We'll have to get one,' Ruth Foster said calmly. 'Otherwise it won't make any difference whether we've got a shelter or not. The bore-pellets were specifically designed to penetrate the surface and seek out warmth. As soon as the Russians have them in production—'

'I'll get one,' Bob Foster said. 'I'll get an anti-pellet grill and whatever else they have. I'll buy everything they put on the market. I'll never stop buying.'

'It's not as bad as that.'

'You know, this game has one real advantage over selling people cars and TV sets. With something like this we *have* to buy. It isn't a luxury, something big and flashy to impress the neighbors, something we could do without. If we don't buy this we die. They always said the way to sell something was create anxiety in people. Create a sense of insecurity – tell them they smell bad or look funny. But this makes a joke out of deodorant and hair oil. You can't escape this. If you don't buy, *they'll kill you*. The perfect sales-pitch. Buy or die – new slogan. Have a shiny new General Electronics H-bomb shelter in your back yard or be slaughtered.'

'Stop talking like that!' Ruth snapped.

Bob Foster threw himself down at the kitchen table. 'All right. I give up. I'll go along with it.'

'You'll get one? I think they'll be on the market by Christmas.'

'Oh, yes,' Foster said. 'They'll be out by Christmas.' There was a strange look on his face. 'I'll buy one of the damn things for Christmas, and so will everybody else.'

The GEC grill-screen adaptors were a sensation.

Mike Foster walked slowly along the crowd-packed December street, through the late-afternoon twilight. Adaptors glittered in every store window. All shapes and sizes, for every kind of shelter. All prices, for every pocket-book. The crowds of people were gay and excited, typical Christmas crowds, shoving good-naturedly, loaded down with packages and heavy overcoats. The air was white with gusts of sweeping snow. Cars nosed cautiously along the jammed streets. Lights and neon displays, immense glowing store windows gleamed on all sides.

His own house was dark and silent. His parents weren't home yet. Both of them were down at the store working; business had been bad and his mother was taking the place of one of the clerks. Mike held his hand up to the code-key, and the front door let him in. The automatic furnace had kept the house warm and pleasant. He removed his coat and put away his schoolbooks.

He didn't stay in the house long. His heart pounding with excitement, he felt his way out the back door and started onto the back porch.

He forced himself to stop, turn around, and reenter the house. It was better if he didn't hurry things. He had worked out every moment of the process, from the first instant he saw the low hinge of the neck reared up hard and firm against the evening sky. He had made a fine art of it; there was no wasted motion. His procedure had been shaped, molded until it was a beautiful thing. The first overwhelming sense of *presence* as the neck of the shelter came around him. Then the blood-freezing rush of air as the descent-lift hurtled down all the way to the bottom.

And the grandeur of the shelter itself.

Every afternoon, as soon as he was home, he made his way down into it, below the surface, concealed and protected in its steel silence, as he had done since the first day. Now the chamber was full, not empty. Filled with endless cans of food, pillows, books, vidtapes, audio-tapes, prints on the walls, bright fabrics, textures and colors, even vases of flowers. The shelter was his place, where he crouched curled up, surrounded by everything he needed.

Delaying things as long as possible, he hurried back through the house and rummaged in the audio-tape file. He'd sit down in the shelter until dinner, listening to *Wind in the Willows*. His parents knew where to find him; he was always down there. Two hours of uninterrupted happiness, alone by himself in the shelter. And then when dinner was over he would hurry back down, to stay until time for bed. Sometimes late at night, when his parents were sound asleep, he got quietly up and made his way outside, to the shelter-neck, and down into its silent depths. To hide until morning.

He found the audio-tape and hurried through the house, out onto the back porch and into the yard. The sky was a bleak gray, shot with streamers of ugly black clouds. The lights of the town were coming on here and there. The yard was cold and hostile. He made his way uncertainly down the steps – and froze.

A vast yawning cavity loomed. A gaping mouth, vacant and toothless, fixed open to the night sky. There was nothing else. The shelter was gone.

He stood for an endless time, the tape clutched in one hand, the other hand on the porch railing. Night came on; the dead hole dissolved in darkness. The whole world gradually collapsed into silence and abysmal gloom. Weak stars came out; lights in nearby houses came on fitfully, cold and faint. The boy saw nothing. He stood unmoving, his body rigid as stone, still facing the great pit where the shelter had been.

Then his father was standing beside him. 'How long have you been here?' his father was saying. 'How long, Mike? Answer me!'

With a violent effort Mike managed to drag himself back. 'You're home early,' he muttered.

'I left the store early on purpose. I wanted to be here when you – got home.'

'It's gone.'

'Yes.' His father's voice was cold, without emotion. 'The shelter's gone. I'm sorry, Mike. I called them and told them to take it back.'

'Why?'

'I couldn't pay for it. Not this Christmas, with those grills everyone's getting. I can't compete with them.' He broke off and then continued wretchedly, 'They were damn decent. They gave me back half the money I put in.' His voice twisted ironically. 'I knew if I made a deal with them before Christmas I'd come out better. They can resell it to somebody else.'

255

Mike said nothing.

'Try to understand,' his father went on harshly. 'I had to throw what capital I could scrape together into the store. I have to keep it running. It was either give up the shelter or the store. And if I gave up the store—'

'Then we wouldn't have anything.'

His father caught hold of his arm. 'Then we'd have to give up the shelter, too.' His thin, strong fingers dug in spasmodically. 'You're growing up – you're old enough to understand. We'll get one later, maybe not the biggest, the most expensive, but something. It was a mistake, Mike. I couldn't swing it, not with the goddamn adaptor things to buck. I'm keeping up the NAT payments, though. And your school tab. I'm keeping that going. This isn't a matter of principle,' he finished desperately. 'I can't help it. Do you understand, Mike? *I had to do it.*'

Mike pulled away.

'Where are you going?' His father hurried after him. 'Come back here!' He grabbed for his son frantically, but in the gloom he stumbled and fell. Stars blinded him as his head smashed into the edge of the house; he pulled himself up painfully and groped for some support.

When he could see again, the yard was empty. His son was gone.

'Mike!' he yelled. 'Where are you?'

There was no answer. The night wind blew clouds of snow around him, a think bitter gust of chilled air. Wind and darkness, nothing else.

Bill O'Neill wearily examined the clock on the wall. It was nine thirty: he could finally close the doors and lock up the big dazzling store. Push the milling, murmuring throngs of people outside and on their way home.

'Thank God,' he breathed, as he held the door open for the last old lady, loaded down with packages and presents. He threw the code bolt in place and pulled down the shade. 'What a mob. I never saw so many people.'

'All done,' Al Conners said, from the cash register. 'I'll count the money – you go around and check everything. Make sure we got all of them out.'

O'Neill pushed his blond hair back and loosened his tie. He lit a cigarette gratefully, then moved around the store, checking light switches, turning off the massive GEC displays and appliances. Finally he approached the huge bomb shelter that took up the center of the floor.

He climbed the ladder to the neck and stepped onto the lift. The lift dropped with a *whoosh* and a second later he stepped out in the cavelike interior of the shelter.

In one corner Mike Foster sat curled up in a tight heap, his knees drawn up against his chin, his skinny arms wrapped around his ankles. His face was pushed down; only his ragged brown hair showed. He didn't move as the salesman approached him, astounded.

'Jesus!' O'Neill exclaimed. 'It's that kid.'

Mike said nothing. He hugged his legs tighter and buried his head as far down as possible.

'What the hell are you doing down here?' O'Neill demanded, surprised and angry. His outrage increased. 'I thought your folks got one of these.' Then he remembered. 'That's right. We had to repossess it.'

Al Conners appeared from the descent-lift. 'What's holding you up? Let's get out of here and—' He saw Mike and broke off. 'What's he doing down here? Get him out and let's go.'

'Come on, kid,' O'Neill said gently. 'Time to go home.'

Mike didn't move.

The two men looked at each other. 'I guess we're going to have to drag him out,' Conners said grimly. He took off his coat and tossed it over a decontamination fixture. 'Come on. Let's get it over with.'

It took both of them. The boy fought desperately, without sound, clawing and struggling and tearing at them with his fingernails, kicking them, slashing at them, biting them when they grabbed him. They half-dragged, half-carried him to the descent-lift and pushed him into it long enough to activate the mechanism. O'Neill rode up with him; Conners came immediately after. Grimly, efficiently, they bundled the boy to the front door, threw him out, and locked the bolts after him.

'Wow,' Conners gasped, sinking down against the counter. His sleeve was torn and his cheek was cut and gashed. His glasses hung from one ear; his hair was rumpled and he was exhausted. 'Think we ought to call the cops? There's something wrong with that kid.'

O'Neill stood by the door, panting for breath and gazing out into the darkness. He could see the boy sitting on the pavement. 'He's still out there,' he muttered. People pushed by the boy on both sides. Finally one of them stopped and got him up. The boy struggled away, and then disappeared into the darkness. The larger figure picked up its packages, hesitated a moment, and then went on. O'Neill turned away. 'What a hell of a thing.' He wiped his face with his handkerchief. 'He sure put up a fight.'

'What was the matter with him? He never said anything, not a goddamn word.'

'Christmas is a hell of a time to repossess something,' O'Neill said. He reached shakily for his coat. 'It's too bad. I wish they could have kept it.'

Conners shrugged. 'No tickie, no laundry.'

'Why the hell can't we give them a deal? Maybe—' O'Neill struggled to get the word out. 'Maybe sell the shelter wholesale, to people like that.'

Conners glared at him angrily. '*Wholesale*? And then everybody wants it wholesale. It wouldn't be fair – and how long would we stay in business? How long would GEC last that way?'

'I guess not very long,' O'Neill admitted moodily.

'Use your head.' Conners laughed sharply. 'What you need is a good stiff drink. Come on in the back closet – I've got a fifty of Haig and Haig in a drawer back there. A little something to warm you up, before you go home. That's what you need.'

Mike Foster wandered aimlessly along the dark street, among the crowds of shoppers hurrying home. He saw nothing; people pushed against him but he was unaware of them. Lights, laughing people, the honking of car horns, the clang of signals. He was blank, his mind empty and dead. He walked automatically, without consciousness or feeling.

To his right a garish neon sign winked and glowed in the deepening night shadows. A huge sign, bright and colorful.

PEACE ON EARTH   GOOD WILL TO MEN
PUBLIC SHELTER   ADMISSION 50¢

Human Is

Jill Herrick's blue eyes filled with tears. She gazed at her husband in unspeakable horror. 'You're – you're hideous!' she wailed.

Lester Herrick continued working, arranging heaps of notes and graphs in precise piles.

'Hideous,' he stated, 'is a value judgment. It contains no factual information.' He sent a report tape on Centauran parasitic life whizzing through the desk scanner. 'Merely an opinion. An expression of emotion, nothing more.'

Jill stumbled back to the kitchen. Listlessly, she waved her hand to trip the stove into activity. Conveyor belts in the wall hummed to life, hurrying the food from the underground storage lockers for the evening meal.

She turned to face her husband one last time. 'Not even a *little* while?' she begged. 'Not even—'

'Not even for a month. When he comes you can tell him. If you haven't the courage, I'll do it. I can't have a child running around here. I have too much work to do. This report on Betelgeuse XI is due in ten days.' Lester dropped a spool on Fomalhautan fossil implements into the scanner. 'What's the matter with your brother? Why can't he take care of his own child?'

Jill dabbed at swollen eyes. 'Don't you understand? I *want* Gus here! I begged Frank to let him come. And now you—'

'I'll be glad when he's old enough to be turned over to the Government.' Lester's thin face twisted in annoyance. 'Damn it, Jill, isn't dinner ready yet? It's been ten minutes! What's wrong with that stove?'

'It's almost ready.' The stove showed a red signal light. The robant waiter had come out of the wall and was waiting expectantly to take the food.

Jill sat down and blew her small nose violently. In the living room, Lester worked on unperturbed. His work. His research. Day after day.

Lester was getting ahead; there was no doubt of that. His lean body was bent like a coiled spring over the tape scanner, cold gray eyes taking in the information feverishly, analyzing, appraising, his conceptual faculties operating like well-greased machinery.

Jill's lips trembled in misery and resentment. Gus – little Gus. How could she tell him? Fresh tears welled up in her eyes. Never to see the chubby little fellow again. He could never come back – because his childish laughter and play bothered Lester. Interfered with his research.

The stove clicked to green. The food slid out, into the arms of the robant. Soft chimes sounded to announce dinner.

'I hear it,' Lester grated. He snapped off the scanner and got to his feet. 'I suppose he'll come while we're eating.'

'I can vid Frank and ask—'

'No. Might as well get it over with.' Lester nodded impatiently to the robant. 'All right. Put it down.' His thin lips set in an angry line. 'Damn it, don't dawdle! I want to get back to my work!'

Jill bit back the tears.

Little Gus came trailing into the house as they were finishing dinner.

Jill gave a cry of joy. 'Gussie!' She ran to sweep him up in her arms. 'I'm so glad to see you!'

'Watch out for my tiger,' Gus muttered. He dropped his little gray kitten onto the rug and it rushed off, under the couch. 'He's hiding.'

Lester's eyes flickered as he studied the little boy and the tip of gray tail extending from under the couch.

'Why do you call it a tiger? It's nothing but an alley cat.'

Gus looked hurt. He scowled. 'He's a tiger. He's got stripes.'

'Tigers are yellow and a great deal bigger. You might as well learn to classify things by their correct names.'

'Lester, please—' Jill pleaded.

'Be quiet,' her husband said crossly. 'Gus is old enough to shed childish illusions and develop a realistic orientation. What's wrong with the psych testers? Don't they straighten this sort of nonsense out?'

Gus ran and snatched up his tiger. 'You leave him alone!'

Lester contemplated the kitten. A strange, cold smile played about his lips. 'Come down to the lab some time, Gus. We'll show you lots of cats. We use them in our research. Cats, guinea pigs, rabbits—'

'Lester!' Jill gasped. 'How can you!'

Lester laughed thinly. Abruptly he broke off and returned to his desk. 'Now clear out of here. I have to finish these reports. And don't forget to tell Gus.'

Gus got excited. 'Tell me what?' His cheeks flushed. His eyes sparkled. 'What is it? Something for me? A *secret*?'

Jill's heart was like lead. She put her hand heavily on the child's shoulder. 'Come on, Gus. We'll go sit out in the garden and I'll tell you. Bring – bring your tiger.'

A click. The emergency vidsender lit up. Instantly Lester was on his feet. 'Be quiet!' He ran to the sender, breathing rapidly. 'Nobody speak!'

Jill and Gus paused at the door. A confidential message was sliding from the slot into the dish. Lester grabbed it up and broke the seal. He studied it intently.

'What is it?' Jill asked. 'Anything bad?'

'Bad?' Lester's face shone with a deep inner glow. 'No, not bad at all.' He glanced at his watch. 'Just time. Let's see, I'll need—'

'What is it?'

'I'm going on a trip. I'll be gone two or three weeks. Rexor IV is into the charted area.'

'Rexor IV? You're going there?' Jill clasped her hands eagerly. 'Oh, I've always wanted to see an old system, old ruins and cities! Lester, can I come along? Can I go with you? We never took a vacation, and you always promised—'

Lester Herrick stared at his wife in amazement. 'You?' he said. '*You* go along?' He laughed unpleasantly. 'Now hurry and get my things together. I've been waiting for this a long time.' He rubbed his hands together in satisfaction. 'You can keep the boy here until I'm back. But no longer. Rexor IV! I can hardly wait!'

'You have to make allowances,' Frank said. 'After all, he's a scientist.'

'I don't care,' Jill said. 'I'm leaving him. As soon as he gets back from Rexor IV. I've made up my mind.'

Her brother was silent, deep in thought. He stretched his feet out, onto the lawn of the little garden. 'Well, if you leave him you'll be free to marry again. You're still classed as sexually adequate, aren't you?'

Jill nodded firmly. 'You bet I am. I wouldn't have any trouble. Maybe I can find somebody who likes children.'

'You think a lot of children,' Frank perceived. 'Gus loves to go visit you. But he doesn't like Lester. Les needles him.'

'I know. This past week has been heaven, with him gone.' Jill patted her soft blonde hair, blushing prettily. 'I've had fun. Makes me feel alive again.'

'When'll he be back?'

'Any day.' Jill clenched her small fists. 'We've been married five years and every year it's worse. He's so – so inhuman. Utterly cold and ruthless. Him and his work. Day and night.'

'Les is ambitious. He wants to get to the top in his field.' Frank lit a cigarette lazily. 'A pusher. Well, maybe he'll do it. What's he in?'

'Toxicology. He works out new poisons for Military. He invented the copper sulphate skin-lime they used against Callisto.'

'It's a small field. Now take me.' Frank leaned contentedly against the wall of the house. 'There are thousands of Clearance lawyers. I could work for years and never create a ripple. I'm content just to be. I do my job. I enjoy it.'

'I wish Lester felt that way.'

'Maybe he'll change.'

'He'll *never* change,' Jill said bitterly. 'I know that, now. That's why I've made up my mind to leave him. He'll always be the same.'

Lester Herrick came back from Rexor IV a different man. Beaming happily, he deposited his anti-grav suitcase in the arms of the waiting robant. 'Thank you.'

Jill gasped speechlessly. 'Les! What—'

Lester moved his hat, bowing a little. 'Good day, my dear. You're looking lovely. Your eyes are clear and blue. Sparkling like some virgin lake, fed by mountain streams.' He sniffed. 'Do I smell a delicious repast warming on the hearth?'

'Oh, Lester.' Jill blinked uncertainly, faint hope swelling in her bosom. 'Lester, what's happened to you? You're so – so different.'

'Am I, my dear?' Lester moved about the house, touching things and sighing. 'What a dear little house. So sweet and friendly. You don't know how wonderful it is to be here. Believe me.'

'I'm afraid to believe it,' Jill said.

'Believe what?'

'That you mean all this. That you're not the way you were. The way you've always been.'

'What way is that?'

'Mean. Mean and cruel.'

'I?' Lester frowned, rubbing his lip. 'Hmm. Interesting.' He brightened. 'Well, that's all in the past. What's for dinner? I'm faint with hunger.'

Jill eyed him uncertainly as she moved into the kitchen. 'Anything you want, Lester. You know our stove covers the maximum select-list.'

'Of course.' Lester coughed rapidly. 'Well, shall we try sirloin steak, medium, smothered in onions? With mushroom sauce. And white rolls. With hot coffee. Perhaps ice cream and apple pie for dessert.'

'You never seemed to care much about food,' Jill said thoughtfully.

'Oh?'

'You always said you hoped eventually they'd make intravenous intake universally applicable.' She studied her husband intently. 'Lester, what's happened?'

'Nothing. Nothing at all.' Lester carelessly took his pipe out and lit it rapidly, somewhat awkwardly. Bits of tobacco drifted to the rug. He bent nervously down and tried to pick them up again. 'Please go about your tasks and don't mind me. Perhaps I can help you prepare – that is, can I do anything to help?'

'No,' Jill said. 'I can do it. You go ahead with your work, if you want.'

'Work?'

'Your research. In toxins.'

'Toxins!' Lester showed confusion. 'Well, for heaven's sake! Toxins. Devil take it!'

'What dear?'

'I mean, I really feel too tired, just now. I'll work later.' Lester moved vaguely around the room. 'I think I'll just sit and enjoy being home again. Off that awful Rexor IV.'

'Was it awful?'

'Horrible.' A spasm of disgust crossed Lester's face. 'Dry and dead. Ancient. Squeezed to a pulp by wind and sun. A dreadful place, my dear.'

'I'm sorry to hear that. I always wanted to visit it.'

'Heaven forbid!' Lester cried feelingly. 'You stay right here, my dear. With me. The – the two of us.' His eyes wandered around the room. 'Two, yes. Terra is a wonderful planet. Moist and full of life.' He beamed happily. 'Just right.'

'I don't understand it,' Jill said.

'Repeat all the things you remember,' Frank said. His robot pencil poised itself alertly. 'The changes you've noticed in him. I'm curious.'

'Why?'

'No reason. Go on. You say you sensed it right away? That he was different?'

'I noticed it at once. The expression on his face. Not that hard, practical look. A sort of mellow look. Relaxed. Tolerant. A sort of calmness.'

'I see,' Frank said. 'What else?'

Jill peered nervously through the back door into the house. 'He can't hear us, can he?'

'No. He's inside playing with Gus. In the living room. They're Venusian otter-men today. Your husband built an otter slide down at his lab. I saw him unwrapping it.'

'His talk.'

'His what?'

'The way he talks. His choice of words. Words he never used before. Whole new phrases. Metaphors. I never heard him use a metaphor in all our five years together. He said metaphors were inexact. Misleading. And—'

'And what?' The pencil scratched busily.

'And they're *strange* words. Old words. Words you don't hear any more.'

'Archaic phraseology?' Frank asked tensely.

'Yes.' Jill paced back and forth across the small lawn, her hands in the pockets of her plastic shorts. 'Formal words. Like something—'

'Something out of a book?'

'Exactly! You've noticed it?'

'I noticed it,' Frank's face was grim. 'Go on.'

Jill stopped pacing. 'What's on your mind? Do you have a theory?'

'I want to know more facts.'

She reflected. 'He plays. With Gus. He plays and jokes. And he – he eats.'

'Didn't he eat before?'

'Not like he does now. Now he *loves* food. He goes in the kitchen and tries endless combinations. He and the stove get together and cook up all sorts of weird things.'

'I thought he'd put on weight.'

'He's gained ten pounds. He eats, smiles and laughs. He's constantly polite.' Jill glanced away coyly. 'He's even – romantic! He always said *that* was irrational. And he's not interested in his work. His research in toxins.'

'I see.' Frank chewed his lip. 'Anything more?'

'One thing puzzles me very much. I've noticed it again and again.'

'What is it?'

'He seems to have strange lapses of—'

A burst of laughter. Lester Herrick, eyes bright with merriment, came rushing out of the house, little Gus close behind.

'We have an announcement!' Lester cried.

'An announzelmen,' Gus echoed.

Frank folded his notes up and slid them into his coat pocket. The pencil hurried after them. He got slowly to his feet. 'What is it?'

'You make it,' Lester said, taking little Gus's hand and leading him forward.

Gus's plump face screwed up in concentration. 'I'm going to come live with you,' he stated. Anxiously he watched Jill's expression. 'Lester says I can. Can I? Can I, Aunt Jill?'

Her heart flooded with incredible joy. She glanced from Gus to Lester. 'Do you – do you really mean it?' Her voice was almost inaudible.

Lester put his arm around her, holding her close to him. 'Of course, we mean it,' he said gently. His eyes were warm and understanding. 'We wouldn't tease you, my dear.'

'No teasing!' Gus shouted excitedly. 'No more teasing!' He and Lester and Jill drew close together. 'Never again!'

Frank stood a little way off, his face grim. Jill noticed him and broke away abruptly. 'What is it?' she faltered. 'Is anything—'

'When you're quite finished,' Frank said to Lester Herrick, 'I'd like you to come with me.'

A chill clutched Jill's heart. 'What is it? Can I come, too?'

Frank shook his head. He moved toward Lester ominously. 'Come on, Herrick. Let's go. You and I are going to take a little trip.'

The three Federal Clearance Agents took up positions a few feet from Lester Herrick, vibro-tubes gripped alertly.

Clearance Director Douglas studied Herrick for a long time. 'You're sure?' he said finally.

'Absolutely,' Frank stated.

'When did he get back from Rexor IV?'

'A week ago.'

'And the change was noticeable at once?'

'His wife noticed it as soon as she saw him. There's no doubt it occurred on Rexor.' Frank paused significantly. 'And you know what that means.'

'I know.' Douglas walked slowly around the seated man, examining him from every angle.

Lester Herrick sat quietly, his coat neatly folded across his knee. He rested his hands on his ivory-topped cane, his face calm and expressionless. He wore a soft gray suit, a subdued necktie, French cuffs, and shiny black shoes. He said nothing.

'Their methods are simple and exact,' Douglas said. 'The original psychic contents are removed and stored – in some sort of suspension. The interjection of the substitute contents is instantaneous. Lester Herrick was probably poking around the Rexor city ruins, ignoring the safety precautions – shield or manual screen – and they got him.'

The seated man stirred. 'I'd like very much to communicate with Jill,' he murmured. 'She surely is becoming anxious.'

Frank turned away, face choked with revulsion. 'God. It's still pretending.'

Director Douglas restrained himself with the greatest effort. 'It's certainly an amazing thing. No physical changes. You could look at it and never know.' He moved toward the seated man, his face hard. 'Listen to me, whatever you call yourself. Can you understand what I say ?'

'Of course,' Lester Herrick answered.

'Did you really think you'd get away with it? We caught the others – the ones before you. All ten of them. Even before they got here.' Douglas grinned coldly. 'Vibro-rayed them one after another.'

The color left Lester Herrick's face. Sweat came out on his forehead. He wiped it away with a silk handkerchief from his breast pocket. 'Oh?' he murmured.

'You're not fooling us. All Terra is alerted for you Rexorians. I'm surprised you got off Rexor at all. Herrick must have been extremely careless. We stopped the others aboard ship. Fried them out in deep space.'

'Herrick had a private ship,' the seated man murmured. 'He bypassed the check station going in. No record of his arrival existed. He was never checked.'

'*Fry it!*' Douglas grated. The three Clearance agents lifted their tubes, moving forward.

'No.' Frank shook his head. 'We can't. It's a bad situation.'

'What do you mean? Why can't we? We fried the others—'

'They were caught in deep space. This is Terra. Terran law, not military law, applies.' Frank waved toward the seated man. 'And it's in a human body. It comes under regular civil laws. We've got to *prove* it's not Lester Herrick — that it's a Rexorian infiltrator. It's going to be tough. But it can be done.'

'How?'

'His wife. Herrick's wife. Her testimony. Jill Herrick can assert the difference between Lester Herrick and this thing. She knows — and I think we can make it stand up in court.'

It was late afternoon. Frank drove his surface cruiser slowly along. Neither he nor Jill spoke.

'So that's it,' Jill said at last. Her face was gray. Her eyes dry and bright, without emotion. 'I knew it was too good to be true.' She tried to smile. 'It seemed so wonderful.'

'I know,' Frank said. 'It's a terrible damn thing. If only—'

'*Why?*' Jill said. 'Why did he — did it do this? Why did it take Lester's body?'

'Rexor IV is old. Dead. A dying planet. Life is dying out.'

'I remember, now. He — it said something like that. Something about Rexor. That it was glad to get away.'

'The Rexorians are an old race. The few that remain are feeble. They've been trying to migrate for centuries. But their bodies are too weak. Some tried to migrate to Venus — and died instantly. They worked out this system about a century ago.'

'But it knows so much. About us. It speaks our language.'

'Not quite. The changes you mentioned. The odd diction. You see, the Rexorians have only a vague knowledge of human beings. A sort of ideal abstraction, taken from Terran objects that have found their way to Rexor. Books mostly. Secondary data like that. The Rexorian idea of Terra is based on centuries-old Terran literature. Romantic novels from our past. Language, custom, manners from old Terran books.

'That accounts for the strange archaic quality to *it*. It had studied Terra, all right. But in an indirect and misleading way.' Frank grinned wryly. 'The Rexorians are two hundred years behind the times — which is a break for us. That's how we're able to detect them.'

'Is this sort of thing — common? Does it happen often? It seems unbelievable.' Jill rubbed her forehead wearily. 'Dreamlike. It's hard to realize that it's actually happened. I'm just beginning to understand what it means.'

'The galaxy is full of alien life forms. Parasitic and destructive entities. Terran ethics don't extend to them. We have to guard constantly against this sort of thing. Lester went in unsuspectingly – and this thing ousted him and took over his body.'

Frank glanced at his sister. Jill's face was expressionless. A stern little face, wide-eyed, but composed. She sat up straight, staring fixedly ahead, her small hands folded quietly in her lap.

'We can arrange it so you won't have to actually appear in court,' Frank went on. 'You can vid a statement and it'll be presented as evidence. I'm certain your statement will do. The Federal courts will help us all they can, but they have to have *some* evidence to go on.'

Jill was silent.

'What do you say?' Frank asked.

'What happens after the court makes its decision?'

'Then we vibro-ray it. Destroy the Rexorian mind. A Terran patrol ship on Rexor IV sends out a party to locate the – er – original contents.'

Jill gasped. She turned toward her brother in amazement. 'You mean—'

'Oh, yes. Lester is alive. In suspension, somewhere on Rexor. In one of the old city ruins. We'll have to force them to give him up. They won't want to, but they'll do it. They've done it before. Then he'll be back with you. Safe and sound. Just like before. And this horrible nightmare you've been living will be a thing of the past.'

'I see.'

'Here we are.' The cruiser pulled to a halt before the imposing Federal Clearance Building. Frank got quickly out, holding the door for his sister. Jill stepped down slowly. 'Okay?' Frank said.

'Okay.'

When they entered the building, Clearance agents led them through the check screens, down the long corridors. Jill's high heels echoed in the ominous silence.

'Quite a place,' Frank observed.

'It's unfriendly.'

'Consider it a glorified police station.' Frank halted. Before them was a guarded door. 'Here we are.'

'Wait.' Jill pulled back, her face twisting in panic. 'I—'

'We'll wait until you're ready.' Frank signaled to the Clearance agent to leave. 'I understand. It's a bad business.'

Jill stood for a moment, her head down. She took a deep breath, her small fists clenched. Her chin came up, level and steady. 'All right.'

'You ready?'

'Yes.'

Frank opened the door. 'Here we are.'

Director Douglas and the three Clearance agents turned expectantly as Jill and Frank entered. 'Good,' Douglas murmured, with relief. 'I was beginning to get worried.'

The sitting man got slowly to his feet, picking up his coat. He gripped his ivory-headed cane tightly, his hands tense. He said nothing. He watched silently as the woman entered the room, Frank behind her. 'This is Mrs Herrick,' Frank said. 'Jill, this is Clearance Director Douglas.'

'I've heard of you,' Jill said faintly.

'Then you know our work.'

'Yes. I know your work.'

'This is an unfortunate business. It's happened before. I don't know what Frank has told you—'

'He explained the situation.'

'Good.' Douglas was relieved. 'I'm glad of that. It's not easy to explain. You understand, then, what we want. The previous cases were caught in deep space. We vibro-tubed them and got the original contents back. But this time we must work through legal channels.' Douglas picked up a vidtape recorder. 'We will need your statement, Mrs Herrick. Since no physical change has occurred we'll have no direct evidence to make our case. We'll have only your testimony of character alteration to present to the court.'

He held the vidtape recorder out. Jill took it slowly.

'Your statement will undoubtedly be accepted by the court. The court will give us the release we want and then we can go ahead. If everything goes correctly we hope to be able to set up things exactly as they were before.'

Jill was gazing silently at the man standing in the corner with his coat and ivory-headed cane. 'Before?' she said. 'What do you mean?'

'Before the change.'

Jill turned toward Director Douglas. Calmly, she laid the vidtape recorder down on the table. 'What change are you talking about?'

Douglas paled. He licked his lips. All eyes in the room were on Jill. 'The change in *him*.' He pointed at the man.

'Jill!' Frank barked. 'What's the matter with you?' He came quickly toward her. 'What the hell are you doing? You know damn well what change we mean!'

'That's odd,' Jill said thoughtfully. 'I haven't noticed any change.'

Frank and Director Douglas looked at each other. 'I don't get it,' Frank muttered, dazed.

'Mrs Herrick—' Douglas began.

Jill walked over to the man standing quietly in the corner. 'Can we go now, dear?' she asked. She took his arm. 'Or is there some reason why my husband has to stay here?'

The man and woman walked silently along the dark street.

'Come on,' Jill said. 'Let's go home.'

The man glanced at her. 'It's a nice afternoon,' he said. He took a deep breath, filling his lungs. 'Spring is coming – I think. Isn't it?'

Jill nodded.

'I wasn't sure. It's a nice smell. Plants and soil and growing things.'

'Yes.'

'Are we going to walk? Is it far?'

'Not too far.'

The man gazed at her intently, a serious expression on his face. 'I am very indebted to you, my dear,' he said.

Jill nodded.

'I wish to thank you. I must admit I did not expect such a—'

Jill turned abruptly. 'What is your name? Your *real* name.'

The man's gray eyes flickered. He smiled a little, a kind, gentle smile. 'I'm afraid you would not be able to pronounce it. The sounds cannot be formed . . .'

Jill was silent as they walked along, deep in thought. The city lights were coming on all around them. Bright yellow spots in the gloom. 'What are you thinking?' the man asked.

'I was thinking perhaps I will still call you Lester,' Jill said. 'If you don't mind.'

'I don't mind,' the man said. He put his arm around her, drawing her close to him. He gazed down tenderly as they walked through the thickening darkness, between the yellow candles of light that marked the way. 'Anything you wish. Whatever will make you happy.'

The Mold of Yancy

Leon Sipling groaned and pushed away his work papers. In an organization of thousands he was the only employee not putting out. Probably he was the only yance-man on Callisto not doing his job. Fear, and the quick pluckings of desperation, made him reach up and wave on the audio circuit to Babson, the over-all office controller.

'Say,' Sipling said hoarsely, 'I think I'm stuck, Bab. How about running the gestalt through, up to my spot? Maybe I can pick up the rhythm . . .' He grinned weakly. 'The hum of other creative minds.'

After a speculative moment, Babson reached for the impulse synapsis, his massive face unsympathetic. 'You holding up progress, Sip? This has to be integrated with the daily by six tonight. The schedule calls for the works to be on the vidlines during the dinner-hour stretch.'

The visual side of the gestalt had already begun to form on the wall screen; Sipling turned his attention to it, grateful of a chance to escape Babson's cold glare.

The screen showed a 3-D of Yancy, the usual three quarter view, from the waist up. John Edward Yancy in his faded workshirt, sleeves rolled up, arms brown and furry. A middle-aged man in his late fifties, his face sunburned, neck slightly red, a good-natured smile on his face, squinting because he was looking into the sun. Behind Yancy was a still of his yard, his garage, his flower garden, lawn, the back of his neat little white plastic house. Yancy grinned at Sipling: a neighbor pausing in the middle of a summer day, perspiring from the heat and the exertion of mowing his lawn, about to launch into a few harmless remarks about the weather, the state of the planet, the condition of the neighborhood.

'Say,' Yancy said, in the audio phones propped up on Sipling's desk. His voice was low, personal. 'The darndest thing happened to my grandson Ralf, the other morning. You know how Ralf is; he's always getting to school half an hour early . . . says he likes to be in his seat before anybody else.'

'That eager-beaver,' Joe Pines, at the next desk, cat-called.

271

From the screen, Yancy's voice rolled on, confident, amiable, undisturbed. 'Well, Ralf saw this squirrel; it was just sitting there on the sidewalk. He stopped for a minute and watched.' The look on Yancy's face was so real that Sipling almost believed him. He could, almost, see the squirrel and the tow-headed youngest grandson of the Yancy family, the familiar child of the familiar son of the planet's most familiar – and beloved – person.

'This squirrel,' Yancy explained, in his homey way, 'was collecting nuts. And by golly, this was just the other day, only the middle of June. And here was this little squirrel—' with his hands he indicated the size, 'collecting these nuts and carrying them off for winter.'

And then, the amused, anecdote-look on Yancy's face faded. A serious, thoughtful look replaced it: the meaningful-look. His blue eyes darkened (good color work). His jaw became more square, more imposing (good dummy-switch by the android crew). Yancy seemed older, more solemn and mature, more impressive. Behind him, the garden-scene had been jerked and a slightly different backdrop filtered in; Yancy now stood firmly planted in a cosmic landscape, among mountains and winds and huge old forests.

'I got to thinking,' Yancy said, and his voice was deeper, slower. 'There was that little squirrel. How did he know winter was coming? There he was, working away, getting prepared for it.' Yancy's voice rose. 'Preparing for a winter he'd never seen.'

Sipling stiffened and prepared *himself*; it was coming. At his desk, Joe Pines grinned and yelled: 'Get set!'

'That squirrel,' Yancy said solemnly, 'had faith. No, he never saw any sign of winter. But he knew winter was coming.' The firm jaw moved; one hand came slowly up . . .

And then the image stopped. It froze, immobile, silent. No words came from it; abruptly the sermon ended, in the middle of a paragraph.

'That's it,' Babson said briskly, filtering the Yancy out. 'Help you any?'

Sipling pawed jerkily at his work papers. 'No,' he admitted, 'actually it doesn't. But – I'll get it worked out.'

'I hope so.' Babson's face darkened ominously and his small mean eyes seemed to grow smaller. 'What's the matter with you? Home problems?'

'I'll be okay,' Sipling muttered, sweating. 'Thanks.'

On the screen a faint impression of Yancy remained, still poised at the word *coming*. The rest of the gestalt was in Sipling's head: the continuing slice of words and gestures hadn't been worked out and fed to the composite. Sipling's contribution was missing, so the entire gestalt was stopped cold in its tracks.

'Say,' Joe Pines said uneasily, 'I'll be glad to take over, today. Cut your desk out of the circuit and I'll cut myself in.'

'Thanks,' Sipling muttered, 'but I'm the only one who can get this damn part. It's the central gem.'

'You ought to take a rest. You've been working too hard.'

'Yes,' Sipling agreed, on the verge of hysteria. 'I'm a little under the weather.'

That was obvious: everybody in the office could see that. But only Sipling knew why. And he was fighting with all his strength to keep from screaming out the reason at the top of his lungs.

Basic analysis of the political milieu at Callisto was laid out by Niplan computing apparatus at Washington, DC; but the final evaluations were done by human technicians. The Washington computers could ascertain that the Callisto political structure was moving toward a totalitarian make-up, but they couldn't say what that indicated. Human beings were required to class the drift as malign.

'It isn't possible,' Taverner protested. 'There's constant industrial traffic in and out of Callisto; except for the Ganymede syndicate they've got out-planet commerce bottled up. We'd know as soon as anything phony got started.'

'How would we know?' Police Director Kellman inquired.

Taverner indicated the data-sheets, graphs and charts of figures and percentages that covered the walls of the Niplan Police offices. 'It would show up in hundreds of ways. Terrorist raids, political prisons, extermination camps. We'd hear about political recanting, treason, disloyalty . . . all the basic props of a dictatorship.'

'Don't confuse a totalitarian society with a dictatorship,' Kellman said dryly. 'A totalitarian state reaches into every sphere of its citizens' lives, forms their opinions on every subject. The government can be a dictatorship, *or* a parliament, *or* an elected president, *or* a council of priests. That doesn't matter.'

'All right,' Taverner said, mollified. 'I'll go. I'll take a team there and see what they're doing.'

'Can you make yourselves look like Callistotes?'

'What are they like?'

'I'm not sure,' Kellman admitted thoughtfully, with a glance at the elaborate wall charts. 'But whatever it is, they're all beginning to turn out alike.'

Among its passengers the interplan commercial liner that settled down at Callisto carried Peter Taverner, his wife, and their two children. With a grimace of concern, Taverner made out the shapes of local officials waiting at the exit hatch. The passengers were going to be carefully screened; as the ramp descended, the clot of officials moved forward.

Taverner got to his feet and collected his family. 'Ignore them,' he told Ruth. 'Our papers will get us by.'

Expertly prepared documents identified him as a speculator in nonferric metals, looking for a wholesale outlet to handle his jobbing. Callisto was a clearing-point for land and mineral operations; a constant flood of wealth-hungry entrepreneurs streamed back and forth, carting raw materials from the underdeveloped moons, hauling mining equipment from the inner planets.

Cautiously, Taverner arranged his topcoat over his arm. A heavyset man, in his middle thirties, he could have passed for a successful business operator. His double-breasted business suit was expensive, but conservative. His big shoes were brightly shined. All things considered, he'd probably get by. As he and his family moved toward the exit ramp, they presented a perfect and exact imitation of the out-planet business-class.

'State your business,' a green-uniformed official demanded, pencil poised. I-d tabs were being checked, photographed, recorded. Brain pattern comparisons were being made: the usual routine.

'Nonferric enterprises,' Taverner began, but a second official cut him abruptly off.

'You're the third cop this morning. What's biting you people on Terra?' The official eyed Taverner intently. 'We're getting more cops than ministers.'

Trying to maintain his poise, Taverner answered evenly: 'I'm here to take a rest. Acute alcoholism – nothing official.'

'That's what your cohorts said.' The official grinned humorously. 'Well, what's one more Terran cop?' He slid the lockbars aside and waved Taverner and his family through. 'Welcome to Callisto. Have fun – enjoy yourselves. Fastest-growing moon in the system.'

'Practically a planet,' Taverner commented ironically.

'Any day now.' The official examined some reports. 'According to our friends in your little organization, you've been pasting up wall graphs and charts about us. Are we that important?'

'Academic interest,' Taverner said; if three spots had been made, then the whole team had been netted. The local authorities were obviously primed to detect infiltration . . . the realization chilled him.

But they were letting him through. Were they *that* confident?

Things didn't look good. Peering around for a cab, he grimly prepared to undertake the business of integrating the scattered team members into a functioning whole.

That evening, at the *Stay-Lit* bar on the main street of the commercial district of town, Taverner met with his two team members. Hunched over their whiskey sours, they compared notes.

'I've been here almost twelve hours,' Eckmund stated, gazing impassively at the rows of bottles in the gloomy depths of the bar. Cigar smoke hovered in the air; the automatic music box in the corner banged away metallically. 'I've been walking around town, looking at things, making observations.'

'Me,' Dorser said, 'I've been at the tape-library. Getting official myth, comparing it to Callistote reality. And talking to the scholars – educated people hanging around the scanning rooms.'

Taverner sipped his drink. 'Anything of interest?'

'You know the primitive rule-of-thumb test,' Eckmund said wryly. 'I loafed around on a slum street corner until I got in a conversation with some people waiting for a bus. I started knocking the authorities: complaining about the bus service, the sewage disposal, taxes, everything. They chimed right in. Heartily. No hesitation. And no fear.'

'The legal government,' Dorser commented, 'is set up in the usual archaic fashion. Two-party system, one a little more conservative than the other – no fundamental difference of course. But both elect candidates at open primaries, ballots circulated to all registered voters.' A spasm of amusement touched him. 'This is a model democracy. I read the text books. Nothing but idealistic slogans: freedom of speech, assembly, religion – the works. Same old grammar school stuff.'

The three of them were temporarily silent.

'There are jails,' Taverner said slowly. 'Every society has law violations.'

'I visited one,' Eckmund said, belching. 'Petty thieves, murderers, claim-jumpers, strong-arm hoods – the usual.'

'No political prisoners?'

'No.' Eckmund raised his voice. 'We might as well discuss this at the top of our lungs. Nobody cares – the authorities don't care.'

'Probably after we're gone they'll clap a few thousand people into prison,' Dorser murmured thoughtfully.

'My God,' Eckmund retorted, 'people can leave Callisto any time they want. If you're operating a police state you have to keep your borders shut. And these borders are wide open. People pour in and out.'

'Maybe it's a chemical in the drinking water,' Dorser suggested.

'How the hell can they have a totalitarian society without terrorism?' Eckmund demanded rhetorically. 'I'll swear to it – there are no thought-control cops here. There is absolutely no fear.'

'Somehow, pressure is being exerted,' Taverner persisted.

'Not by cops,' Dorser said emphatically. 'Not by force and brutality. Not by illegal arrest and imprisonment and forced labor.'

'If this were a police state,' Eckmund said thoughtfully, 'there'd be some kind of resistance movement. Some sort of "subversive" group trying to overthrow the authorities. But in this society you're free to complain; you can buy time on the TV and radio stations, you can buy space in the newspapers – anything you want.' He shrugged. 'So how can there be a clandestine resistance movement? It's silly.'

'Nevertheless,' Taverner said, 'these people are living in a one-party society with a party line, with an official ideology. They show the effects of a carefully controlled totalitarian state. They're guinea pigs – whether they realize it or not.'

'Wouldn't they realize it?'

Baffled, Taverner shook his head. 'I would have thought so. There must be some mechanism we don't understand.'

'It's all open. We can look everything over.'

'We must be looking for the wrong thing.' Idly, Taverner gazed at the television screen above the bar. The nude girlie song-and-dance routine had ended; now the features of a man faded into view. A genial, round-faced man in his fifties, with guileless blue eyes, an almost childish twitch to his lips, a fringe of brown hair playing around his slightly prominent ears.

'Friends,' the TV image rumbled, 'it's good to be with you again, tonight. I thought I might have a little chat with you.'

'A commercial,' Dorser said, signalling the bartending machine for another drink.

'Who is that?' Taverner asked curiously.

'That kindly-looking geezer?' Eckmund examined his notes. 'A sort of popular commentator. Name of Yancy.'

'Is he part of the government?'

'Not that I know of. A kind of home-spun philosopher. I picked up a biography of him on a magazine stand.' Eckmund passed the gaily-colored pamphlet to his boss. 'Totally ordinary man, as far as I can see. Used to be a soldier; in the Mars-Jupiter War he distinguished himself – battlefield commission. Rose to the rank of major.' He shrugged indifferently. 'A sort of talking almanac. Pithy sayings on every topic. Wise old saws: how to cure a chest cold. What the trouble is back on Terra.'

Taverner examined the booklet. 'Yes, I saw his picture around.'

'Very popular figures. Loved by the masses. Man of the people – speaks for them. When I was buying cigarettes I noticed he endorses one particular brand. Very popular brand, now; just about driven the others off the market. Same with beer. The Scotch in this glass is probably the brand Yancy endorses. The same with tennis balls. Only he doesn't play tennis – he plays croquet. All the time, every weekend.' Accepting his fresh drink Eckmund finished, 'So now everybody plays croquet.'

'How can croquet be a planet-wide sport?' Taverner demanded.

'This isn't a planet,' Dorser put in. 'It's a pipsqueak moon.'

'Not according to Yancy,' Eckmund said. 'We're supposed to think of Callisto as a planet.'

'How?' Taverner asked.

'Spiritually, it's a planet. Yancy likes people to take a spiritual view of matters. He's strong on God and honesty in government and being hardworking and clean-cut. Warmed-over truisms.'

The expression on Taverner's face hardened. 'Interesting,' he murmured. 'I'll have to drop by and meet him.'

'Why? He's the dullest, most mediocre man you could dream up.'

'Maybe,' Taverner answered, 'that's why I'm interested.'

Babson, huge and menacing, met Taverner at the entrance of the Yancy Building. 'Of course you can meet Mr Yancy. But he's a busy man – it'll take a while to squeeze in an appointment. Everybody wants to meet Mr Yancy.'

Taverner was unimpressed. 'How long do I have to wait?'

As they crossed the main lobby to the elevators, Babson made a computation. 'Oh, say four months.'

'Four *months*!'

'John Yancy is just about the most popular man alive.'

'Around here, maybe,' Taverner commented angrily, as they entered the packed elevator. 'I never heard of him before. If he's got so much on the ball, why isn't he piped all around Niplan?'

'Actually,' Babson admitted, in a hoarse, confidential whisper, 'I can't imagine what people see in Yancy. As far as I'm concerned he's just a big bag of wind. But people around here enjoy him. After all, Callisto is – provincial. Yancy appeals to a certain type of rural mind – to people who like their world simple. I'm afraid Terra would be too sophisticated for Yancy.'

'Have you tried?'

'Not yet,' Babson said. Reflectively, he added: 'Maybe later.'

While Taverner was pondering the meaning of the big man's words, the elevator ceased climbing. The two of them stepped off into a luxurious, carpeted hall, illuminated by recessed lights. Babson pushed open a door, and they entered a large, active office.

Inside, a screening of a recent Yancy gestalt was in progress. A group of yance-men watched it silently, faces alert and critical. The gestalt showed Yancy sitting at his old-fashioned oak desk, in his study. It was obvious that he had been working on some philosophical thoughts: spread out over the desk were books and papers. On Yancy's face was a thoughtful expression; he sat with his hand against his forehead, features screwed up into a solemn study of concentration.

'This is for next Sunday morning,' Babson explained.

Yancy's lips moved, and he spoke. 'Friends,' he began, in his deep, personal, friendly, man-to-man voice, 'I've been sitting here at my desk – well, about the way you're sitting around your living rooms.' A switch in camera work occurred; it showed the open door of Yancy's study. In the living room was the familiar figure of Yancy's sweet-faced middle-aged homey wife; she was sitting on the comfortable sofa, primly sewing. On the floor their grandson Ralf played the familiar game of jacks. The family dog snoozed in the corner.

One of the watching yance-men made a note on his pad. Taverner glanced at him curiously, baffled.

'Of course, I was in there with them,' Yancy continued, smiling briefly. 'I was reading the funnies to Ralf. He was sitting on my knee.' The background faded, and a momentary phantom scene of Yancy sitting with his grandson on his knee floated into being. Then the desk and the book-lined study returned. 'I'm mighty grateful for my family,' Yancy revealed. 'In these times of stress, it's my family that I turn to, as my pillar of strength.' Another notation was made by a watching yance-man.

'Sitting here, in my study, this wonderful Sunday morning,' Yancy rumbled on, 'I realize how lucky we are to be alive, and to have this lovely planet, and the fine cities and houses, all the things God has given us to enjoy. But we've got to be careful. We've got to make sure we don't lose these things.'

A change had come over Yancy. It seemed to Taverner that the image was subtly altering. It wasn't the same man; the good humor was gone. This was an older man, and larger. A firm-eyed father, speaking to his children.

'My friends,' Yancy intoned, 'there are forces that could weaken this planet. Everything we've built up for our loved ones, for our children, *could be taken away from us overnight*. We must learn to be vigilant. We must protect our liberties, our possessions, our way of life. If we become divided, and fall to bickering among each other, we will be easy prey for our enemies. We must work together, my friends.

'That's what I've been thinking about this Sunday morning. *Co-operation. Teamwork*. We've got to be secure, and to be secure, we must be one united people. That's the key, my friends, the key to a more abundant life.' Pointing out the window at the lawn and garden, Yancy said: 'You know, I was . . .'

The voice trailed off. The image froze. Full room lights came on, and the watching yance-men moved into muttering activity.

'Fine,' one of them said. 'So far, at least. But where's the rest?'

'Sipling, again,' another answered. 'His slice still hasn't come through. What's wrong with that guy?'

Scowling, Babson detached himself. 'Pardon me,' he said to Taverner. 'I'll have to excuse myself – technical matters. You're free to look around, if you care to. Help yourself to any of the literature – anything you want.'

'Thanks,' Taverner said uncertainly. He was confused; everything *seemed* harmless, even trivial. But something basic was wrong.

Suspiciously, he began to prowl.

★

It was obvious that John Yancy had pontificated on every known subject. A Yancy opinion on every conceivable topic was available . . . modern art, or garlic in cooking, or the use of intoxicating beverages, or eating meat, or socialism, or war, or education, or open-front dresses on women, or high taxes, or atheism, or divorce, or patriotism – every shade and nuance of opinion possible.

Was there any subject that Yancy *hadn't* expressed himself on?

Taverner examined the voluminous tapes that lined the walls of the offices. Yancy's utterances had run into billions of tape feet . . . could one man have an opinion on everything in the universe?

Choosing a tape at random, he found himself being addressed on the topic of table manners.

'You know,' the miniature Yancy began, his voice tinny in Taverner's ears, 'at dinner the other night I happened to notice how my grandson Ralf was cutting his steak.' Yancy grinned at the viewer, as an image of the six-year-old boy sawing grimly away floated briefly into sight. 'Well, I got to thinking, there was Ralf working away at that steak, not having any luck with it. And it seemed to me—'

Taverner snapped the tape off and returned it to the slot. Yancy had definite opinions on everything . . . or *were* they so definite?

A strange suspicion was growing in him. On some topics, yes. On minor issues, Yancy had exact rules, specific maxims drawn from mankind's rich storehouse of folklore. But major philosophical and political issues were something else again.

Getting out one of the many tapes listed under War, Taverner ran it through at random.

'. . . I'm against war,' Yancy pronounced angrily. 'And I ought to know; I've done my share of fighting.'

There followed a montage of battle scenes: the Jupiter-Mars War in which Yancy had distinguished himself by his bravery, his concern for his comrades, his hatred of the enemy, his variety of proper emotions.

'But,' Yancy continued staunchly, 'I feel a planet must be strong. We must not surrender ourselves meekly . . . weakness invites attack and fosters aggression. By being weak we promote war. We must gird ourselves and protect those we love. With all my heart and soul I'm against useless wars; but I say again, as I've said many times before, a man must come forward and fight a *just* war. He must not shrink from his responsibility. War is a terrible thing. But sometimes we must . . .'

As he restored the tape, Taverner wondered just what the hell Yancy *had* said. What were his views on war? They took up a hundred separate reels of tape; Yancy was always ready to hold forth on such vital and grandiose subjects as War, the Planet, God, Taxation. But did he *say* anything?

A cold chill crawled up Taverner's spine. On specific – and trivial – items there were absolute opinions: dogs are better than cats, grapefruit is too sour without a dash of sugar, it's good to get up early in the morning, too much drinking is bad. But on big topics . . . an empty vacuum, filled with the vacant roll of high-sounding phrases. A public that agreed with Yancy on war and taxes and God and planet agreed with absolutely nothing. And with everything.

On topics of importance, they had no opinion at all. They only *thought* they had an opinion.

Rapidly, Taverner scanned tapes on various major subjects. It was the same all down the line. With one sentence Yancy gave; with the next he took away. The total effect was a neat cancellation, a skillful negation. But the viewer was left with the illusion of having consumed a rich and varied intellectual feast. It was amazing. And it was professional: the ends were tied up too slickly to be mere accident.

Nobody was as harmless and vapid as John Edward Yancy. He was just too damn good to be true.

Sweating, Taverner left the main reference room and poked his way toward the rear offices, where busy yance-men worked away at their desks and assembly tables. Activity whirred on all sides. The expression on the faces around him was benign, harmless, almost bored. The same friendly, trivial expression that Yancy himself displayed.

Harmless – and in its harmlessness, diabolical. And there wasn't a damn thing he could do. If people liked to listen to John Edward Yancy, if they wanted to model themselves after him – what could the Niplan Police do about it?

What crime was being committed?

No wonder Babson didn't care if the police prowled around. No wonder the authorities had freely admitted them. There weren't any political jails or labor gangs or concentration camps . . . there didn't have to be.

Torture chambers and extermination camps were needed only when persuasion failed. And persuasion was working perfectly. A police state, rule by terror, came about when the totalitarian apparatus began to break down. The earlier totalitarian societies had been incomplete; the authorities hadn't really gotten into every sphere of life. But techniques of communication had improved.

The first really successful totalitarian state was being realized before his eyes: harmless and trivial, it emerged. And the last stage – nightmarish, but perfectly logical – was when all the newborn boys were happily and voluntarily named John Edward.

Why not? They already lived, acted, and thought like John Edward. And there was Mrs Margaret Ellen Yancy, for the women. She had her full range of opinions, too; she had her kitchen, her taste in clothes, her little recipes and advice, for all the women to imitate.

There were even Yancy children for the youth of the planet to imitate. The authorities hadn't overlooked anything.

Babson strolled over, a genial expression on his face. 'How's it going, officer?' he chuckled wetly, putting his hand on Taverner's shoulder.

'Fine,' Taverner managed to answer; he evaded the hand.

'You like our little establishment?' There was genuine pride in Babson's thick voice. 'We do a good job. An artistic job – we have real standards of excellence.'

Shaking with helpless anger, Taverner plunged out of the office and into the hall. The elevator took too long; furiously, he turned toward the stairs. He had to get out of the Yancy Building; he had to get away.

From the shadows of the hall a man appeared, face pale and taut. 'Wait. Can – I talk to you?'

Taverner pushed past him. 'What do you want?'

'You're from the Terran Nipian Police? I—' The man's Adam's apple bobbed. 'I work here. My name's Sipling, Leon Sipling. I have to do something – I can't stand it anymore.'

'Nothing can be done,' Taverner told him. 'If they want to be like Yancy—'

'But there isn't any Yancy,' Sipling broke in, his thin face twitching spasmodically. 'We made him up . . . we invented him.'

Taverner halted. 'You *what*?'

'I've decided.' Voice quavering excitedly, Sipling rushed on: 'I'm going to do something – and I know exactly what.' Catching hold of Taverner's sleeve he grated: 'You've got to help me. I can stop all this, but I can't do it alone.'

★

In Leon Sipling's attractive, well-furnished living room, the two of them sat drinking coffee and watching their children scramble around on the floor, playing games. Sipling's wife and Ruth Taverner were in the kitchen, drying the dishes.

'Yancy is a synthesis,' Sipling explained. 'A sort of composite person. No such individual actually exists. We drew on basic prototypes from sociological records; we based the gestalt on various typical persons. So it's true to life. But we stripped off what we didn't want, and intensified what we did want.' Broodingly, he added: 'There could be a Yancy. There are a lot of Yancy-like people. In fact, that's the problem.'

'You deliberately set out with the idea of remolding people along Yancy's line?' Taverner inquired.

'I can't precisely say what the idea is, at top level. I was an ad writer for a mouth wash company. The Callisto authorities hired me and outlined what they wanted me to do. I've had to guess as to the purpose of the project.'

'By authorities, you mean the governing council?'

Sipling laughed sharply. 'I mean the trading syndicates that own this moon: lock, stock, and barrel. But we're not supposed to call it a moon. It's a planet.' His lips twitched bitterly. 'Apparently, the authorities have a big program built up. It involves absorbing their trade rivals on Ganymede – when that's done, they'll have the out-planets sewed up tight.'

'They can't get at Ganymede without open war,' Taverner protested. 'The Medean companies have their own population behind them.' And then it dawned. 'I see,' he said softly. 'They'd actually start a war. It would be worth a war, to them.'

'You're damn right it would. And to start a war, they have to get the public lined up. Actually, the people here have nothing to gain. A war would wipe out all the small operators – it would concentrate power in fewer hands – and they're few enough already. To get the eighty million people here behind the war, they need an indifferent, sheep-like public. *And they're getting that.* When this Yancy campaign is finished, the people here on Callisto will accept anything. Yancy does all their thinking for them. He tells them how to wear their hair. What games to play. He tells the jokes the men repeat in their back rooms. His wife whips up the meal they all have for dinner. All over this little world – millions of duplicates of Yancy's day. Whatever he does, whatever he believes. We've been conditioning the public for eleven straight years. The important thing is the unvarying monotony of it. A whole generation is growing up looking to Yancy for an answer to everything.'

'It's a big business, then,' Taverner observed. 'This project of creating and maintaining Yancy.'

'Thousands of people are involved in just writing the material. You only saw the first stage – and it goes into every city. Tapes, films, books, magazines, posters, pamphlets, dramatic visual and audio shows, plants in the newspapers, sound trucks, kids' comic strips, word-of-mouth report, elaborate ads . . . the works. A steady stream of Yancy.' Picking up a magazine from the coffee table he indicated the lead article. ' "How is John Yancy's Heart?" Raises the question of what would we do without Yancy? Next week, an article on Yancy's stomach.' Acidly, Sipling finished: 'We know a million approaches. We turn it out of every pore. We're called yance-men; it's a new art-form.'

'How do you – the corps, feel about Yancy?'

'He's a big sack of hot air.'

'None of you is convinced?'

'Even Babson has to laugh. And Babson is at the top; after him come the boys who sign the checks. God, if we ever started believing in Yancy . . . if we got started thinking that trash *meant* something—' An expression of acute agony settled over Sipling's face. 'That's it. That's why I can't stand it.'

'Why?' Taverner asked, deeply curious. His throat-mike was taking it all in, relaying it back to the home office at Washington. 'I'm interested in finding out why you broke away.'

Sipling bent down and called his son. 'Mike, stop playing and come on over here.' To Taverner he explained: 'Mike's nine years old. Yancy's been around as long as he's been alive.'

Mike came dully over. 'Yes, sir?'

'What kind of marks do you get in school?' his father asked.

The boy's chest stuck out proudly; he was a clear-eyed little miniature of Leon Sipling. 'All A's and B's.'

'He's a smart kid,' Sipling said Taverner. 'Good in arithmetic, geography, history, all that stuff.' Turning to the boy he said: 'I'm going to ask you some questions; I want this gentleman to hear your answers. Okay?'

'Yes, sir,' the boy said obediently.

His thin face grim, Sipling said to his son: 'I want to know what you think about war. You've been told about war in school; you know about all the famous wars in history. Right?'

'Yes, sir. We learned about the American Revolution, and the First Global War, and then the Second Global War, and then the First Hydrogen War, and the War between the colonists on Mars and Jupiter.'

'To the schools,' Sipling explained tightly to Taverner, 'we distribute Yancy material – educational subsidies in packet form. Yancy takes children through history, explains the meaning of it all. Yancy explains natural science. Yancy explains good posture and astronomy and every other thing in the universe. But I never thought my own son . . .' His voice trailed off unhappily, then picked up life. 'So you know all about war. Okay, what do you think of war?'

Promptly, the boy answered: 'War is bad. War is the most terrible thing there is. It almost destroyed mankind.'

Eyeing his son intently, Sipling demanded: 'Did anybody tell you to say that?'

The boy faltered uncertainly. 'No, sir.'

'You really believe those things?'

'Yes, sir. It's true, isn't it? Isn't war bad?'

Sipling nodded. 'War is bad. But what about *just* wars?'

Without hesitation the boy answered: 'We have to fight just wars, of course.'

'Why?'

'Well, we have to protect our way of life.'

'Why?'

Again, there was no hesitation in the boy's reedy answer. 'We can't let them walk over us, sir. That would encourage aggressive war. We can't permit a world of brute power. We have to have a world of—' He searched for the exact word. 'A world of *law*.'

Wearily, half to himself, Sipling commented: 'I wrote those meaningless, contradictory words myself, eight years ago.' Pulling himself together with a violent effort he asked: 'So war is bad. But we have to fight just wars. Well, maybe this – *planet*, Callisto, will get into a war with . . . let's pick Ganymede, at random.' He was unable to keep the harsh irony from his voice. 'Just at random. Now, we're at war with Ganymede. Is it a *just* war? Or only a war?'

This time, there was no answer. The boy's smooth face was screwed up in a bewildered, struggling frown.

'No answer?' Sipling inquired icily.

'Why, uh,' the boy faltered. 'I mean . . .' He glanced up hopefully. 'When the time comes won't somebody say?'

'Sure,' Sipling choked. 'Somebody will say. Maybe even Mr Yancy.'

Relief flooded the boy's face. 'Yes, sir. Mr Yancy will say.' He retreated back toward the other children. 'Can I go now?'

As the boy scampered back to his game, Sipling turned miserably to Taverner. 'You know what game they're playing? It's called Hippo-Hoppo. Guess whose grandson just loves it. Guess who invented the game.'

There was silence.

'What do you suggest?' Taverner asked. 'You said you thought something could be done.'

A cold expression appeared on Sipling's face, a flash of deeply-felt cunning. 'I know the project . . . I know how it can be pried apart. But somebody has to stand with a gun at the head of the authorities. In nine years I've come to see the essential key to the Yancy character . . . the key to the new type of person we're growing, here. It's simple. It's the element that makes that person malleable enough to be led around.'

'I'll bite,' Taverner said patiently, hoping the line to Washington was good and clear.

'All Yancy's beliefs are insipid. The key is *thinness*. Every part of his ideology is diluted: nothing excessive. We've come as close as possible to *no* beliefs . . . you've noticed that. Wherever possible we've can- celled attitudes out, left the person apolitical. Without a viewpoint.'

'Sure,' Taverner agreed. 'But with the illusion of a viewpoint.'

'All aspects of personality have to be controlled; we want the total person. So a specific attitude has to exist for each concrete question. In every respect, our rule is: *Yancy believes the least troublesome possibility*. The most shallow. The simple, effortless view, the view that fails to go deep enough to stir any real thought.'

Taverner got the drift. 'Good solid lulling views.' Excitedly he hurried on, 'But if an extreme original view got in, one that took real effort to work out, something that was hard to live . . .'

'Yancy plays croquet. So everybody fools around with a mallet.' Sipling's eyes gleamed. 'But suppose Yancy had a preference for – Kriegspiel.'

'For *what*?'

'Chess played on two boards. Each player has his own board, with a complete set of men. He never sees the other board. A moderator sees both; he tells each player when he's taken a piece, or lost a piece, or moved into an occupied square, or made an impossible move, or checked, or is in check himself.'

'I see,' Taverner said quickly. 'Each player tries to infer his opponent's location on the board. He plays blind. Lord, it would take every mental faculty possible.'

'The Prussians taught their officers military strategy that way. It's more than a game: it's a cosmic wrestling match. What if Yancy sat down in the evening with his wife and grandson, and played a nice lively six-hour game of Kriegspiel? Suppose his favorite books – instead of being western gun-toting anachronisms – were Greek tragedy? Suppose his favorite piece of music was Bach's *Art of the Fugue*, not *My Old Kentucky Home*?'

'I'm beginning to get the picture,' Taverner said, as calmly as possible. 'I think we can help.'

Babson squeaked once. 'But this is – illegal!'

'Absolutely,' Taverner acknowledged. 'That's why we're here.' He waved the squad of Niplan secret-servicemen into the offices of the Yancy Building, ignoring the stunned workers sitting bolt-upright at their desks. Into his throat-mike he said, 'How's it coming with the big-shots?'

'Medium,' Kellman's faint voice came, strengthened by the relay system between Callisto and Earth. 'Some slipped out of bounds to their various holdings, of course. But the majority never thought we'd taken action.'

'You can't!' Babson bleated, his great face hanging down in wattles of white dough. 'What have we done? What law—'

'I think,' Taverner interrupted, 'we can get you on purely commercial grounds alone. You've used the name Yancy to endorse various manufactured products. There's no such person. That's a violation of statutes governing ethical presentation of advertising.'

Babson's mouth closed with a snap, then slid feebly open. 'No – such – person? But everybody knows John Yancy. Why, he's—' Stammering, gesturing, he finished, 'He's everywhere.'

Suddenly a wretched little pistol appeared in his pulpy hand; he was waving it wildly as Dorser stepped up and quietly knocked it skidding across the floor. Babson collapsed into fumbling hysterics.

Disgusted, Dorser clamped handgrapples around him. 'Act like a man,' he ordered. But there was no response; Babson was too far gone to hear him.

Satisfied, Taverner plunged off, past the knot of stunned officials and workers, into the inner offices of the project. Nodding curtly, Taverner made his way up to the desk where Leon Sipling sat surrounded by his work.

The first of the altered gestalts was already flickering through the scanner. Together, the two men stood watching it.

'Well?' Taverner said, when it was done. 'You're the judge.'

'I believe it'll do,' Sipling answered nervously. 'I hope we don't stir up too much . . . it's taken eleven years to build it up; we want to tear it down by degrees.'

'Once the first crack is made, it should start swaying.' Taverner moved toward the door. 'Will you be all right on your own?'

Sipling glanced at Eckmund who lounged at the end of the office, eyes fixed on the uneasily working yance-men. 'I suppose so. Where are you going?'

'I want to watch this as it's released. I want to be around when the public gets its first look at it.' At the door, Taverner lingered. 'It's going to be a big job for you, putting out the gestalt on your own. You may not get much help, for a while.'

Sipling indicated his co-workers; they were already beginning to pick up their tempo where they had left off. 'They'll stay on the job,' he disagreed. 'As long as they get full salaries.'

Taverner walked thoughtfully across the hall to the elevator. A moment later he was on his way downstairs.

At a nearby street corner, a group of people had collected around a public vid-screen. Anticipating the late-afternoon TV cast of John Edward Yancy.

The gestalt began in the regular way. There was no doubt about it: when Sipling wanted to, he could put together a good slice. And in this case he had done practically the whole pie.

In rolled-up shirt sleeves and dirt-stained trousers, Yancy crouched in his garden, a trowel in one hand, straw hat pulled down over his eyes, grinning into the warm glare of the sun. It was so real that Taverner could hardly believe no such person existed. But he had watched Sipling's sub-crews laboriously and expertly constructing the thing from the ground up.

'Afternoon,' Yancy rumbled genially. He wiped perspiration from his steaming, florid face and got stiffly to his feet. 'Man,' he admitted, 'it's a hot day.' He indicated a flat of primroses. 'I was setting them out. Quite a job.'

So far so good. The crowd watched impassively, taking their ideological nourishment without particular resistance. All over the moon, in every house, schoolroom, office, on each street corner, the same gestalt was showing. And it would be shown again.

'Yes,' Yancy repeated, 'it's really hot. Too hot for those primroses – they like shade.' A fast pan-up showed he had carefully planted his primroses in the shadows at the base of his garage. 'On the other hand,' Yancy continued, in his smooth, good-natured, over-the-back-fence conversational voice, 'my dahlias need lots of sun.'

The camera leaped to show the dahlias blooming frantically in the blazing sunlight.

Throwing himself down in a striped lawnchair, Yancy removed his straw hat and wiped his brow with a pocket handkerchief. 'So,' he continued genially, 'if anybody asked me which is better, shade or sun, I'd have to reply it depends on whether you're a primrose or a dahlia.' He grinned his famous guileless boyish grin into the cameras. 'I guess I must be a primrose – I've had all the sun I can stand for today.'

The audience was taking it in without complaint. An inauspicious beginning, but it was going to have long-term consequences. And Yancy was starting to develop them right now.

His genial grin faded. That familiar look, that awaited serious frown showing that deep thoughts were coming, faded into place. Yancy was going to hold forth: wisdom was on the way. But it was nothing ever uttered by him before.

'You know,' Yancy said slowly, seriously, 'that makes a person do some thinking.' Automatically, he reached for his glass of gin and tonic – a glass which up until now would have contained beer. And the magazine beside it wasn't *Dog Stories Monthly*; it was *The Journal of Psychological Review*. The alteration of peripheral props would sink in subliminally; right now, all conscious attention was riveted on Yancy's words.

'It occurs to me,' Yancy orated, as if the wisdom were fresh and brand-new, arriving just now, 'that some people might maintain that, say, sunlight is *good* and shade is *bad*. But that's down-right silly. Sunlight is good for roses and dahlias, but it would darn well finish off my fuchsias.'

The camera showed his ubiquitous prize fuchsias.

'Maybe you know people like that. They just don't understand that—' And as was his custom, Yancy drew on folklore to make his point. 'That one man's meat,' he stated profoundly, 'is another man's poison. Like for instance, for breakfast I like a couple of eggs done sunny-side up, maybe a few stewed prunes, and a piece of toast. But Margaret, she prefers a bowl of cereal. And Ralf, he won't take either. He likes flapjacks. And the fellow down the street, the one with the big front lawn, he likes a kidney pie and a bottle of stout.'

Taverner winced. Well, they would have to feel their way along. But still the audience stood absorbing it, word after word. The first feeble stirrings of a radical idea: that each person had a different set of values, a unique style of life. That each person might believe, enjoy, and approve of different things.

It would take time, as Sipling said. The massive library of tapes would have to be replaced; injunctions built up in each area would have to be broken down. A new type of thinking was being introduced, starting with a trite observation about primroses. When a nine-year-old-boy wanted to find out if a war was just or unjust, he would have to inquire into his own mind. There would be no ready answer from Yancy; a gestalt was already being prepared on that, showing that every war had been called just by some, unjust by others.

There was one gestalt Taverner wished he could see. But it wouldn't be around for a long time; it would have to wait. Yancy was going to change his taste in art, slowly but steadily. One of these days, the public would learn that Yancy no longer enjoyed pastoral calendar scenes.

That now he preferred the art of that fifteenth century Dutch master of macabre and diabolical horror, Hieronymus Bosch.

If There Were No Benny Cemoli

Scampering across the unplowed field the three boys shouted as they saw the ship: it had landed, all right, just where they expected, and they were the first to reach it.

'Hey, that's the biggest I ever saw!' Panting, the first boy halted. 'That's not from Mars; that's from farther. It's from all the way out, I know it is.' He became silent and afraid as he saw the size of it. And then looking up into the sky he realized that an armada had arrived, exactly as everyone had expected. 'We better go tell,' he said to his companions.

Back on the ridge, John LeConte stood by his steam-powered chauffeur-driven limousine, impatiently waiting for the boiler to warm. *Kids got there first*, he said to himself with anger. *Whereas I'm supposed to.* And the children were ragged; they were merely farm boys.

'Is the phone working today?' LeConte asked his secretary.

Glancing at his clipboard, Mr Fall said, 'Yes, sir. Shall I put through a message to Oklahoma City?' He was the skinniest employee ever assigned to LeConte's office. The man evidently took nothing for himself, was positively uninterested in food. And he was efficient.

LeConte murmured, 'The immigration people ought to hear about this outrage.'

He sighed. It had all gone wrong. The armada from Proxima Centauri had after ten years arrived and none of the early-warning devices had detected it in advance of its landing. Now Oklahoma City would have to deal with the outsiders here on home ground – a psychological disadvantage which LeConte felt keenly.

Look at the equipment they've got, he thought as he watched the commercial ships of the flotilla begin to lower their cargos. *Why, hell, they make us look like provincials*. He wished that his official car did not need twenty minutes to warm up; he wished—

Actually, he wished that CURB did not exist.

Centaurus Urban Renewal Bureau, a do-gooding body unfortunately vested with enormous inter-system authority. It had been

291

informed of the Misadventure back in 2170 and had started into space like a phototropic organism, sensitive to the mere physical light created by the hydrogen-bomb explosions. But LeConte knew better than that. Actually the governing organizations in the Centaurian system knew many details of the tragedy because they had been in radio contact with other planets of the Sol system. Little of the native forms on Earth had survived. He himself was from Mars; he had headed a relief mission seven years ago, had decided to stay because there were so many opportunities here on Earth, conditions being what they were . . .

This is all very difficult, he said to himself as he stood waiting for his steam-powered car to warm. *We got here first, but* CURB *does outrank us: we must face that awkward fact. In my opinion, we've done a good job of rebuilding. Of course, it isn't like it was before . . . but ten years is not long. Give us another twenty and we'll have the trains running again. And our recent road-building bonds sold quite successfully, in fact were oversubscribed.*

'Call for you, sir, from Oklahoma City,' Mr Fall said, holding out the receiver of the portable field-phone.

'Ultimate Representative in the Field John LeConte, here,' LeConte said into it loudly. 'Go ahead; I say go ahead.'

'This is Party Headquarters,' the dry official voice at the other end came faintly, mixed with static, in his ear. 'We've received reports from dozens of alert citizens in Western Oklahoma Texas of an immense—'

'It's here,' LeConte said. 'I can see it. I'm just about ready to go out and confer with its ranking members, and I'll file a full report at the usual time. So it wasn't necessary for you to check up on me.' He felt irritable.

'Is the armada heavily armed?'

'Naw,' LeConte said. 'It appears to be comprised of bureaucrats and trade officials and commercial carriers. In other words, vultures.'

The Party desk-man said, 'Well, go and make certain they understand that their presence here is resented by the native population as well as the Relief of War-torn Areas Administrating Council. Tell them that the legislature will be calling to pass a special bill expressing indignation at this intrusion into domestic matters by an inter-system body.'

'I know, I know,' LeConte said. 'It's all been decided; I know.'

His chauffeur called to him, 'Sir, your car is ready now.'

The Party desk-man concluded, 'Make certain they understand that you can't negotiate with them; you have no power to admit them to Earth. Only the Council can do that and of course it's adamantly against that.'

LeConte hung up the phone and hurried to his car.

Despite the opposition of the local authorities, Peter Hood of CURB decided to locate his headquarters in the ruins of the old Terran capital, New York City. This would lend prestige to the CURBmen as they gradually widened the circle of the organization's influence. At last, of course, the circle would embrace the planet. But that would take decades.

As he walked through the ruins of what had once been a major train yard, Peter Hood thought to himself that when the task was done he himself would have long been retired. Not much remained of the pre-tragedy culture here. The local authorities – the political nonentities who had flocked in from Mars and Venus, as the neighboring planets were called – had done little. And yet he admired their efforts.

To the members of his staff walking directly behind him he said, 'You know, they have done the hard part for us. We ought to be grateful. It is not easy to come into a totally destroyed area, as they've done.'

His man Fletcher observed, 'They got back a good return.'

Hood said, 'Motive is not important. They have achieved results.' He was thinking of the official who had met them in his steam car; it had been solemn and formal, carrying complicated trappings. When these locals had first arrived on the scene years ago *they* had not been greeted, except perhaps by radiation-seared, blackened survivors who had stumbled out of cellars and gaped sightlessly. He shivered.

Coming up to him, a CURBman of minor rank saluted and said, 'I think we've managed to locate an undamaged structure in which your staff could be housed for the time being. It's underground.' He looked embarrassed. 'Not what we had hoped for. We'd have to displace the locals to get anything attractive.'

'I don't object,' Hood said. 'A basement will do.'

'The structure,' the minor CURBman said, 'was once a great homeo-static newspaper, the *New York Times*. It printed itself directly below us. At least, according to the maps. We haven't located the newspaper yet; it was customary for the homeopapes to be buried a mile or so down. As yet we don't know how much of this one survived.'

'But it would be valuable,' Hood agreed.

'Yes,' the CURBman said. 'Its outlets are scattered all over the planet; it must have had a thousand different editions which it put out daily. How many outlets function—' He broke off. 'It's hard to believe that the local politicos made no efforts to repair any of the ten or eleven world-wide homeopapes, but that seems to be the case.'

'Odd,' Hood said. Surely it would have eased their task. The post-tragedy job of reuniting people into a common culture depended on newspapers, ionization in the atmosphere making radio and TV reception difficult if not impossible. 'This makes me instantly suspicious,' he said, turning to his staff. 'Are they perhaps not trying to rebuild after all? Is their work merely a pretense?'

It was his own wife Joan who spoke up. 'They may simply have lacked the ability to place the homeopapes on an operational basis.'

Give them the benefit of the doubt, Hood thought. *You're right.*

'So the last edition of the *Times*,' Fletcher said, 'was put on the lines the day the Misadventure occurred. And the entire network of newspaper communication and news-creation had been idle since. I can't respect these politicos; it shows they're ignorant of the basics of a culture. By reviving the homeopapes we can do more to re-establish the pre-tragedy culture than they've done in ten thousand pitiful projects.' His tone was scornful.

Hood said, 'You may misunderstand, but let it go. Let's hope that the cephalon of the pape is undamaged. We couldn't possibly replace it.' Ahead he saw the yawning entrance which the CURBmen crews had cleared. This was to be his first move, here on the ruined planet, restoring this immense self-contained entity to its former authority. Once it had resumed its activity he would be freed for other tasks; the homeopape would take some of the burden from him.

A workman, still clearing debris away, muttered, 'Jeez, I never saw so many layers of junk. You'd think they deliberately bottled it up down here.' In his hands, the suction furnace which he operated glowed and pounded as it absorbed material, converting it to energy, leaving an increasingly enlarged opening.

'I'd like a report as soon as possible as to its condition,' Hood said to the team of engineers who stood waiting to descend into the opening. 'How long it will take to revive it, how much—' He broke off.

Two men in black uniforms had arrived. Police, from the Security ship. One, he saw, was Otto Dietrich, the ranking investigator accompanying the armada from Centaurus, and he felt tense automatically; it was a reflex for all of them – he saw the engineers and the workmen cease momentarily and then, more slowly, resume their work.

'Yes,' he said to Dietrich. 'Glad to see you. Let's go off to this side room and talk there.' He knew beyond a doubt what the investigator wanted; he had been expecting him.

Dietrich said, 'I won't take up too much of your time, Hood. I know you're quite busy. What is this, here?' He glanced about curiously, his scrubbed, round, alert face eager.

In a small side room, converted to a temporary office, Hood faced the two policemen. 'I am opposed to prosecution,' he said quietly. 'It's been too long. Let them go.'

Dietrich tugging thoughtfully at his ear, said, 'But war crimes are war crimes, even four decades later. Anyhow, what argument can there be? We're required by law to prosecute. *Somebody* started the war. They may well hold positions of responsibility now, but that hardly matters.'

'How many police troops have you landed?' Hood asked.

'Two hundred.'

'Then you're ready to go to work.'

'We're ready to make inquiries. Sequester pertinent documents and initiate litigation in the local courts. We're prepared to enforce co-operation, if that's what you mean. Various experienced personnel have been distributed to key points.' Dietrich eyed him. 'All this is necessary; I don't see the problem. Did you intend to protect the guilty parties – make use of their so-called abilities on your staff?'

'No,' Hood said evenly.

Dietrich said, 'Nearly eighty million people died in the Misfortune. Can you forget that? Or is it that since they were merely local people, not known to us personally—'

'It's not that,' Hood said. He knew it was hopeless; he could not communicate with the police mentality. 'I've already stated my objections. I feel it serves no purpose at this late date to have trials and hangings. Don't request use of my staff in this; I'll refuse on the grounds that I can spare no one, not even a janitor. Do I make myself clear?'

'You idealists,' Dietrich sighed. 'This is strictly a noble task confronting us . . . to rebuild, correct? What you don't or won't see is that these people will start it all over again, one day, unless we take steps now. We owe it to future generations. To be harsh now is the most humane method, in the long run. Tell me, Hood. What is this site? What are you resurrecting here with such vigor?'

'The *New York Times*,' Hood said.

'It has, I assume, a morgue? We can consult its backlog of information? That would prove valuable in building up our cases.'

Hood said, 'I can't deny you access to material we uncover.'

Smiling, Dietrich said, 'A day by day account of the political events leading up to the war would prove quite interesting. Who, for instance, held supreme power in the United States at the time of the Misfortune? No one we've talked to so far seems to remember.' His smile increased.

Early the next morning the report from the corps of engineers reached Hood in his temporary office. The power supply of the newspaper had been totally destroyed. But the cephalon, the governing brain-structure which guided and oriented the homeostatic system, appeared to be intact. If a ship were brought close by, perhaps its power supply could be integrated into the newspaper's lines. Thereupon much more would be known.

'In other words,' Fletcher said to Hood, as they sat with Joan eating breakfast, 'it may come on and it may not. Very pragmatic. You hook it up and if it works you've done your job. What if it doesn't? Do the engineers intend to give up at that point?'

Examining his cup, Hood said, 'This tastes like authentic coffee.' He pondered. 'Tell them to bring a ship in and start the homeopape up. And if it begins to print, bring me the edition at once.' He sipped his coffee.

An hour later a ship of the line had landed in the vicinity and its power source had been tapped for insertion into the homeopape. The conduits were placed, the circuits cautiously closed.

Seated in his office, Peter Hood heard far underground a low rumble, a halting, uncertain stirring. They had been successful. The newspaper was returning to life.

The edition, when it was laid on his desk by a bustling CURBman, surprised him by its accuracy. Even in its dormant state, the newspaper had somehow managed not to fall behind events. Its receptors had kept going.

CURB LANDS, TRIP DECADE LONG,
PLANS CENTRAL ADMINISTRATION

Ten years after the Misfortune of a nuclear holocaust, the intersystem rehabilitation agency, CURB, has made its historic appearance on Earth's surface, landing from a veritable armada of craft – a sight which witnesses described as 'overpowering both in scope and in significance.' CURBman Peter Hood, named top coordinator by Centaurian authorities, immediately set up headquarters in the ruins of New York City and conferred with aides, declaring that he had come 'not to punish the guilty but to re-establish the planet-wide culture by every means available, and to restore—

It was uncanny, Hood thought as he read the lead article. The varied news-gathering services of the homeopape had reached into his own life, had digested and then inserted into the lead article even the discussion between himself and Otto Dietrich. The newspaper was – had been – doing its job. Nothing of news-interest escaped it, even a discreet conversation carried on with no outsiders as witnesses. He would have to be careful.

Sure enough, another item, ominous in tone, dealt with the arrival of the black jacks, the police.

SECURITY AGENCY VOWS 'WAR CRIMINALS' TARGET

Captain Otto Dietrich, supreme police investigator arriving with the CURB armada from Proxima Centauri, said today that those responsible for the Misfortune of a decade ago 'would have to pay for their crimes' before the bar of Centaurian justice. Two hundred black-uniformed police, it was learned by the Times, have already begun exploratory activities designed to—

The newspaper was warning Earth about Dietrich, and Hood could not help feeling grim relish. The Times had not been set up to serve merely the occupying hierarchy. It served everyone, including those Dietrich intended to try. Each step of the police activity would no doubt be reported in full detail. Dietrich, who liked to work in anonymity, would not enjoy this. But the authority to maintain the newspaper belonged to Hood.

And he did not intend to shut it off.

One item on the first page of the paper attracted his further notice; he read it, frowning and a little uneasy.

> CEMOLI BACKERS RIOT IN UPSTATE NEW YORK
>
> Supporters of Benny Cemoli, gathered in the familiar tent cities associated with the colorful political figure, clashed with local citizens armed with hammers, shovels, and boards, both sides claiming victory in the two-hour melee which left twenty injured and a dozen hospitalized in hastily-erected first aid stations. Cemoli, garbed as always in his toga-style red robes, visited the injured, evidently in good spirits, joking and telling his supporters that 'it won't be long now' an evident reference to the organization's boast that it would march on New York City in the near future to establish what Cemoli deems 'social justice and true equality for the first time in world history.' It should be recalled that prior to his imprisonment at San Quentin—

Flipping a switch on his intercom system, Hood said, 'Fletcher, check into activities up in the north of the county. Find out about some sort of a political mob gathering there.'

Fletcher's voice came back. 'I have a copy of the *Times*, too, sir. I see the item about this Cemoli agitator. There's a ship on the way up there right now; should have a report within ten minutes.' Fletcher paused. 'Do you think – it'll be necessary to bring in any of Dietrich's people?'

'Let's hope not,' Hood said shortly.

Half an hour later the CURB ship, through Fletcher, made its report. Puzzled, Hood asked that it be repeated. But there was no mistake. The CURB field team had investigated thoroughly. They had found no sign whatsoever of any tent city or any group gathering. And citizens in the area whom they had interrogated had never heard of anyone named 'Cemoli.' And there was no sign of any scuffle having taken place, no first aid stations, no injured persons. Only the peaceful, semi-rural countryside.

Baffled, Hood read the item in the *Times* once more. There it was, in black and white, on the front page, along with the news about the landing of the CURB armada. What did it mean?

He did not like it at all.

Had it been a mistake to revive the great, old, damaged homeostatic newspaper?

★

From a sound sleep that night Hood was awakened by a clanging from far beneath the ground, an urgent racket that grew louder and louder as he sat up in bed, blinking and confused. Machinery roared. He heard the heavy rumbling movement as automatic circuits fitted into place, responding to instructions emanating from within the closed system itself.

'Sir,' Fletcher was saying from the darkness. A light came on as Fletcher located the temporary overhead fixture. 'I thought I should come in and wake you. Sorry, Mr Hood.'

'I'm awake,' Hood muttered, rising from the bed and putting on his robe and slippers. 'What's it doing?'

Fletcher said, 'It's printing an extra.'

Sitting up, smoothing her tousled blonde hair back, Joan said, 'Good Lord. What about?' Wide-eyed, she looked from her husband to Fletcher.

'We'll have to bring in the local authorities,' Hood said. 'Confer with them.' He had an intuition as to the nature of the extra roaring through the presses at this moment. 'Get that LeConte, the politico who met us on our arrival. Wake him up and fly him here immediately. We need him.'

It took almost an hour to obtain the presence of the haughty, ceremonious local potentate and his staff member. The two of them in their elaborate uniforms at last put in an appearance at Hood's office, both of them indignant. They faced Hood silently, waiting to hear what he wanted.

In his bathrobe and slippers Hood sat at his desk, a copy of the *Times'* extra before him; he was reading it once more as LeConte and his man entered.

NEW YORK POLICE REPORT CEMOLI LEGIONS
ON MOVE TOWARD CITY,
BARRICADES ERECTED, NATIONAL GUARD ALERTED

He turned the paper, showing the headlines to the two Earthmen. 'Who is this man?' he said.

After a moment LeConte said, 'I – don't know.'

Hood said, 'Come on, Mr LeConte.'

'Let me read the article,' LeConte said nervously. He scanned it in haste; his hands trembled as he held the newspaper. 'Interesting,' he said at last. 'But I can't tell you a thing. It's news to me. You must understand that our communications have been sparse, since the Misfortune, and it's entirely possible that a political movement could spring up without our—'

'Please,' Hood said. 'Don't make yourself absurd.'

Flushing, LeConte stammered, 'I'm doing the best I can, summoned out of my bed in the middle of the night.'

There was a stir, and through the office doorway came the rapidly-moving figure of Otto Dietrich, looking grim. 'Hood,' he said without preamble, 'there's a *Times* kiosk near my headquarters. It just posted this.' He held up a copy of the extra. 'The damn thing is running this off and distributing it throughout the world, isn't it? However, we have crack teams up in that area and they report absolutely nothing, no road blocks, no militia-style troops on the move, no activity of any sort.'

'I know,' Hood said. He felt weary. And still, from beneath them, the deep rumble continued, the newspaper printing its extra, informing the world of the march by Benny Cemoli's supporters on New York City – a fantasy march, evidently, a product manufactured entirely within the cephalon of the newspaper itself.

'Shut it off,' Dietrich said.

Hood shook his head. 'No. I want to know more.'

'That's no reason,' Dietrich said. 'Obviously, it's defective. Very seriously damaged, not working properly. You'll have to search elsewhere for your world-wide propaganda network.' He tossed the newspaper down on Hood's desk.

To LeConte, Hood said, 'Was Benny Cemoli active before the war?'

There was silence. Both LeConte and his assistant Mr Fall were pale and tense; they faced him tight-lipped, glancing at each other.

'I am not much for police matters,' Hood said to Dietrich, 'but I think you could reasonably step in here.'

Dietrich, understanding, said, 'I agree. You two men are under arrest. Unless you feel inclined to talk a little more freely about this agitator in the red toga.' He nodded to two of his police, who stood by the office doorway; they stepped obediently forward.

As the two policemen came up to him, LeConte said, 'Come to think of it, there was such a person. But – he was very obscure.'

'Before the war?' Hood asked.

'Yes.' LeConte nodded slowly. 'He was a joke. As I recall, and it's difficult . . . a fat, ignorant clown from some backwoods area. He had a little radio station or something over which he broadcast. He peddled some sort of anti-radiation box which you installed in your house, and it made you safe from bomb-test fallout.'

Now his staff member Mr Fall said, 'I remember. He even ran for the UN senate. But he was defeated, naturally.'

'And that was the last of him?' Hood asked.

'Oh yes.' LeConte said. 'He died of Asian flu soon after. He's been dead for fifteen years.'

In a helicopter, Hood flew slowly above the terrain depicted in the *Times* articles, seeing for himself that there was no sign of political activity. He did not feel really assured until he had seen with his own eyes that the newspaper had lost contact with actual events. The reality of the situation did not coincide with the *Times'* articles in any way; that was obvious. And yet – the homeostatic system continued on.

Joan, seated beside him, said, 'I have the third article here, if you want to read it.' She had been looking the latest edition over.

'No,' Hood said.

'It says they're in the outskirts of the city,' she said. 'They broke through the police barricades and the governor has appealed for UN assistance.'

Thoughtfully, Fletcher said, 'Here's an idea. One of us, preferably you, Hood, should write a letter to the *Times.*'

Hood glanced at him.

'I think I can tell you exactly how it should be worded,' Fletcher said. 'Make it a simple inquiry. You've followed the accounts in the paper about Cemoli's movement. Tell the editor—' Fletcher paused. 'That you feel sympathetic *and you'd like to join the movement.* Ask the paper how.'

To himself, Hood thought, *In other words ask the newspaper to put me in touch with Cemoli.* He had to admire Fletcher's idea. It was brilliant, in a crazy sort of way. It was as if Fletcher had been able to match the derangement of the newspaper by a deliberate shift from common sense on his own part. He would participate in the newspaper's delusion. Assuming there was a Cemoli and a march on New York, he was asking a reasonable question.

Joan said, 'I don't want to sound stupid, but how does one go about mailing a letter to a homeopape?'

'I've looked into that,' Fletcher said. 'At each kiosk set up by the paper there's a letter-slot, next to the coin-slot where you pay for your paper. It was the law when the homeopapes were set up originally, decades ago. All we need is your husband's signature.' Reaching into his jacket, he brought out an envelope. 'The letter's written.'

Hood took the letter, examined it. *So we desire to be part of the mythical fat clown's throng,* he said to himself. 'Won't there be a head-line reading CURB CHIEF JOINS MARCH ON EARTH CAPITAL?' he asked Fletcher, feeling a trace of wry amusement. 'Wouldn't a good, enterprising homeopape make front page use of a letter such as this?'

Obviously Fletcher had not thought of that; he looked chagrined. 'I suppose we had better get someone else to sign it,' he admitted. 'Some minor person attached to your staff.' He added, 'I could sign it myself.'

Handing him the letter back, Hood said, 'Do so. It'll be interesting to see what response, if any, there is.' *Letters to the editor,* he thought. *Letters to a vast, complex, electronic organism buried deep in the ground, responsible to no one, guided solely by its own ruling circuits. How would it react to this external ratification of its delusion? Would the newspaper be snapped back to reality?*

It was, he thought, *as if the newspaper, during these years of this enforced silence, had been dreaming, and now, reawakened, it had allowed portions of its former dreams to materialize in its pages along with its accurate, perceptive accounts of the actual situation. A blend of figments and sheer, stark reporting. Which ultimately would triumph? Soon, evidently, the unfolding story of Benny Cemoli would have the toga-wearing spellbinder in New York; it appeared that the march would succeed. And what then? How could this be squared with the arrival of* CURB, *with all its enormous inter-system authority and power? Surely the homeopape, before long, would have to face the incongruity.*

One of the two accounts would have to cease . . . but Hood had an uneasy intuition that a homeopape which had dreamed for a decade would not readily give up its fantasies. *Perhaps,* he thought, *the news of us, of* CURB *and its task of rebuilding Earth, will fade from the pages of the* Times, *will be given a steadily decreasing coverage each day, farther back in the paper. And at last only the exploits of Benny Cemoli will remain.*

It was not a pleasant anticipation. It disturbed him deeply. *As if,* he thought, *we are only real so long as the* Times *writes about us; as if we were dependent for our existence on it.*

★

Twenty-four hours later, in its regular edition, the *Times* printed Fletcher's letter. In print it struck Hood as flimsy and contrived – surely the homeopape could not be taken in by it, and yet here it was. It had managed to pass each of the steps in the pape's processing.

> Dear Editor:
>
> Your coverage of the heroic march on the decadent pluto-cratic stronghold of New York City has fired my enthusiasm. How does an ordinary citizen become a part of this history in the making? Please inform me at once, as I am eager to join Cemoli and endure the rigors and triumphs with the others.
>
> Cordially,
> Rudolf Fletcher

Beneath the letter, the homeopape had given an answer; Hood read it rapidly.

> Cemoli's stalwarts maintain a recruiting office in downtown New York; address, 460 Bleekman St, New York 32. You might apply there, if the police haven't cracked down on these quasi-legal activities, in view of the current crisis.

Touching a button on his desk, Hood opened the direct line to police headquarters. When he had the chief investigator, he said, 'Dietrich, I'd like a team of your men; we have a trip to make and there may be difficulties.'

After a pause Dietrich said dryly, 'So it's not all noble reclamation after all. Well, we've already dispatched a man to keep an eye on the Bleekman Street address. I admire your letter scheme. It may have done the trick.' He chuckled.

Shortly, Hood and four black-uniformed Centaurian policemen flew by 'copter above the ruins of New York City, searching for the remains of what had once been Bleekman Street. By the use of a map they managed after half an hour to locate themselves.

'There,' the police captain in charge of the team said, pointing. 'That would be it, that building used as a grocery store.' The 'copter began to lower.

It was a grocery store, all right. Hood saw no signs of political activity, no persons loitering, no flags or banners. And yet – something ominous seemed to lie behind the commonplace scene below, the bins of vegetables parked out on the sidewalk, the shabby women in long cloth coats who stood picking over the winter potatoes, the elderly proprietor with his white cloth apron sweeping with his broom. It was too natural, too easy. It was *too* ordinary.

'Shall we land?' the police captain asked him.

'Yes,' Hood said. 'And be ready.'

The proprietor, seeing them land in the street before his grocery store, laid his broom carefully to one side and walked toward them. He was, Hood saw, a Greek. He had a heavy mustache and slightly wavy gray hair, and he gazed at them with innate caution, knowing at once that they did not intend him any good. Yet he had decided to greet them with civility; he was not afraid of them.

'Gentlemen,' the Greek grocery store owner said, bowing slightly. 'What can I do for you?' His eyes roved speculatively over the black Centaurian police uniforms, but he showed no expression, no reaction.

Hood said, 'We've come to arrest a political agitator. You have nothing to be alarmed about.' He started toward the grocery store; the team of police followed, their side arms drawn.

'Political agitation here?' the Greek said. 'Come on. It is impossible.' He hurried after them, panting, alarmed now. 'What have I done? Nothing at all; you can look around. Go ahead.' He held open the door of the store, ushering them inside. 'See right away for yourself.'

'That's what we intend to do,' Hood said. He moved with agility, wasting no time on conspicuous portions of the store; he strode directly on through.

The back room lay ahead, the warehouse with its cartons of cans, cardboard boxes stacked up on every side. A young boy was busy making a stock inventory; he glanced up, startled, as they entered. *Nothing here*, Hood thought. *The owner's son at work, that's all.* Lifting the lid of a carton Hood peered inside. Cans of peaches. And beside that a crate of lettuce. He tore off a leaf, feeling futile and – disappointed.

The police captain said to him in a low voice, 'Nothing, sir.'

'I see that,' Hood said, irritably.

A door to the right led to a closet. Opening it, he saw brooms and a mop, a galvanized pail, boxes of detergents. And—

There were drops of paint on the floor.

The closet, some time recently, had been repainted. When he bent down and scratched with his nail he found the paint still tacky.

'Look at this,' he said, beckoning the police captain over.

The Greek, nervously, said, 'What's the matter, gentlemen? You find something dirty and report to the board of health, is that it? Customers have complained – tell me the truth, please. Yes, it is fresh paint. We keep everything spick and span. Isn't that in the public interest?'

Running his hands across the wall of the broom closet, the police captain said quietly, 'Mr Hood, there was a doorway here. Sealed up now, very recently.' He looked expectantly toward Hood, awaiting instructions.

Hood said, 'Let's go in.'

Turning to his subordinates, the police captain gave a series of orders. From the ship, equipment was dragged, through the store, to the closet; a controlled whine arose as the police began the task of cutting into the wood and plaster.

Pale, the Greek said, 'This is outrageous. I will sue.'

'Right,' Hood agreed. 'Take us to court.' Already a portion of the wall had given way. It fell inward with a crash, and bits of rubble spilled down onto the floor. A white cloud of dust rose, then settled.

It was not a large room which Hood saw in the glare of the police flashlights. Dusty, without windows, smelling stale and ancient . . . the room had not been inhabited for a long, long time, be realized, and he warily entered. It was empty. Just an abandoned storeroom of some kind, its wooden walls scaling and dingy. Perhaps before the Misfortune the grocery store had possessed a larger inventory. More stocks had been available then, but now this room was not needed. Hood moved about, flashing his beam of light up to ceiling and then down to the floor. Dead flies, entombed here . . . and, he saw, a few live ones which crept haltingly in the dust.

'Remember,' the police captain said, 'it was boarded up just now, within the last three days. Or at least the painting was just now done, to be absolutely accurate about it.'

'These flies,' Hood said. 'They're not even dead yet.' So it had not even been three days. Probably the boarding-up had been done yesterday.

What had this room been used for? He turned to the Greek, who had come after them, still tense and pale, his dark eyes flickering rapidly with concern. *This is a smart man*, Hood realized. *We will get little out of him.*

At the far end of the storeroom the police flashlights picked out a cabinet, empty shelves of bare, rough wood. Hood walked toward it.

'Okay,' the Greek said thickly, swallowing. 'I admit it. We have kept bootleg gin stored here. We became scared. You Centaurians—' He looked around at them with fear. 'You're not like our local bosses; we know them, they understand us. You! You can't be reached. But we have to make a living.' He spread his hands, appealing to them.

From behind the cabinet the edge of something protruded. Barely visible, it might never have been noticed. A paper which had fallen there, almost out of sight; it had slipped down farther and farther. Now Hood took hold of it and carefully drew it out. Back up the way it had come.

The Greek shuddered.

It was, Hood saw, a picture. A heavy, middle-aged man with loose jowls stained black by the grained beginnings of a beard, frowning, his lips set in defiance. A big man, wearing some kind of uniform. Once this picture had hung on the wall and people had come here and looked at it, paid respect to it. He knew who it was. This was Benny Cemoli, at the height of his political career, the leader glaring bitterly at the followers who had gathered here. So this was the man.

No wonder the *Times* showed such alarm.

To the Greek grocery store owner, Hood said, holding up the picture, 'Tell me. Is this familiar to you?'

'No, no,' the Greek said. He wiped perspiration from his face with a large red handkerchief. 'Certainly not.' But obviously, it was.

Hood said, 'You're a follower of Cemoli, aren't you?'

There was silence.

'Take him along,' Hood said to the police captain. 'And let's start back.' He walked from the room, carrying the picture with him.

As he spread the picture out on his desk, Hood thought, *It isn't merely a fantasy of the* Times. *We know the truth now. The man is real and twenty-four hours ago this portrait of him hung on a wall, in plain sight. It would still be there this moment, if* CURB *had not put in its appearance. We frightened them. The Earth people have a lot to hide from us, and they know it. They are taking steps, rapidly and effectively, and we will be lucky if we can—*

Interrupting his thoughts, Joan said, 'Then the Bleekman Street address really was a meeting place for them. The pape was correct.'

'Yes,' Hood said.

'Where is he now?'

I wish I knew, Hood thought.

'Has Dietrich seen the picture yet?'

'Not yet,' Hood said.

Joan said, 'He was responsible for the war and Dietrich is going to find it out.'

'No one man,' Hood said, 'could be solely responsible.'

'But he figured largely,' Joan said. 'That's why they've gone to so much effort to eradicate all traces of his existence.'

Hood nodded.

'Without the *Times*,' she said, 'would we ever have guessed that such a political figure as Benny Cemoli existed? We owe a lot to the pape. They overlooked it or weren't able to get to it. Probably they were working in such haste; they couldn't think of everything, even in ten years. It must be hard to obliterate *every* surviving detail of a planet-wide political movement, especially when its leader managed to seize absolute power in the final phase.'

'Impossible to obliterate,' Hood said. *A closed-off storeroom in the back of a Greek grocery store . . . that was enough to tell us what we needed to know. Now Dietrich's men can do the rest. If Cemoli is alive they will eventually find him, and if he's dead – they'll be hard to convince, knowing Dietrich. They'll never stop looking now.*

'One good thing about this,' Joan said, 'is that now a lot of innocent people will be off the hook. Dietrich won't go around prosecuting them. He'll be busy tracking down Cemoli.'

True, Hood thought. And that was important. The Centaurian police would be thoroughly occupied for a long time to come, and that was just as well for everyone, including CURB and its ambitious program of reconstruction.

If there had never been a Benny Cemoli, he thought suddenly, *it would almost have been necessary to invent him*. An odd thought . . . he wondered how it happened to come to him. Again he examined the picture, trying to infer as much as possible about the man from this flat likeness. How had Cemoli sounded? Had he gained power through the spoken word, like so many demagogues before him? And his writing . . . Maybe some of it would turn up. Or even tape recordings of speeches he had made, the actual *sound* of the man. And perhaps video tapes as well. Eventually it would all come to light; it was only a question of time. *And then we will be able to experience for ourselves how it was to live under the shadow of such a man*, he realized.

The line from Dietrich's office buzzed. He picked up the phone.

'We have the Greek here,' Dietrich said. 'Under drug-guidance he's made a number of admission; you may be interested.'

'Yes,' Hood said.

Dietrich said, 'He tells us he's been a follower for seventeen years, a real old-timer in the Movement. They met twice a week in the back of his grocery store, in the early days when the Movement was small and relatively powerless. That picture you have – I haven't seen it, of course, but Stavros, our Greek gentleman, told me about it – that portrait is actually obsolete in the sense that several more recent ones have been in vogue among the faithful for some time now. Stavros hung onto it for sentimental reasons. It reminded him of the old days. Later on when the Movement grew in strength, Cemoli stopped showing up at the grocery store, and the Greek lost out in any personal contact with him. He continued to be a loyal dues-paying member, but it became abstract for him.'

'What about the war?' Hood asked.

'Shortly before the war Cemoli seized power in a coup here in North America, through a march on New York City, during a severe economic depression. Millions were unemployed and he drew a good deal of support from them. He tried to solve the economic problems through an aggressive foreign policy – attacked several Latin American republics which were in the sphere of influence of the Chinese. That seems to be it, but Stavros is a bit hazy about the big picture . . . we'll have to fill in more from other enthusiasts as we go along. From some of the younger ones. After all, this one is over seventy years old.'

Hood said, 'You're not going to prosecute him. I hope.'

'Oh, no. He's simply a source of information. When he's told us all he has on his mind we'll let him go back to his onions and canned apple sauce. He's harmless.'

'Did Cemoli survive the war?'

'Yes,' Dietrich said. 'But that was ten years ago. Stavros doesn't know if the man is still alive now. Personally I think he is, and we'll go on that assumption until it's proved false. We have to.'

Hood thanked him and hung up.

As he turned from the phone he heard, beneath him, the low, dull rumbling. The homeopape had once more started into life.

'It's not a regular edition,' Joan said, quickly consulting her wristwatch. 'So it must be another extra. This is exciting, having it happen like this; I can't wait to read the front page.'

What has Benny Cemoli done now? Hood wondered. *According to the* Times, *in its misphased chronicling of the man's epic . . . what stage, actually taking place years ago, has now been reached. Something climatic, deserving of an extra. It will be interesting, no doubt of that. The* Times *knows what is fit to print.*

He, too, could hardly wait.

In downtown Oklahoma City, John LeConte put a coin into the slot of the kiosk which the *Times* had long ago established there. The copy of the *Times*' latest extra slid out, and he picked it up and read the headline briefly, spending only a moment on it to verify the essentials. Then he crossed the sidewalk and stepped once more into the rear seat of his chauffeur-driven steam car.

Mr Fall said circumspectly, 'Sir, here is the primary material, if you wish to make a word-by-word comparison.' The secretary held out the folder, and LeConte accepted it.

The car started up. Without being told, the chauffeur drove in the direction of Party headquarters. LeConte leaned back, lit a cigar and made himself comfortable.

On his lap, the newspaper blazed up its enormous headlines.

CEMOLI ENTERS COALITION UN GOVERNMENT,
TEMPORARY CESSATION OF HOSTILITIES

To his secretary, LeConte said, 'My phone, please.'

'Yes sir.' Mr Fall handed him the portable field-phone. 'But we're almost there. And it's always possible, if you don't mind my pointing it out, that they may have tapped us somewhere along the line.'

'They're busy in New York,' LeConte said. 'Among the ruins.' *In an area that hasn't mattered as long as I can remember,* he said to himself. However, possibly Mr Fall's advice was good; he decided to skip the phone call. 'What do you think of this last item?' he asked his secretary, holding up the newspaper.

'Very success-deserving,' Mr Fall said, nodding.

Opening his briefcase, LeConte brought out a tattered, coverless textbook. It had been manufactured only an hour ago, and it was the next artifact to be planted for the invaders from Proxima Centaurus to discover. This was his own contribution, and he was personally quite proud of it. The book outlined in massive detail Cemoli's program of social change; the revolution depicted in language comprehensible to school children.

'May I ask,' Mr Fall said, 'if the Party hierarchy intends for them to discover a corpse?'

'Eventually,' LeConte said. 'But that will be several months from now.' Taking a pencil from his coat pocket he wrote in the tattered textbook, crudely, as if a pupil had done it:

DOWN WITH CEMOLI.

Or was that going too far? No, he decided. There would be resistance. Certainly of the spontaneous, school boy variety. He added:

WHERE ARE THE ORANGES?

Peering over his shoulder, Mr Fall said, 'What does that mean?'

'Cemoli promises oranges to the youth,' LeConte explained. 'Another empty boast which the revolution never fulfills. That was Stavros's idea . . . he being a grocer. A nice touch.' *Giving it*, he thought, *just that much more semblance of verisimilitude. It's the little touches that have done it.*

'Yesterday,' Mr Fall said, 'when I was at Party headquarters, I heard an audio tape that had been made. Cemoli addressing the UN. It was uncanny; if you didn't know—'

'Who did they get to do it?' LeConte asked, wondering why he hadn't been in on it.

'Some nightclub entertainer here in Oklahoma City. Rather obscure, of course. I believe he specializes in all sorts of characterizations. The fellow gave it a bombastic, threatening quality . . . I must admit I enjoyed it.'

And meanwhile, LeConte thought, *there are no war-crimes trials. We who were leaders during the war, on Earth and on Mars, we who held responsible posts – we are safe, at least for a while. And perhaps it will be forever. If our strategy continues to work. And if our tunnel to the cephalon of the homeopape, which took us five years to complete, isn't discovered. Or doesn't collapse.*

The steam car parked in the reserved space before Party headquarters; the chauffeur came around to open the door and LeConte got leisurely out, stepping forth into the light of day, with no feeling of anxiety. He tossed his cigar into the gutter and then sauntered across the sidewalk, into the familiar building.

The Days of Perky Pat

At ten in the morning a terrific horn, familiar to him, hooted Sam Regan out of his sleep, and he cursed the careboy upstairs; he knew the racket was deliberate. The careboy, circling, wanted to be certain that flukers – and not merely wild animals – got the care parcels that were to be dropped.

We'll get them, we'll get them, Sam Regan said to himself as he zipped his dust-proof overalls, put his feet into boots and then grumpily sauntered as slowly as possible toward the ramp. Several other flukers joined him, all showing similar irritation.

'He's early today,' Tod Morrison complained. 'And I'll bet it's all staples, sugar and flour and lard – nothing interesting like say candy.'

'We ought to be grateful,' Norman Schein said.

'Grateful!' Tod halted to stare at him. 'GRATEFUL?'

'Yes,' Schein said. 'What do you think we'd be eating without them: If they hadn't seen the clouds ten years ago.'

'Well,' Tod said sullenly, 'I just don't like them to come *early*; I actually don't exactly mind their coming, as such.'

As he put his shoulders against the lid at the top of the ramp, Schein said genially, 'That's mighty tolerant of you, Tod boy. I'm sure the careboys would be pleased to hear your sentiments.'

Of the three of them, Sam Regan was the last to reach the surface; he did not like the upstairs at all, and he did not care who knew it. And anyhow, no one could compel him to leave the safety of the Pinole Fluke-pit; it was entirely his business, and he noted now that a number of his fellow flukers had elected to remain below in their quarters, confident that those who did answer the horn would bring them back something.

'It's bright,' Tod murmured, blinking in the sun.

The care ship sparkled close overhead, set against the gray sky as if hanging from an uneasy thread. Good pilot, this drop, Tod decided. He, or rather *it*, just lazily handles it, in no hurry. Tod waved at the care ship, and once more the huge horn burst out its din, making him clap his hands to his ears. Hey, a joke's a joke, he said to himself. And then the horn ceased; the careboy had relented.

'Wave to him to drop,' Norm Schein said to Tod. 'You've got the wigwag.'

'Sure,' Tod said, and began laboriously flapping the red flag, which the Martian creatures had long ago provided, back and forth, back and forth.

A projectile slid from the underpart of the ship, tossed out stabilizers, spiraled toward the ground.

'Sheoot,' Sam Regan said with disgust. 'It is staples; they don't have the parachute.' He turned away, not interested.

How miserable the upstairs looked today, he thought as he surveyed the scene surrounding him. There, to the right, the uncompleted house which someone — not far from their pit — had begun to build out of lumber salvaged from Vallejo, ten miles to the north. Animals or radiation dust had gotten the builder, and so his work remained where it was; it would never be put to use. And, Sam Regan saw, an unusually heavy precipitate had formed since last he had been up here, Thursday morning or perhaps Friday; he had lost exact track. The darn dust, he thought. Just rocks, pieces of rubble, and the dust. World's becoming a dusty object with no one to whisk it off regularly. How about you? he asked silently of the Martian careboy flying in slow circles overhead. Isn't your technology limitless? Can't you appear some morning with a dust rag a million miles in surface area and restore our planet to pristine newness?

Or rather, he thought, to pristine *oldness*, the way it was in the 'ol-days,' as the children call it. We'd like that. While you're looking for something to give to us in the way of further aid, try that.

The careboy circled once more, searching for signs of writing in the dust: a message from the flukers below. I'll write that, Sam thought. BRING DUST RAG, RESTORE OUR CIVILIZATION. Okay, careboy?

All at once the care ship shot off, no doubt on its way back home to its base on Luna or perhaps all the way to Mars.

From the open fluke-pit hole, up which the three of them had come, a further head poked, a woman. Jean Regan, Sam's wife, appeared, shielded by a bonnet against the gray, blinding sun, frowning and saying, 'Anything important? Anything *new*?'

''Fraid not,' Sam said. The care parcel projectile had landed and he walked toward it, scuffing his boots in the dust. The hull of the projectile had cracked open from the impact and he could see the canisters already. It looked to be five thousand pounds of salt – might as well leave it up here so the animals wouldn't starve, he decided. He felt despondent.

How peculiarly anxious the careboys were. Concerned all the time that the mainstays of existence be ferried from their own planet to Earth. They must think we eat all day long, Sam thought. My God . . . the pit was filled to capacity with stored foods. But of course it had been one of the smallest public shelters in Northern California.

'Hey,' Schein said, stooping down by the projectile and peering into the crack opened along its side. 'I believe I see something we can use.' He found a rusted metal pole – once it had helped reinforce the concrete side of an ol-days public building – and poked at the projectile, stirring its release mechanism into action. The mechanism, triggered off, popped the rear half of the projectile open . . . and there lay the contents.

'Looks like radios in that box,' Tod said. 'Transistor radios.' Thoughtfully stroking his short black beard he said, 'Maybe we can use them for something new in our layouts.'

'Mine's already got a radio,' Schein pointed out.

'Well, build an electronic self-directing lawn mower with the parts,' Tod said. 'You don't have that, do you?' He knew the Scheins' Perky Pat layout fairly well; the two couples, he and his wife with Schein and his, had played together a good deal, being almost evenly matched.

Sam Regan said, 'Dibs on the radios, because I can use them.' His layout lacked the automatic garage-door opener that both Schein and Tod had; he was considerably behind them.

'Let's get to work,' Schein agreed. 'We'll leave the staples here and just cart back the radios. If anybody wants the staples, let them come here and get them. Before the do-cats do.'

Nodding, the other two men fell to the job of carting the useful contents of the projectile to the entrance of their fluke-pit ramp. For use in their precious, elaborate Perky Pat layouts.

Seated cross-legged with his whetstone, Timothy Schein, ten years old and aware of his many responsibilities, sharpened his knife, slowly and expertly. Meanwhile, disturbing him, his mother and father noisily quarreled with Mr and Mrs Morrison, on the far side of the partition. They were playing Perky Pat again. As usual.

How many times today they have to play that dumb game? Timothy asked himself. Forever, I guess. He could see nothing in it, but his parents played on anyhow. And they weren't the only ones; he knew from what other kids said, even from other fluke-pits, that their parents, too, played Perky Pat most of the day, and sometimes even on into the night.

His mother said loudly, 'Perky Pat's going to the grocery store and it's got one of those electric eyes that opens the door. Look.' A pause. 'See, it opened for her, and now she's inside.'

'She pushes a cart,' Timothy's dad added, in support.

'No, she doesn't,' Mrs Morrison contradicted. 'That's wrong. She gives her list to the grocer and he fills it.'

'That's only in little neighborhood stores,' his mother explained. 'And this is a supermarket, you can tell because of the electric eye door.'

'I'm sure all grocery stores had electric eye doors,' Mrs Morrison said stubbornly, and her husband chimed in with his agreement. Now the voices rose in anger; another squabble had broken out. As usual.

Aw, cung to them, Timothy said to himself, using the strongest word which he and his friends knew. What's a supermarket anyhow? He tested the blade of his knife – he had made it himself, originally, out of a heavy metal pan – and then hopped to his feet. A moment later he had sprinted silently down the hall and was rapping his special rap on the door of the Chamberlains' quarters.

Fred, also ten years old, answered. 'Hi. Ready to go? I see you got that ol' knife of yours sharpened; what do you think we'll catch?'

'Not a do-cat,' Timothy said. 'A lot better than that, I'm tired of eating do-cat. Too peppery.'

'Your parents playing Perky Pat?'

'Yeah.'

Fred said, 'My mom and dad have been gone for a long time, off playing with the Benteleys.' He glanced sideways at Timothy, and in an instant they had shared their mute disappointment regarding their parents. Gosh, and maybe the darn game was all over the world, by now; that would not have surprised either of them.

'How come your parents play it?' Timothy asked.

'Same reason yours do,' Fred said.

Hesitating, Timothy said, 'Well, why? I don't know why they do; I'm asking you, can't you say?'

'It's because—' Fred broke off. 'Ask them. Come on; let's get upstairs and start hunting.' His eyes shone. 'Let's see what we can catch and kill today.'

Shortly, they had ascended the ramp, popped open the lid, and were crouching amidst the dust and rocks, searching the horizon. Timothy's heart pounded; this moment always overwhelmed him, the first instant of reaching the upstairs. The thrilling initial sight of the expanse. Because it was never the same. The dust, heavier today, had a darker gray color to it than before; it seemed denser, more mysterious.

Here and there, covered by many layers of dust, lay parcels dropped from past relief ships – dropped and left to deteriorate. Never to be claimed. And, Timothy saw, an additional new projectile which had arrived that morning. Most of its cargo could be seen within; the grownups had not had any use for the majority of the contents, today.

'Look,' Fred said softly.

Two do-cats – mutant dogs or cats; no one knew for sure – could be seen, lightly sniffing at the projectile. Attracted by the unclaimed contents.

'We don't want them,' Timothy said.

'That one's sure nice and fat,' Fred said longingly. But it was Timothy that had the knife; all he himself had was a string with a metal bolt on the end, a bull-roarer that could kill a bird or a small animal at a distance – but useless against a do-cat, which generally weighed fifteen to twenty pounds and sometimes more.

High up in the sky a dot moved at immense speed, and Timothy knew that it was a care ship heading for another fluke-pit, bringing supplies to it. Sure are busy, he thought to himself. Those careboys always coming and going; they never stop, because if they did, the grownups would die. Wouldn't that be too bad? he thought ironically. Sure be sad.

Fred said, 'Wave to it and maybe it'll drop something.' He grinned at Timothy, and then they both broke out laughing.

'Sure,' Timothy said. 'Let's see; what do I want?' Again the two of them laughed at the idea of them wanting something. The two boys had the entire upstairs, as far as the eye could see . . . they had even more than the careboys had, and that was plenty, more than plenty.

'Do you think they know,' Fred said, 'that our parents play Perky

Pat with furniture made out of what they drop? I bet they don't know about Perky Pat; they never have seen a Perky Pat doll, and if they did they'd be really mad.'

'You're right,' Timothy said. 'They'd be so sore they'd probably stop dropping stuff.' He glanced at Fred, catching his eye.

'Aw no,' Fred said. 'We shouldn't tell them; your dad would beat you again if you did that, and probably me, too.'

Even so, it was an interesting idea. He could imagine first the surprise and then the anger of the careboys; it would be fun to see that, see the reaction of the eight-legged Martian creatures who had so much charity inside their warty bodies, the cephalopodic univalve mollusk-like organisms who had voluntarily taken it upon themselves to supply succor to the waning remnants of the human race . . . this was how they got paid back for their charity, this utterly wasteful, stupid purpose to which their goods were being put. This stupid Perky Pat game that all the adults played.

And anyhow it would be very hard to tell them; there was almost no communication between humans and careboys. They were too different. Acts, deeds, could be done, conveying something . . . but not mere words, not mere *signs*. And anyhow—

A great brown rabbit bounded by to the right, past the half-completed house. Timothy whipped out his knife. 'Oh boy!' he said aloud in excitement. 'Let's go!' He set off across the rubbly ground, Fred a little behind him. Gradually they gained on the rabbit; swift running came easy to the two boys: they had done much practicing.

'Throw the knife!' Fred panted, and Timothy, skidding to a halt, raised his right arm, paused to take aim, and then hurled the sharpened, weighted knife. His most valuable, self-made possession.

It cleaved the rabbit straight through its vitals. The rabbit tumbled, slid, raising a cloud of dust.

'I bet we can get a dollar for that!' Fred exclaimed, leaping up and down. 'The hide alone – I bet we can get fifty cents just for the darn hide!'

Together, they hurried toward the dead rabbit, wanting to get there before a red-tailed hawk or a day-owl swooped on it from the gray sky above.

Bending, Norman Schein picked up his Perky Pat doll and said sullenly, 'I'm quitting; I don't want to play any more.'

Distressed, his wife protested, 'But we've got Perky Pat all the way downtown in her new Ford hardtop convertible and parked and a dime in the meter and she's shopped and now she's in the analyst's office reading *Fortune* – we're way ahead of the Morrisons! Why do you want to quit, Norm?'

'We just don't agree,' Norman grumbled. 'You say analysts charged twenty dollars an hour and I distinctly remember them charging only ten; nobody could charge twenty. So you're penalizing our side, and for what? The Morrisons agree it was only ten. Don't you?' he said to Mr and Mrs Morrison, who squatted on the far side of the layout which combined both couples' Perky Pat sets.

Helen Morrison said to her husband, 'You went to the analyst more than I did; are you sure he charged only ten?'

'Well, I went mostly to group therapy,' Tod said. 'At the Berkeley State Mental Hygiene Clinic, and they charged according to your ability to pay. And Perky Pat is at a *private* psychoanalyst.'

'We'll have to ask someone else,' Helen said to Norman Schein. 'I guess all we can do now this minute is suspend the game.' He found himself being glared at by her, too, now, because by his insistence on the one point he had put an end to their game for the whole afternoon.

'Shall we leave it all set up?' Fran Schein asked. 'We might as well; maybe we can finish tonight after dinner.'

Norman Schein gazed down at their combined layout, the swanky shops, the well-lit streets with the parked new-model cars, all of them shiny, the split-level house itself, where Perky Pat lived and where she entertained Leonard, her boy friend. It was the *house* that he perpetually yearned for; the house was the real focus of the layout – of all the Perky Pat layouts, however much they might otherwise differ.

Perky Pat's wardrobe, for instance, there in the closet of the house, the big bedroom closet. Her capri pants, her white cotton short-shorts, her two-piece polka dot swimsuit, her fuzzy sweaters . . . and there, in her bedroom, her hi-fi set, her collection of long playing records . . .

It had been this way, once, really been like this in the ol-days. Norm Schein could remember his own l-p record collection, and he had once had clothes almost as swanky as Perky Pat's boy friend Leonard, cashmere jackets and tweed suits and Italian sportshirts and shoes made in England. He hadn't owned a Jaguar XKE sports car, like Leonard did, but he had owned a fine-looking old 1963 Mercedes-Benz, which he had used to drive to work.

We lived then, Norm Schein said to himself, *like Perky Pat and Leonard do now*. This is how it actually was.

To his wife he said, pointing to the clock radio which Perky Pat kept beside her bed, 'Remember our GE clock radio? How it used to wake us up in the morning with classical music from that FM station, KSFR? The "Wolfgangers," the program was called. From six AM to nine every morning.'

'Yes,' Fran said, nodding soberly. 'And you used to get up before me; I knew I should have gotten up and fixed bacon and hot coffee for you, but it was so much fun just indulging myself, not stirring for half an hour longer, until the kids woke up.'

'Woke up, hell; they were awake before we were,' Norm said. 'Don't you remember? They were in the back watching "The Three Stooges" on TV until eight. Then I got up and fixed hot cereal for them, and then I went on to my job at Ampex down at Redwood City.'

'Oh yes,' Fran said. 'The TV.' Their Perky Pat did not have a TV set; they had lost it to the Regans in a game a week ago, and Norm had not yet been able to fashion another one realistic-looking enough to substitute. So, in a game, they pretended now that 'the TV repairman had come for it.' That was how they explained their Perky Pat not having something she really would have had.

Norm thought, Playing this game . . . it's like being back there, back in the world before the war. That's why we play it, I suppose. He felt shame, but only fleetingly; the shame, almost at once, was replaced by the desire to play a little longer.

'Let's not quit,' he said suddenly. 'I'll agree the psychoanalyst would have charged Perky Pat twenty dollars. Okay?'

'Okay,' both the Morrisons said together, and they settled back down once more to resume the game.

Tod Morrison had picked up their Perky Pat; he held it, stroking its blonde hair – theirs was blonde, whereas the Scheins' was a brunette – and fiddling with the snaps of its skirt.

'Whatever are you doing?' his wife inquired.

'Nice skirt she has,' Tod said. 'You did a good job sewing it.'

Norm said, 'Ever know a girl, back in the ol-days, that looked like Perky Pat?'

'No,' Tod Morrison said somberly. 'Wish I had, though. I *saw* girls like Perky Pat, especially when I was living in Los Angeles during the Korean War. But I just could never manage to know them personally. And of course there were really terrific girl singers, like Peggy Lee and Julie London . . . they looked a lot like Perky Pat.'

'Play,' Fran said vigorously. And Norm, whose turn it was, picked up the spinner and spun.

'Eleven,' he said. 'That gets my Leonard out of the sports car repair garage and on his way to the race track.' He moved the Leonard doll ahead.

Thoughtfully, Tod Morrison said, 'You know, I was out the other day hauling in perishables which the careboys had dropped. Bill Ferner was there, and he told me something interesting. He met a fluker from a fluke-pit down where Oakland used to be. And at that fluke-pit you know what they play? Not Perky Pat. They never have heard of Perky Pat.'

'Well, what do they play, then?' Helen asked.

'They have another doll entirely.' Frowning, Tod continued, 'Bill says the Oakland fluker called it a Connie Companion doll. Ever hear of that?'

'A "Connie Companion" doll,' Fran said thoughtfully. 'How strange. I wonder what she's like. Does she have a boy friend?'

'Oh sure,' Tod said. 'His name is Paul. Connie and Paul. You know, we ought to hike down there to that Oakland Fluke-pit one of these days and see what Connie and Paul look like and how they live. Maybe we could learn a few things to add to our own layouts.'

Norm said, 'Maybe we could play them.'

Puzzled, Fran said, 'Could a Perky Pat play a Connie Companion? Is that possible? I wonder what would happen?'

There was no answer from any of the others. Because none of them knew.

As they skinned the rabbit, Fred said to Timothy, 'Where did the name "fluker" come from? It's sure an ugly word; why do they use it?'

'A fluker is a person who lived through the hydrogen war,' Timothy explained. 'You know, by a fluke. A fluke of fate? See? Because almost everyone was killed; there used to be thousands of people.'

'But what's a "fluke," then? When you say a "fluke of fate—" '

'A fluke is when fate has decided to spare you,' Timothy said, and that was all he had to say on the subject. That was all he knew.

Fred said thoughtfully, 'But you and I, we're not flukers because we weren't alive when the war broke out. We were born after.'

'Right,' Timothy said.

'So anybody who calls me a fluker,' Fred said, 'is going to get hit in the eye with my bull-roarer.'

'And "careboy,"' Timothy said, 'that's a made-up word, too. It's from when stuff was dumped from jet planes and ships to people in a disaster area. They were called "care parcels" because they came from people who cared.'

'I know that,' Fred said. 'I didn't ask that.'

'Well, I told you anyhow,' Timothy said.

The two boys continued skinning the rabbit.

Jean Regan said to her husband, 'Have you heard about the Connie Companion doll?' She glanced down the long rough-board table to make sure none of the other families was listening. 'Sam,' she said, 'I heard it from Helen Morrison; she heard it from Tod and he heard it from Bill Ferner, I think. So it's probably true.'

'What's true?' Sam said.

'That in the Oakland Fluke-pit they don't have Perky Pat; they have Connie Companion . . . and it occurred to me that maybe some of this — you know, this sort of emptiness, this boredom we feel now and then — maybe if we saw the Connie Companion doll and how she lives, maybe we could add enough to our own layout to—' She paused, reflecting. 'To make it more complete.'

'I don't care for the name ' Sam Regan said. 'Connie Companion; it sounds cheap.' He spooned up some of the plain, utilitarian grain-mash which the careboys had been dropping, of late. And, as he ate a mouthful, he thought, I'll bet Connie Companion doesn't eat slop like this; I'll bet she eats cheeseburgers with all the trimmings, at a high-type drive-in.

'Could we make a trek down there?' Jean asked.

'To Oakland Fluke-pit?' Sam stared at her. '*It's fifteen miles*, all the way on the other side of the Berkeley Fluke-pit!'

'But this is important,' Jean said stubbornly. 'And Bill says that a fluker from Oakland came all the way up here, in search of electronic parts or something . . . so if he can do it, we can. We've got the dust suits they dropped us. I know we could do it.'

Little Timothy Schein, sitting with his family, had overheard her;

now he spoke up. 'Mrs Regan, Fred Chamberlain and I, we could trek down that far, if you pay us. What do you say?' He nudged Fred, who sat beside him. 'Couldn't we? For maybe five dollars.'

Fred, his face serious, turned to Mrs Regan and said, 'We could get you a Connie Companion doll. For five dollars for *each* of us.'

'Good grief,' Jean Regan said, outraged. And dropped the subject.

But later, after dinner, she brought it up again when she and Sam were alone in their quarters.

'Sam, I've got to see it,' she burst out. Sam, in a galvanized tub, was taking his weekly bath, so he had to listen to her. 'Now that we know it exists we have to play against someone in the Oakland Fluke-pit; at least we can do that. Can't we? Please.' She paced back and forth in the small room, her hands clasped tensely. 'Connie Companion may have a Standard Station and an airport terminal with jet landing strip and color TV and a French restaurant where they serve escargots, like the one you and I went to when we were first married . . . I just have to see her layout.'

'I don't know,' Sam said hesitantly. 'There's something about Connie Companion doll that – makes me uneasy.'

'What could it possibly be?'

'I don't know.'

Jean said bitterly, 'It's because you know her layout is so much better than ours and she's so much more than Perky Pat.'

'Maybe that's it,' Sam murmured.

'If you don't go, if you don't try to make contact with them down at the Oakland Fluke-pit, someone else will – someone with more ambition will get ahead of you. Like Norman Schein. He's not afraid the way you are.'

Sam said nothing; he continued with his bath. But his hands shook.

A careboy had recently dropped complicated pieces of machinery which were, evidently, a form of mechanical computer. For several weeks the computers – if that was what they were – had sat about the pit in their cartons, unused, but now Norman Schein was finding something to do with one. At the moment he was busy adapting some of its gears, the smallest ones, to form a garbage disposal unit for his Perky Pat's kitchen.

Using the tiny special tools – designed and built by inhabitants of the fluke-pit – which were necessary in fashioning environmental items for Perky Pat, he was busy at his hobby bench. Thoroughly engrossed in what he was doing, he all at once realized that Fran was standing directly behind him, watching.

'I get nervous when I'm watched,' Norm said, holding a tiny gear with a pair of tweezers.

'Listen,' Fran said, 'I've thought of something. Does this suggest anything to you?' She placed before him one of the transistor radios which had been dropped the day before.

'It suggests that garage-door opener already thought of,' Norm said irritably. He continued with his work, expertly fitting the miniature pieces together in the sink drain of Pat's kitchen; such delicate work demanded maximum concentration.

Fran said, 'It suggests that there must be radio *transmitters* on Earth somewhere, or the careboys wouldn't have dropped these.'

'So?' Norm said, uninterested.

'Maybe our Mayor has one,' Fran said. 'Maybe there's one right here in our own pit, and we could use it to call the Oakland Fluke-pit. Representatives from there could meet us halfway . . . say at the Berkeley Fluke-pit. And we could play there. So we wouldn't have that long fifteen mile trip.'

Norman hesitated in his work; he set the tweezers down and said slowly, 'I think possibly you're right.' But if their Mayor Hooker Glebe had a radio transmitter, would he let them use it? And if he did—

'We can try,' Fran urged. 'It wouldn't hurt to try.'

'Okay,' Norm said, rising from his hobby bench.

The short, sly-faced man in Army uniform, the Mayor of the Pinole Fluke-pit, listened in silence as Norm Schein spoke. Then he smiled a wise, cunning smile. 'Sure, I have a radio transmitter. Had it all the time. Fifty watt output. But why would you want to get in touch with the Oakland Fluke-pit?'

Guardedly, Norm said, 'That's my business.'

Hooker Glebe said thoughtfully, 'I'll let you use it for fifteen dollars.'

It was a nasty shock, and Norm recoiled. Good Lord; all the money he and his wife had — they needed every bill of it for use in playing Perky Pat. Money was the tender in the game; there was no other criterion by which one could tell if he had won or lost. 'That's too much,' he said aloud.

'Well, say ten,' the Mayor said, shrugging.

In the end they settled for six dollars and a fifty cent piece.

'I'll make the radio contact for you,' Hooker Glebe said. 'Because you don't know how. It will take time.' He began turning a crank at the side of the generator of the transmitter. 'I'll notify you when I've made contact with them. But give me the money now.' He held out his hand for it, and, with great reluctance, Norm paid him.

It was not until late that evening that Hooker managed to establish contact with Oakland. Pleased with himself, beaming in self-satisfaction, he appeared at the Scheins' quarters, during their dinner hour. 'All set,' he announced. 'Say, you know there are actually *nine* fluke-pits in Oakland? I didn't know that. Which you want? I've got one with the radio code of Red Vanilla.' He chuckled. 'They're tough and suspicious down there; it was hard to get any of them to answer.'

Leaving his evening meal, Norman hurried to the Mayor's quarters, Hooker puffing along after him.

The transmitter, sure enough, was on, and static wheezed from the speaker of its monitoring unit. Awkwardly, Norm seated himself at the microphone. 'Do I just talk?' he asked Hooker Glebe.

'Just say, This is Pinole Fluke-pit calling. Repeat that a couple of times and then when they acknowledge, you say what you want to say.' The Mayor fiddled with controls of the transmitter, fussing in an important fashion.

'This is Pinole Fluke-pit,' Norm said loudly into the microphone.

Almost at once a clear voice from the monitor said, 'This is Red Vanilla Three answering.' The voice was cold and harsh; it struck him forcefully as distinctly alien. Hooker was right. 'Do you have Connie Companion down there where you are?'

'Yes we do,' the Oakland fluker answered.

'Well, I challenge you,' Norman said, feeling the veins in his throat pulse with the tension of what he was saying. 'We're Perky Pat in this area; we'll play Perky Pat against your Connie Companion. Where can we meet?'

'Perky Pat,' the Oakland fluker echoed. 'Yeah, I know about her. What would the stakes be, in your mind?'

'Up here we play for paper money mostly,' Norman said, feeling that his response was somehow lame.

'We've got lots of paper money,' the Oakland fluker said cuttingly. 'That wouldn't interest any of us. What else?'

'I don't know.' He felt hampered, talking to someone he could not

323

see; he was not used to that. People should, he thought, be face to face, then you can see the other person's expression. This was not natural. 'Let's meet halfway,' he said, 'and discuss it. Maybe we could meet at the Berkeley Fluke-pit; how about that?'

The Oakland fluker said, 'That's too far. You mean lug our Connie Companion layout all that way? It's too heavy and something might happen to it.'

'No, just to discuss rules and stakes,' Norman said.

Dubiously, the Oakland fluker said, 'Well, I guess we could do that. But you better understand – we take Connie Companion doll pretty damn seriously; you better be prepared to talk terms.'

'We will,' Norm assured him.

All this time Mayor Hooker Glebe had been cranking the handle of the generator; perspiring, his face bloated with exertion, he motioned angrily for Norm to conclude his palaver.

'At the Berkeley Fluke-pit,' Norm finished. 'In three days. And send your best player, the one who has the biggest and most authentic layout. Our Perky Pat layouts are works of art, you understand.'

The Oakland fluker said, 'We'll believe that when we see them. After all, we've got carpenters and electricians and plasterers here, building our layouts; I'll bet you're all unskilled.'

'Not as much as you think,' Norm said hotly, and laid down the microphone. To Hooker Glebe – who had immediately stopped cranking – he said, 'We'll beat them. Wait'll they see the garbage disposal unit I'm making for my Perky Pat; did you know there were people back in the ol-days, I mean real alive human beings, who didn't have garbage disposal units?'

'I remember,' Hooker said peevishly. 'Say, you got a lot of cranking for your money; I think you gypped me, talking so long.' He eyed Norm with such hostility that Norm began to feel uneasy. After all, the Mayor of the pit had the authority to evict any fluker he wished; that was their law.

'I'll give you the fire alarm box I just finished the other day,' Norm said. 'In my layout it goes at the corner of the block where Perky Pat's boy friend Leonard lives.'

'Good enough,' Hooker agreed, and his hostility faded. It was replaced, at once, by desire. 'Let's see it, Norm. I bet it'll go good in my layout; a fire alarm box is just what I need to complete my first block where I have the mailbox. Thank you.'

'You're welcome,' Norm sighed, philosophically.

When he returned from the two-day trek to the Berkeley Fluke-pit his face was so grim that his wife knew at once that the parley with the Oakland people had not gone well.

That morning a careboy had dropped cartons of a synthetic tea-like drink; she fixed a cup of it for Norman, waiting to hear what had taken place eight miles to the south.

'We haggled,' Norm said, seated wearily on the bed which he and his wife and child all shared. 'They don't want money; they don't want goods – naturally not goods, because the darn careboys are dropping regularly down there, too.'

'What will they accept, then?'

Norm said, 'Perky Pat herself.' He was silent, then.

'Oh good Lord,' she said, appalled.

'But if we win,' Norm pointed out, 'we win Connie Companion.'

'And the layouts? What about them?'

'We keep our own. It's just Perky Pat herself, not Leonard, not anything else.'

'But,' she protested, 'what'll we *do* if we lose Perky Pat?'

'I can make another one,' Norm said. 'Given time. There's still a big supply of thermoplastics and artificial hair, here in the pit. And I have plenty of different paints; it would take at least a month, but I could do it. I don't look forward to the job, I admit. But—' His eyes glinted. 'Don't look on the dark side; *imagine what it would be like to win Connie Companion doll.* I think we may well win; their delegate seemed smart and, as Hooker said, tough . . . but the one I talked to didn't strike me as being very flukey. You know, on good terms with luck.'

And, after all, the element of luck, of chance, entered into each stage of the game through the agency of the spinner.

'It seems wrong,' Fran said, 'to put up Perky Pat herself. But if you say so—' She managed to smile a little. 'I'll go along with it. And if you won Connie Companion – who knows? You might be elected Mayor when Hooker dies. Imagine, to have won somebody else's *doll* – not just the game, the money, but the *doll itself.*'

'I can win,' Norm said soberly. 'Because I'm very flukey.' He could feel it in him, the same flukeyness that had got him through the hydrogen war alive, that had kept him alive ever since. You either have it or you don't, he realized. And I do.

His wife said, 'Shouldn't we ask Hooker to call a meeting of everyone in the pit, and send the best player out of our entire group. So as to be the surest of winning.'

'Listen,' Norm Schein said emphatically. 'I'm the best player. I'm going. And so are you; we made a good team, and we don't want to break it up. Anyhow, we'll need at least two people to carry Perky Pat's layout.' All in all, he judged, their layout weighed sixty pounds.

His plan seemed to him to be satisfactory. But when he mentioned it to the others living in the Pinole Fluke-pit he found himself facing sharp disagreement. The whole next day was filled with argument.

'You can't lug your layout all that way yourselves,' Sam Regan said. 'Either take more people with you or carry your layout in a vehicle of some sort. Such as a cart.' He scowled at Norm.

'Where'd I get a cart?' Norm demanded.

'Maybe something could be adapted,' Sam said. 'I'll give you every bit of help I can. Personally, I'd go along but as I told my wife this whole idea worries me.' He thumped Norm on the back. 'I admire your courage, you and Fran, setting off this way. I wish I had what it takes.' He looked unhappy.

In the end, Norm settled on a wheelbarrow. He and Fran would take turns pushing it. That way neither of them would have to carry any load above and beyond their food and water, and of course knives by which to protect them from the do-cats.

As they were carefully placing the elements of their layout in the wheelbarrow, Norm Schein's boy Timothy came sidling up to them. 'Take me along, Dad,' he pleaded. 'For fifty cents I'll go as guide and scout, and also I'll help you catch food along the way.'

'We'll manage fine,' Norm said. 'You stay here in the fluke-pit; you'll be safer here.' It annoyed him, the idea of his son tagging along on an important venture such as this. It was almost – sacreligious.

'Kiss us goodbye,' Fran said to Timothy, smiling at him briefly; then her attention returned to the layout within the wheelbarrow. 'I hope it doesn't tip over,' she said fearfully to Norm.

'Not a chance,' Norm said. 'If we're careful.' He felt confident.

A few moments later they began wheeling the wheelbarrow up the ramp to the lid at the top, to upstairs. Their journey to the Berkeley Fluke-pit had begun.

*

A mile outside the Berkeley Fluke-pit he and Fran began to stumble over empty drop-canisters and some only partly empty: remains of past care parcels such as littered the surface near their own pit. Norm Schein breathed a sigh of relief; the journey had not been so bad after all, except that his hands had become blistered from gripping the metal handles of the wheelbarrow, and Fran had turned her ankle so that now she walked with a painful limp. But it had taken them less time than he had anticipated, and his mood was one of buoyancy.

Ahead, a figure appeared, crouching low in the ash. A boy. Norm waved at him and called, 'Hey, sonny – we're from the Pinole pit; we're supposed to meet a party from Oakland here . . . do you remember me?'

The boy, without answering, turned and scampered off.

'Nothing to be afraid of,' Norm said to his wife. 'He's going to tell their Mayor. A nice old fellow named Ben Fennimore.'

Soon several adults appeared, approaching warily.

With relief, Norm set the legs of the wheelbarrow down into the ash, letting go and wiping his face with his handkerchief. 'Has the Oakland team arrived yet?' he called.

'Not yet,' a tall, elderly man with a white armband and ornate cap answered. 'It's you Schein, isn't it?' he said, peering. This was Ben Fennimore. 'Back already with your layout.' Now the Berkeley flukers had begun crowding around the wheelbarrow, inspecting the Scheins' layout. Their faces showed admiration.

'They have Perky Pat here,' Norm explained to his wife. 'But—' He lowered his voice. 'Their layouts are only basic. Just a house, wardrobe and car . . . they've built almost nothing. No imagination.'

One Berkeley fluker, a woman, said wonderingly to Fran, 'And you made each of the pieces of furniture yourselves?' Marveling, she turned to the man beside her. 'See what they've accomplished, Ed?'

'Yes,' the man answered, nodding. 'Say,' he said to Fran and Norm, 'can we see it all set up? You're going to set it up in our pit, aren't you?'

'We are indeed,' Norm said.

The Berkeley flukers helped push the wheelbarrow the last mile. And before long they were descending the ramp, to the pit below the surface.

'It's a big pit,' Norm said knowingly to Fran. 'Must be two thousand people here. This is where the University of California was.'

'I see,' Fran said, a little timid at entering a strange pit; it was the first

327

time in years – since the war, in fact – that she had seen any strangers. And so many at once. It was almost too much for her; Norm felt her shrink back, pressing against him in fright.

When they had reached the first level and were starting to unload the wheelbarrow, Ben Fennimore came up to them and said softly, 'I think the Oakland people have been spotted; we just got a report of activity upstairs. So be prepared.' He added, 'We're rooting for you, of course, because you're Perky Pat, the same as us.'

'Have you ever seen Connie Companion doll?' Fran asked him.

'No ma'am,' Fennimore answered courteously. 'But naturally we've heard about it, being neighbors to Oakland and all. I'll tell you one thing . . . we hear that Connie Companion doll is a bit older than Perky Pat. You know – more, um, *mature*.' He explained, 'I just wanted to prepare you.'

Norm and Fran glanced at each other. 'Thanks,' Norm said slowly. 'Yes, we should be as much prepared as possible. How about Paul?'

'Oh, he's not much,' Fennimore said. 'Connie runs things; I don't even think Paul has a real apartment of his own. But you better wait until the Oakland flukers get here; I don't want to mislead you – my knowledge is all hearsay, you understand.'

Another Berkeley fluker, standing nearby, spoke up. 'I saw Connie once, and she's much more grown up than Perky Pat.'

'How old do you figure Perky Pat is?' Norm asked him.

'Oh, I'd say seventeen or eighteen,' Norm was told.

'And Connie?' He waited tensely.

'Oh, she might be twenty-five, even.'

From the ramp behind them they heard noises. More Berkeley flukers appeared, and, after them, two men carrying between them a platform on which, spread out, Norm saw a great, spectacular layout.

This was the Oakland team, and they weren't a couple, a man and wife; they were both men, and they were hard-faced with stern, remote eyes. They jerked their heads briefly at him and Fran, acknowledging their presence. And then, with enormous care, they set down the platform on which their layout rested.

Behind them came a third Oakland fluker carrying a metal box, much like a lunch pail. Norm, watching, knew instinctively that in the box lay Connie Companion doll. The Oakland fluker produced a key and began unlocking the box.

'We're ready to begin playing any time,' the taller of the Oakland men said. 'As we agreed in our discussion, we'll use a numbered spinner instead of dice. Less chance of cheating that way.'

'Agreed,' Norm said. Hesitantly he held out his hand. 'I'm Norman Schein and this is my wife and play-partner Fran.'

The Oakland man, evidently the leader, said, 'I'm Walter R. Wynn. This is my partner here, Charley Dowd, and the man with the box, that's Peter Foster. He isn't going to play; he just guards out layout.' Wynn glanced about, at the Berkeley flukers, as if saying, I know you're all partial to Perky Pat, in here. But we don't care; we're not scared.

Fran said, 'We're ready to play, Mr Wynn.' He voice was low but controlled.

'What about money?' Fennimore asked.

'I think both teams have plenty of money,' Wynn said. He laid out several thousand dollars in greenbacks, and now Norm did the same. 'The money of course is not a factor in this, except as a means of conducting the game.'

Norm nodded; he understood perfectly. Only the dolls themselves mattered. And now, for the first time, he saw Connie Companion doll.

She was being placed in her bedroom by Mr Foster who evidently was in charge of her. And the sight of her took his breath away. Yes, she was older. A grown woman, not a girl at all . . . the difference between her and Perky Pat was acute. And so life-like. Carved, not poured; she obviously had been whittled out of wood and then painted – she was not a thermoplastic. And her hair. It appeared to be genuine hair.

He was deeply impressed.

'What do you think of her?' Walter Wynn asked, with a faint grin.

'Very – impressive,' Norm conceded.

Now the Oaklanders were studying Perky Pat. 'Poured thermoplastic,' one of them said. 'Artificial hair. Nice clothes, though; all stitched by hand, you can see that. Interesting; what we heard was correct. Perky Pat isn't a grownup, she's just a teenager.'

Now the male companion to Connie appeared; he was set down in the bedroom beside Connie.

'Wait a minute,' Norm said. 'You're putting Paul or whatever his name is, in her bedroom with her? Doesn't he have his own apartment?'

Wynn said, 'They're married.'

'*Married!*' Norman and Fran stared at him, dumbfounded.

'Why sure,' Wynn said. 'So naturally they live together. Your dolls, they're not, are they?'

'N-no,' Fran said. 'Leonard is Perky Pat's boy friend . . .' Her voice trailed off. 'Norm,' she said, clutching his arm, 'I don't believe him; I think he's just saying they're married to get the advantage. Because if they both start out from the same room—'

Norm said aloud, 'You fellows, look here. It's not fair, calling them married.'

Wynn said, 'We're not "calling" them married; they are married. Their names are Connie and Paul Lathrope, of 24 Arden Place, Piedmont. They've been married for a year, most players will tell you.' He sounded calm.

Maybe, Norm thought, it's true. He was truly shaken.

'Look at them together,' Fran said, kneeling down to examine the Oaklanders' layout. 'In the same bedroom, in the same house. Why, Norm; do you see? There's just the one bed. A big double bed.' Wild-eyed, she appealed to him. 'How can Perky Pat and Leonard play against them?' Her voice shook. 'It's not morally *right.*'

'This is another type of layout entirely,' Norm said to Walter Wynn. 'This, that you have. Utterly different from what we're used to, as you can see.' He pointed to his own layout. 'I insist that in this game Connie and Paul *not* live together and *not* be considered married.'

'But they are,' Foster spoke up. 'It's a fact. Look – their clothes are in the same closet.' He showed them the closet. 'And in the same bureau drawers.' He showed them that, too. 'And look in the bathroom. Two toothbrushes. His and hers, in the same rack. So you can see we're not making it up.'

There was silence.

Then Fran said in a choked voice, 'And if they're married – you mean they've been – intimate?'

Wynn raised an eyebrow, then nodded. 'Sure, since they're married. Is there anything wrong with that?'

'Perky Pat and Leonard have never—' Fran began, and then ceased.

'Naturally not,' Wynn agreed. 'Because they're only going together. We understand that.'

Fran said, 'We just can't play. We can't.' She caught hold of her husband's arm. 'Let's go back to Pinole pit – please, Norman.'

'Wait,' Wynn said, at once. 'If you don't play, you're conceding; you have to give up Perky Pat.'

The three Oaklanders all nodded. And, Norm saw, many of the Berkeley flukers were nodding, too, including Ben Fennimore.

'They're right,' Norm said heavily to his wife. 'We'd have to give her up. We better play, dear.'

'Yes,' Fran said, in a dead, flat voice. 'We'll play.' She bent down and listlessly spun the needle of the spinner. It stopped at six.

Smiling, Walter Wynn knelt down and spun. He obtained a four.

The game had begun.

Crouching behind the strewn, decayed contents of a care parcel that had been dropped long ago, Timothy Schein saw coming across the surface of ash his mother and father, pushing the wheelbarrow ahead of them. They looked tired and worn.

'Hi,' Timothy yelled, leaping out at them in joy at seeing them again; he had missed them very much.

'Hi, son,' his father murmured, nodding. He let go of the handles of the wheelbarrow, then halted and wiped his face with his handkerchief.

Now Fred Chamberlain raced up, panting. 'Hi, Mr Schein; hi, Mrs Schein. Hey, did you win? Did you beat the Oakland flukers? I bet you did, didn't you?' He looked from one of them to the other and then back.

In a low voice Fran said, 'Yes, Freddy. We won.'

Norm said, 'Look in the wheelbarrow.'

The two boys looked. And, there among Perky Pat's furnishings, lay another doll. Larger, fuller-figured, much older than Pat . . . they stared at her and she stared up sightlessly at the gray sky overhead. So this is Connie Companion doll, Timothy said to himself. Gee.

'We were lucky,' Norm said. Now several people had emerged from the pit and were gathering around them, listening. Jean and Sam Regan, Tod Morrison and his wife Helen, and now their Mayor, Hooker Glebe himself, waddling up excited and nervous, his face flushed, gasping for breath from the labor – unusual for him – of ascending the ramp.

Fran said, 'We got a cancellation of debts card, just when we were most behind. We owed fifty thousand, and it made us even with the Oakland flukers. And then, after that, we got an advance ten squares card, and that put us right on the jackpot square, at least in our layout.

We had a very bitter squabble, because the Oaklanders showed us that on their layout it was a tax lien slapped on real estate holdings square, but we had spun an odd number so that put us back on our own board.' She sighed. 'I'm glad to be back. It was hard, Hooker; it was a tough game.'

Hooker Glebe wheezed, 'Let's all get a look at the Connie Companion doll, folks.' To Fran and Norm he said, 'Can I lift her up and show them?'

'Sure,' Norm said, nodding.

Hooker picked up Connie Companion doll. 'She sure is realistic,' he said, scrutinizing her. 'Clothes aren't as nice as ours generally are; they look machine-made.'

'They are,' Norm agreed. 'But she's carved, not poured.'

'Yes, so I see.' Hooker turned the doll about, inspecting her from all angles. 'A nice job. She's – um, more filled-out than Perky Pat. What's this outfit she has on? Tweed suit of some sort.'

'A business suit,' Fran said. 'We won that with her; they had agreed on that in advance.'

'You see, she has a job,' Norm explained. 'She's a psychology consultant for a business firm doing marketing research. In consumer preferences. A high-paying position . . . she earns twenty thousand a year, I believe Wynn said.'

'Golly,' Hooker said. 'And Pat's just going to college; she's still in school.' He looked troubled. 'Well, I guess they were bound to be ahead of us in some ways. What matters is that you won.' His jovial smile returned. 'Perky Pat came out ahead.' He held the Connie Companion doll up high, where everyone could see her. 'Look what Norm and Fran came back with, folks!'

Norm said, 'Be careful with her, Hooker.' His voice was firm.

'Eh?' Hooker said, pausing. 'Why, Norm?'

'Because,' Norm said, 'she's going to have a baby.'

There was a sudden chill silence. The ash around them stirred faintly; that was the only sound.

'How do you know?' Hooker asked.

'They told us. The Oaklanders told us. And we won that, too – after a bitter argument that Fennimore had to settle.' Reaching into the wheelbarrow he brought out a little leather pouch, from it he carefully took a carved pink new-born baby. 'We won this too because Fennimore agreed that from a technical standpoint it's literally part of Connie Companion doll at this point.'

Hooker stared a long, long time.

'She's married,' Fran explained. 'To Paul. They're not just going together. She's three months pregnant, Mr Wynn said. He didn't tell us until after we won; he didn't want to, then, but they felt they had to. I think they were right; it wouldn't have done not to say.'

Norm said, 'And in addition there's actually an embryo outfit—'

'Yes,' Fran said. 'You have to open Connie up, of course, to see—'

'No,' Jean Regan said. 'Please, no.'

Hooker said, 'No, Mrs Schein, don't.' He backed away.

Fran said, 'It shocked us of course at first, but—'

'You see,' Norm put in, 'it's logical; you have to follow the logic. Why, eventually Perky Pat—'

'No,' Hooker said violently. He bent down, picked up a rock from the ash at his feet. 'No,' he said, and raised his arm. 'You stop, you two. Don't say any more.'

Now the Regans, too, had picked up rocks. No one spoke.

Fran said, at last, 'Norm, we've got to get out of here.'

'You're right,' Tod Morrison told them. His wife nodded in grim agreement.

'You two go back down to Oakland,' Hooker told Norman and Fran Schein. 'You don't live here any more. You're different than you were. You – changed.'

'Yes,' Sam Regan said slowly, half to himself. 'I was right; there was something to fear.' To Norm Schein he said, 'How difficult a trip is it to Oakland?'

'We just went to Berkeley,' Norm said. 'To the Berkeley Fluke-pit.' He seemed baffled and stunned by what was happening. 'My God,' he said, 'we can't turn around and push this wheelbarrow back all the way to Berkeley again – we're worn out, we need rest!'

Sam Regan said, 'What if somebody else pushed?' He walked up to the Scheins, then, and stood with them. 'I'll push the darn thing. You lead the way, Schein.' He looked toward his own wife, but Jean did not stir. And she did not put down her handful of rocks.

Timothy Schein plucked at his father's arm. 'Can I come this time, Dad? Please let me come.'

'Okay,' Norm said, half to himself. Now he drew himself together. 'So we're not wanted here.' He turned to Fran. 'Let's go. Sam's going to push the wheelbarrow; I think we can make it back there before

333

nightfall. If not, we can sleep out in the open; Timothy'll help protect us against the do-cats.'

Fran said, 'I guess we have no choice.' Her face was pale.

'And take this,' Hooker said. He held out the tiny carved baby. Fran Schein accepted it and put it tenderly back in its leather pouch. Norm laid Connie Companion back down in the wheelbarrow, where she had been. They were ready to start back.

'It'll happen up here eventually,' Norm said, to the group of people, to the Pinole flukers. 'Oakland is just more advanced; that's all.'

'Go on,' Hooker Glebe said. 'Get started.'

Nodding, Norm started to pick up the handles of the wheelbarrow, but Sam Regan moved him aside and took them himself. 'Let's go,' he said.

The three adults, with Timothy Schein going ahead of them with his knife ready – in case a do-cat attacked – started into motion, in the direction of Oakland and the south. No one spoke. There was nothing to say.

'It's a shame this had to happen,' Norm said at last, when they had gone almost a mile and there was no further sign of the Pinole flukers behind them.

'Maybe not,' Sam Regan said. 'Maybe it's for the good.' He did not seem downcast. And after all, he had lost his wife; he had given up more than anyone else, and yet – he had survived.

'Glad you feel that way,' Norm said somberly.

They continued on, each with his own thoughts.

After a while, Timothy said to his father, 'All these big fluke-pits to the south . . . there's lots more things to do there, isn't there? I mean, you don't just sit around playing that game.' He certainly hoped not.

His father said, 'That's true, I guess.'

Overhead, a care ship whistled at great velocity and then was gone again almost at once; Timothy watched it go but he was not really interested in it, because there was so much more to look forward to, on the ground and below the ground, ahead of them to the south.

His father murmured, 'Those Oaklanders; their game, their particular doll, it taught them something. Connie had to grow and it forced them all to grow along with her. Our flukers never learned about that, not from Perky Pat. I wonder if they ever will. She'd have to grow up the way Connie did. Connie must have been like Perky Pat, once. A long time ago.'

Not interested in what his father was saying — who really cared about dolls and games with dolls? — Timothy scampered ahead, peering to see what lay before them, the opportunities and possibilities, for him and for his mother and dad, for Mr Regan also.

'I can't wait,' he yelled back at his father, and Norm Schein managed a faint, fatigued smile in answer.

Oh, To Be a Blobel!

He put a twenty-dollar platinum coin into the slot and the analyst, after a pause, lit up. Its eyes shone with sociability and it swiveled about in its chair, picked up a pen and pad of long yellow paper from its desk and said,

'Good morning, sir. You may begin.'

'Hello, Dr Jones. I guess you're not the same Dr Jones who did the definitive biography of Freud; that was a century ago.' He laughed nervously; being a rather poverty-stricken man he was not accustomed to dealing with the new fully homeostatic psychoanalysts. 'Um,' he said, 'should I free-associate or give you background material or just what?'

Dr Jones said, 'Perhaps you could begin by telling me who you are und warum mich – why you have selected me.'

'I'm George Minister of catwalk 4, building WEF-395, San Francisco condominium established 1996.'

'How do you do, Mr Munster.' Dr Jones held out its hand, and George Munster shook it. He found the hand to be of a pleasant body-temperature and decidedly soft. The grip, however, was manly.

'You see,' Munster said, 'I'm an ex-GI, a war veteran. That's how I got my condominium apartment at WEF-395; veterans' preference.'

'Ah yes,' Dr Jones said, ticking faintly as it measured the passage of time. 'The war with the Blobels.'

'I fought three years in that war,' Munster said, nervously smoothing his long, black, thinning hair. 'I hated the Blobels and I volunteered; I was only nineteen and I had a good job – but the crusade to clear the Sol System of Blobels came first in my mind.'

'Um,' Dr Jones said, ticking and nodding.

George Munster continued, 'I fought well. In fact I got two decorations and a battlefield citation. Corporal. That's because I single-handedly wiped out an observation satellite full of Blobels; we'll never know exactly how many because of course, being Blobels, they tend to fuse together and unfuse confusingly.' He broke off, then, feeling emotional. Even remembering and talking about the war was too much for him . . . he lay back on the couch, lit a cigarette and tried to become calm.

The Blobels had emigrated originally from another star system, probably Proxima. Several thousand years ago they had settled on Mars and on Titan, doing very well at agrarian pursuits. They were developments of the original unicellular amoeba, quite large and with a highly-organized nervous system, but still amoeba, with pseudopodia, reproducing by binary fission, and in the main offensive to Terran settlers.

The war itself had broken out over ecological considerations. It had been the desire of the Foreign Aid Department of the UN to change the atmosphere on Mars, making it more usable for Terran settlers. This change, however, had made it unpalatable for the Blobel colonies already there; hence the squabble.

And, Munster reflected, it was not possible to change *half* the atmosphere of a planet, the Brownian movement being what it was. Within a period of ten years the altered atmosphere had diffused throughout the planet, bringing suffering – at least so they alleged – to the Blobels. In retaliation, a Blobel armada had approached Terra and had put into orbit a series of technically sophisticated satellites designed eventually to alter the atmosphere of Terra. This alteration had never come about because of course the War Office of the UN had gone into action; the satellites had been detonated by self-instructing missiles . . . and the war was on.

Dr Jones said, 'Are you married, Mr Munster?'

'No sir,' Munster said. 'And—' He shuddered. 'You'll see why when I've finished telling you. See, Doctor—' He stubbed out his cigarette. 'I'll be frank. I was a Terran spy. That was my task; they gave the job to me because of my bravery in the field . . . I didn't ask for it.'

'I see,' Dr Jones said.

'Do you?' Munster's voice broke. 'Do you know what was necessary in those days in order to make a Terran into a successful spy among the Blobels?'

Nodding, Dr Jones said, 'Yes, Mr Munster. You had to relinquish your human form and assume the repellent form of a Blobel.'

Munster said nothing; he clenched and unclenched his fist, bitterly. Across from him Dr Jones ticked.

*

That evening, back in his small apartment at WEF-395, Munster opened a fifth of Teacher's scotch, sat by himself sipping from a cup, lacking even the energy to get a glass down from the cupboard over the sink.

What had he gotten out of the session with Dr Jones today? Nothing, as nearly as he could tell. And it had eaten deep into his meager financial resources . . . meager because—

Because for almost twelve hours out of the day he reverted, despite all the efforts of himself and the Veterans' Hospitalization Agency of the UN, to his old war-time Blobel shape. To a formless unicellular-like blob, right in the middle of his own apartment at WEF-395.

His financial resources consisted of a small pension from the War Office; finding a job was impossible, because as soon as he was hired the strain caused him to revert there on the spot, in plain sight of his new employer and fellow workers.

It did not assist in forming successful work-relationships.

Sure enough, now, at eight in the evening, he felt himself once more beginning to revert; it was an old and familiar experience to him, and he loathed it. Hurriedly, he sipped the last of the cup of scotch, put the cup down on a table . . . and felt himself slide together into a homogenous puddle.

The telephone rang.

'I can't answer,' he called to it. The phone's relay picked up his anguished message and conveyed it to the calling party. Now Munster had become a single transparent gelatinous mass in the middle of the rug; he undulated toward the phone – it was still ringing, despite his statement to it, and he felt furious resentment; didn't he have enough troubles already, without having to deal with a ringing phone?

Reaching it, he extended a pseudopodium and snatched the receiver from the hook. With great effort he formed his plastic substance into the semblance of a vocal apparatus, resonating dully. 'I'm busy,' he resonated in a low booming fashion into the mouthpiece of the phone. 'Call later.' *Call*, he thought as he hung up, *tomorrow morning. When I've been able to regain my human form*.

The apartment was quiet, now.

Sighing, Munster flowed back across the carpet, to the window, where he rose into a high pillar in order to see the view beyond; there was a light-sensitive spot on his outer surface, and although he did not possess a true lens he was able to appreciate – nostalgically – the sight of

San Francisco Bay, the Golden Gate Bridge, the playground for small children which was Alcatraz Island.

Dammit, he thought bitterly. *I can't marry; I can't live a genuine human existence, reverting this way to the form the War Office bigshots forced me into back in the war times . . .*

He had not known then, when he accepted the mission, that it would leave this permanent effect. They had assured him it was 'only temporary, for the duration,' or some such glib phrase. *Duration my ass*, Munster thought with furious, impotent resentment. *It's been* eleven years, *now*.

The psychological problems created for him, the pressure on his psyche, were immense. Hence his visit to Dr Jones.

Once more the phone rang.

'Okay,' Munster said aloud, and flowed laboriously back across the room to it. 'You want to talk to me?' he said as he came closer and closer; the trip, for someone in Blobel form, was a long one. 'I'll talk to you. You can even turn on the vidscreen and *look* at me.' At the phone he snapped the switch which would permit visual communication as well as auditory. 'Have a good look,' he said, and displayed his amorphous form before the scanning tube of the video.

Dr Jones' voice came: 'I'm sorry to bother you at your home, Mr Munster, especially when you're in this, um, awkward condition . . .' The homeostatic analyst paused. 'But I've been devoting time to problem-solving vis-a-vis your condition. I may have at least a partial solution.'

'What?' Munster said, taken by surprise. 'You mean to imply that medical science can now—'

'No, no,' Dr Jones said hurriedly. 'The physical aspects lie out of my domain; you must keep that in mind, Munster. When you consulted me about your problems it was the psychological adjustment that—'

'I'll come right down to your office and talk to you,' Munster said. And then he realized that he could not; in his Blobel form it would take him days to undulate all the way across town to Dr Jones' office. 'Jones,' he said desperately, 'you see the problems I face. I'm stuck here in this apartment every night beginning about eight o'clock and lasting through until almost seven in the morning . . . I can't even visit you and consult you and get help—'

'Be quiet, Mr Munster,' Dr Jones interrupted. 'I'm trying to tell you something. *You're not the only one in this condition*. Did you know that?'

Heavily, Munster said, 'Sure. In all, eighty-three Terrans were made over into Blobels at one time or another during the war. Of the eighty-three—' He knew the facts by heart. 'Sixty-one survived and now there's an organization called Veterans of Unnatural Wars of which fifty are members. I'm a member. We meet twice a month, revert in unison . . .' He started to hang up the phone. So this was what he had gotten for his money, this stale news. 'Goodbye, Doctor,' he murmured.

Dr Jones whirred in agitation. 'Mr Munster, I don't mean other Terrans. I've researched this in your behalf, and I discover that according to captured records at the Library of Congress fifteen *Blobels* were formed into pseudo-Terrans to act as spies for *their* side. Do you understand?'

After a moment Munster said, 'Not exactly.'

'You have a mental block against being helped,' Dr Jones said. 'But here's what I want, Munster; you be at my office at eleven in the morning tomorrow. We'll take up the solution to your problem then. Goodnight.'

Wearily, Munster said, 'When I'm in my Blobel form my wits aren't too keen, Doctor. You'll have to forgive me.' He hung up, still puzzled. So there were fifteen Blobels walking around on Titan this moment, doomed to occupy human forms – so what? How did that help him?

Maybe he would find out at eleven tomorrow.

When he strode into Dr Jones' waiting room he saw, seated in a deep chair in a corner by a lamp, reading a copy of *Fortune*, an exceedingly attractive young woman.

Automatically, Munster found a place to sit from which he could eye her. Stylish dyed-white hair braided down the back of her neck . . . he took in the sight of her with delight, pretending to read his own copy of *Fortune*. Slender legs, small and delicate elbows. And her sharp, clearly-featured face. The intelligent eyes, the thin, tapered nostrils – a truly lovely girl, he thought. He drank in the sight of her . . . until all at once she raised her head and stared coolly back at him.

'Dull, having to wait,' Munster mumbled.

The girl said, 'Do you come to Dr Jones often?'

'No,' he admitted. 'This is just the second time.'

'I've never been here before,' the girl said. 'I was going to another electronic fully-homeostatic psychoanalyst in Los Angeles and then late yesterday Dr Bing, my analyst, called me and told me to fly up here and see Dr Jones this morning. Is this one good?'

'Um,' Munster said. 'I guess so.' *We'll see,* he thought. *That's precisely what we don't know, at this point.*

The inner office door opened and there stood Dr Jones. 'Miss Arrasmith,' it said, nodding to the girl. 'Mr Munster.' It nodded to George. 'Won't you both come in?'

Rising to her feet, Miss Arrasmith said, 'Who pays the twenty dollars then?'

But the analyst had become silent; it had turned off.

'I'll pay,' Miss Arrasmith said, reaching into her purse.

'No, no,' Munster said. 'Let me.' He got out a twenty-dollar piece and dropped it into the analyst's slot.

At once, Dr Jones said, 'You're a gentleman, Mr Munster.' Smiling, it ushered the two of them into its office. 'Be seated, please. Miss Arrasmith, without preamble please allow me to explain your – condition to Mr Munster.' To Munster it said, 'Miss Arrasmith is a Blobel.'

Munster could only stare at the girl.

'Obviously,' Dr Jones continued, 'presently in human form. This, for her, is the state of involuntary reversion. During the war she operated behind Terran lines, acting for the Blobel War League. She was captured and held, but then the war ended and she was neither tried nor sentenced.'

'They released me,' Miss Arrasmith said in a low, carefully-controlled voice. 'Still in human form. I stayed here out of shame. I just couldn't go back to Titan and—' Her voice wavered.

'There is great shame attached to this condition,' Dr Jones said, 'for any high-caste Blobel.'

Nodding, Miss Arrasmith sat, clutching a tiny Irish linen handkerchief and trying to look poised. 'Correct, Doctor. I did visit Titan to discuss my condition with medical authorities there. After expensive and prolonged therapy with me they were able to induce a return to my natural form for a period of—' She hesitated. 'About one-fourth of the time. But the other three-fourths . . . I am as you perceive me now.' She ducked her head and touched the handkerchief to her right eye.

'Jeez,' Munster protested, 'you're lucky; a human form is infinitely superior to a Blobel form – I ought to know. As a Blobel you have to creep along . . . you're like a big jellyfish, no skeleton to keep you erect. And binary fission – it's lousy, I say really lousy, compared to the Terran form of – you know. Reproduction.' He colored.

Dr Jones ticked and stated, 'For a period of about six hours your human forms overlap. And then for about one hour your Blobel forms overlap. So all in all, the two of you possess seven hours out of twenty-four in which you both possess identical forms. In my opinion—' It toyed with its pen and paper. 'Seven hours is not too bad. If you follow my meaning.'

After a moment Miss Arrasmith said, 'But Mr Munster and I are natural enemies.'

'That was years ago,' Munster said.

'Correct,' Dr Jones agreed. 'True, Miss Arrasmith is basically a Blobel and you, Munster, are a Terran, but—' It gestured. 'Both of you are outcasts in either civilization; both of you are stateless and hence gradually suffering a loss of ego-identity. I predict for both of you a gradual deterioration ending finally in severe mental illness. Unless you two can develop a rapprochement.' The analyst was silent, then.

Miss Arrasmith said softly, 'I think we're very lucky, Mr Munster. As Dr Jones said, we do overlap for seven hours a day . . . we can enjoy that time together, no longer in wretched isolation.' She smiled up hopefully at him, rearranging her coat. Certainly, she had a nice figure; the somewhat low-cut dress gave an ideal clue to that.

Studying her, Munster pondered.

'Give him time,' Dr Jones told Miss Arrasmith. 'My analysis of him is that he will see this correctly and do the right thing.'

Still rearranging her coat and dabbing at her large, dark eyes, Miss Arrasmith waited.

The phone in Dr Jones' office rang, a number of years later. He answered it in his customary way. 'Please, sir or madam, deposit twenty dollars if you wish to speak to me.'

A tough male voice on the other end of the line said, 'Listen, this is the UN Legal Office and we don't deposit twenty dollars to talk to anybody. So trip that mechanism inside you, Jones.'

'Yes, sir,' Dr Jones said, and with his right hand tripped the lever behind his ear that caused him to come on free.

'Back in 2037,' the UN legal expert said, 'did you advise a couple to marry? A George Munster and a Vivian Arrasmith, now Mrs Munster?'

'Why yes,' Dr Jones said, after consulting his built-in memory banks.

'Had you investigated the legal ramifications of their issue?'

'Um well,' Dr Jones said, 'that's not my worry.'

'You can be arraigned for advising any action contrary to UN law.'

'There's no law prohibiting a Blobel and a Terran from marrying.'

The UN legal expert said, 'All right, Doctor, I'll settle for a look at their case histories.'

'Absolutely not,' Dr Jones said. 'That would be a breach of ethics.'

'We'll get a writ and sequester them, then.'

'Go ahead.' Dr Jones reached behind his ear to shut himself off.

'Wait. It may interest you to know that the Munsters now have four children. And, following the Mendelian Law, the offspring comprise a strict one, two, one ratio. One Blobel girl, one hybrid boy, one hybrid girl, one Terran girl. The legal problem arises in that the Blobel Supreme Council claims the pure-blooded Blobel girl as a citizen of Titan and also suggests that one of the two hybrids be donated to the Council's jurisdiction.' The UN legal expert explained, 'You see, the Munsters' marriage is breaking up; they're getting divorced and it's sticky finding which laws obtain regarding them and their issue.'

'Yes,' Dr Jones admitted, 'I would think so. What has caused their marriage to breakup?'

'I don't know and don't care. Possibly the fact that both adults and two of the four children rotate daily between being Blobels and Terrans; maybe the strain got to be too much. If you want to give them psychological advice, consult them. Goodbye.' The UN legal expert rang off.

Did I make a mistake, advising them to marry? Dr Jones asked itself. *I wonder if I shouldn't look them up; I owe at least that to them.*

Opening the Los Angeles phone book, it began thumbing through the Ms.

These had been six difficult years for the Munsters.

First, George had moved from San Francisco to Los Angeles; he and Vivian had set up a household in a condominium apartment with three instead of two rooms. Vivian, being in Terran form three-fourths of the time, had been able to obtain a job; right out in public she gave jet flight information at the Fifth Los Angeles Airport. George, however—

His pension comprised an amount only one-fourth that of his wife's salary and he felt it keenly. To augment it, he had searched for a way of earning money at home. Finally in a magazine he had found this valuable ad:

MAKE SWIFT PROFITS IN YOUR OWN CONDO! RAISE GIANT BULL-FROGS FROM JUPITER, CAPABLE OF EIGHTY-FOOT LEAPS. CAN BE USED IN FROG-RACING (where legal) AND . . .

So in 2038 he had bought his first pair of frogs imported from Jupiter and had begun raising them for swift profits, right in his own condominium apartment building, in a corner of the basement that Leopold, the partially-homeostatic janitor, let him use gratis.

But in the relatively feeble Terran gravity the frogs were capable of enormous leaps, and the basement proved too small for them; they ricocheted from wall to wall like green ping pong balls and soon died. Obviously it took more than a portion of the basement at QEK-604 Apartments to house a crop of the damned things, George realized.

And then, too, their first child had been born. It had turned out to be a pure-blooded Blobel; for twenty-four hours a day it consisted of a gelatinous mass and George found himself waiting in vain for it to switch over to a human form, even for a moment.

He faced Vivian defiantly in this matter, during a period when both of them were in human form.

'How can I consider it my child?' he asked her. 'It's – an alien life form to me.' He was discouraged and even horrified. 'Dr Jones should have foreseen this; maybe it's *your* child – it looks just like you.'

Tears filled Vivian's eyes. 'You mean that insultingly.'

'Damn right I do. We fought you creatures – we used to consider you no better than Portuguese sting-rays.' Gloomily, he put on his coat. 'I'm going down to Veterans of Unnatural Wars Headquarters,' he informed his wife. 'Have a beer with the boys.' Shortly, he was on his way to join with his old war-time buddies, glad to get out of the apartment house.

VUW Headquarters was a decrepit cement building in downtown Los Angeles left over from the twentieth century and sadly in need of paint. The VUW had little funds because most of its members were, like George Munster, living on UN pensions. However, there was a pool table and an old 3-D television set and a few dozen tapes of popular music and also a chess set. George generally drank his beer and played chess with his fellow members, either in human form or in Blobel form; this was one place in which both were accepted.

This particular evening he sat with Pete Ruggles, a fellow veteran who also had married a Blobel female, reverting, as Vivian did, to human form.

'Pete, I can't go on. I've got a gelatinous blob for a child. My whole life I've wanted a kid, and now what have I got? Something that looks like it washed up on the beach.'

Sipping his beer – he too was in human form at the moment – Pete answered, 'Criminy, George, I admit it's a mess. But you must have known what you were getting into when you married her. And my God, according to Mendel's Law, the next kid—'

'I mean,' George broke in, 'I don't respect my own wife; that's the basis of it. I think of her as a *thing*. And myself, too. We're both things.' He drank down his beer in one gulp.

Pete said meditatively, 'But from the Blobel standpoint—'

'Listen, whose side are you on?' George demanded.

'Don't yell at me,' Pete said, 'or I'll deck you.'

A moment later they were swinging wildly at each other. Fortunately Pete reverted to Blobel form in the nick of time; no harm was done. Now George sat alone, in human shape, while Pete oozed off somewhere else, probably to join a group of the boys who had also assumed Blobel form.

Maybe we can find a new society somewhere on a remote moon, George said to himself moodily. *Neither Terran nor Blobel.*

I've got to go back to Vivian, George resolved. *What else is there for me? I'm lucky to find her; I'd be nothing but a war veteran guzzling beer here at VUW Headquarters every damn day and night, with no future, no hope, no real life . . .*

He had a new money-making scheme going now. It was a home mail-order business; he had placed an ad in the *Saturday Evening Post* for MAGIC LODE-STONES REPUTED TO BRING YOU LUCK. FROM AN-OTHER STAR-SYSTEM ENTIRELY! The stones had come from Proxima and were obtainable on Titan; it was Vivian who had made the commercial contact for him with her people. But so far, few people had sent in the dollar-fifty.

I'm a failure, George said to himself.

Fortunately the next child, born in the winter of 2039, showed itself to be a hybrid; it took human form fifty percent of the time, and so at last George had a child who was – occasionally, anyhow – a member of his own species.

He was still in the process of celebrating the birth of Maurice when a delegation of their neighbors at QEK-604 Apartments came and rapped on their door.

'We've got a petition here,' the chairman of the delegation said, shuffling his feet in embarrassment, 'asking that you and Mrs Munster leave QEK-604.'

'But why?' George asked, bewildered. 'You haven't objected to us up until now.'

'The reason is that now you've got a hybrid youngster who will want to play with ours, and we feel it's unhealthy for our kids to—'

George slammed the door in their faces.

But still, he felt the pressure, the hostility from the people on all sides of them. *And to think*, he thought bitterly, *that I fought in the war to save these people. It sure wasn't worth it.*

An hour later he was down at VUW Headquarters once more, drinking beer and talking with his buddy Sherman Downs, also married to a Blobel.

'Sherman, it's no good. We're not wanted; we've got to emigrate. Maybe we'll try it on Titan, in Viv's world.'

'Chrissakes,' Sherman protested, 'I hate to see you fold up, George. Isn't your electromagnetic reducing belt beginning to sell, finally?'

For the last few months, George had been making and selling a complex electronic reducing gadget which Vivian had helped him design; it was based in principle on a Blobel device popular on Titan but unknown on Terra. And this had gone over well; George had more orders than he could fill. But—

'I had a terrible experience, Sherm,' George confided. 'I was in a drugstore the other day, and they gave me a big order for my reducing belt, and I got so excited—' He broke off. 'You can guess what happened. I reverted. Right in plain sight of a hundred customers. And when the buyer saw that he canceled the order for the belts. It was what we all fear . . . you should have seen how their attitude toward me changed.'

Sherm said, 'Hire someone to do your selling for you. A full-blooded Terran.'

Thickly, George said, '*I'm* a full-blooded Terran, and don't you forget it. Ever.'

'I just mean—'

'I know what you meant,' George said. And took a swing at Sherman. Fortunately he missed and in the excitement both of them reverted to Blobel form. They oozed angrily into each other for a time, but at last fellow veterans managed to separate them.

'I'm as much Terran as anyone,' George thought-radiated in the Blobel manner to Sherman. 'And I'll flatten anyone who says otherwise.'

In Blobel form he was unable to get home; he had to phone Vivian to come and get him. It was humiliating.

Suicide, he decided. *That's the answer.*

How best to do it? In Blobel form he was unable to feel pain; best to do it then. Several substances would dissolve him . . . he could for instance drop himself into a heavily-chlorinated swimming pool, such as QEK-604 maintained in its recreation room.

Vivian, in human form, found him as he reposed hesitantly at the edge of the swimming pool, late one night.

'George, I beg you – go back to Dr Jones.'

'Naw,' he boomed dully, forming a quasi-vocal apparatus with a portion of his body. 'It's no use, Viv. I don't *want* to go on.' Even the belts; they had been Viv's idea, rather than his. He was second even there . . . behind her, falling constantly farther behind each passing day.

Viv said, 'You have so much to offer the children.'

That was true. 'Maybe I'll drop over to the UN War Office,' he decided. 'Talk to them, see if there's anything new that medical science has come up with that might stabilize me.'

'But if you stabilize as a Terran,' Vivian said, 'what would become of me?'

'We'd have *eighteen entire hours* together a day. All the hours you take human form!'

'But you wouldn't want to stay married to me. Because, George, then you could meet a Terran woman.'

It wasn't fair to her, he realized. So he abandoned the idea.

In the spring of 2041 their third child was born, also a girl, and like Maurice a hybrid. It was Blobel at night and Terran by day.

Meanwhile, George found a solution to some of his problems.

He got himself a mistress.

He and Nina arranged to meet each other at the Hotel Elysium, a rundown wooden building in the heart of Los Angeles.

'Nina,' George said, sipping Teacher's scotch and seated beside her on the shabby sofa which the hotel provided, 'you've made my life worth living again.' He fooled with the buttons of her blouse.

'I respect you,' Nina Glaubman said, assisting him with the buttons. 'In spite of the fact – well, you are a former enemy of our people.'

'God,' George protested, 'we must not think about the old days – we have to close our minds to our pasts.' *Nothing but our future,* he thought.

His reducing belt enterprise had developed so well that now he employed fifteen full-time Terran employees and owned a small, modern factory on the outskirts of San Fernando. If UN taxes had been reasonable he would by now be a wealthy man . . . brooding on that, George wondered what the tax rate was in Blobel-run lands, on Io, for instance. Maybe he ought to look into it.

One night at VUW Headquarters he discussed the subject with Reinholt, Nina's husband, who of course was ignorant of the modus vivendi between George and Nina.

'Reinholt,' George said with difficulty, as he drank his beer, 'I've got big plans. This cradle-to-grave socialism the UN operates . . . it's not for me. It's cramping me. The Munster Magic Magnetic Belt is—' He gestured. 'More than Terran civilization can support. You get me?'

Coldly, Reinholt said, 'But George, you are a Terran; if you emigrate to Blobel-run territory with your factory you'll be betraying your—'

'Listen,' George told him, 'I've got one authentic Blobel child, two half-Blobel children, and a fourth on the way. I've got strong *emotional* ties with those people out there on Titan and Io.'

'You're a traitor,' Reinholt said, and punched him in the mouth. 'And not only that,' he continued, punching George in the stomach, 'you're running around with my wife. I'm going to kill you.'

To escape, George reverted to Blobel form; Reinholt's blows passed harmlessly deep into his moist, jelly-like substance. Reinholt then reverted too, and flowed into him murderously, trying to consume and absorb George's nucleus.

Fortunately fellow veterans pried their two bodies apart before any permanent harm was done.

Later that night, still trembling, George sat with Vivian in the living room of their eight-room suite at the great new condominium apartment building ZGF-900. It had been a close call, and now of course

Reinholt would tell Viv; it was only a question of time. The marriage, as far as George could see, was over. This perhaps was their last moment together.

'Viv,' he said urgently, 'you have to believe me; I love you. You and the children – plus the belt business, naturally – are my complete life.' A desperate idea came to him. 'Let's emigrate now, tonight. Pack up the kids and go to Titan, right this minute.'

'I can't go,' Vivian said. 'I know how my people would treat me, and treat you and the children, too. George, *you go*. Move the factory to Io. I'll stay here.' Tears filled her dark eyes.

'Hell,' George said, 'what kind of life is that? With you on Terra and me on Io – that's no marriage. And who'll get the kids?' Probably Viv would get them . . . but his firm employed top legal talent – perhaps he could use it to solve his domestic problems.

The next morning Vivian found out about Nina. And hired an attorney of her own.

'Listen,' George said, on the phone talking to his top legal talent, Henry Ramarau. 'Get me custody of the fourth child; it'll be a Terran. And we'll compromise on the two hybrids; I'll take Maurice and she can have Kathy. And naturally she gets that blob, the first so-called child. As far as I'm concerned it's hers anyhow.' He slammed the receiver down and then turned to the board of directors of his company. 'Now where were we?' he demanded. 'In our analysis of Io tax laws.'

During the next weeks the idea of a move to Io appeared more and more feasible from a profit and loss standpoint.

'Go ahead and buy land on Io,' George instructed his business agent in the field, Tom Hendricks. 'And get it cheap; we want to start right.' To his secretary, Miss Nolan, he said, 'Now keep everyone out of my office until further notice. I feel an attack coming on. From anxiety over this major move off Terra to Io.' He added, 'And personal worries.'

'Yes, Mr Munster,' Miss Nolan said, ushering Tom Hendricks out of George's private office. 'No one will disturb you.' She could be counted on to keep everyone out while George reverted to his wartime Blobel shape, as he often did, these days; the pressure on him was immense.

When, later in the day, be resumed human form, George learned from Miss Nolan that a Doctor Jones had called.

'I'll be damned,' George said, thinking back to six years ago. 'I thought it'd be in the junk pile by now.' To Miss Nolan he said, 'Call Doctor Jones, notify me when you have it; I'll take a minute off to talk to it.' It was like old times, back in San Francisco.

Shortly, Miss Nolan had Dr Jones on the line.

'Doctor,' George said, leaning back in his chair and swiveling from side to side and poking at an orchid on his desk. 'Good to hear from you.'

The voice of the homeostatic analyst came in his ear, 'Mr Munster, I note that you now have a secretary.'

'Yes,' George said, 'I'm a tycoon. I'm in the reducing belt game; it's somewhat like the flea-collar that cats wear. Well, what can I do for you?'

'I understand you have four children now—'

'Actually three, plus a fourth on the way. Listen, that fourth, Doctor, is vital to me; according to Mendel's Law it's a full-blooded Terran and by God I'm doing everything in my power to get custody of it.' He added, 'Vivian – you remember her – is now back on Titan. Among her own people, where she belongs. And I'm putting some of the finest doctors I can get on my payroll to stabilize me; I'm tired of this constant reverting, night and day; I've got too much to do for such nonsense.'

Dr Jones said, 'From your tone I can see you're an important, busy man, Mr Munster. You've certainly risen in the world, since I saw you last.'

'Get to the point,' George said impatiently. 'Why'd you call?'

'I, um, thought perhaps I could bring you and Vivian together again.'

'Bah,' George said contemptuously. 'That woman? Never. Listen, Doctor, I have to ring off; we're in the process of finalizing on some basic business strategy, here at Munster, Incorporated.'

'Mr Munster,' Dr Jones asked, 'is there another woman?'

'There's another Blobel,' George said, 'if that's what you mean.' And he hung up the phone. *Two Blobels are better than none*, he said to himself. *And now back to business* . . . He pressed a button on his desk and at once Miss Nolan put her head into the office. 'Miss Nolan,' George said, 'get me Hank Ramarau; I want to find out—'

'Mr Ramarau is waiting on the other line,' Miss Nolan said. 'He says it's urgent.'

Switching to the other line, George said, 'Hi, Hank. What's up?'

'I've just discovered,' his top legal advisor said, 'that to operate your factory on Io you must be a citizen of Titan.'

'We ought to be able to fix that up,' George said.

'But to be a citizen of Titan—' Ramarau hesitated. 'I'll break it to you easy as I can, George. You have to be a Blobel.'

'Dammit, I am a Blobel,' George said. 'At least part of the time. Won't that do?'

'No,' Ramarau said, 'I checked into that, knowing of your affliction, and it's got to be one hundred percent of the time. Night *and* day.'

'Hmmm,' George said. 'This is bad. But we'll overcome it, somehow. Listen, Hank, I've got an appointment with Eddy Fullbright, my medical coordinator; I'll talk to you after, okay?' He rang off and then sat scowling and rubbing his jaw. *Well*, he decided, *if it has to be it has to be. Facts are facts, and we can't let them stand in our way.*

Picking up the phone he dialed his doctor, Eddy Fullbright.

The twenty-dollar platinum coin rolled down the chute and tripped the circuit. Dr Jones came on, glanced up and saw a stunning, sharp-breasted young woman whom it recognized – by means of a quick scan of its memory banks – as Mrs George Munster, the former Vivian Arrasmith.

'Good day, Vivian,' Dr Jones said cordially. 'But I understood you were on Titan.' It rose to its feet, offering her a chair.

Dabbing at her large, dark eyes, Vivian sniffled, 'Doctor, everything is collapsing around me. My husband is having an affair with another woman . . . all I know is that her name is Nina and all the boys down at VUW Headquarters are talking about it. Presumably she's a Terran. We're both filing for divorce. And we're having a dreadful legal battle over the children.' She arranged her coat modestly. 'I'm expecting. Our fourth.'

'This I know,' Dr Jones said. 'A full-blooded Terran this time, if Mendel's Law holds . . . although it only applied to litters.'

Mrs Munster said miserably, 'I've been on Titan talking to legal and medical experts, gynecologists, and especially marital guidance counselors; I've had all sorts of advice during the past month. Now I'm back on Terra but I can't find George – he's *gone*.'

'I wish I could help you, Vivian,' Dr Jones said. 'I talked to your husband briefly, the other day, but he spoke only in generalities . . . evidently he's such a big tycoon now that it's hard to approach him.'

'And to think,' Vivian sniffled, 'that he achieved it all because of an idea *I* gave him. A Blobel idea.'

'The ironies of fate,' Dr Jones said. 'Now, if you want to keep your husband, Vivian—'

'I'm determined to keep him, Doctor Jones. Frankly I've undergone therapy on Titan, the latest and most expensive . . . it's because I love George so much, even more than I love my own people or my planet.'

'Eh?' Dr Jones said.

'Through the most modern developments in medical science in the Sol System,' Vivian said, 'I've been stabilized, Doctor Jones. Now I am in human form twenty-four hours a day instead of eighteen. I've renounced my natural form in order to keep my marriage with George.'

'The supreme sacrifice,' Dr Jones said, touched.

'Now, if I can only *find* him, Doctor—'

At the ground-breaking ceremonies on Io, George Munster flowed gradually to the shovel, extended a pseudopodium, seized the shovel, and with it managed to dig a symbolic amount of soil. 'This is a great day,' he boomed hollowly, by means of the semblance of a vocal apparatus into which he had fashioned the slimy, plastic substance which made up his unicellular body.

'Right, George,' Hank Ramarau agreed, standing nearby with the legal documents.

The Ionan official, like George a great transparent blob, oozed across to Ramarau, took the documents and boomed, 'These will be transmitted to my government. I'm sure they're in order, Mr Ramarau.'

'I guarantee you,' Ramarau said to the official, 'Mr Munster does not revert to human form at any time; he's made use of some of the most advanced techniques in medical science to achieve this stability at the unicellular phase of his former rotation. Munster would never cheat.'

'This historic moment,' the great blob that was George Munster thought-radiated to the throng of local Blobels attending the ceremonies, 'means a higher standard of living for Ionans who will be employed; it will bring prosperity to this area, plus a proud sense of national achievement in the manufacture of what we recognize to be a native invention, the Munster Magic Magnetic Belt.'

The throng of Blobels thought-radiated cheers.

'This is a proud day in my life,' George Munster informed them, and began to ooze by degrees back to his car, where his chauffeur waited to drive him to his permanent hotel room at Io City.

Someday he would own the hotel. He was putting the profits from his business in local real estate; it was the patriotic – and the profitable – thing to do, other Ionans, other Blobels, had told him.

'I'm finally a successful man,' George Munster thought-radiated to all close enough to pick up his emanations.

Amid frenzied cheers he oozed up the ramp and into his Titan-made car.

We Can Remember It For You Wholesale

He awoke — and wanted Mars. The valleys, he thought. What would it be like to trudge among them? Great and greater yet: the dream grew as he became fully conscious, the dream and the yearning. He could almost feel the enveloping presence of the other world, which only Government agents and high officials had seen. A clerk like himself? Not likely.

'Are you getting up or not?' his wife Kirsten asked drowsily, with her usual hint of fierce crossness. 'If you are, push the hot coffee button on the darn stove.'

'Okay,' Douglas Quail said, and made his way barefoot from the bedroom of their conapt to the kitchen. There, having dutifully pressed the hot coffee button, he seated himself at the kitchen table, brought out a yellow, small tin of fine Dean Swift snuff. He inhaled briskly, and the Beau Nash mixture stung his nose, burned the roof of his mouth. But still he inhaled; it woke him up and allowed his dreams, his nocturnal desires and random wishes, to condense into a semblance of rationality.

I will go, he said to himself. *Before I die I'll see Mars.*

It was, of course, impossible, and he knew this even as he dreamed. But the daylight, the mundane noise of his wife now brushing her hair before the bedroom mirror — everything conspired to remind him of what he was. *A miserable little salaried employee*, he said to himself with bitterness. Kirsten reminded him of this at least once a day and he did not blame her; it was a wife's job to bring her husband down to Earth. *Down to Earth*, he thought, and laughed. The figure of speech in this was literally apt.

'What are you sniggering about?' his wife asked as she swept into the kitchen, her long busy-pink robe wagging after her. 'A dream, I bet. You're always full of them.'

'Yes,' he said, and gazed out the kitchen window at the hover-cars and traffic runnels, and all the little energetic people hurrying to work. In a little while he would be among them. As always.

'I'll bet it had to do with some woman,' Kirsten said witheringly.

'No,' he said. 'A god. The god of war. He has wonderful craters with every kind of plant-life growing deep down in them.'

'Listen.' Kirsten crouched down beside him and spoke earnestly, the harsh quality momentarily gone from her voice. 'The bottom of the ocean – *our* ocean is much more, an infinity of times more beautiful. You know that; everyone knows that. Rent an artificial gill-outfit for both of us, take a week off from work, and we can descend and live down there at one of those year-round aquatic resorts. And in addition—' She broke off. 'You're not listening. You should be. Here is something a lot better than that compulsion, that obsession you have about Mars, and you don't even listen!' Her voice rose piercingly. 'God in heaven, you're doomed, Doug! What's going to become of you?'

'I'm going to work,' he said, rising to his feet, his breakfast forgotten. 'That's what's going to become of me.'

She eyed him. 'You're getting worse. More fanatical every day. Where's it going to lead?'

'To Mars,' he said, and opened the door to the closet to get down a fresh shirt to wear to work.

Having descended from the taxi Douglas Quail slowly walked across three densely-populated foot runnels and to the modern, attractively inviting doorway. There he halted, impeding mid-morning traffic, and with caution read the shifting-color neon sign. He had, in the past, scrutinized this sign before . . . but never had he come so close. This was very different; what he did now was something else. Something which sooner or later had to happen.

REKAL, INCORPORATED

Was this the answer? After all, an illusion, no matter how convincing, remained nothing more than an illusion. At least objectively. But subjectively – quite the opposite entirely.

And anyhow he had an appointment. Within the next five minutes.

Taking a deep breath of mildly smog-infested Chicago air, he walked through the dazzling polychromatic shimmer of the doorway and up to the receptionist's counter.

The nicely-articulated blonde at the counter, bare-bosomed and tidy, said pleasantly, 'Good morning, Mr Quail.'

'Yes,' he said. 'I'm here to see about a Rekal course. As I guess you know.'

'Not "rekal" but *re*call,' the receptionist corrected him. She picked up the receiver of the vidphone by her smooth elbow and said into it, 'Mr Douglas Quail is here, Mr McClane. May he come inside, now? Or is it too soon?'

'Giz wetwa wum-wum wamp,' the phone mumbled.

'Yes, Mr Quail,' she said. 'You may go in; Mr McClane is expecting you.' As he started off uncertainly she called after him, 'Room D, Mr Quail. To your right.'

After a frustrating but brief moment of being lost he found the proper room. The door hung open and inside, at a big genuine walnut desk, sat a genial-looking man, middle-aged, wearing the latest Martian frog-pelt gray suit; his attire alone would have told Quail that he had come to the right person.

'Sit down, Douglas,' McClane said, waving his plump hand toward a chair which faced the desk. 'So you want to have gone to Mars. Very good.'

Quail seated himself, feeling tense. 'I'm not so sure this is worth the fee,' he said. 'It costs a lot and as far as I can see I really get nothing.' *Costs almost as much as going*, he thought.

'You get tangible proof of your trip,' McClane disagreed emphatically. 'All the proof you'll need. Here; I'll show you.' He dug within a drawer of his impressive desk. 'Ticket stub.' Reaching into a manila folder, he produced a small square of embossed cardboard. 'It proves you went – and returned. Postcards.' He laid out four franked picture 3-D full-color postcards in a neatly-arranged row on the desk for Quail to see. 'Film. Shots you took of local sights on Mars with a rented moving camera.' To Quail he displayed those, too. 'Plus the names of people you met, two hundred poscreds' worth of souvenirs, which will arrive – from Mars – within the following month. And passport, certificates listing the shots you received. And more.' He glanced up keenly at Quail. 'You'll know you went, all right,' he said. 'You won't remember us, won't remember me or ever having been here. It'll be a real trip in your mind; we guarantee that. A full two weeks of recall; every last piddling detail. Remember this: if at any time you doubt that you really took an extensive trip to Mars you can return here and get a full refund. You see?'

'But I didn't go,' Quail said. 'I won't have gone, no matter what proofs you provide me with.' He took a deep, unsteady breath. 'And I never was a secret agent with Interplan.' It seemed impossible to him that Rekal, Incorporated's extra-factual memory implant would do its job – despite what he had heard people say.

'Mr Quail,' McClane said patiently. 'As you explained in your letter to us, you have no chance, no possibility in the slightest, of ever actually getting to Mars; you can't afford it, and what is much more important, you could never qualify as an undercover agent for Interplan or anybody else. This is the only way you can achieve your, ahem, life-long dream; am I not correct, sir? You can't be this; you can't actually do this.' He chuckled. 'But you can *have been* and *have done*. We see to that. And our fee is reasonable; no hidden charges.' He smiled encouragingly.

'Is an extra-factual memory that convincing?' Quail asked.

'More than the real thing, sir. Had you really gone to Mars as an Interplan agent, you would by now have forgotten a great deal; our analysts of true-mem systems – authentic recollections of major events in a person's life – shows that a variety of details are very quickly lost to the person. Forever. Part of the package we offer you is such deep implantation of recall that nothing is forgotten. The packet which is fed to you while you're comatose is the creation of trained experts, men who have spent years on Mars; in every case we verify details down to the last iota. And you've picked a rather easy extra-factual system; had you picked Pluto or wanted to be Emperor of the Inner Planet Alliance we'd have much more difficulty . . . and the charges would be considerably greater.'

Reaching into his coat for his wallet, Quail said, 'Okay. It's been my life-long ambition and so I see I'll never really do it. So I guess I'll have to settle for this.'

'Don't think of it that way,' McClane said severely. 'You're not accepting second-best. The actual memory, with all its vagueness, omissions and ellipses, not to say distortions – that's second-best.' He accepted the money and pressed a button on his desk. 'All right, Mr Quail,' he said, as the door of his office opened and two burly men swiftly entered. 'You're on your way to Mars as a secret agent.' He rose, came over to shake Quail's nervous, moist hand. 'Or rather, you have been on your way. This afternoon at four-thirty you will, um, arrive back here on Terra; a cab will leave you off at your conapt and as I say you will never remember seeing me or coming here; you won't, in fact, even remember having heard of our existence.'

His mouth dry with nervousness, Quail followed the two technicians from the office; what happened next depended on them.

Will I actually believe I've been on Mars? he wondered. *That I managed to fulfill my lifetime ambition?* He had a strange, lingering intuition that something would go wrong. But just what – he did not know.

He would have to wait and find out.

The intercom on McClane's desk, which connected him with the work area of the firm, buzzed and a voice said, 'Mr Quail is under sedation now, sir. Do you want to supervise this one, or shall we go ahead?'

'It's routine,' McClane observed. 'You may go ahead, Lowe; I don't think you'll run into any trouble.' Programming an artificial memory of a trip to another planet – with or without the added fillip of being a secret agent – showed up on the firm's work-schedule with monotonous regularity. *In one month*, he calculated wryly, *we must do twenty of these . . . ersatz interplanetary travel has become our bread and butter.*

'Whatever you say, Mr McClane,' Lowe's voice came, and thereupon the intercom shut off.

Going to the vault section in the chamber behind his office, McClane searched about for a Three packet – trip to Mars – and a Sixty-two packet: secret Interplan spy. Finding the two packets, he returned with them to his desk, seated himself comfortably, poured out the contents – merchandise which would be planted in Quail's conapt while the lab technicians busied themselves installing false memory.

A one-poscred sneaky-pete side arm, McClane reflected; *that's the largest item. Sets us back financially the most.* Then a pellet-sized transmitter, which could be swallowed if the agent were caught. Code book that astonishingly resembled the real thing . . . the firm's models were highly accurate: based, whenever possible, on actual US military issue. Odd bits which made no intrinsic sense but which would be woven into the warp and woof of Quail's imaginary trip, would coincide with his memory: half an ancient silver fifty cent piece, several quotations from John Donne's sermons written incorrectly, each on a separate piece of transparent tissue-thin paper, several match folders from bars on Mars, a stainless steel spoon engraved PROPERTY OF DOME-MARS NATIONAL KIBBUZIM, a wire tapping coil which—

The intercom buzzed. 'Mr McClane, I'm sorry to bother you but something rather ominous has come up. Maybe it would be better if you were in here after all. Quail is already under sedation; he reacted well to the narki-drine; he's completely unconscious and receptive. But—'

'I'll be in.' Sensing trouble, McClane left his office; a moment later he emerged in the work area.

On a hygienic bed lay Douglas Quail, breathing slowly and regularly, his eyes virtually shut; he seemed dimly – but only dimly – aware of the two technicians and now McClane himself.

'There's no space to insert false memory-patterns?' McClane felt irritation. 'Merely drop out two work weeks; he's employed as a clerk at the West Coast Emigration Bureau, which is a government agency, so he undoubtedly has or had two weeks' vacation within the last year. That ought to do it.' Petty details annoyed him. And always would.

'Our problem,' Lowe said sharply, 'is something quite different.' He bent over the bed, said to Quail, 'Tell Mr McClane what you told us.' To McClane he said, 'Listen closely.'

The gray-green eyes of the man lying supine in the bed focused on McClane's face. The eyes, he observed uneasily, had become hard; they had a polished, inorganic quality, like semi-precious tumbled stones. He was not sure that he liked what he saw; the brilliance was too cold. 'What do you want now?' Quail said harshly. 'You've broken my cover. Get out of here before I take you all apart.' He studied McClane. 'Especially you,' he continued. 'You're in charge of this counter-operation.'

Lowe said, 'How long were you on Mars?'

'One month,' Quail said gratingly.

'And your purpose there?' Lowe demanded.

The meager lips twisted; Quail eyed him and did not speak. At last, drawling the words out so that they dripped with hostility, he said, 'Agent for Interplan. As I already told you. Don't you record everything that's said? Play your vid-aud tape back for your boss and leave me alone.' He shut his eyes, then; the hard brilliance ceased. McClane felt, instantly, a rushing splurge of relief.

Lowe said quietly, 'This is a tough man, Mr McClane.'

'He won't be,' McClane said, 'after we arrange for him to lose his memory-chain again. He'll be as meek as before.' To Quail he said, 'So *this* is why you wanted to go to Mars so terribly bad.'

Without opening his eyes Quail said, 'I never wanted to go to Mars. I was assigned it – they handed it to me and there I was: stuck. Oh yeah, I admit I was curious about it; who wouldn't be?' Again he opened his eyes and surveyed the three of them, McClane in particular. 'Quite a truth drug you've got here; it brought up things I had absolutely no memory of.' He pondered. 'I wonder about Kirsten,' he said, half to himself. 'Could she be in on it? An Interplan contact keeping an eye on me . . . to be certain I didn't regain my memory? No wonder she's been so derisive about my wanting to go there.' Faintly, he smiled; the smile — one of understanding — disappeared almost at once.

McClane said, 'Please believe me, Mr Quail; we stumbled onto this entirely by accident. In the work we do—'

'I believe you,' Quail said. He seemed tired, now; the drug was continuing to pull him under, deeper and deeper. 'Where did I say I'd been?' he murmured. 'Mars? Hard to remember — I know I'd like to see it; so would everybody else. But me—' His voice trailed off. 'Just a clerk, a nothing clerk.'

Straightening up, Lowe said to his superior. 'He wants a false memory implanted that corresponds to a trip he actually took. And a false reason which is the real reason. He's telling the truth; he's a long way down in the narkidrine. The trip is very vivid in his mind – at least under sedation. But apparently he doesn't recall it otherwise. Someone, probably at a government military-sciences lab, erased his conscious memories; all he knew was that going to Mars meant something special to him, and so did being a secret agent. They couldn't erase that; it's not a memory but a desire, undoubtedly the same one that motivated him to volunteer for the assignment in the first place.'

The other technician, Keeler, said to McClane, 'What do we do? Graft a false memory-pattern over the real memory? There's no telling what the results would be; he might remember some of the genuine trip, and the confusion might bring on a psychotic interlude. He'd have to hold two opposite premises in his mind simultaneously: that he went to Mars and that he didn't. That he's a genuine agent for Interplan and he's not, that it's spurious. I think we ought to revive him without any false memory implantation and send him out of here; this is hot.'

'Agreed,' McClane said. A thought came to him. 'Can you predict what he'll remember when he comes out of sedation?'

'Impossible to tell,' Lowe said. 'He probably will have some dim, diffuse memory of his actual trip, now. And he'd probably be in grave doubt as to its validity; he'd probably decide our programming slipped a gear-tooth. And he'd remember coming here; that wouldn't be erased – unless you want it erased.'

'The less we mess with this man,' McClane said, 'the better I like it. This is nothing for us to fool around with; we've been foolish enough to – or unlucky enough to – uncover a genuine Interplan spy who has a cover so perfect that up to now even he didn't know what he was – or rather is.' The sooner they washed their hands of the man calling himself Douglas Quail the better.

'Are you going to plant packets Three and Sixty-two in his conapt?' Lowe said.

'No,' McClane said. 'And we're going to return half his fee.'

' "Half"! Why half?'

McClane said lamely, 'It seems to be a good compromise.'

As the cab carried him back to his conapt at the residential end of Chicago, Douglas Quail said to himself, *It's sure good to be back on Terra.*

Already the month-long period on Mars had begun to waver in his memory; he had only an image of profound gaping craters, an ever-present ancient erosion of hills, of vitality, of motion itself. A world of dust where little happened, where a good part of the day was spent checking and rechecking one's portable oxygen source. And then the life forms, the unassuming and modest gray-brown cacti and maw-worms.

As a matter of fact he had brought back several moribund examples of Martian fauna; he had smuggled them through customs. After all, they posed no menace; they couldn't survive in Earth's heavy atmosphere.

Reaching into his coat pocket, he rummaged for the container of Martian maw-worms—

And found an envelope instead.

Lifting it out, he discovered, to his perplexity, that it contained five hundred and seventy poscreds, in cred bills of low denomination.

Where'd I get this? he asked himself. *Didn't I spend every 'cred I had on my trip?*

With the money came a slip of paper marked: *One-half fee ret'd. By McClane.* And then the date. Today's date.

'Recall,' he said aloud.

'Recall what, sir or madam?' the robot driver of the cab inquired respectfully.

'Do you have a phone book?' Quail demanded.

'Certainly, sir or madam.' A slot opened; from it slid a microtape phone book for Cook County.

'It's spelled oddly,' Quail said as he leafed through the pages of the yellow section. He felt fear, then; abiding fear. 'Here it is,' he said. 'Take me there, to Rekal, Incorporated. I've changed my mind; I don't want to go home.'

'Yes, sir or madam, as the case may be,' the driver said. A moment later the cab was zipping back in the opposite direction.

'May I make use of your phone?' he asked.

'Be my guest,' the robot driver said. And presented a shiny new emperor 3-D color phone to him.

He dialed his own conapt. And after a pause found himself confronted by a miniature but chillingly realistic image of Kirsten on the small screen. 'I've been to Mars,' he said to her.

'You're drunk.' Her lips writhed scornfully. 'Or worse.'

''S God's truth.'

'When?' she demanded.

'I don't know.' He felt confused. 'A simulated trip, I think. By means of one of those artificial or extra-factual or whatever it is memory places. It didn't take.'

Kirsten said witheringly, 'You *are* drunk.' And broke the connection at her end. He hung up, then, feeling his face flush. *Always the same tone*, he said hotly to himself. *Always the retort, as if she knows everything and I know nothing. What a marriage. Keerist*, he thought dismally.

A moment later the cab stopped at the curb before a modern, very attractive little pink building, over which a shifting polychromatic neon sign read: REKAL, INCORPORATED.

The receptionist, chic and bare from the waist up, started in surprise, then gained masterful control of herself. 'Oh, hello, Mr Quail,' she said nervously. 'H-how are you? Did you forget something?'

'The rest of my fee back,' he said.

More composed now, the receptionist said, 'Fee? I think you are mistaken, Mr Quail. You were here discussing the feasibility of an extra-factual trip for you, but—' She shrugged her smooth pale shoulders. 'As I understand it, no trip was taken.'

Quail said, 'I remember everything, miss. My letter to Rekal, Incorporated, which started this whole business off. I remember my arrival here, my visit with Mr McClane. Then the two lab technicians taking me in tow and administering a drug to put me out.' No wonder the firm had returned half his fee. The false memory of his 'trip to Mars' hadn't taken – at least not entirely, not as he had been assured.

'Mr Quail,' the girl said, 'although you are a minor clerk you are a good-looking man and it spoils your features to become angry. If it would make you feel any better, I might, ahem, let you take me out . . .'

He felt furious, then. 'I remember you,' he said savagely. 'For instance the fact that your breasts are sprayed blue; that stuck in my mind. And I remember Mr McClane's promise that if I remembered my visit to Rekal, Incorporated I'd receive my money back in full. Where is Mr McClane?'

After a delay – probably as long as they could manage – he found himself once more seated facing the imposing walnut desk, exactly as he had been an hour or so earlier in the day.

'Some technique you have,' Quail said sardonically. His disappointment – and resentment – was enormous, by now. 'My so-called "memory" of a trip to Mars as an undercover agent for Interplan is hazy and vague and shot full of contradictions. And I clearly remember my dealings here with you people. I ought to take this to the Better Business Bureau.' He was burning angry, at this point; his sense of being cheated had overwhelmed him, had destroyed his customary aversion to participating in a public squabble.

Looking morose, as well as cautious, McClane said, 'We capitulate, Quail . We'll refund the balance of your fee. I fully concede the fact that we did absolutely nothing for you.' His tone was resigned.

Quail said accusingly, 'You didn't even provide me with the various artifacts that you claimed would "prove" to me I had been on Mars. All that song-and-dance you went into – it hasn't materialized into a damn thing. Not even a ticket stub. Nor postcards. Nor passport. Nor proof of immunization shots. Nor—'

'Listen, Quail,' McClane said. 'Suppose I told you—' He broke off. 'Let it go.' He pressed a button on his intercom. 'Shirley, will you disburse five hundred and seventy more 'creds in the form of a cashier's check made out to Douglas Quail? Thank you.' He released the button, then glared at Quail.

Presently the check appeared; the receptionist placed it before McClane and once more vanished out of sight, leaving the two men alone, still facing each other across the surface of the massive walnut desk.

'Let me give you a word of advice,' McClane said as he signed the check and passed it over. 'Don't discuss your, ahem, recent trip to Mars with anyone.'

'What trip?'

'Well, that's the thing.' Doggedly, McClane said, 'The trip you partially remember. Act as if you don't remember; pretend it never took place. Don't ask me why; just take my advice: it'll be better for all of us.' He had begun to perspire. Freely. 'Now, Mr Quail, I have other business, other clients to see.' He rose, showed Quail to the door.

Quail said, as he opened the door, 'A firm that turns out such bad work shouldn't have any clients at all.' He shut the door behind him.

On the way home in the cab Quail pondered the wording of his letter of complaint to the Better Business Bureau, Terra Division. As soon as he could get to his typewriter he'd get started; it was clearly his duty to warn other people away from Rekal, Incorporated.

When he got back to his conapt he seated himself before his Hermes Rocket portable, opened the drawers and rummaged for carbon paper – and noticed a small, familiar box. A box which he had carefully filled on Mars with Martian fauna and later smuggled through customs.

Opening the box he saw, to his disbelief, six dead maw-worms and several varieties of the unicellular life on which the Martian worms fed. The protozoa were dried-up, dusty, but he recognized them; it had taken him an entire day picking among the vast dark alien boulders to find them. A wonderful, illuminated journey of discovery.

But I didn't go to Mars, he realized.

Yet on the other hand—

Kirsten appeared at the doorway to the room, an armload of pale brown groceries gripped. 'Why are you home in the middle of the day?' Her voice, in an eternity of sameness, was accusing.

'*Did I go to Mars?*' he asked her. 'You would know.'

'No, of course you didn't go to Mars; *you* would know that, I would think. Aren't you always bleating about going?'

He said, 'By God, I think I went.' After a pause he added, 'And simultaneously I think I didn't go.'

'Make up your mind.'

'How can I?' He gestured. 'I have both memory-tracks grafted inside my head; one is real and one isn't but I can't tell which is which. Why can't I rely on you? They haven't tinkered with you.' She could do this much for him at least – even if she never did anything else.

Kirsten said in a level, controlled voice, 'Doug, if you don't pull yourself together, we're through. I'm going to leave you.'

'I'm in trouble.' His voice came out husky and coarse. And shaking. 'Probably I'm heading into a psychotic episode; I hope not, but – maybe that's it. It would explain everything, anyhow.'

Setting down the bag of groceries, Kirsten stalked to the closet. 'I was not kidding,' she said to him quietly. She brought out a coat, got it on, walked back to the door of the conapt. 'I'll phone you one of these days soon,' she said tonelessly. 'This is goodbye, Doug. I hope you pull out of this eventually; I really pray you do. For your sake.'

'Wait,' he said desperately. 'Just tell me and make it absolute; I did go or I didn't – tell me which one.' *But they may have altered your memory-track also*, he realized.

The door closed. His wife had left. Finally!

A voice behind him said, 'Well, that's that. Now put up your hands, Quail. And also please turn around and face this way.'

He turned, instinctively, without raising his hands.

The man who faced him wore the plum uniform of the Interplan Police Agency, and his gun appeared to be UN issue. And, for some odd reason, he seemed familiar to Quail; familiar in a blurred, distorted fashion which he could not pin down. So, jerkily, he raised his hands.

'You remember,' the policeman said, 'your trip to Mars. We know all your actions today and all your thoughts – in particular your very important thoughts on the trip home from Rekal, Incorporated.' He explained, 'We have a tele-transmitter wired within your skull; it keeps us constantly informed.'

A telepathic transmitter; use of a living plasma that had been discovered ou Luna. He shuddered with self-aversion. The thing lived inside him, within his own brain, feeding, listening, feeding. But the Interplan police used them; that had come out even in the homeopapes. So this was probably true, dismal as it was.

'Why me?' Quail said huskily. What had he done – or thought? And what did this have to do with Rekal, Incorporated?

'Fundamentally,' the Interplan cop said, 'this has nothing to do with Rekal; it's between you and us.' He tapped his right ear. 'I'm still picking up your mentational processes by way of your cephalic transmitter.' In the man's ear Quail saw a small white-plastic plug. 'So I have to warn you: any thing you think may be held against you.' He smiled. 'Not that it matters now; you've already thought and spoken yourself into oblivion. What's annoying is the fact that under narki-drine at Rekal, Incorporated you told them, their technicians and the owner, Mr McClane, about your trip – where you went, for whom, some of what you did. They're very frightened. They wish they had never laid eyes on you.' He added reflectively, 'They're right.'

Quail said, 'I never made any trip. It's a false memory-chain improperly planted in me by McClane's technicians.' But then he thought of the box, in his desk drawer, containing the Martian life forms. And the trouble and hardship he had had gathering them. The memory seemed real. And the box of life forms; that certainly was real. Unless McClane had planted it. Perhaps this was one of the 'proofs' which McClane had talked glibly about.

The memory of my trip to Mars, he thought, *doesn't convince me – but unfortunately it has convinced the Interplan Police Agency. They think I really went to Mars and they think I at least partially realize it.*

'We not only know you went to Mars,' the Interplan cop agreed, in answer to his thoughts, 'but we know that you now remember enough to be difficult for us. And there's no use expunging your conscious memory of all this, because if we do you'll simply show up at Rekal, Incorporated again and start over. And we can't do anything about McClane and his operation because we have no jurisdiction over anyone except our own people. Anyhow, McClane hasn't committed any crime.' He eyed Quail, 'Nor, technically, have you. You didn't go to Rekal, Incorporated with the idea of regaining your memory; you went, as we realize, for the usual reason people go there – a love by plain, dull people for adventure.' He added, 'Unfortunately you're not plain, not dull, and you've already had too much excitement; the last thing in the universe you needed was a course from Rekal, Incorpo-rated. Nothing could have been more lethal for you or for us. And, for that matter, for McClane.'

Quail said, 'Why is it "difficult" for you if I remember my trip – my alleged trip – and what I did there?'

'Because,' the Interplan harness bull said, 'what you did is not in accord with our great white all-protecting father public image. You did, for us, what we never do. As you'll presently remember – thanks to narkidrine. That box of dead worms and algae has been sitting in your desk drawer for six months, ever since you got back. And at no time have you shown the slightest curiosity about it. We didn't even know you had it until you remembered it on your way home from Rekal; then we came here on the double to look for it.' He added, unnecessarily, 'Without any luck; there wasn't enough time.'

A second Interplan cop joined the first one; the two briefly conferred. Meanwhile, Quail thought rapidly. He did remember more, now; the cop had been right about narkidrine. They – Interplan – probably used it themselves. Probably? He knew darn well they did; he had seen them putting a prisoner on it. Where would *that* be? Somewhere on Terra? More likely on Luna, he decided, viewing the image rising from his highly defective – but rapidly less so – memory.

And he remembered something else. Their reason for sending him to Mars; the job he had done.

No wonder they had expunged his memory.

'Oh, God,' the first of the two Interplan cops said, breaking off his conversation with his companion. Obviously, he had picked up Quail's thoughts. 'Well, this is a far worse problem, now; as bad as it can get.' He walked toward Quail, again covering him with his gun. 'We've got to kill you,' he said. 'And right away.'

Nervously, his fellow officer said, 'Why right away? Can't we simply cart him off to Interplan New York and let them—'

'*He* knows why it has to be right away,' the first cop said; he too looked nervous, now, but Quail realized that it was for an entirely different reason. His memory had been brought back almost entirely, now. And he fully understood the officer's tension.

'On Mars,' Quail said hoarsely, 'I killed a man. After getting past fifteen bodyguards. Some armed with sneaky-pete guns, the way you are.' He had been trained, by Interplan, over a five year period to be an assassin. A professional killer. He knew ways to take out armed adversaries . . . such as these two officers; and the one with the ear-receiver knew it, too.

If he moved swiftly enough—

The gun fired. But he had already moved to one side, and at the same time he chopped down the gun-carrying officer. In an instant he had possession of the gun and was covering the other, confused, officer.

'Picked my thoughts up,' Quail said, panting for breath. 'He knew what I was going to do, but I did it anyhow.'

Half sitting up, the injured officer grated, 'He won't use that gun on you, Sam; I pick that up, too. He knows he's finished, and he knows we know it, too. Come on, Quail.' Laboriously, grunting with pain, he got shakily to his feet. He held out his hand. 'The gun,' he said to Quail. 'You can't use it, and if you turn it over to me I'll guarantee not to kill you; you'll be given a hearing, and someone higher up in Interplan will decide, not me. Maybe they can erase your memory once more, I don't know. But you know the thing I was going to kill you for; I couldn't keep you from remembering it. So my reason for wanting to kill you is in a sense past.'

Quail, clutching the gun, bolted from the conapt, sprinted for the elevator. *If you follow me*, he thought, *I'll kill you. So don't.* He jabbed at the elevator button and, a moment later, the doors slid back.

The police hadn't followed him. Obviously they had picked up his terse, tense thoughts and had decided not to take the chance.

With him inside the elevator descended. He had gotten away – for a time. But what next? Where could he go?

The elevator reached the ground floor; a moment later Quail had joined the mob of peds hurrying along the runnels. His head ached and he felt sick. But at least he had evaded death; they had come very close to shooting him on the spot, back in his own conapt.

And they probably will again, he decided. *When they find me. And with this transmitter inside me, that won't take too long.*

Ironically, he had gotten exactly what he had asked Rekal, Incorporated for. Adventure, peril, Interplan police at work, a secret and dangerous trip to Mars in which his life was at stake – everything he had wanted as a false memory.

The advantages of it being a memory – and nothing more – could now be appreciated.

On a park bench, alone, he sat dully watching a flock of perts: a semi-bird imported from Mars' two moons, capable of soaring flight, even against Earth's huge gravity.

Maybe I can find my way back to Mars, he pondered. But then what? It would be worse on Mars; the political organization whose leader he had assassinated would spot him the moment he stepped from the ship; he would have Interplan and *them* after him, there.

Can you hear me thinking? he wondered. Easy avenue to paranoia; sitting here alone he felt them tuning in on him, monitoring, recording, discussing . . . He shivered, rose to his feet, walked aimlessly, his hands deep in his pockets. *No matter where I go*, he realized, *you'll always be with me. As long as I have this device inside my head.*

I'll make a deal with you, he thought to himself – and to them. *Can you imprint a false-memory template on me again, as you did before, that I lived an average, routine life, never went to Mars? Never saw an Interplan uniform up close and never handled a gun?*

A voice inside his brain answered, 'As has been carefully explained to you: that would not be enough.'

Astonished, he halted.

'We formerly communicated with you in this manner,' the voice continued. 'When you were operating in the field, on Mars. It's been months since we've done it; we assumed, in fact, that we'd never have to do so again. Where are you?'

'Walking,' Quail said, 'to my death.' *By your officers' guns*, he added as an afterthought. 'How can you be sure it wouldn't be enough?' he demanded. 'Don't the Rekal techniques work?'

'As we said. If you're given a set of standard, average memories you get – restless. You'd inevitably seek out Rekal or one of its competitors again. We can't go through this a second time.'

'Suppose,' Quail said, 'once my authentic memories have been canceled, something more vital than standard memories are implanted. Something which would act to satisfy my craving,' he said. 'That's been proved; that's probably why you initially hired me. But you ought to be able to come up with something else – something equal. I was the richest man on Terra but I finally gave all my money to educational foundations. Or I was a famous deep-space explorer. Anything of that sort; wouldn't one of those do?'

Silence.

'Try it,' he said desperately. 'Get some of your top-notch military psychiatrists; explore my mind. Find out what my most expansive daydream is.' He tried to think. 'Women,' he said. 'Thousands of them, like Don Juan had. An interplanetary playboy – a mistress in every city on Earth, Luna and Mars. Only I gave that up, out of exhaustion. Please,' he begged. 'Try it.'

'You'd voluntarily surrender, then?' the voice inside his head asked. 'If we agreed, to arrange such a solution? *If* it's possible?'

After an interval of hesitation he said, 'Yes.' *I'll take the risk*, he said to himself, *that you don't simply kill me.*

'You make the first move,' the voice said presently. 'Turn yourself over to us. And we'll investigate that line of possibility. If we can't do it, however, if your authentic memories begin to crop up again as they've done at this time, then—' There was silence and then the voice finished, 'We'll have to destroy you. As you must understand. Well, Quail, you still want to try?'

'Yes,' he said. Because the alternative was death now – and for certain. At least this way he had a chance, slim as it was.

'You present yourself at our main barracks in New York,' the voice of the Interplan cop resumed. 'At 580 Fifth Avenue, floor twelve. Once you've surrendered yourself, we'll have our psychiatrists begin on you; we'll have personality-profile tests made. We'll attempt to determine your absolute, ultimate fantasy wish – then we'll bring you back to Rekal, Incorporated, here; get them in on it, fulfilling that wish in vicarious surrogate retrospection. And – good luck. We do owe you something; you acted as a capable instrument for us.' The voice lacked malice; if anything, they – the organization – felt sympathy toward him.

'Thanks,' Quail said. And began searching for a robot cab.

'Mr Quail,' the stern-faced, elderly Interplan psychiatrist said, 'you possess a most interesting wish-fulfillment dream fantasy. Probably nothing such as you consciously entertain or suppose. This is commonly the way; I hope it won't upset you too much to hear about it.'

The senior ranking Interplan officer present said briskly, 'He better not be too much upset to hear about it, not if he expects not to get shot.'

'Unlike the fantasy of wanting to be an Interplan undercover agent,' the psychiatrist continued, 'which, being relatively speaking a product of maturity, had a certain plausibility to it, this production is a grotesque dream of your childhood; it is no wonder you fail to recall it. Your fantasy is this: you are nine years old, walking alone down a rustic lane. An unfamiliar variety of space vessel from another star system lands directly in front of you. No one on Earth but you, Mr Quail, sees it. The creatures within are very small and helpless, somewhat on the order of field mice, although they are attempting to invade Earth; tens of thousands of other ships will soon be on their way, when this advance party gives the go-ahead signal.'

'And I suppose I stop them,' Quail said, experiencing a mixture of amusement and disgust. 'Single-handed I wipe them out. Probably by stepping on them with my foot.'

'No,' the psychiatrist said patiently. 'You halt the invasion, but not by destroying them Instead, you show them kindness and mercy, even though by telepathy – their mode of communication – you know why they have come. They have never seen such humane traits exhibited by any sentient organism, and to show their appreciation they make a covenant with you.'

Quail said, 'They won't invade Earth as long as I'm alive.'

'Exactly.' To the Interplan officer the psychiatrist said, 'You can see it does fit his personality, despite his feigned scorn.'

'So by merely existing,' Quail said, feeling a growing pleasure, 'by simply being alive, I keep Earth safe from alien rule. I'm in effect, then, the most important person on Terra. Without lifting a finger.'

'Yes, indeed, sir,' the psychiatrist said. 'And this is bedrock in your psyche; this is a life-long childhood fantasy. Which, without depth and drug therapy, you never would have recalled. But it has always existed in you; it went underneath, but never ceased.'

To McClane, who sat intently listening, the senior police official said, 'Can you implant an extra-factual memory pattern that extreme in him?'

'We get handed every possible type of wish-fantasy there is,' McClane said. 'Frankly, I've heard a lot worse than this. Certainly we can handle it. Twenty-four hours from now he won't just *wish* he'd saved Earth; he'll devoutly believe it really happened.'

The senior police official said, 'You can start the job, then. In preparation we've already once again erased the memory in him of his trip to Mars.'

Quail said, 'What trip to Mars?'

No one answered him, so reluctantly, he shelved the question. And anyhow a police vehicle had now put in its appearance; he, McClane and the senior police officer crowded into it, and presently they were on their way to Chicago and Rekal, Incorporated.

'You had better make no errors this time,' the police officer said to heavy-set, nervous-looking McClane.

'I can't see what could go wrong,' McClane mumbled, perspiring. 'This has nothing to do with Mars or Interplan. Single-handedly stopping an invasion of Earth from another star-system.' He shook his head at that. 'Wow, what a kid dreams up. And by pious virtue, too;

not by force. It's sort of quaint.' He dabbed at his forehead with a large linen pocket handkerchief.

Nobody said anything.

'In fact,' McClane said, 'it's touching.'

'But arrogant,' the police official said starkly. 'Inasmuch as when he dies the invasion will resume. No wonder he doesn't recall it; it's the most grandiose fantasy I ever ran across.' He eyed Quail with disapproval. 'And to think we put this man on our payroll.'

When they reached Rekal, Incorporated the receptionist, Shirley, met them breathlessly in the outer office. 'Welcome back, Mr Quail,' she fluttered, her melon-shaped breasts – today painted an incandescent orange – bobbing with agitation. 'I'm sorry everything worked out so badly before; I'm sure this time it'll go better.'

Still repeatedly dabbing at his shiny forehead with his neatly folded Irish linen handkerchief, McClane said, 'It better.' Moving with rapidity he rounded up Lowe and Keeler, escorted them and Douglas Quail to the work area, and then, with Shirley and the senior police officer, returned to his familiar office. To wait.

'Do we have a packet made up for this, Mr McClane?' Shirley asked, bumping against him in her agitation, then coloring modestly.

'I think we do.' He tried to recall, then gave up and consulted the formal chart. 'A combination,' he decided aloud, 'of packets Eighty-one, Twenty, and Six.' From the vault section of the chamber behind his desk he fished out the appropriate packets, carried them to his desk for inspection. 'From Eight-one,' he explained, 'a magic healing rod given him – the client in question, this time Mr Quail – by the race of beings from another system. A token of their gratitude.'

'Does it work?' the police officer asked curiously.

'It did once,' McClane explained. 'But he, ahem, you see, used it up years ago, healing right and left. Now it's only a memento. But he remembers it working spectacularly.' He chuckled, then opened packet Twenty. 'Document from the UN Secretary General thanking him for saving Earth; this isn't precisely appropriate, because part of Quail's fantasy is that no one knows of the invasion except himself, but for the sake of verisimilitude we'll throw it in.' He inspected packet Six, then. What came from this? He couldn't recall; frowning, he dug into the plastic bag as Shirley and the Interplan police officer watched intently.

'Writing,' Shirley said. 'In a funny language.'

'This tells who they were,' McClane said, 'and where they came from. Including a detailed star map logging their flight here and the system of origin. Of course it's in *their* script, so he can't read it. But he remembers them reading it to him in his own tongue.' He placed the three artifacts in the center of the desk. 'These should be taken to Quail's conapt,' he said to the police officer. 'So that when he gets home he'll find them. And it'll confirm his fantasy. SOP – standard operating procedure.' He chuckled apprehensively, wondering how matters were going with Lowe and Keeler.

The intercom buzzed. 'Mr McClane, I'm sorry to bother you.' It was Lowe's voice; he froze as he recognized it, froze and became mute. 'But something's come up. Maybe it would be better if you came in here and supervised. Like before, Quail reacted well to the narkidrine; he's unconscious, relaxed and receptive. But—'

McClane sprinted for the work area.

On a hygienic bed Douglas Quail lay breathing slowly and regularly, eyes half-shut, dimly conscious of those around him.

'We started interrogating him,' Lowe said, white-faced. 'To find out exactly when to place the fantasy-memory of him single-handedly having saved Earth. And strangely enough—'

'They told me not to tell,' Douglas Quail mumbled in a dull drug-saturated voice. 'That was the agreement. I wasn't even supposed to remember. But how could I forget an event like that?'

I guess it would be hard, McClane reflected. *But you did – until now.*

'They even gave me a scroll,' Quail mumbled, 'of gratitude. I have it hidden in my conapt; I'll show it to you.'

To the Interplan officer who had followed after him, McClane said, 'Well, I offer the suggestion that you better not kill him. If you do they'll return.'

'They also gave me a magic invisible destroying rod,' Quail mumbled, eyes totally shut now. 'That's how I killed that man on Mars you sent me to take out. It's in my drawer along with the box of Martian maw-worms and dried-up plant life.'

Wordlessly, the Interplan officer turned and stalked from the work area.

I might as well put those packets of proof-artifacts away, McClane said to himself resignedly. He walked, step by step, back to his office. *Including the citation from the UN Secretary General. After all—*

The real one probably would not be long in coming.

The Electric Ant

At four-fifteen in the afternoon, TST, Garson Poole woke up in his hospital bed, knew that he lay in a hospital bed in a three-bed ward and realized in addition two things: that he no longer had a right hand and that he felt no pain.

They had given me a strong analgesic, he said to himself as he stared at the far wall with its window showing downtown New York. Webs in which vehicles and peds darted and wheeled glimmered in the late afternoon sun, and the brilliance of the aging light pleased him. It's not yet out, he thought. And neither am I.

A fone lay on the table beside his bed; he hesitated, then picked it up and dialed for an outside line. A moment later he was faced by Louis Danceman, in charge of Tri-Plan's activities while he, Garson Poole, was elsewhere.

'Thank God you're alive,' Danceman said, seeing him; his big, fleshy face with its moon's surface of pock marks flattened with relief. 'I've been calling all—'

'I just don't have a right hand,' Poole said.

'But you'll be okay. I mean, they can graft another one on.'

'How long have I been here?' Poole said. He wondered where the nurses and doctors had gone to; why weren't they clucking and fussing about him making a call?

'Four days,' Danceman said. 'Everything here at the plant is going splunkishly. In fact we've splunked orders from three separate police systems, all here on Terra. Two in Ohio, one in Wyoming. Good solid orders, with one third in advance and the usual three-year lease-option.'

'Come get me out of here,' Poole said.

'I can't get you out until the new hand—'

'I'll have it done later.' He wanted desperately to get back to familiar surroundings; memory of the mercantile squib looming grotesquely on the pilot screen careened at the back of his mind; if he shut his eyes he felt himself back in his damaged craft as it plunged from one vehicle to another, piling up enormous damage as it went. The kinetic sensations . . . he winced, recalling them. I guess I'm lucky, he said to himself.

'Is Sarah Benton there with you?' Danceman asked.

'No.' Of course; his personal secretary – if only for job considerations – would be hovering close by, mothering him in her jejune, infantile way. All heavy-set women like to mother people, he thought. And they're dangerous; if they fall on you they can kill you. 'Maybe that's what happened to me,' he said aloud. 'Maybe Sarah fell on my squib.'

'No, no; a tie rod in the steering fin of your squib split apart during the heavy rush-hour traffic and you—'

'I remember.' He turned in his bed as the door of the ward opened; a white-clad doctor and two blue-clad nurses appeared, making their way toward his bed. 'I'll talk to you later,' Poole said and hung up the fone. He took a deep, expectant breath.

'You shouldn't be foning quite so soon,' the doctor said as he studied his chart. 'Mr Garson Poole, owner of Tri-Plan Electronics. Maker of random ident darts that track their prey for a circle-radius of a thousand miles, responding to unique enceph wave patterns. You're a successful man, Mr Poole, But, Mr Poole, you're not a man. You're an electric ant.'

'Christ,' Poole said, stunned.

'So we can't really treat you here, now that we've found out. We knew, of course, as soon as we examined your injured right hand; we saw the electronic components and then we made torso x-rays and of course they bore out our hypothesis.'

'What,' Poole said, 'is an "electric ant"?' But he knew; he could decipher the term.

A nurse said, 'An organic robot.'

'I see,' Poole said. Frigid perspiration rose to the surface of his skin, across all his body.

'You didn't know,' the doctor said.

'No.' Poole shook his head.

The doctor said, 'We get an electric ant every week or so. Either brought in here from a squib accident – like yourself – or one seeking voluntary admission . . . one who, like yourself, has never been told, who has functioned alongside humans, believing himself – itself – human. As to your hand—' He paused.

'Forget my hand,' Poole said savagely.

'Be calm.' The doctor leaned over him, peered acutely down into Poole's face. 'We'll have a hospital boat convey you over to a service facility where repairs, or replacement, on your hand can be made at a reasonable expense, either to yourself, if you're self-owned, or to your owners, if such there are. In any case you'll be back at your desk at Tri-Plan functioning just as before.'

'Except,' Poole said, 'now I know.' He wondered if Danceman or Sarah or any of the others at the office knew. Had they – or one of them – purchased him? Designed him? A figurehead, he said to himself; that's all I've been. I must never really have run the company; it was a delusion implanted in me when I was made . . . along with the delusion that I am human and alive.

'Before you leave for the repair facility,' the doctor said, 'could you kindly settle your bill at the front desk?'

Poole said acidly, 'How can there be a bill if you don't treat ants here?'

'For our services,' the nurse said. 'Up until the point we knew.'

'Bill me,' Poole said, with furious, impotent anger. 'Bill my firm.' With massive effort he managed to sit up; his head swimming, he stepped haltingly from the bed and onto the floor. 'I'll be glad to leave here,' he said as he rose to a standing position. 'And thank you for your humane attention.'

'Thank you, too, Mr Poole,' the doctor said. 'Or rather I should say just Poole.'

At the repair facility he had his missing hand replaced.

It proved fascinating, the hand; he examined it for a long time before he let the technicians install it. On the surface it appeared organic – in fact on the surface, it was. Natural skin covered natural flesh, and true blood filled the veins and capillaries. But, beneath that, wires and circuits, miniaturized components, gleamed . . . looking deep into the wrist he saw surge gates, motors, multi-stage valves, all very small. Intricate. And – the hand cost forty frogs. A week's salary, insofar as he drew it from the company payroll.

'Is this guaranteed?' he asked the technicians as they fused the 'bone' section of the hand to the balance of his body.

'Ninety days, parts and labor,' one of the technicians said. 'Unless subjected to unusual or intentional abuse.'

'That sounds vaguely suggestive,' Poole said.

The technician, a man – all of them were men – said, regarding him keenly, 'You've been posing?'

'Unintentionally,' Poole said.

'And now it's intentional?'

Poole said, 'Exactly.'

'Do you know why you never guessed? There must have been signs . . . clickings and whirrings from inside you, now and then. You never guessed because you were programmed not to notice. You'll now have the same difficulty finding out why you were built and for whom you've been operating.'

'A slave,' Poole said. 'A mechanical slave.'

'You've had fun.'

'I've lived a good life,' Poole said. 'I've worked hard.'

He paid the facility its forty frogs, flexed his new fingers, tested them out by picking up various objects such as coins, then departed. Ten minutes later he was aboard a public carrier, on his way home. It had been quite a day.

At home, in his one-room apartment, he poured himself a shot of Jack Daniel's Purple Label – sixty years old – and sat sipping it, meanwhile gazing through his sole window at the building on the opposite side of the street. Shall I go to the office? he asked himself. If so, why? If not, why? Choose one. Christ, he thought, it undermines you, knowing this. I'm a freak, he realized. An inanimate object mimicking an animate one. But – he felt alive. Yet . . . he felt differently, now. About himself. Hence about everyone, especially Danceman and Sarah, everyone at Tri-Plan.

I think I'll kill myself, he said to himself. But I'm probably programmed not to do that; it would be a costly waste which my owner would have to absorb. And he wouldn't want to.

Programmed. In me somewhere, he thought, there is a matrix fitted in place, a grid screen that cuts me off from certain thoughts, certain actions. And forces me into others. I am not free. I never was, but now I know it; that makes it different.

Turning his window to opaque, he snapped on the overhead light, carefully set about removing his clothing, piece by piece. He had watched carefully as the technicians at the repair facility had attached his new hand: he had a rather clear idea, now, of how his body had been assembled. Two major panels, one in each thigh; the technicians had removed the panels to check the circuit complexes beneath. If I'm programmed, he decided, the matrix probably can be found there.

The maze of circuitry baffled him. I need help, he said to himself. Let's see . . . what's the fone code for the class BBB computer we hire at the office?

He picked up the fone, dialed the computer at its permanent location in Boise, Idaho.

'Use of this computer is prorated at a five frogs per minute basis,' a mechanical voice from the fone said. 'Please hold your mastercredit-chargeplate before the screen.'

He did so.

'At the sound of the buzzer you will be connected with the computer,' the voice continued. 'Please query it as rapidly as possible, taking into account the fact that its answer will be given in terms of a microsecond, while your query will—' He turned the sound down, then. But quickly turned it up as the blank audio input of the computer appeared on the screen. At this moment the computer had become a giant ear, listening to him – as well as fifty thousand other queriers throughout Terra.

'Scan me visually,' he instructed the computer. 'And tell me where I will find the programming mechanism which controls my thoughts and behavior.' He waited. On the fone's screen a great active eye, multi-lensed, peered at him; he displayed himself for it, there in his one-room apartment.

The computer said, 'Remove your chest panel. Apply pressure at your breastbone and then ease outward.'

He did so. A section of his chest came off; dizzily, he set it down on the floor.

'I can distinguish control modules,' the computer said, 'but I can't tell which—' It paused as its eye roved about on the fone screen. 'I distinguish a roll of punched tape mounted above your heart mechanism. Do you see it?' Poole craned his neck, peered. He saw it, too. 'I will have to sign off,' the computer said. 'After I have examined the data available to me I will contact you and give you an answer. Good day.' The screen died out.

I'll yank the tape out of me, Poole said to himself. Tiny . . . no larger than two spools of thread, with a scanner mounted between the delivery drum and the take-up drum. He could not see any sign of motion; the spools seemed inert. They must cut in as override, he reflected, when specific situations occur. Override to my encephalic processes. And they've been doing it all my life.

He reached down, touched the delivery drum. All I have to do is tear this out, he thought, and—

The fone screen relit. 'Mastercreditchargeplate number 3-BNX-882-HQR446-T,' the computer's voice came. 'This is BBB-307DR recontacting you in response to your query of sixteen seconds lapse, November 4,1992. The punched tape roll above your heart mechanism is not a programming turret but is in fact a reality–supply construct. All sense stimuli received by your central neurological system emanate from that unit and tampering with it would be risky if not terminal.' It added, 'You appear to have no programming circuit. Query answered. Good day.' It flicked off.

Poole, standing naked before the fone screen, touched the tape drum once again, with calculated, enormous caution. I see, he thought wildly. Or do I see? This unit—

If I cut the tape, he realized, my world will disappear. Reality will continue for others, but not for me. Because my reality, my universe, is coming to me from this minuscule unit. Fed into the scanner and then into my central nervous system as it snailishly unwinds.

It has been unwinding for years, he decided.

Getting his clothes, he redressed, seated himself in his big armchair – a luxury imported into his apartment from Tri–Plan's main offices – and lit a tobacco cigarette. His hands shook as he laid down his initialed lighter; leaning back, he blew smoke before himself, creating a nimbus of gray.

I have to go slowly, he said to himself. What am I trying to do? Bypass my programming? But the computer found no programming circuit. Do I want to interfere with the reality tape? And if so, *why*?

Because, he thought, if I control that, I control reality. At least so far as I'm concerned. My subjective reality . . . but that's all there is. Objective reality is a synthetic construct, dealing with a hypothetical universalization of a multitude of subjective realities.

My universe is lying within my fingers, he realized. If I can just figure out how the damn thing works. All I set out to do originally was to search for and locate my programming circuit so I could gain true homeostatic functioning: control of myself. But with this—

With this he did not merely gain control of himself; he gained control over everything.

And this sets me apart from every human who ever lived and died, he thought somberly.

Going over to the fone he dialed his office. When he had Danceman on the screen he said briskly, 'I want you to send a complete set of microtools and enlarging screen over to my apartment. I have some microcircuitry to work on.' Then he broke the connection, not wanting to discuss it.

A half hour later a knock sounded on his door. When he opened up he found himself facing one of the shop foremen, loaded down with microtools of every sort. 'You didn't say exactly what you wanted,' the foreman said, entering the apartment. 'So Mr Danceman had me bring everything.'

'And the enlarging-lens system?'

'In the truck, up on the roof.'

Maybe what I want to do, Poole thought, is die. He lit a cigarette, stood smoking and waiting as the shop foreman lugged the heavy enlarging screen, with its power-supply and control panel, into the apartment. This is suicide, what I'm doing here. He shuddered.

'Anything wrong, Mr Poole?' the shop foreman said as he rose to his feet, relieved of the burden of the enlarging-lens system. 'You must still be rickety on your pins from your accident.'

'Yes,' Poole said quietly. He stood tautly waiting until the foreman left.

Under the enlarging-lens system the plastic tape assumed a new shape: a wide track along which hundreds of thousands of punch-holes worked their way. I thought so, Poole thought. Not recorded as charges on a ferrous oxide layer but actually punched-free slots.

Under the lens the strip of tape visibly oozed forward. Very slowly, but it did, at uniform velocity, move in the direction of the scanner.

The way I figure it, he thought, is that the punched holes are *on* gates. It functions like a player piano; solid is no, punch-hole is yes. How can I test this?

Obviously by filling in a number of holes.

He measured the amount of tape left on the delivery spool, calculated – at great effort – the velocity of the tape's movement, and then came up with a figure. If he altered the tape visible at the in-going edge of the scanner, five to seven hours would pass before that particular time period arrived. He would in effect be painting out stimuli due a few hours from now.

With a microbrush he swabbed a large — relatively large — section of tape with opaque varnish . . . obtained from the supply kit accompanying the microtools. I have smeared out stimuli for about half an hour, he pondered. Have covered at least a thousand punches.

It would be interesting to see what change, if any, overcame his environment, six hours from now.

Five and a half hours later he sat at Krackter's, a superb bar in Manhattan, having a drink with Danceman.

'You look bad,' Danceman said.

'I am bad,' Poole said. He finished his drink, a Scotch sour, and ordered another.

'From the accident?'

'In a sense, yes.'

Danceman said, 'Is it — something you found out about yourself?'

Raising his head, Poole eyed him in the murky light of the bar. 'Then you know.'

'I know,' Danceman said, 'that I should call you "Poole" instead of "Mr Poole." But I prefer the latter, and will continue to do so.'

'How long have you known?' Poole said.

'Since you took over the firm. I was told that the actual owners of Tri-Plan, who are located in the Prox System, wanted Tri-Plan run by an electric ant whom they could control. They wanted a brilliant and forceful—'

'The real owners?' This was the first he had heard about that. 'We have two thousand stockholders. Scattered everywhere.'

'Marvis Bey and her husband Ernan, on Prox 4, control fifty-one percent of the voting stock. This has been true from the start.'

'Why didn't I know?'

'I was told not to tell you. You were to think that you yourself made all company policy. With my help. But actually I was feeding you what the Beys fed to me.'

'I'm a figurehead,' Poole said.

'In a sense, yes.' Danceman nodded. 'But you'll always be "Mr Poole" to me.'

A section of the far wall vanished. And with it, several people at tables nearby. And—

Through the big glass side of the bar, the skyline of New York City flickered out of existence.

Seeing his face, Danceman said, 'What is it?'

Poole said hoarsely, 'Look around. Do you see any changes?'

After looking around the room, Danceman said, 'No. What like?'

'You still see the skyline?'

'Sure. Smoggy as it is. The lights wink—'

'Now I know,' Poole said. He had been right; every punch-hole covered up meant the disappearance of some object in his reality world. Standing, he said, 'I'll see you later, Danceman. I have to get back to my apartment; there's some work I'm doing. Goodnight.' He strode from the bar and out onto the street, searching for a cab.

No cabs.

Those, too, he thought. I wonder what else I painted over. Prostitutes? Flowers? Prisons?

There, in the bar's parking lot, Danceman's squib. I'll take that, he decided. There are still cabs in Danceman's world; he can get one later. Anyhow it's a company car, and I hold a copy of the key.

Presently he was in the air, turning toward his apartment.

New York City had not returned. To the left and right vehicles and buildings, streets, ped-runners, signs . . . and in the center nothing. How can I fly into that? he asked himself. I'd disappear.

Or would I? He flew toward the nothingness.

Smoking one cigarette after another he flew in a circle for fifteen minutes . . . and then, soundlessly, New York reappeared. He could finish his trip. He stubbed out his cigarette (a waste of something so valuable) and shot off in the direction of his apartment.

If I insert a narrow opaque strip, he pondered as he unlocked his apartment door, I can—

His thoughts ceased. Someone sat in his living room chair, watching a captain kirk on the TV. 'Sarah,' he said, nettled.

She rose, well-padded but graceful. 'You weren't at the hospital, so I came here. I still have that key you gave me back in March after we had that awful argument. Oh . . . you look so depressed.' She came up to him, peeped into his face anxiously. 'Does your injury hurt that badly?'

'It's not that.' He removed his coat, tie, shirt, and then his chest panel; kneeling down he began inserting his hands into the microtool gloves. Pausing, he looked up at her and said, 'I found out I'm an electric ant. Which from one standpoint opens up certain possibilities, which I am exploring now.' He flexed his fingers and, at the far end of the left waldo, a micro screwdriver moved, magnified into visibility by the enlarging-lens system. 'You can watch,' he informed her. 'If you so desire.'

She had begun to cry.

'What's the matter?' he demanded savagely, without looking up from his work.

'I – it's just so sad. You've been such a good employer to all of us at Tri–Plan. We respect you so. And now it's all changed.'

The plastic tape had an unpunched margin at top and bottom; he cut a horizontal strip, very narrow, then, after a moment of great concentration, cut the tape itself four hours away from the scanning head. He then rotated the cut strip into a right-angle piece in relation to the scanner, fused it in place with a micro heat element, then reattached the tape reel to its left and right sides. He had, in effect, inserted a dead twenty minutes into the unfolding flow of his reality. It would take effect – according to his calculations – a few minutes after midnight.

'Are you fixing yourself?' Sarah asked timidly.

Poole said, 'I'm freeing myself!' Beyond this he had several alterations in mind. But first he had to test his theory; blank, unpunched tape meant no stimuli, in which case the *lack* of tape . . .

'That look on your face,' Sarah said. She began gathering up her purse, coat, rolled-up aud-vid magazine. 'I'll go; I can see how you feel about finding me here.'

'Stay,' he said. 'I'll watch the captain kirk with you.' He got into his shirt. 'Remember years ago when there were – what was it? – twenty or twenty-two TV channels? Before the government shut down the independents?'

She nodded.

'What would it have looked like,' he said, 'if this TV set projected all channels onto the cathode ray screen *at the same time*? Could we have distinguished anything, in the mixture?'

'I don't think so.'

'Maybe we could learn to. Learn to be selective; do our own job of perceiving what we wanted to and what we didn't. Think of the possibilities, if our brain could handle twenty images at once; think of the amount of knowledge which could be stored during a given period. I wonder if the brain, the human brain—' He broke off. 'The human brain couldn't do it,' he said, presently, reflecting to himself. 'But in theory a quasi-organic brain might.'

'Is that what you have?' Sarah asked.

'Yes,' Poole said.

They watched the captain kirk to its end, and then they went to bed. But Poole sat up against his pillows, smoking and brooding. Beside him, Sarah stirred restlessly, wondering why he did not turn off the light.

Eleven-fifty. It would happen anytime, now.

'Sarah,' he said. 'I want your help. In a very few minutes something strange will happen to me. It won't last long, but I want you to watch me carefully. See if I—' He gestured. 'Show any changes. If I seem to go to sleep, or if I talk nonsense, or—' He wanted to say, if I disappear. But he did not. 'I won't do you any harm, but I think it might be a good idea if you armed yourself. Do you have your anti-mugging gun with you?'

'In my purse.' She had become fully awake now; sitting up in bed, she gazed at him with wild fright, her ample shoulders tanned and freckled in the light of the room.

He got her gun for her.

The room stiffened into paralyzed immobility. Then the colors began to drain away. Objects diminished until, smoke-like, they flitted away into shadows. Darkness filmed everything as the objects in the room became weaker and weaker.

The last stimuli are dying out, Poole realized. He squinted, trying to see. He made out Sarah Benton, sitting in the bed: a two-dimensional figure that doll-like had been propped up, there to fade and dwindle. Random gusts of dematerialized substance eddied about in unstable clouds; the elements collected, fell apart, then collected once again. And then the last heat, energy and light dissipated; the room closed over and fell into itself, as if sealed off from reality. And at that point absolute blackness replaced everything, space without depth, not nocturnal but rather stiff and unyielding. And in addition he heard nothing.

Reaching, he tried to touch something. But he had nothing to reach with. Awareness of his own body had departed along with everything else in the universe. He had no hands, and even if he had, there would be nothing for them to feel.

I am still right about the way the damn tape works, he said to himself, using a nonexistent mouth to communicate an invisible message.

Will this pass in ten minutes? he asked himself. Am I right about that, too? He waited . . . but knew intuitively that his time sense had departed with everything else. I can only wait, he realized. And hope it won't be long.

To pace himself, he thought, I'll make up an encyclopedia; I'll try to list everything that begins with an 'a.' Let's see. He pondered. Apple, automobile, acksetron, atmosphere, Atlantic, tomato aspic, advertising – he thought on and on, categories slithering through his fright-haunted mind.

All at once light flickered on.

He lay on the couch in the living room, and mild sunlight spilled in through the single window. Two men bent over him, their hands full of tools. Maintenance men, he realized. They've been working on me.

'He's conscious,' one of the technicians said. He rose, stood back; Sarah Benton, dithering with anxiety, replaced him.

'Thank God!' she said, breathing wetly in Poole's ear. 'I was so afraid; I called Mr Danceman finally about—'

'What happened?' Poole broke in harshly. 'Start from the beginning and for God's sake speak slowly. So I can assimilate it all.'

Sarah composed herself, paused to rub her nose, and then plunged on nervously, 'You passed out. You just lay there, as if you were dead. I waited until two-thirty and you did nothing. I called Mr Danceman, waking him up unfortunately, and he called the electric-ant main-tenance – I mean, the organic-roby maintenance people, and these two men came about four forty-five, and they've been working on you ever since. It's now six fifteen in the morning. And I'm very cold and I want to go to bed; I can't make it in to the office today; I really can't.' She turned away, sniffling. The sound annoyed him.

One of the uniformed maintenance men said, 'You've been playing around with your reality tape.'

'Yes,' Poole said. Why deny it? Obviously they had found the inserted solid strip. 'I shouldn't have been out that long,' he said. 'I inserted a ten minute strip only.'

'It shut off the tape transport,' the technician explained. 'The tape stopped moving forward; your insertion jammed it, and it automatically shut down to avoid tearing the tape. Why would you want to fiddle around with that? Don't you know what you could do?'

'I'm not sure,' Poole said.

'But you have a good idea.'

Poole said acridly, 'That's why I'm doing it.'

'Your bill,' the maintenance man said, 'is going to be ninety-five frogs. Payable in installments, if you so desire.'

'Okay,' he said; he sat up groggily, rubbed his eyes and grimaced. His head ached and his stomach felt totally empty.

'Shave the tape next time,' the primary technician told him. 'That way it won't jam. Didn't it occur to you that it had a safety factor built into it? So it would stop rather than—'

'What happens,' Poole interrupted, his voice low and intently careful, 'if no tape passed under the scanner? No tape – nothing at all. The photocell shining upward without impedance?'

The technicians glanced at each other. One said, 'All the neuro circuits jump their gaps and short out.'

'Meaning what?' Poole said.

'Meaning it's the end of the mechanism.'

Poole said, 'I've examined the circuit. It doesn't carry enough voltage to do that. Metal won't fuse under such slight loads of current, even if the terminals are touching. We're talking about a millionth of a watt along a cesium channel perhaps a sixteenth of an inch in length. Let's assume there are a billion possible combinations at one instant arising from the punch-outs on the tape. The total output isn't cumulative; the amount of current depends on what the battery details for that module, and it's not much. With all gates open and going.'

'Would we lie?' one of the technicians asked wearily.

'Why not?' Poole said. 'Here I have an opportunity to experience everything. Simultaneously. To know the universe and its entirety, to be momentarily in contact with all reality. Something that no human can do. A symphonic score entering my brain outside of time, all notes, all instruments sounding at once. And all symphonies. Do you see?'

'It'll burn you out,' both technicians said, together.

'I don't think so,' Poole said.

Sarah said, 'Would you like a cup of coffee, Mr Poole?'

'Yes,' he said; he lowered his legs, pressed his cold feet against the floor, shuddered. He then stood up. His body ached. They had me lying all night on the couch, he realized. All things considered, they could have done better than that.

At the kitchen table in the far corner of the room, Garson Poole sat sipping coffee across from Sarah. The technicians had long since gone.

'You're not going to try any more experiments on yourself, are you?' Sarah asked wistfully.

Poole grated, 'I would like to control time. To reverse it.' I will cut a segment of tape out, he thought, and fuse it in upside down. The causal sequences will then flow the other way. Thereupon I will walk backward down the steps from the roof field, back up to my door, push a locked door open, walk backward to the sink, where I will get out a stack of dirty dishes. I will seat myself at this table before the stack, fill each dish with food produced from my stomach . . . I will then transfer the food to the refrigerator. The next day I will take the food out of the refrigerator, pack it in bags, carry the bags to a supermarket, distribute the food here and there in the store. And at last, at the front counter, they will pay me money for this, from their cash register. The food will be packed with other food in big plastic boxes, shipped out of the city into the hydroponic plants on the Atlantic, there to be joined back to trees and bushes or the bodies of dead animals or pushed deep into the ground. But what would all that prove? A video tape running backward . . . would know 'no more than I know now, which is not enough.

What I want, he realized, is ultimate and absolute reality, for one micro-second. After that it doesn't matter, because all will be known; nothing will be left to understand or see.

I might try one other change, he said to himself. Before I try cutting the tape. I will prick new punch-holes in the tape and see what presently emerges. It will be interesting because I will not know what the holes I make mean.

Using the tip of a microtool, he punched several holes, at random, on the tape. As close to the scanner as he could manage . . . he did not want to wait.

'I wonder if you'll see it,' he said to Sarah. Apparently not, insofar as he could extrapolate. 'Something may show up,' he said to her. 'I just want to warn you; I don't want you to be afraid.'

'Oh dear,' Sarah said tinnily.

He examined his wristwatch. One minute passed, then a second, a third. And then—

In the center of the room appeared a flock of green and black ducks. They quacked excitedly, rose from the floor, fluttered against the ceiling in a dithering mass of feathers and wings and frantic in their vast urge, their instinct, to get away.

'Ducks,' Poole said, marveling. 'I punched a hole for a flight of wild ducks.'

Now something else appeared. A park bench with an elderly, tattered man seated on it, reading a torn, bent newspaper. He looked up, dimly made out Poole, smiled briefly at him with badly made dentures, and then returned to his folded-back newspaper. He read on.

'Do you see him?' Poole asked Sarah. 'And the ducks.' At that moment the ducks and the park bum disappeared. Nothing remained of them. The interval of their punch-holes had quickly passed.

'They weren't real,' Sarah said. 'Were they? So how—'

'You're not real,' he told Sarah. 'You're a stimulus-factor on my reality tape. A punch-hole that can be glazed over. Do you also have an existence in another reality tape, or one in an objective reality?' He did not know; he couldn't tell. Perhaps Sarah did not know, either. Perhaps she existed in a thousand reality tapes; perhaps on every reality tape ever manufactured. 'If I cut the tape,' he said, 'you will be everywhere and nowhere. Like everything else in the universe. At least as far as I am aware of it.'

Sarah faltered, 'I am real.'

'I want to know you completely,' Poole said. 'To do that I must cut the tape. If I don't do it now, I'll do it some other time; it's inevitable that eventually I'll do it.' So why wait? he asked himself. And there is always the possibility that Danceman has reported back to my maker, that they will be making moves to head me off. Because, perhaps, I'm endangering their property – myself.

'You make me wish I had gone to the office after all,' Sarah said, her mouth turned down with dimpled gloom.

'Go,' Poole said.

'I don't want to leave you alone.'

'I'll be fine,' Poole said.

'No, you're not going to be fine. You're going to unplug yourself or something, kill yourself because you've found out you're just an electric ant and not a human being.'

He said, presently, 'Maybe so.' Maybe it boiled down to that.

'And I can't stop you,' she said.

'No.' He nodded in agreement.

'But I'm going to stay,' Sarah said. 'Even if I can't stop you. Because if I do leave and you do kill yourself, I'll always ask myself for the rest of my life what would have happened if I had stayed. You see?'

Again he nodded.

'Go ahead,' Sarah said.

He rose to his feet. 'It's not pain I'm going to feel,' he told her. 'Although it may look like that to you. Keep in mind the fact that organic robots have minimal pain-circuits in them. I will be experiencing the most intense—'

'Don't tell me any more,' she broke in. 'Just do it if you're going to, or don't do it if you're not.'

Clumsily – because he was frightened – he wriggled his hands into the microglove assembly, reached to pick up a tiny tool: a sharp cutting blade. 'I am going to cut a tape mounted inside my chest panel,' he said, as he gazed through the enlarging-lens system. 'That's all.' His hand shook as it lifted the cutting blade. In a second it can be done, he realized. All over. And – I will have time to fuse the cut ends of the tape back together, he realized. A half hour at least. If I change my mind.

He cut the tape.

Staring at him, cowering, Sarah whispered, 'Nothing happened.'

'I have thirty or forty minutes.' He reseated himself at the table, having drawn his hands from the gloves. His voice, he noticed, shook; undoubtedly Sarah was aware of it, and he felt anger at himself, knowing that he had alarmed her. 'I'm sorry,' he said, irrationally; he wanted to apologize to her. 'Maybe you ought to leave,' he said in panic; again he stood up. So did she, reflexively, as if imitating him; bloated and nervous she stood there palpitating. 'Go away,' he said thickly. 'Back to the office where you ought to be. Where we both ought to be.' I'm going to fuse the tape-ends together, he told himself; the tension is too great for me to stand.

Reaching his hands toward the gloves he groped to pull them over his straining fingers. Peering into the enlarging screen, he saw the beam from the photoelectric gleam upward, pointed directly into the scanner; at the same time he saw the end of the tape disappearing under the scanner . . . he saw this, understood it; I'm too late, he realized. It has passed through. God, he thought, help me. It has begun winding at a rate greater than I calculated. So it's *now* that—

He saw apples, and cobblestones and zebras. He felt warmth, the silky texture of cloth; he felt the ocean lapping at him and a great wind, from the north, plucking at him as if to lead him somewhere. Sarah was all around him, so was Danceman. New York glowed in the night, and the squibs about him scuttled and bounced through night skies and

389

daytime and flooding and drought. Butter relaxed into liquid on his tongue, and at the same time hideous odors and tastes assailed him: the bitter presence of poisons and lemons and blades of summer grass. He drowned; he fell; he lay in the arms of a woman in a vast white bed which at the same time dinned shrilly in his ear: the warning noise of a defective elevator in one of the ancient, ruined downtown hotels. I am living, I have lived, I will never live, he said to himself, and with his thoughts came every word, every sound; insects squeaked and raced, and he half sank into a complex body of homeostatic machinery located somewhere in Tri-Plan's labs.

He wanted to say something to Sarah. Opening his mouth he tried to bring forth words – a specific string of them out of the enormous mass of them brilliantly lighting his mind, scorching him with their utter meaning.

His mouth burned. He wondered why.

Frozen against the wall, Sarah Benton opened her eyes and saw the curl of smoke ascending from Poole's half-opened mouth. Then the roby sank down, knelt on elbows and knees, then slowly spread out in a broken, crumpled heap. She knew without examining it that it had 'died.'

Poole did it to itself, she realized. And it couldn't feel pain; it said so itself. Or at least not very much pain; maybe a little. Anyhow, now it is over.

I had better call Mr Danceman and tell him what's happened, she decided. Still shaky, she made her way across the room to the fone; picking it up, she dialed from memory.

It thought I was a stimulus-factor on its reality tape, she said to herself. So it thought I would die when it 'died.' How strange, she thought. Why did it imagine that? It had never been plugged into the real world; it had 'lived' in an electronic world of its own. How bizarre.

'Mr Danceman,' she said when the circuit to his office had been put through. 'Poole is gone. It destroyed itself right in front of my eyes. You'd better come over.'

'So we're finally free of it.'

'Yes, won't it be nice?'

Danceman said, 'I'll send a couple of men over from the shop.' He saw past her, made out the sight of Poole lying by the kitchen table.

'You go home and rest,' he instructed Sarah. 'You must be worn out by all this.'

'Yes,' she said. 'Thank you, Mr Danceman.' She hung up and stood, aimlessly.

And then she noticed something.

My hands, she thought. She held them up. Why is it I can see through them?

The walls of the room, too, had become ill-defined.

Trembling, she walked back to the inert roby, stood by it, not knowing what to do. Through her legs the carpet showed, and then the carpet became dim, and she saw, through it, farther layers of disintegrating matter beyond.

Maybe if I can fuse the tape-ends back together, she thought. But she did not know how. And already Poole had become vague.

The wind of early morning blew about her. She did not feel it; she had begun, now, to cease to feel.

The winds blew on.

A Little Something For Us Tempunauts

        Wearily, Addison Doug plodded up the long path of synthetic redwood rounds, step by step, his head down a little, moving as if he were in actual physical pain. The girl watched him, wanting to help him, hurt within her to see how worn and unhappy he was, but at the same time she rejoiced that he was there at all. On and on, toward her, without glancing up, going by feel . . . like he's done this many times, she thought suddenly. Knows the way too well. Why?

'Addi,' she called, and ran toward him. 'They said on the TV you were dead. All of you were killed!'

He paused, wiping back his dark hair, which was no longer long; just before the launch they had cropped it. But he had evidently forgotten. 'You believe everything you see on TV?' he said, and came on again, haltingly, but smiling now. And reaching up for her.

God, it felt good to hold him, and to have him clutch at her again, with more strength than she had expected. 'I was going to find somebody else,' she gasped. 'To replace you.'

'I'll knock your head off if you do,' he said. 'Anyhow, that isn't possible; nobody could replace me.'

'But what about the implosion?' she said. 'On reentry; they said—'

'I forget,' Addison said, in the tone he used when he meant, I'm not going to discuss it. The tone had always angered her before, but not now. This time she sensed how awful the memory was. 'I'm going to stay at your place a couple of days,' he said, as together they moved up the path toward the open front door of the tilted A-frame house. 'If that's okay. And Benz and Crayne will be joining me, later on; maybe even as soon as tonight. We've got a lot to talk over and figure out.'

'Then all three of you survived.' She gazed up into his careworn face. 'Everything they said on TV . . .' She understood, then. Or believed she did. 'It was a cover story. For – political purposes, to fool the Russians. Right? I mean, the Soviet Union'll think the launch was a failure because on reentry—'

'No,' he said. 'A chrononaut will be joining us, most likely. To help figure out what happened. General Toad said one of them is already on his way here; they got clearance already. Because of the gravity of the situation.'

'Jesus,' the girl said, stricken. 'Then who's the cover story for?'

'Let's have something to drink,' Addison said. 'And then I'll outline it all for you.'

'Only thing I've got at the moment is California brandy.'

Addison Doug said, 'I'd drink anything right now, the way I feel.' He dropped to the couch, leaned back, and sighed a ragged, distressed sigh, as the girl hurriedly began fixing both of them a drink.

The FM-radio in the car yammered, '. . . grieves at the stricken turn of events precipitating out of an unheralded . . .'

'Official nonsense babble,' Crayne said, shutting off the radio. He and Benz were having trouble finding the house, having been there only once before. It struck Crayne that this was somewhat informal a way of convening a conference of this importance, meeting at Addison's chick's pad out here in the boondocks of Ojai. On the other hand, they wouldn't be pestered by the curious. And they probably didn't have much time. But that was hard to say; about that no one knew for sure.

The hills on both sides of the road had once been forests, Crayne observed. Now housing tracts and their melted, irregular, plastic roads marred every rise in sight. 'I'll bet this was nice once,' he said to Benz, who was driving.

'The Los Padres National Forest is near here,' Benz said. 'I got lost in there when I was eight. For hours I was sure a rattler would get me. Every stick was a snake.'

'The rattler's got you now,' Crayne said.

'All of us,' Benz said.

'You know,' Crayne said, 'it's a hell of an experience to be dead.'

'Speak for yourself.'

'But technically—'

'If you listen to the radio and TV.' Benz turned toward him, his big gnome face bleak with admonishing sternness. 'We're no more dead than anyone else on the planet. The difference for us is that our death date is in the past, whereas everyone else's is set somewhere at an uncertain time in the future. Actually, some people have it pretty damn well set, like people in cancer wards; they're as certain as we are. More so. For example, how long can we stay here before we go back? We have a margin, a latitude that a terminal cancer victim doesn't have.'

Crayne said cheerfully, 'The next thing you'll be telling us to cheer us up is that we're in no pain.'

'Addi is. I watched him lurch off earlier today. He's got it psycho-somatically – made it into a physical complaint. Like God's kneeling on his neck; you know, carrying a much-too-great burden that's unfair, only he won't complain out loud . . . just points now and then at the nail hole in his hand.' He grinned.

'Addi has got more to live for than we do.'

'Everyman has more to live for than any other man. I don't have a cute chick to sleep with, but I'd like to see the semis rolling along Riverside Freeway at sunset a few more times. It's not what you have to live for; it's that you want to live to see it, to be there – that's what is so damn sad.'

They rode on in silence.

In the quiet living room of the girl's house the three tempunauts sat around smoking, taking it easy; Addison Doug thought to himself that the girl looked unusually foxy and desirable in her stretched-tight white sweater and micro-skirt and he wished, wistfully, that she looked a little less interesting. He could not really afford to get embroiled in such stuff, at this point. He was too tired.

'Does she know,' Benz said, indicating the girl, 'what this is all about? I mean, can we talk openly? It won't wipe her out?'

'I haven't explained it to her yet,' Addison said.

'You goddam well better,' Crayne said.

'What is it?' the girl said, stricken, sitting upright with one hand directly between her breasts. As if clutching at a religious artifact that isn't there, Addison thought.

'We got snuffed on reentry,' Benz said. He was, really, the cruelest of the three. Or at least the most blunt. 'You see, Miss . . .'

'Hawkins,' the girl whispered.

'Glad to meet you, Miss Hawkins.' Benz surveyed her in his cold, lazy fashion. 'You have a first name?'

'Merry Lou.'

'Okay, Merry Lou,' Benz said. To the other two men he observed, 'Sounds like the name a waitress has stitched on her blouse. Merry Lou's my name and I'll be serving you dinner and breakfast and lunch and dinner and breakfast for the next few days or however long it is before you all give up and go back to your own time; that'll be fifty-three dollars and eight cents, please, not including tip And I hope y'all never come back, y'hear?' His voice had begun to shake; his cigarette, too. 'Sorry, Miss Hawkins,' he said then. 'We're all screwed up by the implosion at reentry. As soon as we got here in ETA we learned about it. We've known longer than anyone else; we knew as soon as we hit Emergence Time.'

'But there's nothing we could do,' Crayne said.

'There's nothing anyone can do,' Addison said to her, and put his arm around her. It felt like a déjà vu thing but then it hit him. We're in a closed time loop, he thought, we keep going through this again and again, trying to solve the reentry problem, each time imagining it's the first time, the only time . . . and never succeeding. Which attempt is this? Maybe the millionth; we have sat here a million times, raking the same facts over and over again and getting nowhere. He felt bone-weary, thinking that. And he felt a sort of vast philosophical hate toward all other men, who did not have this enigma to deal with. We all go to one place, he thought, as the Bible says. But . . . for the three of us, we have been there already. Are lying there now. So it's wrong to ask us to stand around on the surface of Earth afterward and argue and worry about it and try to figure out what malfunctioned. That should be, rightly, for our heirs to do. We've had enough already.

He did not say this aloud, though – for their sake.

'Maybe you bumped into something,' the girl said.

Glancing at the others, Benz said sardonically, 'Maybe we "bumped into something."'

'The TV commentators kept saying that,' Merry Lou said, 'about the hazard in reentry of being out of phase spatially and colliding right down to the molecular level with tangent objects, any one of which—' She gestured. 'You know. "No two objects can occupy the same space at the same time." So everything blew up, for that reason.' She glanced around questioningly.

'That is the major risk factor,' Crayne acknowledged. 'At least theoretically, as Dr Fein at Planning calculated when they got into the hazard question. But we had a variety of safety locking devices provided that functioned automatically. Reentry couldn't occur unless these assists had stabilized us spatially so we would not overlap. Of course, all those devices, in sequence, might have failed. One after the other. I was watching my feedback metric scopes on launch, and they agreed, every one of them, that we were phased properly at that time. And I heard no warning tones. Saw none, neither.' He grimaced. 'At least it didn't happen then.'

Suddenly Benz said, 'Do you realize that our next of kin are now rich? All our Federal and commercial life-insurance payoff. Our "next of kin" — God forbid, that's us, I guess. We can apply for tens of thousands of dollars, cash on the line. Walk into our brokers' offices and say, "I'm dead; lay the heavy bread on me." '

Addison Doug was thinking, The public memorial services. That they have planned, after the autopsies. That long line of black-draped Cads going down Pennsylvania Avenue, with all the government dignitaries and double-domed scientist types — *and we'll be there.* Not once but twice. Once in the oak hand-rubbed brass-fitted flag-draped caskets, but also . . . maybe riding in open limos, waving at the crowds of mourners.

'The ceremonies,' he said aloud.

The others stared at him, angrily, not comprehending. And then, one by one, they understood; he saw it on their faces.

'No,' Benz grated. 'That's — impossible.'

Crayne shook his head emphatically. 'They'll order us to be there, and we will be. Obeying orders.'

'Will we have to *smile*?' Addison said. 'To fucking *smile*?'

'No,' General Toad said slowly, his great wattled head shivering about on his broomstick neck, the color of his skin dirty and mottled, as if the mass of decorations on his stiff-board collar had started part of him decaying away. 'You are not to smile, but on the contrary are to adopt a properly grief-stricken manner. In keeping with the national mood of sorrow at this time.'

'That'll be hard to do,' Crayne said.

The Russian chrononaut showed no response; his thin beaked face, narrow within his translating earphones, remained strained with concern.

'The nation,' General Toad said, 'will become aware of your presence among us once more for this brief interval; cameras of all major TV networks will pan up to you without warning, and at the same time, the various commentators have been instructed to tell their audiences something like, the following.' He got out a piece of typed material, put on his glasses, cleared his throat and said, ' "We seem to be focusing on three figures riding together. Can't quite make them out. Can you?" ' General Toad lowered the paper. 'At this point they'll inter-rogate their colleagues extempore. Finally they'll exclaim, "Why, Roger," or Walter or Ned, as the case may be, according to the individual network—'

'Or Bill,' Crayne said. 'In case it's the Bufonidae network, down there in the swamp.'

General Toad ignored him. 'They will severally exclaim, "Why Roger I believe we're seeing the three tempunauts themselves! Does this indeed mean that somehow the difficulty—?" And then the colleague commentator says in his somewhat more somber voice, "What we're seeing at this time, I think, David," or Henry or Pete or Ralph, whichever it is, "consists of mankind's first verified glimpse of what the technical people refer to as Emergence Time Activity or ETA. Contrary to what might seem to be the case at first sight, these are *not* – repeat, not – our three valiant tempunauts as such, as we would ordinarily experience them, but more likely picked up by our cameras as the three of them are temporarily suspended in their voyage to the future, which we initially had reason to hope would take place in a time continuum roughly a hundred years from now . . . but it would seem that they somehow undershot and are here now, at this moment, which of course is, as we know, our present." '

Addison Doug closed his eyes and thought, Crayne will ask him if he can be panned up on by the TV cameras holding a balloon and eating cotton candy. I think we're all going nuts from this, all of us. And then he wondered, How many times have we gone through this idiotic exchange?

I can't prove it, he thought wearily. But I know it's true. We've sat here, done this minuscule scrabbling, listened to and said all this crap, many times. He shuddered. Each rinky-dink word . . .

'What's the matter?' Benz said acutely.

The Soviet chrononaut spoke up for the first time. 'What is the maximum interval of ETA possible to your three-man team? And how large a per cent has been exhausted by now?'

After a pause Crayne said, 'They briefed us on that before we came in here today. We've consumed approximately one-half of our maximum total ETA interval.'

'However,' General Toad rumbled, 'we have scheduled the Day of

National Mourning to fall within the expected period remaining to them of ETA time. This required us to speed up the autopsy and other forensic findings, but in view of public sentiment, it was felt . . .'

The autopsy, Addison Doug thought, and again he shuddered; this time he could not keep his thoughts within himself and he said, 'Why don't we adjourn this nonsense meeting and drop down to pathology and view a few tissue sections enlarged and in color, and maybe we'll brainstorm a couple of vital concepts that'll aid medical science in its quest for explanations? Explanations – that's what we need. Explanations for problems that don't exist yet; we can develop the problems later.' He paused. 'Who agrees?'

'I'm not looking at my spleen up there on the screen,' Benz said. 'I'll ride in the parade but I won't participate in my own autopsy.'

'You could distribute microscopic purple-stained slices of your own gut to the mourners along the way,' Crayne said. 'They could provide each of us with a doggy bag; right, General? We can strew tissue sections like confetti. I still think we should smile.'

'I have researched all the memoranda about smiling,' General Toad said, riffling the pages stacked before him, 'and the consensus at policy is that smiling is not in accord with national sentiment. So that issue must be ruled closed. As far as your participating in the autopsical procedures which are now in progress—'

'We're missing out as we sit here,' Crayne said to Addison Doug. 'I always miss out.'

Ignoring him, Addison addressed the Soviet chrononaut. 'Officer N. Gauki,' he said into his microphone, dangling on his chest, 'what in your mind is the greatest terror facing a time traveler? That there will be an implosion due to coincidence on reentry, such as has occurred in our launch? Or did other traumatic obsessions bother you and your comrade during your own brief but highly successful time flight?'

N. Gauki, after a pause, answered, 'R. Plenya and I exchanged views at several informal times. I believe I can speak for us both when I respond to your question by emphasizing our perpetual fear that we had inadvertently entered a closed time loop and would never break out.'

'You'd repeat it forever?' Addison Doug asked.

'Yes, Mr A. Doug,' the chrononaut said, nodding somberly.

A fear that he had never experienced before overcame Addison

Doug. He turned helplessly to Benz and muttered, 'Shit.' They gazed at each other.

'I really don't believe this is what happened,' Benz said to him in a low voice, putting his hand on Doug's shoulder; he gripped hard, the grip of friendship. 'We just imploded on reentry, that's all. Take it easy.'

'Could we adjourn soon?' Addison Doug said in a hoarse, strangling voice, half rising from his chair. He felt the room and the people in it rushing in at him, suffocating him. Claustrophobia, he realized. Like when I was in grade school, when they flashed a surprise test on our teaching machines, and I saw I couldn't pass it. 'Please,' he said simply, standing. They were all looking at him, with different expressions. The Russian's face was especially sympathetic, and deeply lined with care. Addison wished – 'I want to go home,' he said to them all, and felt stupid.

He was drunk. It was late at night, at a bar on Hollywood Boulevard; fortunately, Merry Lou was with him, and he was having a good time. Everyone was telling him so, anyhow. He clung to Merry Lou and said, 'The great unity in life, the supreme unity and meaning, is man and woman. Their absolute unity; right?'

'I know,' Merry Lou said. 'We studied that in class.' Tonight, at his request, Merry Lou was a small blonde girl, wearing purple bellbottoms and high heels and an open midriff blouse. Earlier she had had a lapis lazuli in her navel, but during dinner at Ting Ho's it had popped out and been lost. The owner of the restaurant had promised to keep on searching for it, but Merry Lou had been gloomy ever since. It was, she said, symbolic. But of what she did not say. Or anyhow he could not remember; maybe that was it. She had told him what it meant, and he had forgotten.

An elegant young black at a nearby table, with an Afro and striped vest and overstuffed red tie, had been staring at Addison for some time. He obviously wanted to come over to their table but was afraid to; meanwhile, he kept on staring.

'Did you ever get the sensation,' Addison said to Merry Lou, 'that you knew exactly what was about to happen? What someone was going to say? Word for word? Down to the slightest detail. As if you had already lived through it once before?'

'Everybody gets into that space,' Merry Lou said. She sipped a Bloody Mary.

The black rose and walked toward them. He stood by Addison. 'I'm sorry to bother you, sir.'

Addison said to Merry Lou, 'He's going to say, "Don't I know you from somewhere? Didn't I see you on TV?"'

'That was precisely what I intended to say,' the black said.

Addison said, 'You undoubtedly saw my picture on page forty-six of the current issue of *Time*, the section on new medical discoveries. I'm the GP from a small town in Iowa catapulted to fame by my invention of a widespread, easily available cure for eternal life. Several of the big pharmaceutical houses are already bidding on my vaccine.'

'That might have been where I saw your picture,' the black said, but he did not appear convinced. Nor did he appear drunk; he eyed Addison Doug intensely. 'May I seat myself with you and the lady?'

'Sure,' Addison Doug said. He now saw, in the man's hand, the ID of the US security agency that had ridden herd on the project from the start.

'Mr Doug,' the security agent said as he seated himself beside Addison, 'you really shouldn't be here shooting off your mouth like this. If I recognized you some other dude might and break out. It's all classified until the Day of Mourning. Technically, you're in violation of a Federal Statute by being here; did you realize that? I should haul you in. But this is a difficult situation; we don't want to do something uncool and make a scene. Where are your two colleagues?'

'At my place,' Merry Lou said. She had obviously not seen the ID. 'Listen,' she said sharply to the agent, 'why don't you get lost? My husband here has been through a grueling ordeal, and this is his only chance to unwind.'

Addison looked at the man. 'I knew what you were going to say before you came over here.' Word for word, he thought. I am right, and Benz is wrong and this will keep happening, this replay.

'Maybe,' the security agent said, 'I can induce you to go back to Miss Hawkins' place voluntarily. Some info arrived' – he tapped the tiny earphone in his right ear – 'just a few minutes ago, to all of us, to deliver to you, marked urgent, if we located you. At the launchsite ruins . . . they've been combing through the rubble, you know?'

'I know,' Addison said.

'They think they have their first clue. Something was brought back by one of you. From ETA, over and above what you took, in violation of all your pre-launch training.'

'Let me ask you this,' Addison Doug said. 'Suppose somebody does see me? Suppose somebody does recognize me? So what?'

'The public believes that even though reentry failed, the flight into time, the first American time-travel launch, was successful. Three US tempunauts were thrust a hundred years into the future – roughly twice as far as the Soviet launch of last year. That you only went a *week* will be less of a shock if it's believed that you three chose deliberately to remanifest at this continuum because you wished to attend, in fact felt compelled to attend—'

'We wanted to be in the parade,' Addison interrupted. 'Twice.'

'You were drawn to the dramatic and somber spectacle of your own funeral procession, and will be glimpsed there by the alert camera crews of all major networks. Mr Doug, really, an awful lot of high-level planning and expense have gone into this to help correct a dreadful situation; trust us, believe me. It'll be easier on the public, and that's vital, if there's ever to be another US time shot. And that is, after all, what we all want.'

Addison Doug stared at him. 'We want what?'

Uneasily, the security agent said, 'To take further trips into time. As you have done. Unfortunately, you yourself cannot ever do so again, because of the tragic implosion and death of the three of you. But other tempunauts—'

'We want what? Is that what we want?' Addison's voice rose; people at nearby tables were watching now. Nervously.

'Certainly,' the agent said. 'And keep your voice down.'

'I don't want that,' Addison said. 'I want to stop. To stop forever. To just lie in the ground, in the dust, with everyone else. To see no more summers – the *same* summer.'

'Seen one, you've seen them all,' Merry Lou said hysterically. 'I think he's right, Addi; we should get out of here. You've had too many drinks, and it's late, and this news about the—'

Addison broke in, 'What was brought back? How much extra mass?'

The security agent said, 'Preliminary analysis shows that machinery weighing about one hundred pounds was lugged back into the time-field of the module and picked up along with you. This much mass—' The agent gestured. 'That blew up the pad right on the spot. It couldn't begin to compensate for that much more than had occupied its open area at launch time.'

'Wow!' Merry Lou said, eyes wide. 'Maybe somebody sold one of you a quadraphonic phono for a dollar ninety-eight including fifteen-inch air-suspension speakers and a lifetime supply of Neil Diamond records.' She tried to laugh, but failed; her eyes dimmed over. 'Addi,' she whispered, 'I'm sorry. But it's sort of – weird. I mean, it's absurd; you all were briefed, weren't you, about your return weight? You weren't even to add so much as a piece of paper to what you took. I even saw Dr Fein demonstrating the reasons on TV. And one of you hoisted a hundred pounds of machinery into that field? You must have been trying to self-destruct, to do that!' Tears slid from her eyes; one tear rolled out onto her nose and hung there. He reached reflexively to wipe it away, as if helping a little girl rather than a grown one.

'I'll fly you to the analysis site,' the security agent said, standing up. He and Addison helped Merry Lou to her feet; she trembled as she stood a moment, finishing her Bloody Mary. Addison felt acute sorrow for her, but then, almost at once, it passed. He wondered why. One can weary even of that, he conjectured. Of caring for someone. If it goes on too long – on and on. Forever. And, at last, even after that, into something no one before, not God Himself, maybe, had ever had to suffer and in the end, for all His great heart, succumb to.

As they walked through the crowded bar toward the street, Addison Doug said to the security agent, 'Which one of us—'

'They know which one,' the agent said as he held the door to the street open for Merry Lou. The agent stood, now, behind Addison, signaling for a gray Federal car to land at the red parking area. Two other security agents, in uniform, hurried toward them.

'Was it me?' Addison Doug asked.

'You better believe it,' the security agent said.

The funeral procession moved with aching solemnity down Pennsylvania Avenue, three flag-draped caskets and dozens of black limousines passing between rows of heavily coated, shivering mourners. A low haze hung over the day, gray outlines of buildings faded into the rain-drenched murk of the Washington March day.

Scrutinizing the lead Cadillac through prismatic binoculars, TV's top news and public-events commentator, Henry Cassidy, droned on at his vast unseen audience, '. . . sad recollections of that earlier train among the wheatfields carrying the coffin of Abraham Lincoln back to burial and the nation's capital. And what a sad day this is, and what appropriate weather, with its dour overcast and sprinkles!' In his monitor he saw the zoomar lens pan up on the fourth Cadillac, as it followed those with the caskets of the dead tempunauts.

His engineer tapped him on the arm.

'We appear to be focusing on three unfamiliar figures so far not identified, riding together,' Henry Cassidy said into his neck mike, nodding agreement. 'So far I'm unable to quite make them out. Are your location and vision any better from where you're placed, Everett?' he inquired of his colleague and pressed the button that notified Everett Branton to replace him on the air.

'Why, Henry,' Branton said in a voice of growing excitement, 'I believe we're actually eyewitness to the three American tempunauts as they remanifest themselves on their historic journey into the future!'

'Does this signify,' Cassidy said, 'that somehow they have managed to solve and overcome the—'

'Afraid not, Henry,' Branton said in his slow, regretful voice. 'What we're eyewitnessing to our complete surprise consists of the Western world's first verified glimpse of what the technical people refer to as Emergence Time Activity.'

'Ah, yes, ETA,' Cassidy said brightly, reading it off the official script the Federal authorities had handed to him before air time.

'Right, Henry. Contrary to what *might* seem to be the case at first sight, these are not – repeat *not* – our three brave tempunauts as such, as we would ordinarily experience them—'

'I grasp it now, Everett,' Cassidy broke in excitedly, since his authorized script read CASS BREAKS IN EXCITEDLY. 'Our three tempunauts have momentarily suspended in their historic voyage to the future, which we believe will span across a time-continuum roughly a century from now . . . It would seem that the overwhelming grief and drama of this unanticipated day of mourning has caused them to—'

'Sorry to interrupt, Henry,' Everett Branton said, 'but I think, since the procession has momentarily halted on its slow march forward, that we might be able to—'

'No!' Cassidy said, as a note was handed him in a swift scribble, reading: *Do not interview nauts. Urgent. Dis. previous inst.* 'I don't think we're going to be able to . . .' he continued, '. . . to speak briefly with tempunauts Benz, Crayne, and Doug, as you had hoped, Everett. As we had all briefly hoped to.' He wildly waved the boom-mike back; it had already begun to swing out expectantly toward the stopped

Cadillac. Cassidy shook his head violently at the mike technician and his engineer.

Perceiving the boom-mike swinging at them Addison Doug stood up in the back of the open Cadillac. Cassidy groaned. He wants to speak, he realized. Didn't they reinstruct *him*? Why am I the only one they get across to? Other boom-mikes representing other networks plus radio station interviewers on foot now were rushing out to thrust up their microphones into the faces of the three tempunauts, especially Addison Doug's. Doug was already beginning to speak, in response to a question shouted up to him by a reporter. With his boom-mike off, Cassidy couldn't hear the question, nor Doug's answer. With reluctance, he signaled for his own boom-mike to trigger on.

'. . . before,' Doug was saying loudly.

'In what manner, "All this has happened before"?' the radio reporter, standing close to the car, was saying.

'I mean,' US tempunaut Addison Doug declared, his face red and strained, 'that I have stood here in this spot and said again and again, and all of you have viewed this parade and our deaths at reentry endless times, a closed cycle of trapped time which must be broken.'

'Are you seeking,' another reporter jabbered up at Addison Doug, 'for a solution to the reentry implosion disaster which can be applied in retrospect so that when you do return to the past you will be able to correct the malfunction and avoid the tragedy which cost – or for you three, will cost – your lives?'

Tempunaut Benz said, 'We are doing that, yes.'

'Trying to ascertain the cause of the violent implosion and eliminate the cause before we return,' tempunaut Crayne added, nodding. 'We have learned already that, for reasons unknown, a mass of nearly one hundred pounds of miscellaneous Volkswagen motor parts, including cylinders, the head . . .'

This is awful, Cassidy thought. 'This is amazing!' he said aloud, into his neck mike. 'The already tragically deceased US tempunauts, with a determination that could emerge only from the rigorous training and discipline to which they were subjected – and we wondered why at the time but can clearly see why now – have already analyzed the mechanical slip-up responsible, evidently, for their own deaths, and have begun the laborious process of sifting through and eliminating causes of that slip-up so that they can return to their original launch site and reenter without mishap.'

'One wonders,' Branton mumbled onto the air and into his feed-back earphone, 'what the consequences of this alteration of the near past will be. If in reentry they do *not* implode and are *not* killed, then they will not – well, it's too complex for me, Henry, these time paradoxes that Dr Fein at the Time Extrusion Labs in Pasadena has so frequently and eloquently brought to our attention.'

Into all the microphones available, of all sorts, tempunaut Addison Doug was saying, more quietly now, 'We must not eliminate the cause of reentry implosion. The only way out of this trip is for us to die. Death is the only solution for this. For the three of us.' He was interrupted as the procession of Cadillacs began to move forward.

Shutting off his mike momentarily, Henry Cassidy said to his engineer, 'Is he nuts?'

'Only time will tell,' his engineer said in a hard-to-hear voice.

'An extraordinary moment in the history of the United States' involvement in time travel,' Cassidy said, then, into his now live mike. 'Only time will tell – if you will pardon the inadvertent pun – whether tempunaut Doug's cryptic remarks, uttered impromptu at this moment of supreme suffering for him, as in a sense to a lesser degree it is for all of us, are the words of a man deranged by grief or an accurate insight into the macabre dilemma that in theoretical terms we knew all along might eventually confront – confront and strike down with its lethal blow – a time-travel launch, either ours or the Russians'.'

He segued, then, to a commercial.

'You know,' Branton's voice muttered in his ear, not on the air but just to the control room and to him, 'if he's right they ought to let the poor bastards die.'

'They ought to release them,' Cassidy agreed. 'My God, the way Doug looked and talked, you'd imagine he'd gone through this for a thousand years and then some! I wouldn't be in his shoes for anything.'

'I'll bet you fifty bucks,' Branton said, 'they have gone through this before. Many times.'

'Then we have, too,' Cassidy said.

Rain fell now, making all the lined-up mourners shiny. Their faces, their eyes, even their clothes – everything glistened in wet reflections of broken, fractured light, bent and sparkling, as, from gathering gray formless layers above them, the day darkened.

'Are we on the air?' Branton asked.

Who knows? Cassidy thought. He wished the day would end.

405

*

The Soviet chrononaut N. Gauki lifted both hands impassionedly and spoke to the Americans across the table from him in a voice of extreme urgency. 'It is the opinion of myself and my colleague R. Plenya, who for his pioneering achievements in time travel has been certified a Hero of the Soviet People, and rightly so, that based on our own experience and on theoretical material developed both in your own academic circles and in the soviet Academy of Sciences of the USSR, we believe that tempunaut A. Doug's fears may be justified. And his deliberate destruction of himself and his teammates at reentry, by hauling a huge mass of auto back with him from ETA, in violation of his orders, should be regarded as the act of a desperate man with no other means of escape. Of course, the decision is up to you. We have only advisory position in this matter.'

Addison Doug played with his cigarette lighter on the table and did not look up. His ears hummed, and he wondered what that meant. It had an electronic quality. Maybe we're within the module again, he thought. But he didn't perceive it; he felt the reality of the people around him, the table, the blue plastic lighter between his fingers. No smoking in the module during reentry, he thought. He put the light carefully away in his pocket.

'We've developed no concrete evidence whatsoever,' General Toad said, 'that a closed time loop has been set up. There's only the subjective feelings of fatigue on the part of Mr Doug. Just his belief that he's done all this repeatedly. As he says, it is very probably psychological in nature.' He rooted, piglike, among the papers before him. 'I have a report, not disclosed to the media, from four psychiatrists at Yale on his psychological makeup. Although unusually stable, there is a tendency toward cyclothymia on his part, culminating in acute depression. This naturally was taken into account long before the launch, but it was calculated that the joyful qualities of the two others in the team would offset this functionally. Anyhow, that depressive tendency in him is exceptionally high, now.' He held the paper out, but no one at the table accepted it. 'Isn't it true, Dr Fein,' he said, 'that an acutely depressed person experiences time in a peculiar way, that is, circular time, time repeating itself, getting nowhere, around and around? The person gets so psychotic that he refuses to let go of the past. Reruns it in his head constantly.'

'But you see,' Dr Fein said, 'this subjective sensation of being trapped is perhaps all we would have.' This was the research physicist whose basic work had laid the theoretical foundation for the project. 'If a closed loop did unfortunately lock into being.'

'The general,' Addison Doug said, 'is using words he doesn't understand.'

'I researched the one I was unfamiliar with,' General Toad said. 'The technical psychiatric terms . . . know what they mean.'

To Addison Doug, Benz said, 'Where'd you get all those VW parts, Addi?'

'I don't have them yet,' Addison Doug said.

'Probably picked up the first junk he could lay his hands on,' Crayne said. 'Whatever was available, just before we started back.'

'Will start back,' Addison Doug corrected.

'Here are my instructions to the three of you,' General Toad said. 'You are not in any way to attempt to cause damage or implosion or malfunction during reentry, either by lugging back extra mass or by any other method that enters your mind. You are to return as scheduled and in replica of the prior simulations. This especially applies to you, Mr Doug.' The phone by his right arm buzzed. He frowned, picked up the receiver. An interval passed, and then he scowled deeply and set the receiver back down, loudly.

'You've been overruled,' Dr Fein said.

'Yes, I have,' General Toad said. 'And I must say at this time that I am personally glad because my decision was an unpleasant one.'

'Then we can arrange for implosion at reentry,' Benz said after a pause.

'The three of you are to make the decision,' General Toad said. 'Since it involves your lives. It's been entirely left up to you. Whichever way you want it. If you're convinced you're in a closed time loop, and you believe a massive implosion at reentry will abolish it—' He ceased talking, as tempunaut Doug rose to his feet. 'Are you going to make another speech, Doug?' he said.

'I just want to thank everyone involved,' Addison Doug said. 'For letting us decide.' He gazed haggard-faced and wearily around at all the individuals seated at the table. 'I really appreciate it.'

'You know,' Benz said slowly, 'blowing us up at reentry could add nothing to the chances of abolishing a closed loop. In fact that could do it, Doug.'

'Not if it kills us all,' Crayne said.

407

'You agree with Addi?' Benz said.

'Dead is dead,' Crayne said. 'I've been pondering it. What other way is more likely to get us out of this? Than if we're dead? What possible other way?'

'You may be in no loop,' Dr Fein pointed out.

'But we may be,' Crayne said.

Doug, still on his feet, said to Crayne and Benz, 'Could we include Merry Lou in our decision-making?'

'Why?' Benz said.

'I can't think too clearly any more,' Doug said. 'Merry Lou can help me; I depend on her.'

'Sure,' Crayne said. Benz, too, nodded.

General Toad examined his wristwatch stoically and said, 'Gentlemen, this concludes our discussion.'

Soviet chrononaut Gauki removed his headphones and neck mike and hurried toward the three US tempunauts, his hand extended; he was apparently saying something in Russian, but none of them could understand it. They moved away somberly, clustering close.

'In my opinion you're nuts, Addi,' Benz said. 'But it would appear that I'm the minority now.'

'If he *is* right,' Crayne said, 'if – one chance in a billion – if we are going back again and again forever, that would justify it.'

'Could we go see Merry Lou?' Addison Doug said. 'Drive over to her place now?'

'She's waiting outside,' Crayne said.

Striding up to stand beside the three tempunauts, General Toad said, 'You know, what made the determination go the way it did was the public reaction to how you, Doug, looked and behaved during the funeral procession. The NSC advisors came to the conclusion that the public would, like you, rather be certain it's over for all of you. That it's more of a relief to them to know you're free of your mission than to save the project and obtain a perfect reentry. I guess you really made a lasting impression on them, Doug. That whining you did.' He walked away, then, leaving the three of them standing there alone.

'Forget him,' Crayne said to Addison Doug. 'Forget everyone like him. We've got to do what we have to.'

'Merry Lou will explain it to me,' Doug said. She would know what to do, what would be right.

'I'll go get her,' Crayne said, 'and after that the four of us can drive somewhere, maybe to her place, and decide what to do. Okay?'

'Thank you,' Addison Doug said, nodding; he glanced around for her hopefully, wondering where she was. In the next room, perhaps, somewhere close. 'I appreciate that,' he said.

Benz and Crayne eyed each other. He saw that, but did not know what it meant. He knew only that he needed someone, Merry Lou most of all, to help him understand what the situation was. And what to finalize on to get them out of it.

Merry Lou drove them north from Los Angeles in the superfast lane of the freeway toward Ventura, and after that inland to Ojai. The four of them said very little. Merry Lou drove well, as always; leaning against her, Addison Doug felt himself relax into a temporary sort of peace.

'There's nothing like having a chick drive you,' Crayne said, after many miles had passed in silence.

'It's an aristocratic sensation,' Benz murmured. 'To have a woman do the driving. Like you're nobility being chauffeured.'

Merry Lou said, 'Until she runs into something. Some big slow object.'

Addison Doug said, 'When you saw me trudging up to your place . . . up the redwood round path the other day. What did you think? Tell me honestly.'

'You looked,' the girl said, 'as if you'd done it many times. You looked worn and tired and – ready to die. At the end.' She hesitated. 'I'm sorry, but that's how you looked, Addi. I thought to myself, he knows the way too well.'

'Like I'd done it too many times.'

'Yes,' she said.

'Then you vote for implosion,' Addison Doug said.

'Well—'

'Be honest with me,' he said.

Merry Lou said, 'Look in the back seat. The box on the floor.'

With a flashlight from the glove compartment the three men examined the box. Addison Doug, with fear, saw its contents. VW motor parts, rusty and worn. Still oily.

'I got them from behind a foreign-car garage near my place,' Merry Lou said. 'On the way to Pasadena. The first junk I saw that seemed as if it'd be heavy enough. I had heard them say on TV at launch time that anything over fifty pounds up to—'

'It'll do it,' Addison Doug said. 'It did do it.'

'So there's no point in going to your place,' Crayne said. 'It's decided. We might as well head south toward the module. And initiate the procedure for getting out of ETA. And back to reentry.' His voice was heavy but evenly pitched. 'Thanks for your vote, Miss Hawkins.'

She said, 'You are all so tired.'

'I'm not,' Benz said. 'I'm mad. Mad as hell.'

'At me?' Addison Doug said.

'I don't know,' Benz said. 'It's just— Hell.' He lapsed into brooding silence then. Hunched over, baffled and inert. Withdrawn as far as possible from the others in the car.

At the next freeway junction she turned the car south. A sense of freedom seemed now to fill her, and Addison Doug felt some of the weight, the fatigue, ebbing already.

On the wrist of each of the three men the emergency alert receiver buzzed its warning tone; they all started.

'What's that mean?' Merry Lou said, slowing the car.

'We're to contact General Toad by phone as soon as possible,' Crayne said. He pointed. 'There's a Standard Station over there; take the next exit, Miss Hawkins. We can phone in from there.'

A few minutes later Merry Lou brought her car to a halt beside the outdoor phone booth. 'I hope it's not bad news,' she said.

'I'll talk first,' Doug said, getting out. Bad news, he thought with labored amusement. Like what? He crunched stiffly across to the phone booth, entered, shut the door behind him, dropped in a dime and dialed the toll-free number.

'Well, do I have news!' General Toad said when the operator had put him on the line. 'It's a good thing we got hold of you. Just a minute – I'm going to let Dr Fein tell you this himself. You're more apt to believe him than me.' Several clicks, and then Dr Fein's reedy, precise, scholarly voice, but intensified by urgency.

'What's the bad news?' Addison Doug said.

'Not bad, necessarily,' Dr Fein said. 'I've had computations run since our discussion, and it would appear – by that I mean it is statistically probable but still unverified for a certainty – that you are right, Addison. You are in a closed time loop.'

Addison Doug exhaled raggedly. You nowhere autocratic mother, he thought You probably knew all along.

'However,' Dr Fein said excitedly, stammering a little, 'I also calculate – we jointly do, largely through Cal Tech – that the greatest likelihood of maintaining the loop is to implode on reentry. Do you understand, Addison? If you lug all those rusty VW parts back and implode, then your statistical chances of closing the loop forever is greater than if you simply reenter and all goes well.'

Addison Doug said nothing.

'In fact, Addi – and this is the severe part that I have to stress – implosion at reentry, especially a massive, calculated one of the sort we seem to see shaping up – do you grasp all this, Addi? Am I getting through to you? For Chrissake, Addi? Virtually *guarantees* the locking in of an absolutely unyielding loop such as you've got in mind. Such as we've all been worried about from the start.' A pause. 'Addi? Are you there?'

Addison Doug said, 'I want to die.'

'That's your exhaustion from the loop. God knows how many repetitions there've been already of the three of you—'

'No,' he said and started to hang up.

'Let me speak with Benz and Crayne,' Dr Fein said rapidly. 'Please, before you go ahead with reentry. Especially Benz; I'd like to speak with him in particular. Please, Addison. For their sake; your almost total exhaustion has—'

He hung up. Left the phone booth, step by step.

As he climbed back into the car, he heard their two alert receivers still buzzing. 'General Toad said the automatic call for us would keep your two receivers doing that for a while,' he said. And shut the car door after him. 'Let's take off.'

'Doesn't he want to talk to us?' Benz said.

Addison Doug said, 'General Toad wanted to inform us that they have a little something for us. We've been voted a special Congressional Citation for valor or some damn thing like that. A special medal they never voted anyone before. To be awarded posthumously.'

'Well, hell – that's about the only way it can be awarded,' Crayne said.

Merry Lou, as she started up the engine, began to cry.

'It'll be a relief,' Crayne said presently, as they returned bumpily to me freeway, 'when it's over.'

It won't be long now, Addison Doug's mind declared.

On their wrists the emergency alert receivers continued to put out their combined buzzing.

'They will nibble you to death,' Addison Doug said. 'The endless wearing down by various bureaucratic voices.'

The others in the car turned to gaze at him inquiringly, with uneasiness mixed with perplexity.

'Yeah,' Crayne said. 'These automatic alerts are really a nuisance.' He sounded tired. As tired as I am, Addison Doug thought. And, realizing this, he felt better. It showed how right he was.

Great drops of water struck the windshield; it had now begun to rain. That pleased him too. It reminded him of that most exalted of all experiences within the shortness of his life: the funeral procession moving slowly down Pennsylvania Avenue, the flag-draped caskets. Closing his eyes he leaned back and felt good at last. And heard, all around him once again, the sorrow-bent people. And, in his head, dreamed of the special Congressional Medal. For weariness, he thought. A medal for being tired.

He saw, in his head, himself in other parades too, and in the deaths of many. But really it was one death and one parade. Slow cars moving along the street in Dallas and with Dr King as well . . . He saw himself return again and again, in his closed cycle of life, to the national mourning that he could not and they could not forget. He would be there; they would always be there; it would always be, and every one of them would return together again and again forever. To the place, the moment, they wanted to be. The event which meant the most to all of them.

This was his gift to them, the people, his country. He had bestowed upon the world a wonderful burden. The dreadful and weary miracle of eternal life.

The Pre-Persons

        Past the grove of cypress trees Walter – he had been playing king of the mountain – saw the white truck, and he knew it for what it was. He thought, That's the abortion truck. Come to take some kid in for a postpartum down at the abortion place.

And he thought, Maybe my folks called it. For me.

He ran and hid among the blackberries, feeling the scratching of the thorns but thinking, It's better than having the air sucked out of your lungs. That's how they do it; they perform all the PPs on all the kids there at the same time. They have a big room for it. For the kids nobody wants.

Burrowing deeper into the blackberries, he listened to hear if the truck stopped; he heard its motor.

'I am invisible,' he said to himself, a line he had learned at the fifth-grade play of *Midsummer Night's Dream*, a line Oberon, whom he had played, had said. And after that no one could see him. Maybe that was true now. Maybe the magic saying worked in real life; so he said it again to himself, 'I am invisible.' But he knew he was not. He could still see his arms and legs and shoes, and he knew they – everyone, the abortion truck man especially, and his mom and dad – they could see him too. If they looked.

If it was him they were after this time.

He wished he was a king; he wished he had magic dust all over him and a shining crown that glistened, and ruled fairyland and had Puck to confide to. To ask for advice from, even. Advice even if he himself was a king and bickered with Titania, his wife.

I guess, he thought, saying something doesn't make it true.

Sun burned down on him and he squinted, but mostly he listened to the abortion truck motor; it kept making its sound, and his heart gathered hope as the sound went on and on. Some other kid, turned over to the abortion clinic, not him; someone up the road.

He made his difficult exit from the berry brambles shaking and in many places scratched and moved step by step in the direction of his house. And as he trudged he began to cry, mostly from the pain of the scratches but also from fear and relief.

'Oh, good Lord,' his mother exclaimed, on seeing him. 'What in the name of God have you been doing?'

He said stammeringly, 'I – saw – the abortion – truck.'

'And you thought it was for you?'

Mutely, he nodded.

'Listen, Walter,' Cynthia Best said, kneeling down and taking hold of his trembling hands, 'I promise, your dad and I both promise, you'll never be sent to the County Facility. Anyhow you're too old. They only take children up to twelve.'

'But Jeff Vogel—'

'His parents got him in just before the new law went into effect. They couldn't take him now, legally. They couldn't take you now. Look – you have a soul; the law says a twelve-year-old boy has a soul. So he can't go to the County Facility. See? You're safe. Whenever you see the abortion truck, it's for someone else, not you. Never for you. Is that clear? It's come for another younger child who doesn't have a soul yet, a pre-person.'

Staring down, not meeting his mother's gaze, he said, 'I don't feel like I got a soul; I feel like I always did.'

'It's a legal matter,' his mother said briskly. 'Strictly according to age. And you're past the age. The Church of Watchers got Congress to pass the law – actually they, those church people, wanted a lower age; they claimed the soul entered the body at three years old, but a compromise bill was put through. The important thing for you is that you are legally safe, however you feel inside; do you see?'

'Okay,' he said, nodding.

'You knew that.'

He burst out with anger and grief, 'What do you think it's like, maybe waiting every day for someone to come and put you in a wire cage in a truck and—'

'Your fear is irrational,' his mother said.

'I saw them take Jeff Vogel that day. He was crying, and the man just opened the back of the truck and put him in and shut the back of the truck.'

'That was two years ago. You're weak.' His mother glared at him. 'Your grandfather would whip you if he saw you now and heard you talk this way. Not your father. He'd just grin and say something stupid.

414

Two years later, and intellectually you know you're past the legal maximum age! How—' She struggled for the word. 'You are being *depraved*.'

'And he never came back.'

'Perhaps someone who wanted a child went inside the County Facility and found him and adopted him. Maybe he's got a better set of parents who really care for him. They keep them thirty days before they destroy them.' She corrected herself. 'Put them to sleep, I mean.'

He was not reassured. Because he knew 'put him to sleep' or 'put them to sleep' was a Mafia term. He drew away from his mother, no longer wanting her comfort. She had blown it, as far as he was concerned; she had shown something about herself or, anyhow, the source of what she believed and thought and perhaps did. What all of them did. I know I'm no different, he thought, than two years ago when I was just a little kid; if I have a soul now like the law says, then I had a soul then, or else we have no souls – the only real thing is just a horrible metallic-painted truck with wire over its windows carrying off kids their parents no longer want, parents using an extension of the old abortion law that let them kill an unwanted child before it came out: because it had no 'soul' or 'identity,' it could be sucked out by a vacuum system in less than two minutes. A doctor could do a hundred a day, and it was legal because the unborn child wasn't 'human.' He was a pre-person. Just like this truck now; they merely set the date forward as to when the soul entered.

Congress had inaugurated a simple test to determine the approximate age at which the soul entered the body: the ability to formulate higher math like algebra. Up to then, it was only body, animal instincts and body, animal reflexes and responses to stimuli. Like Pavlov's dogs when they saw a little water seep in under the door of the Leningrad laboratory; they 'knew' but were not human.

I guess I'm human, Walter thought, and looked up into the gray, severe face of his mother, with her hard eyes and rational grimness. I guess I'm like you, he thought. Hey, it's neat to be a human, he thought; then you don't have to be afraid of the truck coming.

'You feel better,' his mother observed. 'I've lowered your threshold of anxiety.'

'I'm not so freaked,' Walter said. It was over; the truck had gone and not taken him.

But it would be back in a few days. It cruised perpetually.

415

Anyhow he had a few days. And then the sight of it – if only I didn't know they suck the air out of the lungs of the kids they have there, he thought. Destroy them that way. Why? Cheaper, his dad had said. Saves the taxpayers money.

He thought then about taxpayers and what they would look like. Something that scowled at all children, he thought. That did not answer if the child asked them a question. A thin face, lined with watch-worry grooves, eyes always moving. Or maybe fat; one or the other. It was the thin one that scared him; it didn't enjoy life nor want life to be. It flashed the message, 'Die, go away, sicken, don't exist.' And the abortion truck was proof – or the instrument – of it.

'Mom,' he said, 'how do you shut a County Facility? You know, the abortion clinic where they take the babies and little kids.'

'You go and petition the county legislature,' his mother said.

'You know what I'd do?' he said. 'I'd wait until there were no kids in there, only county employees, and I'd firebomb it.'

'Don't talk like that!' his mother said severely, and he saw on her face the stiff lines of the thin taxpayer. And it frightened him; his own mother frightened him. The cold and opaque eyes mirrored nothing, no soul inside, and he thought, *It's you who don't have a soul*, you and your skinny messages not-to-be. Not us.

And then he ran outside to play again.

A bunch more kids had seen the truck; he and they stood around together, talking now and then, but mostly kicking at rocks and dirt, and occasionally stepping on a bad bug.

'Who'd the truck come for?' Walter said.

'Fleischhacker. Earl Fleischhacker.'

'Did they get him?'

'Sure, didn't you hear the yelling?'

'Was his folks home at the time?'

'Naw, they split earlier on some shuck about "taking the car in to be greased." '

'*They* called the truck?' Walter said.

'Sure, it's the law; it's gotta be the parents. But they were too chickenshit to be there when the truck drove up. Shit, he really yelled; I guess you're too far away to hear, but he really yelled.'

Walter said, 'You know what we ought to do? Firebomb the truck and snuff the driver.'

All the other kids looked at him contemptuously. 'They put you in the mental hospital for life if you act out like that.'

'Sometimes for life,' Pete Bride corrected. 'Other times they "build up a new personality that is socially viable."'

'Then what should we do?' Walter said.

'You're twelve; you're safe.'

'But suppose they change the law.' Anyhow it did not assuage his anxiety to know that he was technically safe; the truck still came for others and still frightened him. He thought of the younger kids down at the Facility now, looking through the Cyclone fence hour by hour, day after day, waiting and marking the passage of time and hoping someone would come in and adopt them.

'You ever been down there?' he said to Pete Bride. 'At the County Facility? All those really little kids, like babies some of them, just maybe a year old. And they don't even know what's in store.'

'The babies get adopted,' Zack Yablonski said. 'It's the old ones that don't stand a chance. They're the ones that get you; like, they talk to people who come in and put on a good show, like they're desirable. But people know they wouldn't be there if they weren't – you know, undesirable.'

'Let the air out of the tires,' Walter said, his mind working.

'Of the truck? Hey, and you know if you drop a mothball in the gas tank, about a week later the motor wears out. We could do that.'

Ben Blaire said, 'But then they'd be after us.'

'They're after us now,' Walter said.

'I think we ought to firebomb the truck,' Harry Gottlieb said, 'but suppose there're kids in it. It'll burn them up. The truck picks up maybe – shit, I don't know. Five kids a day from different parts of the county.'

'You know they even take dogs too?' Walter said. 'And cats; you see the truck for that only about once a month. The pound truck it's called. Otherwise it's the same; they put them in a big chamber and suck the air out of their lungs and they die. They'd do that even to animals! Little animals!'

'I'll believe that when I see it,' Harry Gottlieb said, derision on his face, and disbelief. 'A truck that carries off dogs.'

He knew it was true, though. Walter had seen the pound truck two different times. Cats, dogs, and mainly us, he thought glumly. I mean, if they'd start with us, it's natural they'd wind up taking people's pets, too; we're not that different. But what kind of a person would do that, even if it is the law? 'Some laws are made to be kept, and some to be broken,' he remembered from a book he had read. We ought to firebomb the pound truck first, he thought; that's the worst, that truck.

Why is it, he wondered, that the more helpless a creature, the easier it was for some people to snuff it? Like a baby in the womb; the original abortions, 'pre-partums,' or 'pre-persons' they were called now. How could they defend themselves? Who would speak for them? All those lives, a hundred by each doctor a day . . . and all helpless and silent and then just dead. The fuckers, he thought. That's why they do it; they know they can do it; they get off on their macho power. And so a little thing that wanted to see the light of day is vacuumed out in less than two minutes. And the doctor goes on to the next chick.

There ought to be an organization, he thought, similar to the Mafia. Snuff the snuffers, or something. A contract man walks up to one of those doctors, pulls out a tube, and sucks the doctor into it, where he shrinks down like an unborn baby. An unborn baby doctor, with a stethoscope the size of a pinhead . . . he laughed, thinking of that.

Children don't know. But children know everything, knew too much. The abortion truck, as it drove along, played a Good Humor Man's jingle:

> Jack and Jill
> Went up the hill
> To fetch a pail of water

A tape loop in the sound system of the truck, built especially by Ampex for GM, blared that out when it wasn't actively nearing a seize. Then the driver shut off the sound system and glided along until he found the proper house. However, once he had the unwanted child in the back of the truck, and was either starting back to the County Facility or beginning another pre-person pick-up, he turned back on:

> Jack and Jill
> Went up the hill
> To fetch a pail of water

Thinking of himself, Oscar Ferris, the driver of truck three, finished, 'Jack fell down and broke his crown and Jill came tumbling after.' What the hell's a crown? Ferris wondered. Probably a private part. He grinned. Probably Jack had been playing with it, or Jill, both of them together. Water, my ass, he thought. I know what they went off into the bushes for. Only, Jack fell down, and his thing broke right off. 'Tough luck, Jill,' he said aloud as he expertly drove the four-year-old truck along the winding curves of California Highway One.

Kids are like that, Ferris thought. Dirty and playing with dirty things, like themselves.

This was still wild and open country, and many stray children scratched about in the canyons and fields; he kept his eye open, and sure enough – off to his right scampered a small one, about six, trying to get out of sight. Ferris at once pressed the button that activated the siren of the truck. The boy froze, stood in fright, waited as the truck, still playing 'Jack and Jill,' coasted up beside him and came to a halt.

'Show me your D papers,' Ferris said, without getting out of the truck; he leaned one arm out the window, showing his brown uniform and patch; his symbols of authority.

The boy had a scrawny look, like many strays, but, on the other hand, he wore glasses. Tow-headed, in jeans and T-shirt, he stared up in fright at Ferris, making no move to get out his identification.

' You got a D card or not?' Ferris said.

'W-w-w-what's a "D card"?'

In his official voice, Ferris explained to the boy his rights under the law. 'Your parent, either one, or legal guardian, fills out form 36-W, which is a formal statement of desirability. That they or him or her regard you as desirable. You don't have one? Legally, that makes you a stray, even if you have parents who want to keep you; they are subject to a fine of $500.'

'Oh,' the boy said. 'Well, I lost it.'

'Then a copy would be on file. They microdot all those documents and records. I'll take you in—'

'To the County Facility?' Pipe-cleaner legs wobbled in fear.

'They have thirty days to claim you by filling out the 36-W form. If they haven't done it by then—'

'My mom and dad never agree. Right now I'm staying with my dad.'

'He didn't give you a D card to identify yourself with.' Mounted transversely across the cab of the truck was a shotgun. There was always the possibility that trouble might break out when he picked up a stray. Reflexively, Ferris glanced up at it. It was there, all right, a pump shotgun. He had used it only five times in his law-enforcement career. It could blow a man into molecules. 'I have to take you in,' he said, opening the truck door and bringing out his keys. 'There's another kid back there; you can keep each other company.'

'No,' the boy said. 'I won't go.' Blinking, he confronted Ferris, stubborn and rigid as stone.

'Oh, you probably heard a lot of stories about the County Facility. It's only the warpies, the creepies, that get put to sleep; any nice normal-looking kid'll be adopted – we'll cut your hair and fix you up so you look professionally groomed. We want to find you a home. That's the whole idea. It's just a few, those who are – you know – ailing mentally or physically that no one wants. Some well-to-do individual will snap you up in a minute; you'll see. Then you won't be running around out here alone with no parents to guide you. You'll have new parents, and listen – they'll be paying heavy bread for you; hell, they'll *register* you. Do you see? It's more a temporary lodging place where we're taking you right now, to make you available to prospective new parents.'

'But if nobody adopts me in a month—'

'Hell, you could fall off a cliff here at Big Sur and kill yourself. Don't worry. The desk at the Facility will contact your blood parents, and most likely they'll come forth with the Desirability Form (I5A) sometime today even. And meanwhile you'll get a nice ride and meet a lot of new kids. And how often—'

'No,' the boy said.

'This is to inform you,' Ferris said, in a different tone, 'that I am a County Official.' He opened his truck door, jumped down, showed his gleaming metal badge to the boy. 'I am Peace Officer Ferris and I now order you to enter by the rear of the truck.'

A tall man approached them, walking with wariness; he, like the boy, wore jeans and a T-shirt, but no glasses.

'You the boy's father?' Ferris said.

The man, hoarsely, said, 'Are you taking him to the pound?'

'We consider it a child protection shelter,' Ferris said. 'The use of the term "pound" is a radical hippie slur, and distorts – deliberately – the overall picture of what we do.'

Gesturing toward the truck, the man said, 'You've got kids locked in there in those cages, have you?'

'I'd like to see your ID,' Ferris said. 'And I'd like to know if you've ever been arrested before.'

'Arrested and found innocent? Or arrested and found guilty?'

'Answer my question, sir,' Ferris said, showing his black flatpack that he used with adults to identify him as a County Peace Officer. 'Who are you? Come on, let's see your ID.'

The man said, 'Ed Gantro is my name and I have a record. When I was eighteen, I stole four crates of Coca-Cola from a parked truck.'

'You were apprehended at the scene?'

'No,' the man said. 'When I took the empties back to cash in on the refunds. That's when they seized me. I served six months.'

'Have you a Desirability Card for your boy here?' Ferris asked.

'We couldn't afford the $90 it cost.'

'Well, now it'll cost you five hundred. You should have gotten it in the first place. My suggestion is that you consult an attorney.' Ferris moved toward the boy, declaring officially. 'I'd like you to join the other juveniles in the rear section of the vehicle.' To the man he said, 'Tell him to do as instructed.'

The man hesitated and then said. 'Tim, get in the goddamn truck. And we'll get a lawyer; we'll get the D card for you. It's futile to make trouble – technically you're a stray.'

' "A stray," ' the boy said, regarding his father.

Ferris said, 'Exactly right. You have thirty days, you know, to raise the—'

'Do you also take cats?' the boy said. 'Are there any cats in there? I really like cats; they're all right.'

'I handle only PP cases,' Ferris said. 'Such as yourself.' With a key he unlocked the back of the truck. 'Try not to relieve yourself while you're in the truck; it's hard as hell to get the odor and stains out.'

The boy did not seem to understand the word; he gazed from Ferris to his father in perplexity.

'Just don't go to the bathroom while you're in the truck,' his father explained. 'They want to keep it sanitary, because that cuts down their maintenance costs.' His voice was savage and grim.

'With stray dogs or cats,' Ferris said, 'they just shoot them on sight, or put out poison bait.'

'Oh, yeah, I know that Warfarin,' the boy's father said. 'The animal eats it over a period of a week, and then he bleeds to death internally.'

'With no pain,' Ferris pointed out.

'Isn't that better than sucking the air from their lungs?' Ed Gantro said. 'Suffocating them on a mass basis?'

'Well, with animals the county authorities—'

'I mean the children. Like Tim.' His father stood beside him, and they both looked into the rear of the truck. Two dark shapes could be dimly discerned, crouching as far back as possible, in the starkest form of despair.

'Fleischhacker!' the boy Tim said. 'Didn't you have a D card?'

'Because of energy and fuel shortages,' Ferris was saying, 'population must be radically cut. Or in ten years there'll be no food for anyone. This is one phase of—'

'I had a D card,' Earl Fleischhacker said, 'but my folks took it away from me. They didn't want me any more; so they took it back, and then they called for the abortion truck.' His voice croaked; obviously he had been secretly crying.

'And what's the difference between a five-month-old fetus and what we have here?' Ferris was saying. 'In both cases what you have is an unwanted child. They simply liberalized the laws.'

Tim's father, staring at him, said, 'Do you agree with these laws?'

'Well, it's really all up to Washington and what they decide will solve our needs in these days of crises,' Ferris said. 'I only enforce their edicts. If this law changed – hell. I'd be trucking empty milk cartons for recycling or something and be just as happy.'

'*Just* as happy? You enjoy your work?'

Ferris said, mechanically. 'It gives me the opportunity to move around a lot and to meet people.'

Tim's father Ed Gantro said, 'You are insane. This postpartum abortion scheme and the abortion laws before it where the unborn child had no legal rights – it was removed like a tumor. Look what it's come to. If an unborn child can be killed without due process, why not a born one? What I see in common in both cases is their helplessness; the organism that is killed had no chance, no ability, to protect itself. You know what? I want you to take me in, too. In back of the truck with the three children.'

'But the President and Congress have declared that when you're past twelve you have a soul,' Ferris said. 'I can't take you. It wouldn't be right.'

'I have no soul,' Tim's father said. 'I got to be twelve and nothing happened. Take me along, too. Unless you can find my soul.'

'Jeez,' Ferris said.

'Unless you can show me my soul,' Tim's father said, 'unless you can specifically locate it, then I insist you take me in as no different from these kids.'

Ferris said, 'I'll have to use the radio to get in touch with the County Facility, see what they say.'

'You do that,' Tim's father said, and laboriously clambered up into the rear of the truck, helping Tim along with him. With the other two boys they waited while Peace Officer Ferris, with all his official identification as to who he was, talked on his radio.

'I have here a Caucasian male, approximately thirty, who insists that he be transported to the County Facility with his infant son,' Ferris was saying into his mike. 'He claims to have no soul, which he maintains puts him in the class of subtwelve-year-olds. I don't have with me or know any test to detect the presence of a soul, at least any I can give out here in the boondocks that'll later on satisfy a court. I mean, he probably can do algebra and higher math; he seems to possess an intelligent mind. But—'

'Affirmative as to bringing him in,' his superior's voice on the two-way radio came back to him. 'We'll deal with him here.'

'We're going to deal with you downtown,' Ferris said to Tim's father, who, with the three smaller figures, was crouched down in the dark recesses of the rear of the truck. Ferris slammed the door, locked it – an extra precaution, since the boys were already netted by electronic bands – and then started up the truck.

> Jack and Jill went up the hill
> To fetch a pail of water
> Jack fell down
> And broke his crown

Somebody's sure going to get their crown broke, Ferris thought as he drove along the winding road, and it isn't going to be me.

'I can't do algebra,' he heard Tim's father saying to the three boys. 'So I can't have a soul.'

The Fleischhacker boy said, snidely, 'I can, but I'm only nine. So what good does it do me?'

'That's what I'm going to use as my plea at the Facility,' Tim's father continued. 'Even long division was hard for me. I don't have a soul. I belong with you three little guys.'

Ferris, in a loud voice, called back, 'I don't want you soiling the truck, you understand? It costs us—'

'Don't tell me,' Tim's father said, 'because I wouldn't understand. It would be too complex, the proration and accrual and fiscal terms like that.'

I've got a weirdo back there, Ferris thought, and was glad he had the pump shotgun mounted within easy reach. 'You know the world is running out of everything,' Ferris called back to them, 'energy and apple juice and fuel and bread; we've got to keep the population down, and the embolisms from the Pill make it impossible—'

'None of us knows those big words,' Tim's father broke in.

Angrily, and feeling baffled, Ferris said. 'Zero population growth; that's the answer to the energy and food crisis. It's like – shit, it's like when they introduced the rabbit in Australia, and it had no natural enemies, and so it multiplied until, like people—'

'I do understand multiplication,' Tim's father said. 'And adding and subtraction. But that's all.'

Four crazy rabbits flopping across the road, Ferris thought. People pollute the natural environment, he thought. What must this part of the country have been like before man? Well, he thought, with the postpartum abortions taking place in every county in the US of A we may see that day; we may stand and look once again upon a virgin land.

We, he thought. I guess there won't be any we. I mean, he thought, giant sentient computers will sweep out the landscape with their slotted video receptors and find it pleasing.

The thought cheered him up.

'Let's have an abortion!' Cynthia declared excitedly as she entered the house with an armload of synthogroceries. 'Wouldn't that be neat? Doesn't that turn you on?'

Her husband Ian Best said dryly, 'But first you have to get pregnant. So make an appointment with Dr Guido – that should cost me only fifty or sixty dollars – and have your IUD removed.'

'I think it's slipping down anyhow. Maybe, if—' Her pert dark shag-haired head tossed in glee. 'It probably hasn't worked properly since last year. So I could be pregnant now.'

Ian said caustically. 'You could put an ad in the *Free Press*; "Man wanted to fish out IUD with coathanger." '

'But you see,' Cynthia said, following him as he made his way to the master closet to hang up his status-tie and class-coat, 'it's the in thing now, to have an abortion. Look, what do we have? A kid. We have Walter. Every time someone comes over to visit and sees him, I know they're wondering. "Where did you screw up?" It's embarrassing.' She added, 'And the kind of abortions they give now, for women in early stages – it only costs one hundred dollars . . . the price of ten gallons of gas! And you can talk about it with practically everybody who drops by for hours '

Ian turned to face her and said in a level voice. 'Do you get to keep the embryo? Bring it home in a bottle or sprayed with special luminous paint so it glows in the dark like a night light?'

'In any color you want!'

'The *embryo?*'

'No, the bottle. And the color of the fluid. It's in a preservative solution, so really it's a lifetime acquisition. It even has a written guarantee, I think.'

Ian folded his arms to keep himself calm: alpha state condition. 'Do you know that there are people who would want to have a child? Even an ordinary dumb one? That go to the County Facility week after week looking for a little newborn baby? These ideas – there's been this world panic about overpopulation. Nine trillion humans stacked like kindling in every block of every city. Okay, if that were going on—' He gestured. 'But what we have now is not *enough* children. Or don't you watch TV or read the *Times?*'

'It's a drag,' Cynthia said. 'For instance, today Walter came into the house freaked out because the abortion truck cruised by. It's a drag taking care of him. *You* have it easy; you're at work. But *me*—'

'You know what I'd like to do to the Gestapo abortion wagon? Have two ex-drinking buddies of mine armed with BARs, one on each side of the road. And when the wagon passes by—'

'It's a ventilated air-conditioned truck, not a wagon.'

He glared at her and then went to the bar in the kitchen to fix himself a drink. Scotch will do, he decided. Scotch and milk, a good before-'dinner' drink.

As he mixed his drink, his son Walter came in. He had, on his face, an unnatural pallor.

'The 'bort truck went by today, didn't it?' Ian said.

'I thought maybe—'

'No way. Even if your mother and I saw a lawyer and had a legal document drawn up, an un-D Form, you're too old. So relax.'

'I know intellectually,' Walter said, 'but—'

' "Do not seek to know for whom the bell tolls; it tolls for thee," ' Ian quoted (inaccurately). 'Listen, Walt, let me lay something on you.' He took a big, long drink of Scotch and milk. 'The name of all this is, *kill me*. Kill them when they're the size of a fingernail, or a baseball, or later on, if you haven't done it already, suck the air out of the lungs of a ten-year-old boy and let him die. It's a certain kind of woman advocating this all. They used to call them "castrating females." Maybe that was once the right term, except that these women, these hard cold women, didn't just want to – well, they want to do in the *whole* boy or man, make all of them dead, not just the part that makes him a man. Do you see?'

'No,' Walter said, but in a dim sense, very frightening, he did.

After another hit of his drink, Ian said, 'And we've got one living right here, Walter. Here in our very house.'

'What do we have living here?'

'What the Swiss psychiatrists call a *kindermorder*,' Ian said, deliberately choosing a term he knew his boy wouldn't understand. 'You know what,' he said, 'you and I could get onto an Amtrak coach and head north and just keep on going until we reached Vancouver, British Columbia, and we could take a ferry to Vancouver Island and never be seen by anybody down here again.'

'But what about Mom?'

'I would send her a cashier's check,' Ian said. 'Each month. And she would be quite happy with that.'

'It's cold up there, isn't it?' Walter said. 'I mean, they have hardly any fuel and they wear—'

'About like San Francisco. Why? Are you afraid of wearing a lot of sweaters and sitting close to the fireplace? What did you see today that frightened you a hell of a lot more?'

'Oh, yeah.' He nodded somberly.

'We could live on a little island off Vancouver Island and raise our own food. You can plant stuff up there and it grows. And the truck won't come there; you'll never see it again. They have different laws. The women up there are different. There was this one girl I knew when I was up there for a while, a long time ago; she had long black hair and smoked Players cigarettes all the time and never ate anything or ever stopped talking. Down here we're seeing a civilization in which the desire by women to destroy their own—' Ian broke off; his wife had walked into the kitchen.

'If you drink any more of that stuff,' she said to him, 'you'll barf it up.'

'Okay,' Ian said irritably. 'Okay!'

'And don't yell,' Cynthia said. 'I thought for dinner tonight it'd be nice if you took us out. Dal Rey's said on TV they have steak for early comers.'

Wrinkling his nose, Walter said, 'They have raw oysters.'

'Blue points,' Cynthia said. 'In the half shell, on ice. I love them. All right, Ian? Is it decided?'

To his son Walter, Ian said. 'A raw blue point oyster looks like nothing more on earth than what the surgeon—' He became silent, then. Cynthia glared at him, and his son was puzzled. 'Okay,' he said, 'but I get to order steak.'

'Me too,' Walter said.

Finishing his drink, Ian said more quietly, 'When was the last time you fixed dinner here in the house? For the three of us?'

'I fixed you that pigs' ears and rice dish on Friday,' Cynthia said. 'Most of which went to waste because it was something new and on the nonmandatory list. Remember, *dear*?'

Ignoring her, Ian said to his son, 'Of course, that type of woman will sometimes, even often, be found up there, too. She has existed throughout time and all cultures. But since Canada has no law permitting postpartum—' He broke off. 'It's the carton of milk talking,' he explained to Cynthia. 'They adulterate it these days with sulfur. Pay no attention or sue somebody; the choice is yours.'

Cynthia, eyeing him, said, 'Are you running a fantasy number in your head again about splitting?'

'Both of us,' Walter broke in. 'Dad's taking me with him.'

'Where?' Cynthia said, casually.

Ian said. 'Wherever the Amtrak track leads us.'

'We're going to Vancouver Island in Canada,' Walter said.

'Oh, really?' Cynthia said.

After a pause Ian said, 'Really.'

'And what the shit am I supposed to do when you're gone? Peddle my ass down at the local bar? How'll I meet the payments on the various—'

'I will continually mail you checks,' Ian said. 'Bonded by giant banks.'

'Sure. You bet. Yep. Right.'

'You could come along,' Ian said, 'and catch fish by leaping into English Bay and grinding them to death with your sharp teeth. You could rid British Columbia of its fish population overnight. All those ground-up fish, wondering vaguely what happened . . . swimming along one minute and then this – ogre, this fish-destroying monster with a single luminous eye in the center of its forehead, falls on them and grinds them into grit. There would soon be a legend. News like that spreads. At least among the last surviving fish.'

'Yeah, but Dad,' Walter said, 'suppose there are no surviving fish.'

'Then it will have been all in vain,' Ian said, 'except for your mother's own personal pleasure at having bitten to death an entire species in British Columbia, where fishing is the largest industry anyhow, and so many other species depend on it for survival.'

'But then everyone in British Columbia will be out of work,' Walter said.

'No,' Ian said, 'they will be cramming the dead fish into cans to sell to Americans. You see, Walter, in the olden days, before your mother multi-toothedly bit to death all the fish in British Columbia, the simple rustics stood with stick in hand, and when a fish swam past, they whacked the fish over the head. This will *create* jobs, not eliminate them. Millions of cans of suitably marked—'

'You know,' Cynthia said quickly, 'he believes what you tell him.'

Ian said, 'What I tell him is true.' Although not, he realized, in a literal sense. To his wife he said, 'I'll take you out to dinner. Get our ration stamps, put on that blue knit blouse that shows off your boobs; that way you'll get a lot of attention and maybe they won't remember to collect the stamps.'

'What's a "boob"?' Walter asked.

'Something fast becoming obsolete,' Ian said, 'like the Pontiac GTO. Except as an ornament to be admired and squeezed. Its function is dying away.' As is our race, he thought, once we gave full rein to those who would destroy the unborn – in other words, the most helpless creatures alive.

'A boob,' Cynthia said severely to her son, 'is a mammary gland that ladies possess which provides milk to their young.'

'Generally there are two of them,' Ian said. 'Your operational boob and then your backup boob, in case there is power failure in the operational one. I suggest the elimination of a step in all this pre-person abortion mania,' he said. 'We will send all the boobs in the world to the County Facilities. The milk, if any, will be sucked out of them, by mechanical means of course; they will become useless and empty, and then the young will die naturally, deprived of many and all sources of nourishment.'

'There's formula,' Cynthia said, witheringly. 'Similac and those. I'm going to change so we can go out.' She turned and strode toward their bedroom.

'You know,' Ian said after her, 'if there was any way you could get me classified as a pre-person, you'd send me there. To the Facility with the greatest facility.' And, he thought, I'll bet I wouldn't be the only husband in California who went. There'd be plenty others. In the same bag as me, then as now.

'Sounds like a plan,' Cynthia's voice came to him dimly; she had heard.

'It's not just a hatred for the helpless,' Ian Best said. 'More is involved. Hatred of what? Of everything that grows?' You blight them, he thought, before they grow big enough to have muscle and the tactics and skill for fight – big like I am in relation to you, with my fully developed musculature and weight. So much easier when the other person – I should say pre-person – is floating and dreaming in the amniotic fluid and knows nothing about how to nor the need to hit back.

Where did the motherly virtues go to? he asked himself. When mothers *especially* protected what was small and weak and defenseless?

Our competitive society, he decided. The survival of the strong. Not the fit, he thought; just those who hold the *power*. And are not going to surrender it to the next generation: it is the powerful and evil old against the helpless and gentle new.

'Dad,' Walter said, 'are we really going to Vancouver Island in Canada and raise real food and not have anything to be afraid of any more?'

Half to himself, Ian said, 'Soon as I have the money.'

'I know what that means. It's a "we'll see" number you say. We aren't going, are we?' He watched his father's face intently. 'She won't let us, like taking me out of school and like that; she always brings up that . . . right?'

'It lies ahead for us someday,' Ian said doggedly. 'Maybe not this month but someday, sometime. I promise.'

'And there's no abortion trucks there.'

'No. None. Canadian law is different.'

'Make it soon, Dad. Please.'

His father fixed himself a second Scotch and milk and did not answer; his face was somber and unhappy, almost as if he was about to cry.

In the rear of the abortion truck three children and one adult huddled, jostled by the turning of the truck. They fell against the restraining wire that separated them, and Tim Gantro's father felt keen despair at being cut off mechanically from his own boy. A nightmare during day, he thought. Caged like animals; his noble gesture had brought only more suffering to him.

'Why'd you say you don't know algebra?' Tim asked, once. 'I know you know even calculus and trig-something; you went to Stanford University.'

'I want to show,' he said, 'that either they ought to kill all of us or none of us. But not divide along these bureaucratic arbitrary lines. "When does the soul enter the body?" What kind of rational question is that in this day and age? It's Medieval.' In fact, he thought, it's a pretext – a pretext to prey on the helpless. And he was not helpless. The abortion truck had picked up a fully grown man, with all his knowledge, all his cunning. How are they going to handle me? he asked himself. Obviously I have what all men have; if they have souls, then so do I. If not, then I don't, but on what real basis can they 'put me to sleep'? I am not weak and small, not an ignorant child cowering defenselessly. I can argue the sophistries with the best of the county lawyers; with the DA himself, if necessary.

If they snuff me, he thought, they will have to snuff everyone, including themselves. And that is not what this is all about. This is a con game by which the established, those who already hold all the key economic and political posts, keep the youngsters out of it – murder them if necessary. There is, he thought, in the land, a hatred by the old of the young, a hatred and a fear. So what will they do with me? I am in their age group, and I am caged up in the back of this abortion truck. I pose, he thought, a different kind of threat; I am one of them but on the other side, with stray dogs and cats and babies and infants.

Let them figure it out; let a new St Thomas Aquinas arise who can unravel this.

'All I know,' he said aloud, 'is dividing and multiplying and subtracting. I'm even hazy on my fractions.'

'But you used to know that!' Tim said.

'Funny how you forget it after you leave school,' Ed Gantro said. 'You kids are probably better at it than I am.'

'Dad, they're going to *snuff* you,' his son Tim said, wildly. 'Nobody'll adopt you. Not at your age. You're too *old*.'

'Let's see,' Ed Gantro said. 'The binomial theorem. How does that go? I can't get it all together: something about a and b.' And as it leaked out of his head, as had his immortal soul . . . he chuckled to himself. I cannot pass the soul test, he thought. At least not talking like that. I am a dog in the gutter, an animal in a ditch.

The whole mistake of the pro-abortion people from the start, he said to himself, was the *arbitrary* line they drew. An embryo is not entitled to American Constitutional rights and can be killed, legally, by a doctor. But a fetus was a 'person,' with rights, at least for a while; and then the pro-abortion crowd decided that even a seven-month fetus was not 'human' and could be killed, legally, by a licensed doctor. And, one day, a newborn baby – it is a vegetable; it can't focus its eyes, it understands nothing, nor talks . . . the pro-abortion lobby argued in court, and won, with their contention that a newborn baby was only a fetus expelled by accident or organic processes from the womb. But, even then, where was the line to be drawn finally? When the baby smiled its first smile? When it spoke its first word or reached for its initial time for a toy it enjoyed? The legal line was relentlessly pushed back and back. And now the most savage and arbitrary definition of all: when it could perform 'higher math.'

That made the ancient Greeks, of Plato's time, nonhumans, since arithmetic was unknown to them, only geometry; and algebra was an Arab invention, much later in history. *Arbitrary*. It was not a theological arbitrariness either; it was a mere legal one. The Church had long since – from the start, in fact – maintained that even the zygote, and the embryo that followed, was as sacred a life form as any that walked the earth. They had seen what would come of arbitrary definitions of 'Now the soul enters the body,' or in modern terms, 'Now it is a person entitled to the full protection of the law like everyone else.' What was so sad was the sight now of the small child playing bravely in his yard day by day, trying to hope, trying to pretend a security he did not have.

Well, he thought, we'll see what they do with me; I am thirty-five years old, with a Master's Degree from Stanford. Will they put me in a cage for thirty days, with a plastic food dish and a water source and a place – in plain sight – to relieve myself, and if no one adopts me will they consign me to automatic death along with the others?

I am risking a lot, he thought. But they picked up my son today, and the risk began then, when they had him, not when I stepped forward and became a victim myself.

He looked about at the three frightened boys and tried to think of something to tell them – not just his own son but all three.

' "Look," ' he said, quoting. ' "I tell you a sacred secret. We shall not all sleep in death. We shall—" ' But then he could not remember the rest. Bummer, he thought dismally. ' "We shall wake up," ' he said, doing the best he could. ' "In a flash. In the twinkling of an eye." '

'Cut the noise,' the driver of the truck, from beyond his wire mesh, growled. 'I can't concentrate on this fucking road.' He added, 'You know, I can squirt gas back there where you are, and you'll pass out; it's for obstreperous pre-persons we pick up. So you want to knock it off, or have me punch the gas button?'

'We won't say anything,' Tim said quickly, with a look of mute terrified appeal at his father. Urging him silently to conform.

His father said nothing. The glance of urgent pleading was too much for him, and he capitulated. Anyhow, he reasoned, what happened in the truck was not crucial. It was when they reached the County Facility – where there would be, at the first sign of trouble, newspaper and TV reporters.

So they rode in silence, each with his own fears, his own schemes. Ed Gantro brooded to himself, perfecting in his head what he would do – what he *had* to do. And not just for Tim but all the PP abortion candidates; he thought through the ramifications as the truck lurched and rattled on.

As soon as the truck parked in the restricted lot of the County Facility and its rear doors had been swung open, Sam B. Carpenter, who ran the whole goddamn operation, walked over, stared, said, 'You've got a grown man in there, Ferris. In fact, you comprehend what you've got? A protester, that's what you've latched onto.'

'But he insisted he doesn't know any math higher than adding,' Ferris said.

To Ed Gantro, Carpenter said, 'Hand me your wallet. I want your actual name. Social Security number, police region stability ident – come on, I want to know who you really are.'

'He's just a rural type,' Ferris said, as he watched Gantro pass over his lumpy wallet.

'And I want confirm prints offa his feet,' Carpenter said. 'The full set. Right away – priority A.' He liked to talk that way.

An hour later he had the reports back from the jungle of inter-locking security-data computers from the fake-pastoral restricted area in Virginia. 'This individual graduated from Stanford College with a degree in math. And then got a master's in psychology, which he has, no doubt about it, been subjecting us to. We've got to get him out of here.'

'I did have a soul,' Gantro said, 'but I lost it.'

'How?' Carpenter demanded, seeing nothing about that on Gantro's official records.

'An embolism. The portion of my cerebral cortex, where my soul was, got destroyed when I accidentally inhaled the vapors of insect spray. That's why I've been living out in the country eating roots and grubs, with my boy here, Tim.'

'We'll run an EEG on you,' Carpenter said.

'What's that?' Gantro said. 'One of those brain tests?'

To Ferris, Carpenter said. 'The law says the soul enters at twelve years. And you bring this individual male adult well over thirty. We could be charged with murder. We've got to get rid of him. You drive him back to exactly where you found him and dump him off. If he won't voluntarily exit from the truck, gas the shit out of him and then throw him out. That's a national security order. Your job depends on it, also your status with the penal code of this state.'

'I belong here,' Ed Gantro said. 'I'm a dummy.'

'And his kid,' Carpenter said. 'He's probably a mathematical mental mutant like you see on TV. They set you up; they've probably already alerted the media. Take them all back and gas them and dump them wherever you found them or, barring that, anyhow out of sight.'

'You're getting hysterical,' Ferris said, with anger. 'Run the EEG and the brain scan on Gantro, and probably we'll have to release him, but these three juveniles—'

'All geniuses,' Carpenter said. 'All part of the setup, only you're too stupid to know. Kick them out of the truck and off our premises, and deny – you get this? – deny you ever picked any of the four of them up. Stick to that story.'

'Out of the vehicle,' Ferris ordered, pressing the button that lifted the wire mesh gates.

The three boys scrambled out. But Ed Gantro remained.

'He's not going to exit voluntarily,' Carpenter said. 'Okay, Gantro, we'll physically expel you.' He nodded to Ferris, and the two of them entered the back of the truck. A moment later they had deposited Ed Gantro on the pavement of the parking lot.

'Now you're just a plain citizen,' Carpenter said, with relief. 'You can claim all you want, but you have no proof.'

'Dad,' Tim said, 'how are we going to get home?' All three boys clustered around Ed Gantro.

'You could call somebody from up there,' the Fleischhacker boy said. 'I bet if Walter Best's dad has enough gas he'd come and get us. He takes a lot of long drives; he has a special coupon.'

'Him and his wife, Mrs Best, quarrel a lot,' Tim said. 'So he likes to go driving at night alone; I mean, without her.'

Ed Gantro said, 'I'm staying here. I want to be locked up in a cage.'

'But we can go,' Tim protested. Urgently, he plucked at his dad's sleeve. 'That's the whole point, isn't it? They let us go when they saw you. We did it!'

Ed Gantro said to Carpenter, 'I insist on being locked up with the other pre-persons you have in there.' He pointed at the gaily imposing, esthetic solid-green-painted Facility Building.

To Mr Sam B. Carpenter, Tim said, 'Call Mr Best, out where we were, on the peninsula. It's a 669 prefix number. Tell him to come and get us, and he will. I promise. Please.'

The Fleischhacker boy added, 'There's only one Mr Best listed in the phone book with a 669 number. Please, mister.'

Carpenter went indoors, to one of the Facility's many official phones, looked up the number. Ian Best. He punched the number.

'You have reached a semiworking, semiloafing number,' a man's voice, obviously that of someone half-drunk, responded. In the background Carpenter could hear the cutting tones of a furious woman, excoriating Ian Best.

'Mr Best,' Carpenter said, 'several persons whom you know are stranded down at Fourth and A Streets in Verde Gabriel, an Ed Gantro and his son, Tim, a boy identified as Ronald or Donald Fleischhacker, and another unidentified minor boy. The Gantro boy suggested you would not object to driving down here to pick them up and take them home.'

'Fourth and A Streets,' Ian Best said. A pause. 'Is that the pound?'

'The County Facility,' Carpenter said.

'You son of a bitch,' Best said. 'Sure I'll come get them; expect me in twenty minutes. You have *Ed* Gantro there as a pre-person? Do you know he graduated from Stanford University?'

'We are aware of this,' Carpenter said stonily. 'But they are not being detained; they are merely – here. Not – I repeat not – in custody.'

Ian Best, the drunken slur gone from his voice, said, 'There'll be reporters from all the media there before I get there.' Click. He had hung up.

Walking back outside, Carpenter said to the boy Tim, 'Well, it seems you mickey-moused me into notifying a rabid anti-abortionist activist of your presence here. How neat, how really neat.'

A few moments passed, and then a bright-red Mazda sped up to the entrance of the Facility. A tall man with a light beard got out, unwound camera and audio gear, walked leisurely over to Carpenter. 'I understand you may have a Stanford MA in math here at the Facility,' he said in a neutral, casual voice. 'Could I interview him for a possible story?'

Carpenter said, 'We have booked no such person. You can inspect our records.' But the reporter was already gazing at the three boys clustered around Ed Gantro.

In a loud voice the reporter called, 'Mr Gantro?'

'Yes, sir,' Ed Gantro replied.

Christ, Carpenter thought. We did lock him in one of our official vehicles and transport him here; it'll hit all the papers. Already a blue van with the markings of a TV station had rolled onto the lot. And, behind it, two more cars.

> ABORTION FACILITY SNUFFS
> STANFORD GRAD

That was how it read in Carpenter's mind. Or

> COUNTY ABORTION FACILITY
> FOILED IN ILLEGAL ATTEMPT TO . . .

And so forth. A spot on the 6:00 evening TV news. Gantro, and when he showed up, Ian Best who was probably an attorney, surrounded by tape recorders and mikes and video cameras.

We have mortally fucked up, he thought. Mortally fucked up. They at Sacramento will cut our appropriation; we'll be reduced to hunting down stray dogs and cats again, like before. Bummer.

When Ian Best arrived in his coal-burning Mercedes-Benz, he was still a little stoned. To Ed Gantro he said, 'You mind if we take a scenic roundabout route back?'

'By way of what?' Ed Gantro said. He wearily wanted to leave now. The little flow of media people had interviewed him and gone. He had made his point, and now he felt drained, and he wanted to go home.

Ian Best said, 'By way of Vancouver Island, British Columbia.'

With a smile, Ed Gantro said, 'These kids should go right to bed. My kid and the other two. Hell, they haven't even had any dinner.'

'We'll stop at a McDonald's stand,' Ian Best said. 'And then we can take off for Canada, where the fish are, and lots of mountains that still have snow on them, even this time of year.'

'Sure,' Gantro said, grinning. 'We can go there.'

'You want to?' Ian Best scrutinized him. 'You really want to?'

'I'll settle a few things, and then, sure, you and I can take off together.'

'Son of a bitch,' Best breathed. 'You mean it.'

'Yes,' he said. 'I do. Of course, I have to get my wife's agreement. You can't go to Canada unless your wife signs a document in writing where she won't follow you. You become what's called a "landed Immigrant." '

'Then I've got to get Cynthia's written permission.'

'She'll give it to you. Just agree to send support money.'

'You think she will? She'll let me go?'

'Of course,' Gantro said.

'You actually think our wives will let us go,' Ian Best said as he and Gantro herded the children into the Mercedes-Benz. 'I'll bet you're right; Cynthia'd love to get rid of me. You know what she calls me, right in front of Walter? "An aggressive coward," and stuff like that. She has no respect for me.'

'Our wives,' Gantro said, 'will let us go.' But he knew better.

He looked back at the Facility manager, Mr Sam B. Carpenter, and at the truck driver, Ferris, who, Carpenter had told the press and TV, was as of this date fired and was a new and inexperienced employee anyhow.

'No,' he said. 'They won't let us go. None of them will.'

Clumsily, Ian Best fiddled with the complex mechanism that controlled the funky coal-burning engine. 'Sure they'll let us go; look, they're just standing there. What can they do, after what you said on TV and what that one reporter wrote up for a feature story?'

'I don't mean them,' Gantro said tonelessly.

'We could just run.'

'We are caught,' Gantro said. 'Caught and can't get out. You ask Cynthia, though. It's worth a try.'

'We'll never see Vancouver Island and the great ocean-going ferries steaming in and out of the fog, will we?' Ian Best said.

'Sure we will, eventually.' But he knew it was a lie, an absolute lie, just like you know sometimes when you say something that for no rational reason you know is absolutely true.

They drove from the lot, out onto the public street.

'It feels good,' Ian Best said, 'to be free . . . right?' The three boys nodded, but Ed Gantro said nothing. Free, he thought. Free to go home. To be caught in a larger net, shoved into a greater truck than the metal mechanical one the County Facility uses.

'This is a great day,' Ian Best said.

'Yes,' Ed Gantro agreed. 'A great day in which a noble and effective blow has been struck for all helpless things, anything of which you could say, "It is alive." '

Regarding him intently in the narrow trickly light, Ian Best said, 'I don't want to go home; I want to take off for Canada now.'

'We *have* to go home,' Ed Gantro reminded him. 'Temporarily, I mean. To wind things up. Legal matters, pick up what we need.'

Ian Best, as he drove, said, 'We'll never get there, to British Columbia and Vancouver Island and Stanley Park and English Bay and where they grow food and keep horses and where they have the ocean-going ferries.'

'No, we won't,' Ed Gantro said.

'Not now, not even later?'

'Not ever,' Ed Gantro said.

'That's what I was afraid of.' Best said and his voice broke and his driving got funny. 'That's what I thought from the beginning.'

They drove in silence, then, with nothing to say to each other. There was nothing left to say.

Philip K. Dick was born in the USA in 1928. His twin sister Jane died in infancy. He started his writing career publishing short stories in magazines. The first of these was 'Beyond Lies the Wub' in 1952. While publishing SF prolifically during the 1950s, Dick also wrote a series of mainstream novels, only one of which, *Confessions of a Crap Artist*, achieved publication during his lifetime. These included titles such as *Mary and the Giant* and *In Milton Lumky Territory*. During the 1960s Dick produced an extraordinary succession of novels, including *The Man in the High Castle*, which won a Hugo Award, *Martian Time-Slip*, *Dr Bloodmoney*, *The Three Stigmata of Palmer Eldritch*, *Do Androids Dream of Electric Sheep?* and *Ubik*. In the 1970s, Dick started to concern himself more directly with metaphysical and theological issues, experiencing a moment of revelation – or breakdown – in March 1974 which became the basis for much of his subsequent writing, in particular *Valis*, as he strove to make sense of what had happened. He died in 1982, a few weeks before the film *Blade Runner* opened and introduced his vision to a wider audience.